Published by Champlain Avenue Books, Inc.,
Las Vegas, Nevada

WhatWouldGrandpaSay@gmail.com
John F. Weber

International Standard Book Number ISBN- 978-1-943063-54-3
Library of Congress LCN: 2018952577

FIRST EDITION
2018

Printed in the United States of America

WHAT WOULD GRANDPA SAY?

Stories Like None Other
From the Minnesota River Valley

John F. Weber

Champlain Avenue Books, Inc.
Las Vegas, Nevada, USA

WHAT WOULD GRANDPA SAY?

Stories Like None Other
From the Minnesota River Valley

DEDICATION

To my parents, Allie and Geri Weber. Dad provided stories,
Mom provided research, and as always,
both provided guidance.

CONTENTS

INTRODUCTION

During the glorious steamship era, paddle wheelers brought self-reliant settlers up the Minnesota River to start a new life in the wilds of southern Minnesota. They used the abundant natural resources to build towns throughout the virgin valleys of the Minnesota River and its tributaries. Rugged farmers grubbed out the Big Woods and discovered the loamy soil yielded a bountiful harvest of grain.

In 1858 my great-great-grandfather, Anton Weber from Germany, ended up in Minnesota, Land of 10,000 Lakes (later changed by politicians to Land of 10,000 Taxes). Of all places, Anton settled in Minnesota's first Irish farming settlement in Jessenland Township in the Lower Minnesota River Valley. He cleared the land he claimed and started farming. Succeeding generations of Webers continue to till the land settled by Anton.

Along with a little malarkey, this one-of-a-kind book chronicles events and people, including my ancestors and living relatives in the greater Minnesota River Valley. Stories of national and world events that influenced life in the Valley are included. Accounts are given of politicians' behavior—no shortage of lowbrow material, fer sure. Political correctness is cast aside and a little history is put forth, *dontcha know*. If you come about some not-so-good grammar it's Minnesotan, *dern-tootin'*.

Not all was peaceful in the Valley. The contemptuous attitude of settlers and politicians toward Indians and their brutal treatment of them led to the Sioux Uprising. It was America's bloodiest Indian war and it led to our country's largest mass execution. President Abraham Lincoln intervened or more Indians would have been hanged. Grave robbers led by Dr. William Mayo dug up and dissected bodies of those hanged.

Noted slaves, Dred Scott and Harriet Robinson, got married in the Minnesota River Valley. The James-Younger gang rode through the Valley. Charles Lindbergh flew through the Valley, and Archbishop John Ireland traversed it seeking pledges to give up "demon rum." A congressman's daughter from the Valley kept 30 years of letters sent to her by FBI Director J. Edgar Hoover. The Ku Klux Klan set crosses on fire. The Valley was the site of mob lynchings, executions, a slavery trial, an Army intelligence school for Japanese-American soldiers, and a German prison camp. The Valley was home to one of President Nixon's men, and to Dan Patch, one of the greatest racehorses of all time. Pop star Prince hailed from the Valley and Olympic skier Lindsey Vonn was raised there, too.

In the beginning, God looked down on his creation and saw his people were miserable. He blessed the world with Irishmen and even Norwegians started having fun. Father McGinnis, fresh out of the seminary, came to St. Thomas Church in Jessenland to practice up before the bishop assigned him his own parish. After a few days, the priest at St. Thomas asked Father McGinnis how things were stacking up. Father McGinnis said, "I was hearing confessions last Saturday when a young lad got in the box and confessed he's been bootlegging moonshine down from Stearns County to the speakeasies in Belle Plaine and Jordan. The penitent said he was using the money to buy his granny spectacles and a set of false teeth. I didn't know what to give him." The parish priest told the greenhorn, "Ya know that 'Minnesota 13' dem Germans cook up there in Stearns County tis some of the finest moon in all the land. I give the young feller $5.00 for a quart jar."

Told in mostly chronological order, these stories from the Minnesota River Valley aren't found in national history books. Except for the obvious humor, (much of which was inspired by actual events) the stories are historical. Most stories have local color, a quirky side or an interesting tidbit of history.

Watch for the "Time for a Pint Book Tour" at your local watering hole and I'll sign your copy of What Would Grandpa Say?
John F. Weber

Chapter One
Settlers Arrive

Louisiana Purchase

In 1803 the author of the Declaration of Independence, Thomas Jefferson, was president and the "neighborhood" doubled in size when the United States purchased the Louisiana Territory. In New Orleans, the French flag came down, and the stars and stripes were run up the flagpole. One of the greatest land purchases in history, which included the Minnesota River Valley, became part of the United States. [1]

Dakota Indians

Slave owner President Jefferson sent a party of men from St. Louis, led by Army Lieutenant Zebulon Pike, up the Mississippi River to acquire land for a future Army fort. In 1805 Pike gave the Dakota Indians trinkets, and in exchange the Dakota agreed to a treaty ceding to the U.S. strategic land, including acreage at the confluence of the Minnesota and Mississippi Rivers. [2]

Dakota and Sioux are different names for the same Indians. The Dakota were among the Northern Plains Indians and bands of them lived in the greater Minnesota River Valley. The Dakota's hereditary enemy to the north, the Ojibwe, called them "Nadouësse," meaning "snake in the grass." The French

1

called them "Nadouësioux," then shortened it to Sioux so the Dakota didn't know they were talking about them.[3] The Dakota and Ojibwe were two of the most powerful Indian nations in North America.[4]

The Dakota and Ojibwe, also known as the Chippewa, had an unquenchable thirst for each other's blood. Sometimes after a battle, the Dakota placed their victims' heads on a row of stakes, and performed scalp dances around the bloody trophies, howling, hooting, and yelling. [5]

Dakota means "alliance of friends."[6] They were hunters and gatherers with a communal lifestyle.[7] Life for the Dakota was about the hunt and war. [8] A chief usually inherited his position, but he had to exhibit leadership to maintain it. He didn't make laws nor did he enforce them. At councils, tribesmen argued matters and votes were taken. The Chief Soldier led the Dakota in battle.[9]

Dakota men looked upon women as slaves.[10] Squaws performed all labor connected with Dakota life. They set up buffalo skin wigwams, gathered firewood, prepared the meals, raised small patches of Indian corn, tanned furs, hewed out canoes, and cared for the children. [11] If a husband discovered his wife committed adultery it was common for him to cut off the tip of her nose.[12]

To the Dakota, nature was filled with spirits. They were at peace with Mother Earth and they revered her.[13] The Dakota couldn't grasp the concept of private property, especially when it came to food. When a Dakota was hungry and he saw someone with belly grub, he expected to eat. The Dakota ate every type of animal. If they saw a dead cow or horse they'd have a feast and gorge themselves. Dog meat was a delicacy.[14]

John Calhoun

In 1819, Secretary of War John Calhoun from South Carolina sent Lieutenant Colonel Henry Leavenworth up the Mississippi River to build a fort on the land Pike acquired from the Dakota. Leavenworth named two nearby lakes, one, Harriet, after his wife, and the other, Calhoun, after the Secretary of War.[15] Calhoun owned slaves and took the view slavery was a positive good.[16] He wasn't the one getting whipped. Calhoun's attempt to pass a federal statute prohibiting the distribution of abolitionists' images and writings failed.[17]

Josiah Snelling

Leavenworth's successor, Josiah Snelling, who served from approximately 1820 to 1824, oversaw the building of the fort on the edge of the wilderness. Local limestone was used to build the imposing fortress where the Minnesota River joined the Mississippi. For doing a bang-up job, the War Department named the fort after Snelling.[18]

Dred Scott and Harriet Robinson

In 1836, while at Fort Snelling, Dred Scott met Harriet Robinson. The slaves were married by the Army officer who was also Harriet's master. Dred Scott's owner acquired Harriet.[19] At the time, Fort Snelling was part of the Wisconsin Territory, which by the terms of the Missouri Compromise banned slavery. However, Army officers weren't questioned for bringing their household slaves to Fort Snelling.[20]

James Thompson

In 1837, Father Brunson established a mission at Kaposia. He soon realized he couldn't converse with Indians. When he discovered an officer's religious slave at Fort Snelling fluent in the Dakota tongue, Father Brunson raised $1,200 and purchased James Thompson from his owner. Thompson was given his "free papers" and interpreted for Father Brunson.[21] Thompson married an Indian and operated a ferry boat. He had a good reputation and was regarded as an equal among whites and Indians.[22]

Pierre Parrant

One-eyed French fur trapper and bootlegger, Pierre "Pig's Eye" Parrant, sold the devil's brew to tough-fisted frontiersmen and soldiers at Pig's Eye, his tavern in the vicinity of Fort Snelling, where card playing and dancing contributed to the debauchery. One day in 1839 a carpenter at the watering hole needed to send a letter to Joseph Brown on Grey Cloud Island. The carpenter looked up, saw Parrant, and because the new settlement had not yet been named, wrote the return address as Pig's Eye. Joseph Brown responded with a letter to the carpenter addressed to Pig's Eye. Henceforth the community around Parrant's whiskey hovel was called Pig's Eye.[23] The name stuck until 1848 when a Catholic priest, who despised the loathsome Parrant, changed the name to St. Paul.[24]

In 1844 "Pig's Eye" Parrant and his neighbor Michael LeClaire got in a row over the borders of their land claims. Neither would back down and they ended up in front of the Honorable Joseph Brown, Justice of the Peace. Brown decided neither litigant had a valid claim to the lands in dispute as neither party staked his claim in front of witnesses. Whoever first properly staked his claim would be entitled to the disputed land. LeClaire won the eight-mile foot race and he was the first to drive stakes down in front of witnesses. Pig's Eye was ridiculed for losing the race. He got angry and took off for Sault Saint Marie; however, on the way he died from intemperance.[25]

Fur Trade

The Minnesota River Valley had a robust fur trade driven by demand in Europe and America. French was the language of the fur trade as French men easily adapted to the manner and customs of Indian life. It was common for French fur traders to purchase an Indian wife in exchange for a few gifts to her parents. Fur traders were hardy adventurers who joined Indians in hunting expeditions that lasted 12 to 18 months. They returned in mackinaw boats teeming with valuable furs.[26]

The fur trade medium of exchange in the Minnesota River Valley was a muskrat skin. The pelts were traded with merchants for food, twists of tobacco, clothes, guns, knives, axes, gun powder, and other goods. A wool shirt went for 30 skins, 150 skins fetched a flintlock rifle. A muskrat pelt in the Valley was worth about a nickel; by the time it reached New York City it was worth a dime.[27]

Henry Hastings Sibley

In 1834, the American Fur Company entered into a partnership with the adventuresome Henry Hastings Sibley and others to establish a fur trading post near Fort Snelling.[28] In his bachelor days the "Princely Pioneer" fathered his first child, Helen, with Red Blanket Woman, a young Dakota squaw. [29] It was common for traders, soldiers, and government agents to take advantage of Indian and half-breed women. Uncommon, was Sibley supporting and maintaining a close relationship with his half-breed daughter. [30] Helen married a doctor and they lived in Racine County, Wisconsin where her husband set up practice. Two days after giving birth to her first child, Helen died from scarlet fever and a week later her baby girl died. [31]

In 1836, Sibley built the first stone house in Minnesota, in Mendota. [32] In 1843 he married a general's daughter at Fort Snelling. [33] All six of the couple's children were born in the stone house.[34]

My great-great-grandmother, Margaret Green, was a handmaid at parties hosted by Henry Hastings Sibley. She met my great-great-grandfather, John Desmond, while he was a livery boy and worked for Henry Hastings Sibley on occasion. Margaret Green and John Desmond were married by John Ireland, then a priest, at the old log cathedral in St. Paul. For their wedding Sibley gave them a set of white ironstone china.[35]

Minnesota Territory

In 1841, pro-slavery President John Tyler occupied the White House. He had fifteen kids, seven with his second wife who was younger than three of his daughters.[36] Also that year while serving in the Wisconsin Territorial Legislature, it appears Joseph Brown came up with the name Minnesota for a new territory to the west.[37]

When Wisconsin became a state in May 1848, Congress left out the portion of the Wisconsin Territory between the St. Croix and Mississippi Rivers, which included settlements. Since Congress didn't formally recognize the continued existence of the Wisconsin Territory, this no man's land between the two rivers was without a government and laws.

Henry Hastings Sibley, Joseph Brown, and others attended a convention in Stillwater in August 1848. They chose Sibley to lobby the politicians in Washington, D.C. for the creation of the Minnesota Territory. In December 1848, after Sibley gave a stately speech to a House committee, he was seated as a delegate in the House of Representatives. The plan for another northern territory was opposed by southern politicians who didn't want to upset the balance between slave and free states. In March 1949, with strong support from Senator Stephen Douglas from Illinois, Congress created the Minnesota Territory. Slower than getting a note pinned to a donkey's tail, a month later, news of the new territory reached St. Paul by steamboat.[38]

President Zachary Taylor was against slavery. Somehow he justified having over one hundred slaves as a "necessary evil."[39] He appointed Alexander Ramsey, a congressman from Pennsylvania, to govern the Minnesota territory.[40] St. Paul became the capital and Stillwater housed the territory's prison. As a member of Minnesota's Territorial Legislature, Joseph Brown introduced a bill to prohibit the sale of alcohol in the territory and to outlaw hanging underwear on clotheslines.[41]

In 1849 Sibley procured a slab of red pipestone from southwestern Minnesota and it was placed in the Washington

Monument as the marker from the Minnesota Territory.[42] The pipestone quarry is one of the most sacred Indian sites in North America. Indians still carve ceremonial pipes out of the soft red pipestone.[43]

At the time it was created, only a small portion of the land in the Minnesota Territory had been ceded by the Indians to the U.S. The northern climate promoted diligence, and newcomers willing to work hard poured into the new territory they called the Suland. Newspaper editor, Horace Greeley, popularized the slogan of the day, "Go west, young man!"[44]

Traverse des Sioux

Sibley and other traders were anxious to get paid on their credit accounts with the Dakota. The traders ran into a snag in 1843 when Congress prohibited clauses in treaties providing payment directly to traders.[45] Nevertheless, politicians and traders pressured and tricked Dakota chiefs into the charade of signing treaties. Sibley bragged, "the Indians are all prepared to make a treaty when we tell them to do so, and such as one as I may dictate."[46]

In early July of 1851, Dakota chiefs and tribesmen, representatives from the U.S. government, territorial politicians, traders, missionaries, a newspaper man, an artist from Baltimore and many others, gathered for negotiations and the signing of a treaty at an area in the Lower Minnesota River Valley known as Traverse des Sioux near the present day city of St. Peter.[47] Torrential rains delayed the arrival of several bands of Dakota.[48] During the almost three-week waiting period, the Dakota played games of lacrosse, and Indians and whites wagered on the outcome.[49] One game ended with firearms drawn.[50] Food at the gathering included dog, buffalo tail, muskrat, elk, and swan.[51] A missionary at the gathering who couldn't swim took a bath in the river. He stepped in a hole and became a floater.[52]

The highlight prior to the treaty negotiations being called to order was the marriage of 30-year-old mixed-blood, David

Faribault, to Nancy Winona McClure, a highly sought after fresh 14-year-old mixed-blood. Educated at a secluded mission school, she spoke English and the Dakota language, but she wasn't familiar with white society. After an Episcopal ceremony by a justice of the peace, the groom broke out lemonade for all and Indian trader Joe La Framboise gave a toast.[53]

On July 18, 1851 the chiefs painted their faces, government representatives put on straight faces, and the treaty session finally got under way. To lure the chiefs into signing the treaty, politicians told strings of lies to the Dakota about how the Great Father in Washington, D.C. would take care of them and their children. The chiefs figured it was better to get something for their land than have the white man take it and get nothing.[54] Using a goose quill, the chiefs scrawled their signatures or marked an "X" on the treaty.[55]

Immediately after the treaty was signed, the chiefs were directed to a spot where trader Joseph Brown was perched on a barrel. He "tugged on the Chiefs' blankets" to sign a separate document that became known as the notorious Traders' Papers, which was not read or explained to the chiefs.[56] To give the appearance of being detached, Sibley stood off to the side as the chiefs signed the document.[57]

Shortly after the chiefs signed the Traders' Papers, they discovered $431,735.78 was to be paid directly to Sibley and his fellow traders from the Dakota's payment under the treaty. After the Dakota objected, a committee of traders reduced the amount to $210,000. The next day, a paper listing the amount owed each trader was attached to the Traders' Papers."[58] In it, Joseph Brown was due $6,564 and Henry Hastings Sibley, as agent for the American Fur Company, was due $66,459.[59]

As a result of the treaty at Traverse des Sioux and a treaty signed a fortnight later at Mendota, most of the rich farmland of southern Minnesota was open for immigration. The treaty at Traverse des Sioux provided payment to the Dakota of $1,665,000 of which $1,360,000 was to be paid in annual installments over 50 years.[60] An article in each treaty prohibited the sale of spirituous liquors in the Indian country in the land ceded unless otherwise directed by the president or Congress.[61]

Many of the Dakota lived on a narrow strip of land in the Upper Minnesota River Valley that comprised two reservations. The north reservation was administered by the Upper Sioux Agency and the southern reservation by the Lower Sioux Agency.[62] The Dakota went from blanket Indians to reservation Indians. To keep an eye on the Dakota, the U.S. built Fort Ridgely near the reservations.[63]

Firewater

Despite attempts to curb its sale, firewater flowed to Indians and settlers on the land ceded by the treaties at Traverse des Sioux and Mendota. Under the influence of the devil's brew, Dakota men fought and killed more than ever. Many gave up their primary source of subsistence—hunting and trapping—to stay drunk, sometimes traveling several miles to get a bottle of ardent spirits. Many Indian men neglected their women who were left to beg for food. In 1850 in St. Paul in Ramsey County, a famished squaw was seen chewing on the head of a dead dog.[64]

Under pressure from the temperance lobby, in 1852 the Minnesota Territorial Legislature passed a law allowing each county to decide by popular vote whether or not to make it a crime to manufacture, sell, or possess alcohol. If passed, counties could no longer issue liquor licenses and liquor dealers couldn't sit on juries. Voters in Ramsey County enacted the law. Unfazed, the Ramsey County Commissioners put their spin on the new law and continued to issue liquor licenses. In St. Paul, Indians continued to swig white man's devil water and settlers stayed on their bar stools. In short order the matter was taken up by a judge of the Territorial Supreme Court. He declared the law unconstitutional, finding the legislature didn't have the power to delegate its authority to the voters in each county to enact the law in question.[65]

9

Doheny Brothers

Early in the summer of 1852, bold prospectors in search of land came up the Minnesota River on the steamboat Black Oak from St. Paul, the last city in the east. Some 50 miles upriver, the water was too shallow for the full-sized Black Oak to continue. She docked at an outcropping of rocks. Carrying an axe and a ham, brothers Thomas, Walter, and Dennis Doheny from Tipperary County, Ireland, went ashore to explore the wilderness. The Black Oak turned around and wound its way back to St. Paul. In a few days the Doheny brothers planned to return to St. Paul on a smaller steamer. The brothers were so impressed with the area's timberland that they each marked a claim with their axe. The Doheny brothers nearly starved to death as the steamer going to St. Paul was a month late.[66]

The next spring the Doheny brothers, along with other sod cutters, returned in the Black Oak to the rocky outcrop that became known as Doheny's Landing. They went ashore and settled on their claims, starting the first permanent Irish settlement in Minnesota.[67] At Doheny's Landing, Thomas Doheny built and operated a general store where sales of whiskey and salt were brisk.[68]

Jessenland

Most believe the area founded by the Dohenys was given the name Jessenland by a visiting bishop who was so impressed with the picturesque Minnesota River Valley he remarked, "This must be what the biblical land of Gessen was like."[69] The book of Genesis tells how Jacob and his descendants migrated to Egypt when their homeland was struck with a famine. Jacob's son, Joseph, who had a position of great importance in Egypt, gave his father the best land in Egypt known as the land of Gessen. Nepotism has been around a long time.

From the beginning there were some French-Canadians from the Acadia region and German settlers in Jessenland, but the vast majority were Celtic Irish. Most were "two-boat" Irish who took a boat across the Atlantic and a boat up the Minnesota River. Many relocated from the Ohio River Valley.[70] The Irish picked Jessenland because the lush green Minnesota River Valley with its wooded bluffs and glens reminded them of their native land. It was even better—no potato famine and no Englishmen.

St. Thomas' First Church

In 1855, near Doheny's Landing, settlers established St. Thomas Catholic Parish and built a log church.[71] The parishioners at St. Thomas, like most churches on the frontier, often heard sermons on temperance because there was a need.[72] According to folklore, St. Thomas' first cemetery was on river bottomland across from the church. When a grave was dug it filled with water causing the wooden coffin to float. After a couple of years the cemetery was moved a little closer to heaven on the steep bluff behind the church. One wintery day, pallbearers were carrying a coffin up an icy slope to the grave when one of them slipped and fell, causing the others to fall. The coffin hit the ground and burst open. The clothes on the corpse had been cut open and draped over the body, and the naked corpse slid down the icy slope.[73]

Paddy

When he was a youngster, Paddy boarded a ship in Sligo, Ireland bound to the "land of the brave." He got so sick the captain thought he was dead. Twice Paddy was wrapped up to be thrown overboard. His mother pleaded to spare him a watery grave. Paddy was 15 years old when he arrived in Jessenland. He went on to have a brood of 20 kids, including several Irish twins, that is, two children born in the same calendar year.

At a ripe old age, Paddy was stricken with illness and confined to bed. After he took last rites he told his wife he had settled up with the undertaker. A day later Paddy slipped into a coma. After a day and a half he came to, smelled ham and said to his wife, "Cut me off a slab of ham." His wife responded,

"Paddy, after all these years you're still giving me the devil, you dasn't have any ham, it's for your wake." A few days later Paddy's name appeared in the newspaper under "Death's Harvest." After the wake his corpse was laid in a plain wood coffin and loaded into a wagon. On the trip to St. Thomas Church for the funeral and burial, turkey vultures circled above the horse drawn wagon. A few weeks after Paddy's burial his widow got a letter from the undertaker saying, "If payment isn't received for Paddy's box up he comes."

Joseph Brown–Restless Frontiersman

Some men (prim and proper women rarely make history) do more in a lifetime than what seems possible; Joseph Brown was one of them. In addition to being the "Pioneer Town Builder of Minnesota," he was a soldier, Indian trader, lumberman, pioneer, legislator, justice of the peace, editor, and inventor.[74] He had a reputation for dealing whiskey.[75] Brown married three times and claimed fifteen kids. By an act of the Wisconsin Territorial Legislature he obtained a divorce from his second wife.[76] As he traveled throughout the western frontier, he was involved in several of its historical events. Throughout the frontier his penchant for Indian and mixed-blood women remained a topic of conversation.[77] "He never drank, he never swore, he never played cards; he did smoke cigars occasionally."[78]

Henderson

In the summer of 1852, Joseph Brown came up the Minnesota River in a steamer. Some five miles upriver from Doheny's Landing, Brown founded the town of Henderson, named in honor of his aunt, Margaret Henderson, who raised him from a young boy after his mother died.[79] Brown planned Henderson to be a transportation hub for roads, stagecoaches, river boats, and as a ferry crossing.[80]

Sibley County

In 1853 the Minnesota Territorial Council established the Sibley County borders. Brown came up with the name Sibley to honor his buddy, Henry Hastings Sibley. The territorial legislature designated Henderson as the Sibley county seat.[81] In 1854 an election was held to choose county officers and Joseph Brown was elected County Recorder.[82] Two years later Joseph Brown was elected President of the Sibley County branch of the American Bible Society.[83]

At a territorial council meeting in 1856 Penn and Round Grove Townships were removed from Sibley County and added to McLeod County. There appeared to be no good reason to put a break in the straight-line border between the two counties. According to legend, the transfer of the two townships was the result of Henry Hastings Sibley losing a bet to Indian trader Martin McLeod.[84]

New Ulm

From 1848-49, the middle class in Germany revolted against the elite ruling class. Those supporting the March Revolution wanted more liberal principles, and better living and working conditions. The revolt was crushed. To escape government persecution, the Forty-Eighters as they were called, began leaving in droves for America. Many planned to return to their beloved Germany when the situation improved.[85]

In the 1850s, in disease-ridden Chicago, German immigrants in search of a better life formed the Chicago Land Society. Its members pooled money to buy land.[86] To avoid conflict the society banned ministers and lawyers.[87] The Chicago Land Society's search for the perfect townsite in Michigan and Iowa turned up empty.[88] In 1854 while scouts were looking for a suitable location in Minnesota, a Norwegian told them to see a frog named Joe La Framboise, a man who spent most of his life with the Dakota. [89] His second and third wives were Sleepy Eye's daughters.[90] La Framboise took the scouts to his house and fed

13

them muskrat meat. After supper they passed around a pipe. The next day La Framboise gave the scouts directions to the best townsite on the Minnesota River.[91]

In 1855 the new Mayor of Chicago, blaming German immigrants for the country's problems, ordered the police to enforce Sunday bar closing laws and he pushed through a large increase in the liquor license fee. When German immigrants opened taverns on Sunday and sold beer without a license, all hell broke loose. Fed up with police crackdowns, protests, shootings and riots, some 30 members of the Chicago Land Society left for the perfect townsite on the Minnesota River.[92] The town of New Ulm—where the bars never close—would be built on a glacial bench high above any floodwaters. It's the best planned and platted city on the Minnesota River.[93]

A popular destination for Forty-Eighters was Cincinnati, where a small group of German immigrants formed a Turner Society.[94] Turner clubs flourished wherever Germans settled, except in New York where the legislature refused to incorporate them, fearing they might be anarchists.[95] The Turners were patriotic to their new country and believed in a sound mind and a sound body. They emphasized gymnastics and a healthy spiritual life free from prejudice, bringing physical education to public schools. They fought for women's suffrage, and against slavery and prohibition.[96]

In 1855, Turners from Cincinnati, at the Turner National Convention in Buffalo, New York, introduced a plan to start settlement societies away from Anglo-American disciplinarians. The plan was approved and the Turner Colonization Society of Cincinnati was formed. While searching for land, they visited New Ulm and liked what they saw. In 1857 the Chicago Land Society and the Turner group merged and became the German Land Company of Minnesota.[97] New Ulm became a German utopia of freethinkers and workers. Freethinkers form their own opinions on how to practice religion and they support separation of church and state.[98]

The Germans of New Ulm are fond of saying, "work makes life sweet."[99] The strong German work ethic and their love for order contributed to the fabric of our great nation. New Ulm Germans often relax on Sunday afternoons by drinking beer and dancing to polka music. Zicke Zacke, Hoi Hoi Hoi!

Bohemian Triangle

From 1850-1890, starving Bohemian peasants left for America with no intention of returning to their homeland.[100] Many came up the Mississippi River and got off the boat in Iowa. In 1856, to get away from Old Stock Americans, four Bohemians headed up the Mississippi River. They turned onto the Minnesota River and ended up in Scott and Le Sueur Counties.[101] It wasn't long before Bohemians settled in or near the Minnesota River Valley in Scott, Le Sueur, and Rice counties, creating the "Bohemian Triangle." At the center of the triangle were the towns of New Prague and Montgomery.[102] Bohemian settlers called rats "German mice."[103] Like the Irish and Germans, the Bohemians were against restrictions on alcohol.[104] Many Bohemian families ate from one bowl placed in the center of a split-log table. To attract a husband, Bohemian girls learned to milk cows, pluck geese, and mix up a savory batch of dumplings.[105]

Frontier courting by Bohemian boys usually occurred on Sunday afternoons. After church, farm boys walked to a girl's home to spend time with her. If a girl became pregnant her father pointed his shotgun at the boy until he said there'd be a wedding. Shotgun weddings weren't uncommon. If a man's wife died leaving him with small children, shortly after her death it was common for the community to subtly urge a young single lady to step up and become his wife. Some brides were chosen by family members in the old country and sent to America for arranged marriages.[106]

Joseph Rolette

In 1857, Nicollet Island, Faribault, Henderson, and St. Peter were all vying to become the capital of the Minnesota Territory.[107] Minnesota's territorial governor, Willis Gorman, backed a bill to move the capital from St. Paul to St. Peter in the Lower Minnesota River Valley, where Gorman happened to have considerable investments. Both houses of the legislature passed the bill.[108] Footloose legislator, Joseph Rolette, left the capital with the original bill and disappeared. Some thought he mushed his dog team back to his home in Pembina near the Canadian border. "Jolly Joe" gloriously waddled into the legislator's chamber too late for the bill to become law. A city historian said, "Rolette became St. Paul's mascot."[109]

Those with investments in St. Peter sought relief from the Territorial Supreme Court. After a lengthy review of the evidence, the court concluded no law had passed to move the capital to St. Peter.[110] During the next go round for a nut house, in 1866, St. Peter won out when the legislature passed a bill establishing Minnesota's first hospital for the insane there.[111]

For voting to move the capital to St. Peter, the citizens of Henderson hanged their territorial representative Francis Bassen in effigy. They printed on his "body" "FRANCIS BASSEN," "TRAITOR" which after a few days, was taken from the scaffold and put in a horse drawn cart. Four to five hundred mourners followed the wagon as a fife and drum unit played and the village bell rang out.[112] The ceremony ended with a mock funeral.[113]

Minnesota Becomes a State

Before becoming a state, Minnesota elected its first governor and other state officials in 1857. With help from "Joe the Juggler" Brown, the ballot box count showed Henry Hastings Sibley nudged out Alexander Ramsey by 240 votes to become the state's first governor elect. The ballot box in Pembina contained 316 votes for Sibley and none for Ramsey.[114] In May 1858, by an act of Congress, the eastern half of the Minnesota Territory became the 32nd star on old glory. Henry Hastings Sibley was sworn in as the North Star State's first governor.[115] Ironically, Pembina wasn't part of the new state. Upon hearing the glorious news of statehood, 100 guns were fired in Winona, Minnesota.[116]

Anton and Margaret Weber

In 1852, while in the German army, my great-great-grandfather, Anton Weber from Heuchlingen in Wurtenburg, Germany, was thrown in prison for leaving his post. His lily-livered commander deserted his troops. While locked up, Anton learned to weave wet tree branches into baskets. Three cohorts joined Anton in a prison break, which may have been aided by Anton's training as a locksmith.[117]

At age 19, Anton made it to Le Havre, France where he paid cash to the Union Line for steerage class passage to the land of opportunity (later changed by politicians to the "land of handouts.") In 1853, with Anton on board, the crowded and stinky Havre, sailed into New York harbor.[118] Anton and other immigrants disembarked from the Havre directly onto a wharf with no processing.[119] With sea legs and an empty stomach, Anton started a new life where they spoke English. All Anton brought to the melting pot was his German hunting rifle. In 1853 to become a U.S. citizen Anton signed a declaration "renouncing forever allegiance and fidelity" to the King of Wurtenburg. The declaration was filed in the Superior Court of the City of New York.

In 1858, Anton went to the federal land office in Henderson and claimed a 144 acre plot in Jessenland that drains into the lower Minnesota River. A good portion of the land borders a shallow 750 acre lake with some sand and rocks on the shore. Legend has it, when the first group of white men discovered the lake, one of them tossed a silver coin in the water and the lake got its name. Silver lake takes 16 acres out of the quarter section Anton claimed. The land had been passed over by early settlers because it contained two large swamps originally called meander land.[120] The land was previously surveyed using the Township and Range System devised by Thomas Jefferson.

Anton's claim was located in the Big Woods, an area covering 5,000 square miles heavily covered with oak, elm, ash, maple, cottonwood, butternut, and other deciduous trees, some 100 feet tall and five feet in diameter.[121] The undergrowth included frost grape, raspberry, wild rose, gooseberry, black currant, hazelnut, and honeysuckle.[122] Wild cranberries grew in marshes and most lake shores were lined with wild rice. [123] Before the trees of the Big Woods were felled and the roots removed with a grub hoe, tons of fiery-tasting ginseng roots were exported from Minnesota to China.[124] At the time, Henderson had seven "sang" dealers.[125]

When my great-great-great-grandfather Nicolaus Mörsch from Stroech in Prussia, Germany, arrived at Waterloo, Belgium, Napoleon had already lost the battle. Nicolaus Mörsch and his four daughters immigrated to the U.S. In 1857 they moved from swampy Chicago to flood-prone Henderson. In 1860, Margaret, Nicolaus' daughter, and Anton Weber united in marriage.

In 1860 Anton received a deed to his claim. Anton and Margaret's first child, Anna, was born in 1860 in a log shanty Anton built on a hill. Their next eight children were born in a new two-story frame house with a rock foundation and a dirt floor cellar built by a carpenter. The lathed and plastered house was fitted with a woodstove for cooking and a wood burning furnace. There was no running water. To take a bath, buckets of water were pumped by hand outside, heated on the stove, and poured in a tub. On Saturday evenings everyone in the house took a bath in the same water; men first, then women and children. By the time the baby got in the water it was so dirty they had to be careful not to throw the baby out with the bath water.

The resourceful Margaret spun wool on a spinning wheel, and then wove and knitted it into clothes and blankets. She washed clothes on a washboard. She sprinkled starchy water from boiled potatoes onto garments, and after placing three flatirons on the woodstove would use one until it cooled off. She then used another, continuing the rotation until the clothes were ironed.

Margaret canned fruits and vegetables, and sealed the jars with wax. The canned goods were stored in the house's root cellar along with potatoes, cabbage, rutabagas, and carrots. She made jam from wild grapes, plums, raspberries, and chokecherries. She used a churn to make butter. To make brooms, Margaret wound twine around bundles of oat straw that she attached to the bottom of a straight stick. She put tallow and wicks in a mold to make candles. She made soap from sugar, salt, ammonia, lard, and lye she leached from ashes.

Anton carved fields out of the Big Woods and tilled the black loam soil to grow fields of small grain and grass to feed horses and livestock. After he butchered livestock, he soaked beef and pork in a salt brine or rubbed it with salt until the salt penetrated the meat. He smoked meat in a hollow log. Pork that wasn't smoked was put in crock jars, preserved with saltpeter and covered with lard. Pig intestines provided casing for German sausages. Poultry was usually butchered a few hours before Sunday dinner or supper, then soaked in cold salt water before it was fried. The women used the feathers to make pillows and feather beds.

The self-made Anton studied grafting and pruning. He planted and tended to an orchard of winter-hardy varieties of apple, pear, plum, peach, and cherry trees. He picked the ripe fruit and put it in baskets he wove from wet willow branches. Careful not to get stung, he gathered honey from hollow trees. Additional food, clothes, and other sundries were purchased from the general store near Silver Lake. Peddlers came to the farm with wagons containing their wares. A door-to-door Jewish salesman named Spielekarl called on the farm selling musical instruments.[126] At Christmas time Spielekarl could be heard singing, "Oh, what a friend I have in Jesus."

As was the custom for German men at the time, Anton ate with other men or alone, and he was served first. The women and children ate at a separate table. When the weather turned warm, the women cooked meals in the summer kitchen to avoid heating up the house. In the evening, Anton enjoyed sipping tea from his mustache cup and often lit up a Major Brown cigar, rolled from a press in Henderson.[127] The stogie was advertised as "the best five cent cigar on the market."[128]

Civic-minded, Anton held several positions in local government including Treasurer at nearby Silver Lake School, Jessenland Township Assessor, and the thankless job of Tax Collector. To attend Mass, Anton laced up his shiny black boots and hitched his team of horses to a surrey and moseyed four miles to St. Thomas Church. When they came to the steep hill descending into the Minnesota River Valley, Anton put a chain through the spokes of a rear wheel and the surrey's frame. The skidding wheel kept the surrey under control. The horses—used to pulling—got skittish when the surrey pushed them from behind. During the winter Anton shod his horses with "never slip" shoes so they didn't fall on the ice and snow. On the trip home from church, the men and children, wearing horsehide robes, walked up the hill so the horses didn't steam up from pulling the sled up the steep grade.[129]

Joseph Brown's Steam Powered Wagon

Voyagers brought supplies on flatboats up the Minnesota River to Henderson. The supplies were loaded onto carts and pulled by horses or oxen some 45 miles to the Army's Fort Ridgely in the Upper Minnesota River Valley. Joseph Brown came up with the idea to use a self-propelled steam powered wagon to deliver the supplies. In 1859, Brown traveled to New York City and placed an order for a steam powered wagon.

In May 1860 the unassembled machine arrived on a packet to Henderson where longshoremen unloaded it.[130] On Independence Day, Anton Weber hitched his team to a rack in Henderson and watched Joseph Brown fire up and drive up and down the dirt streets in his steam powered wagon he called "Mazomanie," Dakota for Walking Metal.[131] In the fall of 1860, Mazomanie belched black smoke from its wood burning steam engine as it climbed the long grade out of the Minnesota River Valley at Henderson. After 28 long days, the steam powered wagon got within four miles of Fort Ridgely.[132] As it forded a small creek, it got mired in the mud and over time was stripped of its parts.[133]

Thomas and Emily Madden

In 1855 my great-great-grandparents, Emily Payne and Thomas Madden, tied the knot at a Catholic church in Susquehanna, Pennsylvania. Two days later Emily was baptized. After the birth of their first child, the family left with other families in Conestoga wagons for the Minnesota Territory.

Thomas Madden claimed 80 acres of bounty land in Jessenland where, in 1860, my great-grandfather, John "Jack" Madden, was born. In 1871, Thomas Madden died. Two years later Emily married her hired man, Thomas Donovan, twelve years her junior. She had ten children and buried two husbands, worked on the farm in Jessenland, and found time to be the countryside midwife.

Emily kept a jar of "orange jam" made from wild plums. When someone came to her with a sore that wasn't healing she'd smear a little of the moldy jam on the sore and it healed—a rudimentary form of penicillin. When she died at age 85, her funeral procession in Jessenland was five miles long.[134]

Wendelin Grimm

In 1857 Wendelin Grimm along with his wife and three kids took passage from the Tauber Valley in Franconia, Germany to the land of hope. A steamboat took Grimm and his family up the Minnesota River to Chaska. From there he purchased a farm in Carver County, some 25 miles northeast of the Lower Minnesota River Valley.[135]

Grimm brought a small wooden box containing "everlasting clover" seeds to America. Over the next fifteen years Grimm accomplished what George Washington and Thomas Jefferson failed to achieve at their Virginia plantations. He selected alfalfa seeds that survived harsh winters.[136] The process produced sturdy and flourishing perennial fields of alfalfa. Grimm's winter-hardy alfalfa's big yields and high protein content made excellent feed for milk cows. Grimm's farm became known as the birthplace of the Dairy Belt. Dairy farmers in Carver County were called "the golden buckle on the dairy belt."[137]

When Grimm died in 1890 his obituary failed to mention the alfalfa he developed. In 1903, Grimm's alfalfa was acknowledged by the U.S. Department of Agriculture. The Secretary of Agriculture in 1938 said, "The production of a forage plant so hardy as Grimm alfalfa is almost without parallel in plant history...it is impossible to compute in dollars and cents what it has meant to the nation."[138]

Charles Rheinhardt

In 1858, Charles Rheinhardt showed up in Lexington in Le Sueur County some seven miles east of the Lower Minnesota River Valley. The tight-lipped Rheinhardt boarded in a small hotel. That spring a Frenchman from Milwaukee named Burdell arrived in Lexington to purchase land. He stayed at the same hotel as Rheinhardt. For several days Rheinhardt escorted Burdell on trips to inspect the lay of the land. One morning Burdell settled up with the hotel and left with Rheinhardt. When Rheinhardt returned to the hotel he said Burdell was on his way back to Milwaukee.

Rheinhardt's actions after Burdell left aroused suspicions in the minds of some. After Rheinhardt disappeared, a search party formed to comb the vicinity. They found Burdell's body in a shallow grave at a nearby lakeshore. A local citizen tore out after Rheinhardt. He caught him near Winona, Minnesota and brought him back to the scene of the murder. Rheinhardt denied any knowledge of the murder. For having the dead man's watch on his person Rheinhardt was tossed in a log jail.

When the leader of a mob entered the jail, Rheinhardt struck him with a stove leg. The avengers backed off and secured the jail door. Three men climbed to the top of the jail and using an axe chopped a hole in the roof. They used poles to punch and jab Rheinhardt until he became bone weary. Rheinhardt squealed like a pig caught under a gate when the mob dragged him from the jail and hanged him from a scrub oak. His body was buried in a shallow unboxed grave.[139]

Ann Bilansky

In 1859 Ann Bilansky found herself living in St. Paul married to an abusive old Polander who took refuge in the bottle. Ann found refuge in the arms of a young lover. Convinced Ann used arsenic to poison her husband, the jury found her guilty of murder. The Minnesota Supreme Court upheld her conviction.

When a jailer went to get his keys Ann made a break for freedom. She escaped through a window and went on the lam. A week later, two deputies spotted her disguised as a man as she walked in St. Paul with her lover. Their plans to go west were foiled.

The judge gave Ann the rope-around-the-neck sentence. A slew of people petitioned Governor Sibley to commute her sentence to life in prison. Sibley left office without making a decision. In an unusual move the State Legislature passed a bill commuting her sentence to life in prison. Minnesota's second Governor, Alexander Ramsey, feeling the bill usurped his power to pardon those convicted of a crime, vetoed it. [140] The day before

Ann was scheduled to swing, the man who prosecuted her wrote Ramsey expressing "grave and serious doubts as to whether the defendant has had a fair trial." [141]

Just prior to feeling the rope, Ann Bilansky said in part, "I die without having had any mercy shown me, or justice. I die for the good of my soul, and not for murder...Your courts of justice are not courts of justice—but I will get justice in Heaven." After a deputy sheriff slipped the noose over her head and covered her head with a black cap, the sheriff released the drop, the rope went tight and she died without incident. Her corpse was cut down and tucked in a black coffin. Spectators scrambled for a piece of the hanging rope for a souvenir or to cure the sick. [142] She was the first white person and the only woman legally hanged in Minnesota. [143]

Chapter Two
Sioux Uprising and the Civil War

James Shields

James Shields was born in 1810 in County Tyrone, Ireland. At age 16 he immigrated to the U.S.[1] In 1842 while serving as the Illinois State Auditor, Shields was belittled politically and personally in a satirical essay titled "The Rebecca Letter" written by Abraham Lincoln with help from Mary Todd. When Shields discovered Lincoln wrote the essay he challenged him to a duel. Since Lincoln in his youth swung a broad axe to split logs into rails, he chose broadswords for the duel. [2] Shields was an adept swordsman who previously taught fencing.[3] Dueling was illegal in Illinois, so in September 1842 the two men crossed the Mississippi River into Missouri. Before it got bloody, the belligerents' common sense kicked in and the "affair of honor" was over.[4] Lincoln said of the event, "If all the good things I have ever done are remembered as long and as well as my scrape with Shields, it is plain I shall not be forgotten."

James "Dirty Dick" Shields was a General in the Mexican-American War. His unit was the first to enter Mexico City and raise Old Glory in the halls of the Montezumas. In 1855, some 30 miles east of the Minnesota River Valley, Shields founded the town of Shieldsville. It was soon populated by Irishmen, some who fought under Shields in Mexico.[5]

At the outbreak of the Civil War, James Shields tendered his services to President Lincoln who appointed him Brigadier General. Shields was the only man in history to defeat Confederate General Thomas "Stonewall" Jackson.[6] Shields was elected to the U.S. Senate from Illinois, Minnesota, and Missouri.[7]

Underground Railroad

The Underground Railroad was the code word for secret routes, meeting spots, transportation, and safe houses. It was largely run by Quakers, the first group in America to organize against slavery, to help runaway slaves attain freedom.[8] Aided by "conductors," fleeing slaves hid among the freight on riverboats coming up the Mississippi River to St. Paul. Some slaves escaped when planters brought their human chattel with them to St. Paul. At the "St. Paul Station" slaves on the run were given shelter, food, disguises and for many, help with passage to the "promise land"—Canada.[9] Those giving aid to runaway slaves took the risk of being punished under the Fugitive Slave Act.

Harriet Beecher Stowe

Angered by the Fugitive Slave Act, Harriet Beecher Stowe wrote *Uncle Tom's Cabin*.[10] Published in 1852, the anti-slave novel and the ensuing plays called "Tom Shows," often performed in a tent, were wildly popular in the Minnesota River Valley and throughout the north. It energized those against the peculiar institution and rallied support for the Civil War. *Uncle Tom's Cabin* has been in the Weber family since the mid-1850s.

Dred and Harriet Scott's Supreme Court Case

In 1846 the Scotts each filed a petition in the Missouri Circuit Court in St. Louis. They claimed they should be free because they lived at Fort Snelling where slavery was prohibited. In addition, Dred Scott spent time with his owner in the free state of Illinois.[11] After a back and forth legal battle, Dred and Harriet Scott's case for freedom went before the U.S. Supreme Court. Some of the legal fees were paid by the sons and son-in-law of Dred Scott's original owner.[12] In 1857, in *Scott v. Sandford*, the court, including two "doughface" justices from the north sympathetic to slavery, decided blacks were inferior and had no rights, and as non-citizens couldn't bring suit in federal court. Dred and Harriet Scott didn't obtain their freedom by being taken to Fort Snelling in the "free" territory of Wisconsin. The Court ruled the Missouri Compromise unconstitutional and held the federal government didn't have the power to prohibit slavery in its territories. The Court reasoned slaves were a form of chattel and Congress had no business telling people what to do with their property. The Court's deplorable decision invigorated Abraham Lincoln and united those opposed to slavery.[13]

John North

Some 45 miles east of the Minnesota River Valley is the city of Northfield, Minnesota. Its founder, John North, inserted in Northfield deeds, "No intoxicating drinks shall be sold or in any manner furnished as a beverage on said premises."[14] If caught providing alcohol on the premises the deed was forfeited.[15] In 1860, North was chairman of the Minnesota delegation to the Chicago convention that nominated Lincoln for President. From Chicago, North, along with others, traveled by train to Springfield, Illinois to announce to Abraham Lincoln his nomination for President.[16]

Abraham Lincoln's severe depression did not suppress his thoughts about the U.S. being a great experiment in the ability of people to rule themselves.[17] If the U.S. failed, dictators and monarchs would proclaim that people couldn't govern themselves.[18] Lincoln supposedly said, "I am a firm believer in the people. If given the truth, they can be depended upon to meet any national crisis. The great point is to bring them the real facts and beer."

President Lincoln appointed rip-roaring abolitionist John North Surveyor-General of the Nevada Territory.[19] When the position ended, the rail splitter named North to the Nevada Territorial Supreme Court and judge of a district court based in Virginia City.[20]

While residing in the Nevada Territory, journalist Samuel Clemens agreed to a duel. Judge North warned Clemens that if he didn't leave town he'd give him a two-year sentence under Nevada's new law making dueling illegal. Clemens, realizing North was not a man to be trifled with, left town.[21] It was the duel that never was. After a powerful attorney accused Judge North of taking a bribe in a mining case, he resigned his judgeship. North was later found innocent. North ended-up in California where he founded the towns of Oleander and Riverside. He's pushing daisies in Riverside.[22]

Hutchinson

Before and during the Civil War the singing Hutchinson family from New Hampshire was the best propagandist group for abolition. Their repertoire included 50 songs in support of Abraham Lincoln for President. During the Civil War, the Hutchinson family sang at Union troop camps and at the White House, where President Lincoln requested they sing "The Ship on Fire."[23]

While barnstorming their way towards Kansas, an old friend in Wisconsin asked them, "Why not skip all that blood and poetry, go to Minnesota, the most favored country on earth and found a city you will always be proud of?" Three of the singing Hutchinsons picked a townsite some 40 miles west of the Minnesota River Valley they named Hutchinson.[24] It's believed Hutchinson's original Articles of Agreement called for equal rights for women and created the second oldest park system in the U.S., behind only New York City.[25]

Henry David Thoreau

In the summer of 1861, Henry David Thoreau traveled up the Minnesota River to improve his declining health. At Traverse des Sioux, Thoreau wrote: "A council was held with the Indians, who have come in on their ponies...The most prominent chief was named Little Crow. They were quite dissatisfied with the white man's treatment of them & probably had reason to be so."[26]

Sioux Uprising

In 1862 the politicians in Washington, D.C. were tardy in appropriating money to the Dakotas' annuity as called for under the treaty at Traverse des Sioux. Food was so scarce on the reservations in the Upper Minnesota River Valley that crows were packing a lunch when they flew in the area. With the traders' stores full of food, the famished Dakota couldn't understand Federal Indian Agent Major Thomas Galbraith not giving them eats until their annuity payment from the government arrived.[27]

At a meeting with the Dakota and traders, Galbraith was trying to convince the traders to release food to the Dakota on credit.[28] Upset that warriors wouldn't let the traders be at the pay table when the annuity money was divvied up, Trader Andrew Myrick responded, "So far as I am concerned, if they are hungry, let them eat grass." Myrick's statement left the Dakota speechless, causing them to walk out of the meeting. As they vanished in the distance they whooped and made wild gestures.[29]

On August 17, 1862 four half-starved young Dakota were traveling on the Pembina-Henderson trail in Acton Township in Meeker County, Minnesota when they came upon a hen's nest belonging to a settler. The four Dakota got into a dare contest about taking an egg from the nest. The dares and bravado led the Dakota to kill five settlers.[30] The episode has been called "the most tragic event in Minnesota history." The next day, partly out of fear of retribution for the killings and realizing a larger number of settlers were in the Union Army, the redskins donned their feathered headgear and went on the warpath. During the Uprising the Dakota killed trader Andrew Myrick and stuffed grass in his mouth.[31]

Anton and Margaret Weber

At the onset of the Uprising settlers living on farms and in small towns sought protection in larger towns. Upon being warned of the Uprising by a horseback rider, my great-great-grandfather, Anton Weber, whipped up his team of horses. Anton, Margaret, their toddler Anna, and screaming six-week-old son, Henry, rode on the buckboard some 35 miles down the Lower Minnesota River Valley to Shakopee. Anton butchered livestock to feed the refugees. There weren't many men in Shakopee as most were fighting the Rebels. From sleeping under a wagon on a rainy night, Anton was taken down with winter fever which ailed him the rest of his years.[32]

John Other Day

While on business in Washington, D.C., Christian Indian, John Other Day, stopped at a hotel. A white waitress gave the handsome Other Day "glad eyes," and when the other women took notice, they badgered her to marry him. Through an interpreter, the women told Other Day the waitress wanted to marry him. He said yes and, a short time later they said, "I do," and left for Minnesota.[33]

John Other Day and his wife farmed near the reservations in the Upper Minnesota River Valley. Early in the Uprising he warned settlers their lives were in danger. Hiding in the woods during the day and traveling under the cover of darkness, Other Day led 62 whites, including his wife and Major Galbraith's family to safety in Henderson.[34]

Sioux Uprising – Response

To put down the Sioux Uprising, Minnesota's second elected Governor, Alexander Ramsey, gave the state's first elected Governor, Henry Hastings Sibley, a Colonel's commission in the state militia. Sibley had no previous military experience, but as the "fur lord" he knew the Dakota's habits. Sibley assembled 1,400 mostly green troops and volunteers to quash the Indian outbreak.[35] John Other Day was a scout in Sibley's makeshift army.[36] To deal with the uprising, the Feds sent washed-up Civil War General John Pope to Minnesota. The War Department was punishing him for losing the Second Battle of Bull Run.[37]

Governor Ramsey wrote a letter to President Lincoln saying the draft in Minnesota for the Union couldn't continue because of the panic caused by the Sioux Uprising. Lincoln's response: "Yours received. Attend to the Indians. If the draft cannot proceed, of course it will not proceed. Necessity knows no law."[38]

Attacks and battles of the Uprising took place at the Upper and Lower Sioux Agencies, at New Ulm, Fort Ridgely, Redwood Ferry, Birch Coulee, Wood Lake, and in several other southwestern Minnesota locations. When panic-stricken New Ulm evacuated, merchants left barrels of whiskey and food laced with strychnine.[39] Upon hearing of the uprising, the Turners in Cincinnati sent New Ulm a Howitzer cannon.[40]

During the Sioux Uprising two soldiers from Company D, 10th Minnesota Infantry, were thrown in the log jail in Henderson for drunkenness. Hoping to escape, the soldiers set the jail on fire. Instead, they died as a key wasn't readily available to unlock the door. Both soldiers are buried in Brown Cemetery in Henderson.[41]

Mary McDonald

In August of 1862, Colonel Sibley, along with 300 troops, boarded two steamboats and headed up the Minnesota River, docking before the Carver Rapids. From there Sibley marched his troops up the Lower Minnesota River Valley to Belle Plaine where they set up camp.

Mary McDonald, a 19-year-old lass from the Oak Savanna area in Faxon Township in Sibley County, crossed the Minnesota River to take a gander at Sibley's camp. Shortly after seeing the camp she wanted to "hunt down the Indians." Mary snuck off to Fort Snelling where she disguised herself as a man and enlisted in the Army. A doctor, known for his "love of drinks," gave her an enlistment physical and signed a statement, "...to the best of my judgment and belief, he is of lawful age."

An exemplary soldier, Mary held herself out to be her brother Abraham. Her father finally caught up with her at Fort Snelling. The colonel in charge, not wanting to release his model soldier, was ordered to appear with Mary at a hearing in front of a judge in Hennepin County. The judge was clued in on the facts and issued an order discharging Mary from the Army. Mary and her father returned to their farm in Faxon Township and disappeared into the mists of history.[42]

Joseph Brown and William Kahlow

In late August 1862 at Fort Ridgely, people were bellyaching to Colonel Sibley that slain persons weren't being buried. Sibley sent Major Joseph Brown out with a detail of men to bury the bodies.[43] They put the dead in the ground where they found them. Despite being told by Sibley to camp in the prairie, the troops set up camp in Birch Coulee so they could have water and wood.[44] Brown assured his men they'd "Sleep as soundly as if in their mothers' feather beds."[45]

Henderson frontiersman, William Kahlow, in 1925 related his experience to the Henderson Independent newspaper of the 31-hour siege at Birch Coulee. Early in the morning he heard the guards shout, "Indians!" About 500 Indians fired from all sides. Kahlow said they lost 22 men and 45 were wounded. Of their 108 horses, 106 were killed and the other two were wounded. He said they suffered keenly from lack of water. Kahlow tells of a Sioux warrior taking four shots at him, hitting his shoulder with the last shot. Kahlow played dead. The warrior came out in the open to reload his gun and Kahlow said, "I drew a fine bead on him and fired." He shot him near the heart.[46] Colonel Sibley sent forces from Fort Ridgely to put down the siege. To assess the damage, Sibley rode his horse into Birch Coulee and saw the heaviest military casualties of the Uprising. The stench of rotting men and horses was unbearable.[47]

Dakota Surrender

On September 26, 1862 America's largest and bloodiest Indian uprising came to an end as the Dakota surrendered at a camp dubbed Camp Release near the town of Montevideo in the Upper Minnesota River Valley.[48] No one kept a tally of the Sioux Uprising's casualties. An estimate of white civilian deaths ranges between 400-500. An estimated 60 white soldiers met their demise.[49] The Dakota carried off their dead and wouldn't tell how many were killed.[50] Shortly after the Dakota surrendered, Sibley received word of his promotion to General in the U.S. Army.[51] Sibley's army was now under the command of President Lincoln.

If the politicians in Congress had acted timely in getting the Dakota their payment, the Uprising would have been avoided. The payment was desperately needed by the starving Dakota to buy food from traders. The payment of $71,000 in gold coins in a wood barrel weighing 220 pounds arrived at Fort Ridgely in a money wagon six hours after the Sioux Uprising started.[52] The Dakota unsuccessfully attacked Fort Ridgely to get their gold.[53]

Dakota Interned

After the Uprising approximately 1,700 Dakota consisting of men, women, and children, from the Minnesota River Valley were rounded up by Sibley's army and put on wagons that formed a train four miles long.[54] In early November 1862, the wagon train left the Lower Sioux Agency near Morton bound for Fort Snelling. As the four-mile-long train passed through Henderson, an angry mob with knives, guns, clubs, and stones rushed and beat the Dakota. A white woman grabbed a Dakota baby from its mother's breast and threw the infant to the ground. The baby died a few hours later. The body was placed in the crotch of a tree.[55] The wagon train passed through Jessenland on the stage and mail route and came within three to four miles of the Weber farm. At Fort Snelling, the prisoners were confined to Pike's Island internment camp. During the winter the Dakota dropped like flies from measles, starvation, and exposure. They were buried in long trenches.[56]

Dakota on Trial

A five-member military commission arranged by Sibley, tried 392 Dakota and mixed-bloods who participated in the Uprising. Some of the trials lasted less than five minutes. The commission handed out 307 death sentences. Eventually the number was pared down to 303. Pope and Sibley wanted to hang the condemned Dakota immediately but they didn't think their authority went that far.[57]

For about a month, the condemned Indians were held at Camp Lincoln in South Bend, near Mankato. After troops prevented whites from murdering the prisoners, they were moved to a safer facility in Mankato.[58] While in Mankato, General Sibley received complaints that his troops were pestering the Dakota women cooking for the prisoners. In response, Sibley ordered a surprise raid. The swoop netted one soldier—tepee creeper Major Joseph Brown.[59]

Rather than spend $400 to send a telegram, President Lincoln sent a letter by mail to General Pope stating he wanted the trial records of all 303 Dakota condemned to death. Lincoln had his deputies draw a distinction between rapists and wanton murderers, and the Dakota who participated in the Uprising.[60]

Lincoln was urged by many in Minnesota to execute all the convicted Dakota. The only effective protest came from Henry Benjamin Whipple, at the time the most detested pale-face in Minnesota.[61] He was the first Episcopal bishop of Minnesota.[62] He wanted the Dakota, whom he considered heathens, to be "cut hairs"–to speak English and convert to Christianity.[63] The Dakota called Whipple "Straight Tongue."[64] Bishop Whipple was a harsh critic of a system that provided money to the Indians but ended up in the pockets of Indian traders and purveyors of whiskey.[65]

Soon after the Uprising ended Whipple traveled to Washington, D.C. and met with President Lincoln. Whipple believed the guilty should be punished; he was concerned innocent Indians would be executed.[66] Lincoln said to a friend about his meeting with Whipple, "He came here the other day and talked with me about the rascality of this Indian business until I felt it down to my boots. If we get through this war, and I live, this Indian system shall be reformed!"[67]

Possibly influenced by Bishop Whipple, President Lincoln, whose grandfather was killed by Indians, commuted all but 39 Dakota who were sentenced to be hanged. Lincoln (he saw Indians as barbaric wards of the State) hand wrote the names of the 39 Dakota to be executed at Mankato on White House stationery. At the last minute the number was reduced to 38 when the President gave Round Wind a reprieve because his conviction was based on the testimony of two young boys.[68] When Lincoln was told his decision to hang only 38 Dakota cost him votes in Minnesota, Lincoln said, "I could not afford to hang men for votes."[69]

Dakota Hanged

The day after Christmas in 1862—the ugliest day in Minnesota history—a crowd of 3,000 onlookers gathered at the public square in Mankato where the Minnesota River makes a bend. On the unseasonably warm day Major Joseph Brown provided a slow drumbeat. The Dakota chanted "hi-yi-yi, -hi-yi-yi" as they were led to the gallows. Just before the hanging, one of the Dakota with a noose around his neck managed to get his trousers to drop and undulate his genitals to the crowd.[70] The executioner whacked the rope with his axe to hang the 38 Dakota who stood on a single scaffold; however, the blow didn't sever the rope, which prompted an angry settler to rush up and cut it with his pocket knife.[71]

In a single drop, all Dakota were dangling from a rope, except one—Rattling Runner, the rope broke. To kill him he was hanged a second time.[72] It was our country's largest mass execution.[73] Jessenland resident and Henderson physician, Dr. H.J. Seigneuret, served as the coroner at the hanging.[74] He wrote a letter to President Lincoln telling him he witnessed the mass hanging and after examining the bodies, he certified, "They are now severely dead."[75]

One of those hanged, Chaska, was the victim of mistaken identity. One Dakota was hanged for telling a harmless lie. For lying, an officer said, "We hung the rascal."[76] If politicians were noosed for telling a lie they'd be an endangered species.

Dr. William Mayo

The dangling bodies were cut down and buried in a mass grave at the edge of the Minnesota River. During the night of the hangings, grave robbers, including Dr. William Mayo, bribed the guard and dug up all 38 bodies—probably still warm. They hauled the corpses in wagons 12 miles down the Minnesota River Valley to a barn in St. Peter. From the barn they prepared and shipped the bodies to various locations, including Chicago.[77]

Dr. Mayo kept the body of a giant brave named Cut Nose. During the Uprising, Cut Nose killed five men and 18 women and children.[78] Once, Cut Nose struggled with Dr. Mayo in an attempt to steal the doctor's horse on the way to a house call.[79] The "Little Doctor" took Cut Nose's corpse to his house/office in Le Sueur in the Lower Minnesota River Valley. He skinned Cut

Nose's corpse and sold pieces as souvenirs. While other doctors looked on, Dr. Mayo dissected the body. He kept Cut Nose's skeleton in a kettle in his office.[80]

In Rochester, Minnesota, Dr. Mayo gave physicals to Union recruits during much of the Civil War. In 1864, Dr. Mayo moved his family from Le Sueur to Rochester where he built a small office and displayed a plaster bust of President Lincoln.[81] As a Protestant originally from England, Dr. Mayo was criticized in Rochester for being pro-Catholic and pro-immigrant.[82] Dr. Mayo's two doctor sons developed a multi-specialty group practice to treat patients with all types of ailments under one roof. The facility became the Mayo Clinic. The organizational structure they developed is used by medical centers around the world. The Mayo brothers were also on the cutting edge of medical research and training for specialists.[83]

Little Crow

Rather than feel a rope on his neck, the leader of the Dakota, the bold and wily Little Crow, after a battle slipped into the Dakota prairies and then he went to Canada. In the summer of 1863, Little Crow, 16 men, a squaw and his 16-year-old son returned to Minnesota to steal horses. As Little Crow and his son were picking berries six miles northwest of Hutchinson, they were spotted by two hunters. A shoot-out ensued and Little Crow took a bullet in the chest. His body was easily identifiable as he had a double set of teeth and displaced wrist bones in both arms.[84] On Independence Day, Little Crow's body was dragged to Main Street in Hutchinson where boys stuck firecrackers up his nose and in his ears, and lit them. His body was thrown in a pile of livestock guts and a cavalry officer cut off Little Crow's head. The man who shot Little Crow collected a $500 reward offered by General Pope.[85]

Shakopee and Medicine Bottle

In 1864, Dakota Chiefs Shakopee and Medicine Bottle, who both fought in the Sioux Uprising, were liquored up by conspirators in Canada, then bound up and delivered to St. Paul. At Fort Snelling, the two Chiefs were tried and got the rope-around-the-neck treatment. Just before he was hanged Chief Shakopee, who had boasted of killing thirteen women and children during the Uprising, pointed to a steam locomotive blowing its whistle and was said to exclaim, "As the white man comes in the Indian goes out."[86] No truer words were ever spoken.

Dakota Banished

The settlers and their politicians were so bitter about the Sioux Uprising they demanded the banishment of Indians from the borders of southern Minnesota. Part of the hatred stemmed from the Dakota killing and mutilating women and children. Before or after many victims were killed, their legs and arms were chopped off and their heart ripped out. Cut Nose used a tomahawk to carve up women and children.[87]

Madder than a tomcat with a knot in his tail, Governor Alexander Ramsey said, "The Sioux Indians of Minnesota must be exterminated or driven forever beyond the borders of the State." The mob mentality drove most of the Indians to surrounding states and to western territories. The peace-loving Winnebago Indians who didn't participate in the Uprising were shoved off their reservation near Mankato.[88]

Congress agreed to banish the Dakota from Minnesota. They cancelled the payment portion of the Indian treaties and used the money to generously compensate victims of the Uprising. David Faribault's and his wife Nancy's claim were rejected because they were half breeds.[89] Congress gave "the faithful Indian," John Other Day, $2,500 for his heroism. He used the money to purchase a farm near Henderson, Minnesota.[90]

Two attacks during the Uprising left New Ulm in ruins. In 1863 the Minnesota legislature authorized New Ulm to form an artillery unit to protect its citizens from future attacks. The New Ulm Battery never fired a shot in anger.[91]

The cruel and inhumane treatment of the Dakota went on for many years. People on the frontier embraced manifest destiny. Politicians and settlers believed they had the God-given right to take Indian land and treat them as inferior people.[92]

Clara Judd

In 1859, Burritt and Clara Judd moved from Chanhassen in the Lower Minnesota River Valley to Tennessee. Burritt died in 1861, leaving Clara with seven children and no means of support. In 1862 as the Union and the Rebels fought for control of Kentucky and Tennessee, Clara made several trips between the lines and became "friendly" with Mr. Forsythe. In the fall of 1862, while on a train to Kentucky, Clara and Forsythe were snagged for being Confederate spies, and subsequently held at a Nashville hotel under the watchful eye of a guard. When told Forsythe would be hanged the next day, Clara confessed to being a spy to save his life. Forsythe turned out to be a double spy.

For several months Clara was locked up in the Union prison in Alton, Illinois. Eventually she was loose as the prison didn't have facilities for women. Clara denied guilt for her role, saying she was duped. She was never tried for spying. When she returned to Minnesota, the newspapers had a field day with her.[93]

First Minnesota Volunteers

Minnesota was the first state to volunteer soldiers in response to President Lincoln's call for troops.[94] A statue of Josias King near the Minnesota State Capitol in St. Paul reads: "The first man to volunteer in the First Minnesota Infantry the first regiment of 1,000 men tendered the government for the suppression of the rebellion."[95] The First Minnesota Regiment included Nels Nelson and Edward Price from the Rifle Guards of Sibley County. They got their first taste of the Civil War at the battle of Bull Run.[96]

In the summer of 1863 the footsore men of the First Minnesota Volunteer Infantry gathered at Gettysburg. Before the battle they were told any soldier leaving would immediately meet his maker.[97] From July 1-3, they took part in the largest land battle ever fought in North America.[98]

During the second day of fighting, political General Daniel Sickles, without orders moved his soldiers from Cemetery Ridge to higher ground. The shift left his flanks disconnected from the Union line and vulnerable to enemy attack, he spent years trying to justify his action. After a fierce battle, the Confederates broke through Sickles' line and his men ran off. The First Minnesota, numbering about 262, were caught between advancing Confederates and the rear of the Union line. If the Confederates had gotten over Cemetery Ridge, the battlefield would have been lost. General Winfield Hancock sent for reserves but it would take time for them to arrive to fill the void left by Sickles' retreating troops. As Confederates rapidly advanced, General Hancock ordered the Minnesotans to "Charge those lines!" The First Minnesota's rush stunned 1,600 Alabamians and stalled their advance in time for reinforcements to arrive.[99] Their forever famous charge saved the line on Cemetery Ridge leading to Union victory at Gettysburg.

As General Sickles' troops fled, he took a cannonball to the leg. As "Devil Dan" was carried off the battlefield, he puffed on a cigar. He donated his amputated leg to an Army medical museum where he often visited his old leg.[100]

On the third day of battle, while helping mow down Pickett's charge, the First Minnesota captured the 28th Virginia Regiment battle flag. The flag is kept at the Minnesota Historical Society in St. Paul. Some in the old slave state of Virginia have asked for the return of the flag. It's not leaving the Minnesota Historical Society.[101]

General "Hancock the Superb" said of the First Minnesota charge, "There is no more gallant deed recorded in history."[102] A monument at Gettysburg referring to the First Minnesota charge says, "In self-sacrificing desperate valor this charge has no parallel in any war."[103] President Calvin Coolidge said of the revered Minnesota "Immortal First" at Gettysburg, "...the first Minnesota are entitled to rank as the saviors of their country."[104] Who'd a ever thunk volunteers from the last state admitted to the Union before the Civil War would be among the saviors of our "trust in God Nation?" The rebels were coming off a string of victories. If Lee won at Gettysburg, it's likely he would have marched into Washington, D.C. and our country as we know it wouldn't exist.

Colonel William Colvill

In 1928, a graveside ceremony was held in Cannon Falls, Minnesota to honor Colonel William Colvill, commander of the First Minnesota at Gettysburg. A bronze statue of Colvill was unveiled and President Calvin Coolidge gave a speech. A passage from the dedication program states, "In the final analysis, Col. Colvill, perhaps, saved not only the Union Army and the day at Gettysburg, but turned back 'the high tide of the Confederacy' and saved the Union."[105]

George Armstrong Custer

Two days before the Battle at Gettysburg, George Armstrong Custer (he was idolized by President Lincoln), got word of his promotion to a brevet brigadier general. After the promotion, "the boy general" fancied up his uniform. At Gettysburg, Custer was part of what experts consider the finest cavalry charge of the war.[106]

Edwin Aldritt

Edwin Aldritt, a soldier from Chanhassen, located in the Lower Minnesota River Valley, enlisted in the fall of 1861. In

41

March 1862 he became a member of the Second U.S. Sharpshooters. The day before the three-day dance at Gettysburg, a Rebel sharpshooter and Aldritt caught one another's eye. They simultaneously shot and wounded each other. Aldritt reloaded faster and yelled at the Reb to throw up his hands. The Reb asked Aldritt where he was from. Aldritt said Minnesota. The Reb said, "You're one of them Minnesota woodsmen. No wonder you got the drop on me."

During the second day at Gettysburg, Aldritt fired against the Alabama regiment, preventing them from taking strategic Cemetery Ridge. The next day, Aldritt helped mow down Pickett's charge. Aldritt said of that third day, "I expected to be killed and pretended to be dead twice and it took some time to make myself believe that I really wasn't." After seeing action in 42 battles, the gritty Aldritt came home to Chanhassen.[107]

Gettysburg Casualties

Gettysburg was the bloodiest battle of the Civil War. The "butcher's bill" was 23,000 Union troops and 27,000 Confederate troops killed, wounded, or missing.[108] Of the 262 soldiers of the First Minnesota who made the gallant rush to save the line on Cemetery Ridge, only 47 were unscathed.[109] Edward Price, from the Rifle Guards of Sibley County, is listed as wounded at Gettysburg.[110] After Gettysburg, the First Minnesota Volunteers were sent to New York City to put down draft riots where downtrodden Irish mobs, afraid of losing their jobs to freed slaves, were lynching blacks.[111]

Anton Weber Receives Draft Notice

In 1864, President Lincoln's call for more troops reached the Weber Farm. Anton Weber, at age 41 and suffering from winter fever, received a conscription notice into the Union Army. After reading the notice Anton said, "I saw enough war." To raise money to pay the $300 exemption fee, he mortgaged a portion of the farm, and sold a cow and a yoke of oxen.[112]

Whandelin Berger

Anton's neighbor, Martin Berger, also got a "ticket to Dixie." Because Martin had a family, his younger brother Whandelin, feeling a sense of duty to preserve the Union, volunteered to fight in his brother's stead. Whandelin joined Minnesota's Second Regiment. He fought under General William Sherman on the March to the Sea. While on the march, Whandelin foraged for food and did his own butchering as it took the mule train a few days to catch up to his unit. The mule train carried rations of square flour biscuits called hardtack or "teeth dullers" and if he was lucky, salted mule meat or dried vegetables called "baled hay." At night he laid his bedroll on a mound of dirt over a Confederate soldier's grave so if it rained he didn't wake up in a puddle of water. Whandelin and other bummers were issued matches and ordered to burn all buildings. The effects of total war made Georgia howl. While singing General William Sherman's theme song, "Marching Through Georgia," he reached Savannah in December 1864. The Johnny Rebs evacuated the city and the war was wound down.[113]

Washington Lake Shooting

An Irishman in Washington Lake Township in Sibley County ignored his draft notice. When the Provost Marshall and his two assistants came for him, he took off running. After he was warned to halt, he was shot in the back of the head and fell in the snow. He died a few days later.[114]

Appomattox Court House

Surrounded by Union troops including the First Minnesota Volunteers, Confederate General Robert E. Lee surrendered the Army of Northern Virginia to General Ulysses S. Grant on April 9, 1865. Other Confederate commanders soon surrendered their armies. The terms of surrender were written out in the parlor of the McLeans' house (behind the house were slave quarters) in the crossroads village of Appomattox Court

43

House, Virginia. Drafted by military secretary, Colonel Ely Parker, an Indian Chief from the Seneca tribe in western New York, the terms of the gentlemen's agreement in essence was take your horses, go home and plant crops.[115] Lincoln's vow to take back the rebels with "malice toward none and charity for all" was carried out by General Grant. After the Dakota Indians lost the Sioux Uprising, which is considered part of the Civil War, they were hanged, exhumed, skinned, dissected, interned, beaten, starved, and banished from their land.

General Lee, nicknamed the "Ace of Spades," was against slavery and secession; but, his steadfast loyalty was to Virginia. As a paroled prisoner of war, Lee rode his horse home to Richmond, Virginia.

While the drafting and signing of the surrender document took place in the McLean house, General George Armstrong Custer (he graduated last in his class at West Point) was outside shooting the breeze with a Confederate colonel. The table on which the surrender was drafted was purchased by General Sheridan from the McLeans for 20 dollars in gold. The table was given to General Custer's wife as a gift.[116]

New Auburn

With their husbands, brothers, and sons fighting on southern battlefields, the pioneer women in Minnesota had to do work usually done by men—chop wood, milk cows, and work in the fields. In 1863 six pioneer women in the small town of New Auburn, on a tributary of the lower Minnesota River, found time to meet every afternoon to sew a flag to use when the Civil War was over and the boys came home. The flag was 20 feet in length and contained 36 stars representing the 36 states that fought in the Civil War. The stars form a huge "US" on a blue field. "'US' for the North and South together, one flag, one nation, forever." The flag was used for celebrations when the victors arrived home and for festivities on Decoration Day, later changed to Memorial Day.[117]

America's Deadliest War

The war over the issue of slavery (being slavery is not mentioned in the Constitution, southern states believed the issue of slavery was for each state to decide) lasted four years and was America's deadliest war taking over 618,000 lives![118] In 1865 the last public auction of slaves in the U.S. took place in St. Louis.[119] Union troops won what Southerners called the "War of Northern Aggression." Lincoln freed the slaves, but that didn't break the Confederates' resolve. In 1865 the Ku Klux Klan got its start in the old slave state of Tennessee.[120]

Chapter Three
Post Civil War

Abraham Lincoln Assassinated

The "Great Emancipator" didn't get a chance to reform the Indian system or to fulfill his dream to see California. On Good Friday, April 14, 1865, five days after Lee's surrender, Shakespearean actor, John Wilkes Booth, shot Lincoln in the head during a third-rate comedy at the Ford Theatre in Washington, D.C. Lincoln was a sitting duck as John Parker, the man charged with protecting the President, snuck away from his post to have a couple of belts. He was also known to frequent brothels.[1] For men guarding the President, the tradition of getting drunk and patronizing houses of entertainment continues to this day.

In the Lower Minnesota River Valley in Shakopee, the Methodist Episcopal Church held a memorial service for President Lincoln. The memorial was interrupted when a man from the congregation shouted, "I want to hear no apologies for our public men here. Eighteen hundred years ago Jesus Christ was killed, and how many tears are shed for Him here today?" Before the man could be tackled he jumped out of a window. The man soon said his remarks were indiscreet. A threat the man received in a letter telling him he would be tarred and feathered if he didn't leave town was never carried out.[2]

Fifty years after Lincoln's assassination the publisher of the *Belle Plaine Herald* recalled how he, at age eleven, received the news of the saddest event in the history of our country. At the time, Belle Plaine, in the Lower Minnesota River Valley, was on the outer edge of the frontier unconnected by rail or wire. At noon on April 16, 1865, as he and a friend watched the gathering and boiling of maple sap at McNally's maple sugar camp, a man on a horse foaming at the mouth drew near the group shouting, "President Lincoln has been assassinated." Mrs. McNally fainted. She had three sons in the Union Army, two of them dangerously ill in hospitals. The courier went from town to town spreading the news to settlers. Along the way he received fresh horses.

Upon receiving the news of Lincoln's assassination Belle Plaine went into mourning. All commercial buildings in the borough hung folds of black cloth in their windows and homes displayed an object of mourning. A liberty pole was draped in black and the flag hung at half-mast. The townspeople gathered and anxiously awaited the arrival of a stagecoach for further particulars of the tragedy.[3]

After John Wilkes Booth assassinated President Lincoln, he went on the lam. Twelve days later, a man, who may or may not have been Booth, refused to come out of a tobacco drying barn near Port Royal, Virginia. The barn was set on fire. The man refused to surrender and Sergeant Boston Corbett, without orders, shot him through an opening in the barn. The man died about an hour later. Corbett took the name "Boston" because it's where he found Jesus. After ladies of the night attempted to seduce him, he castrated himself.[4]

Grand Review

After President Lincoln's assassination, Whandelin Berger traveled from North Carolina to Washington, D.C. On May 23rd and 24th, 1865, while the band played "The Battle Hymn of the Republic," he marched with Union veterans in the Grand Review before the new President, Andrew Johnson. From the capital city, Berger, with history written on his face, returned to the soggy fields of his farm in Jessenland.[5] Raised a quarter-mile from the

Weber farm, a young Mary Scully sat on her great uncle Whandelin Berger's knee to listen to his stories. At age 97, the sharp-minded Mary told me Whandelin's Civil War stories.

Grand Army of the Republic

After the Civil War, veterans of the Union military founded the Grand Army of the Republic (GAR). Local GAR posts were formed throughout the country, including several in the Minnesota River Valley. Membership swelled to over 400,000 members and was limited to "veterans of the late unpleasantness." The GAR had one woman member, Canadian born Sarah "Emma" Edmonds.[6] She disguised herself as a man and served as a spy in the Michigan Volunteers Second Regiment.[7] In 1949, the GAR dissolved as it was down to a handful of members. In 1956 its last member, Albert Woolson, at age 109, went "room temperature" in Duluth, Minnesota.[8]

John Campbell

In May 1865 in Blue Earth County, Minnesota, half-breed John Campbell killed a family of four and their hired man using a firearm and a tomahawk. Only the baby, who was left for dead, survived. Campbell was arrested and jailed in Mankato where he was tortured. Some 800 people showed up and two factions formed, one for stringing him up and one for law and order. The factions decided on an outdoor court, including a judge, prosecutor, defense attorney, and a jury of twelve men. Campbell pleaded not guilty. The kangaroo court jury found Campbell guilty but recommended he be tried by a legitimate court.

The string-him-up faction dragged Campbell toward a basswood tree. The law and order faction intercepted Campbell to put him in jail, and with guns and knives drawn, the two factions struggled until the law and order faction receded. A wagon with Campbell in it was run under a tree. A rope was tied to a branch and the noose was placed around Campbell's neck. The wagon pulled away and Campbell raised his arms and grabbed the rope above his head. On the second try Campbell's hands were tied behind his back and his mother got his corpse.[9]

Charles Campbell and George Liscom

On Christmas Day in 1866, two trappers from Mankato, Charles Campbell and George Liscom, dressed up like Indians and paid a visit to a saloon in New Ulm. They pretended to be taking scalps. A local hero of the Sioux Uprising had enough and whacked Liscom in the head with a hatchet. Campbell knifed the local hero to death. The sheriff tossed Campbell and Liscom in the clink. A mob formed and drug Campbell and Liscom out of jail. Led by AWOL soldier John Gut, Campbell and Liscom took a severe beating before they were hanged from a ladder leaned up against the jailhouse. As Campbell's corpse dangled from the rope, Gut repeatedly stabbed him. The corpses were taken down and slid under the ice on the Minnesota River.

John Gut was tried for murder. His attorney argued that Gut mistook Campbell and Liscom for half-breeds and he was attempting to collect a bounty from the state for their scalps. The jury didn't buy the defense and recommended mercy. Judge Horace Austin, ignoring the jury's recommendation, sentenced Gut to be hanged. After a new law passed giving the jury the power to decide the death penalty, now as Governor, Horace Austin commuted Gut's sentence to life in prison.[10]

Laura Ingalls Wilder

Laura Ingalls was born in 1867 in Pepin, Wisconsin. She was two years old when her Pa moved his family to the Kansas prairie. When the Ingalls family suffered from fever 'n ague, now called malaria, they were doctored to by black physician Dr. George Tann.[11] After moving around, in 1874, Pa, in his prairie schooner with his gun near the seat, moved his family to the high grasses of the vast prairie near Walnut Grove, Minnesota. The schooner contained the family's treasures including Sunday best clothes, quilts, and Pa's fiddle. At first the family lived in a one-room dugout house with a sod roof on the banks of Plum Creek, that drains into the Minnesota River.[12] In the summers of 1875 and 1876, grasshoppers devoured Pa's wheat crop. Disgusted, Pa sold his farm, packed up his family, and moved to Burr Oak, Iowa.[13] Two years later Pa got itchy feet and moved his family back to be with the sodbusters of Walnut Grove.[14]

In 1885, Laura Ingalls began her 64-year marriage to Almanzo "Manly" Wilder. She removed the word "obey" from their wedding vows.[15] They spent most of their years at their beloved Rocky Ridge farm outside Mansfield, Missouri.[16] In her sixties, Laura, with editing help from her daughter Rose, wrote a series of children's books based on her childhood experiences on the frontier.[17] She had no idea she was writing history. Loosely based on Laura's books, the beloved television series *Little House on the Prairie* (passed up by Walt Disney) ran from 1974 to 1983.[18]

James J. Hill

In 1867 with southern racist President Andrew Johnson in the White House, gandy dancers pounded spikes into Mother Earth to lay railroad tracks two miles east of Henderson.[19] The iron horse running through the Minnesota River Valley marked the beginning of the end of the glorious steamboat era. Unlike the river, railroad tracks didn't freeze up during the winter, and locomotives didn't have to deal with low water in the summer.[20]

During the Gilded Age, James J. Hill, the epitome of a self-made man, from an out in the sticks farm in Ontario, Canada, was best known for building the First Transcontinental Railroad line without public funds or land grants. The Protestant Scots-Irishman who had nine years of schooling and was blind in one eye became known as "the greatest empire builder of the new world." He said his secret to success was "work, hard work, intelligent work, and then more work." He filled his mansion on Summit Avenue in St. Paul with ten children from his devout Irish Catholic wife.[21]

Across the Minnesota River from Blakeley, Hill had his eye on a stand of hardwood trees. He hired a logging crew to saw the timbers into ties, bridge timbers, and pilings. To feed and outfit the loggers, Hill set up his friend, Michael Shiely, with a store at Walker's Landing in Faxon Township in Sibley County. From Walker's Landing, river rats rafted the timbers down river to the Mississippi. Hill used the lumber to build the Milwaukee railroad from the Twin Cities to La Crosse, Wisconsin.[22]

St. Thomas' New Church

Five years after the Civil War ended, my great-great-grandfather Anton Weber and other men from Jessenland took a walk in the woods looking for choice oak trees. The trees were felled to build the frame for St. Thomas' new church. The church was built using pioneer construction. Posts and beams were hand-hewn by a top-notch axeman and fastened together with wood pegs. Siding from Louisiana was affixed to the log frame to put the finishing touch on the fine example of Colonial American architecture. The first Mass was celebrated on All Saints Day, November 1, 1870.[23]

When the "jewel of the Minnesota River Valley" opened, it was the finest structure in the Valley.[24] Each family was assigned a pew and pew rent was paid annually. Each year when it came time to pay pew rent, a rumor was floated that if you didn't pay your rent, you wouldn't be buried in the cemetery. The Webers sat in the middle of the new church next to the heat register in the floor. My great-great-grandmother Margaret Weber liked to stay warm on cold Minnesota mornings.[25]

John Ireland's Irish Colonies

As a boy, John Ireland immigrated to America with his parents from County Kilkenney, Ireland, stepping off the boat in St. Paul in 1852. While he was the Archbishop of St. Paul, he had the ear of Presidents Benjamin Harrison, William McKinley, Theodore Roosevelt, and William Taft. The headstrong

Archbishop didn't care for President Woodrow Wilson's racist ways. The Archbishop lobbied for religion in public schools and to end racism. He was a leader in promoting temperance, which really meant total abstinence.[26] Ireland never forgot his childhood memories of suffering discrimination for being Irish Catholic.[27] He worked hard to dispel the belief Catholics weren't good citizens. Full of gumption, he built St. Mary's Basilica in Minneapolis and the St. Paul Cathedral, the national shrine to apostle Paul.[28] He had a close relationship with railroad tycoon James J. Hill.[29]

Believing in the yeoman farmer and free enterprise, Ireland came up with the Irish colonization plan. From 1876 to 1881 Catholics, mostly Irish, from eastern states and Europe were encouraged to purchase farmland in western Minnesota at bargain prices. Overall the program was a success. However, Ireland was disappointed with the low number of impoverished Irish coming to Minnesota.[30] It was people already on the path to success (willing to work hard) who jumped at the opportunity to buy cheap land.

Joseph Brown Dies

Joseph Brown's wanderlust took him to Nebraska where he made trial runs with a new version of his steam-powered wagon. In 1870 while in New York working on the new version, Brown suddenly "gave up the ghost."[31] My great-great-grandfather, Anton Weber, at Brown's funeral in Henderson, heard Henry Hasting Sibley in his eulogy say "No man stands forth more prominent as the untiring friend of Minnesota in all phases of her existence than does Major Brown."[32] At that time, a tombstone wasn't set to mark Brown's grave.[33]

Northern Plains Indians

In June 1876 my great-grandfather, Jack Madden, at age 15, walked eight miles to Henderson to read newspaper accounts of Civil War hero George Armstrong Custer's abrupt demise.[34]

After the Battle of the Little Big Horn in the Montana Territory, the Dakota, Cheyenne, and Arapaho Indians took all the cavalry's horses that weren't wounded. When U.S. soldiers arrived they discovered the Indians had stamped out "Long Hair" and all his men. The only living horse found was a badly injured claybank gelding named Comanche who liked to drink beer.[35] The Plains Indians won the battle at Custer's Last Stand, but it was inevitable they would lose the war. In 1890, at Wounded Knee in South Dakota, the U.S. Army mowed the Plains Indians down with withering gunfire. After the slaughter, the Indian wars were over and the Northern Plains Indians were all but forced onto reservations.[36] Their struggle to preserve their culture and way of life came to a bitter end.

James-Younger Gang Ride Through the Minnesota River Valley

During the War Between the States, Cole Younger and Jesse and Frank James, and other bushwhackers from Missouri, usually without orders, fought a guerilla war against those in the free-soil state of Kansas. The bushwhackers killed those loyal to President Lincoln, captured and killed blacks, and raided and destroyed towns, including massacring the anti-slavery Jayhawkers of Lawrence, Kansas, and burning the city to the ground.[37]

After the Civil War, Union Army General Benjamin "Silver Spoons" Butler was the first federal military governor of New Orleans. Butler ordered the hanging of a New Orleans man who desecrated Old Glory in public. While sitting in a hotel, Cole Younger overheard a conversation that the detested Butler had taken $300,000 from the South and deposited the money in a bank in Northfield, Minnesota. Though untrue, Cole Younger believed it was true and he was preoccupied with getting the loot back.[38]

Jesse James and Cole Younger established a gang of cold-blooded killers who robbed trains, stage coaches, and banks mostly in Missouri and Kansas. In the summer of 1876 the James-Younger gang rode through the Minnesota River Valley to case banks. According to lore, the James gang watered their horses at Tom Doheny's farm near St. Thomas Church. During their trips through the Minnesota River Valley members of the James-Younger gang were polite to everyone.[39]

As the story goes, the sheriff of Carver County sat in his usual chair at a hotel in Chaska in the Lower Minnesota River Valley. He was throwing spotted papers with his cronies when a trio of strangers staying at the hotel were invited to sit in. After a pleasant evening of poker, the game broke up. The next morning, wearing long linen dusters to conceal their weapons, the three fellas mounted their fine steeds from a livery stable. They rode down the valley to a blacksmith shop in Shakopee where they requested their horses be shoed backwards. The farrier complied. The leader, later identified as Jesse James, tipped the smithy and the trio rode off.[40]

In early September 1876 the James-Younger gang rode into Mankato intending to rob the First National Bank. The gang called off the robbery as they feared their plan to rob the bank may have been discovered as a group of men were in front of the bank. The gang's fear was unfounded as a group of men were attending a meeting.[41] The highwaymen decided to ride to Northfield, Minnesota.[42]

James-Younger Gang Ride to Northfield

On September 7, 1876, Frank and Jesse James, the three Younger brothers, along with Clell Miller, William Stiles aka Bill Chadwick, and Charles Pitts rode into Northfield. Three of the ruffians planned to rob the First National Bank while the other five would provide cover and blaze a trail for the getaway.[43] The villains began shooting up a storm and yelling at citizens to clear the streets. During the gunplay a Swede who didn't understand English was shot for not leaving. Four days later he kicked the bucket.[44] As worthless as a politician's promise, Northfield's chief of police hid in a box of dry goods.[45]

Reeking of alcohol, the trio of bandits in the bank were frustrated with employees who couldn't unlock the safe. The safe couldn't be unlocked because it was already unlocked. All the robbers had to do was turn the latch and open the door. As the robbers in the bank were giving up, bank employee James Heywood, who a few minutes earlier had been pistol-whipped, staggered to his feet and, presumably, Frank James lodged a lead ball in his head.[46] On the streets, quick-thinking and fast-acting citizens Henry Wheeler and Anselm Manning dropped outlaws Clell Miller and William Stiles. A choice horse, used by one of the outlaws as a breastwork, also became worm food.[47]

After the shootout, lookie-loos came out to see the dead bodies of Miller, Stiles and the horse. The horse got the most pity.[48] Merchants sold pictures showing the bullet holes in Miller and Stiles.[49] The stiffs were buried in a potter's field in the Northfield Cemetery. That night, accompanied by a black wagon driver, Henry Wheeler and two of his fellow medical students dug up Miller and Stiles and nailed them in barrels marked "paint." The barrels were placed on a train to Michigan. University of Michigan medical students cheered when the cadavers arrived. When asked how he got his cadaver, Wheeler responded, "I shot him."[50]

James Heywood

Banks throughout the U.S. and a few in Canada donated $17,600 to James Heywood's widow and daughter. Banks in the northeast kicked in pretty good as Northfield was largely settled by hardy New Englanders, including Heywood, who was from Fitzwilliam, New Hampshire.[51] Being the broth of a boy, Heywood became a martyr in Northfield.[52]

James-Younger Gang on the Run

After the foiled bank raid, the warm body members of the James-Younger gang went on the run, causing the largest manhunt in U.S. history up to that time.[53] A rivalry between St. Paul and Minneapolis police departments prevented them from cooperating during the pursuit.[54] While on the loose, Jesse and Frank James broke away from Charlie Pitts and the three Younger brothers.[55]

Two weeks after the failed caper, Pitts and the Youngers found themselves in a tight spot in the Hanska Slough on the north fork of the Watonwan River, a tributary of the Minnesota River near the present-day city of LaSalle. A gun battle ensued; Charles Pitts was smoked, and Jim and Cole Younger each took a bullet leaving them unconscious. Bob Younger surrendered.[56] As Charlie Pitts' corpse was loaded onto a wagon, Bob Younger asked for a chew of tobacco and one of the captors gave him a plug.[57]

Pitts' embalmed body lay on display for two days at the state capital. Visitors, including school children, viewed the bullet hole in his naked chest. Pitts' corpse was given to a medical student who dissected the body. To bleach the bones, he put them in a box and sank them with rocks in Lake Como in St. Paul. A year and a half later a muskrat hunter saw a corner of a box protruding from the frozen lake. The hunter slashed the box open with his hatchet and saw the bones. He told his father about the box. Curious, his father went to the lake and when he kicked off the end of the box, out rolled Pitts' skull.[58]

Younger Brothers Sent to Stillwater

To cheat the gallows the three Younger brothers plead guilty to murder and the judge sentenced them to the long grind of life in prison at the Stillwater yard. Women cried, and one rushed up the aisle to kiss the prisoners.[59] A St. Louis newspaper ran an article in which Missouri thanked Minnesota.

After thirteen years of life inside, Bob Younger died of tuberculosis.[60] In 1901, after 25 years at the boys' school, model prisoners James and Cole Younger, were given their civilian clothes and told by the warden, "Put these clothes on. And you won't have to go back." Suffering from depression, James Younger put a bullet in his brain when the Board of Pardons wouldn't let him marry his sweetheart. Cole Younger worked odd jobs, including supervising workers at the home of St. Paul Police Chief, John "The Big Fellow" O'Connor. In 1903 Cole Younger was allowed to go home to Missouri where he ran a Wild West show with Frank James. Cole Younger, known as the "Last Great Outlaw of the West," took his last breath in 1916.[61] From all his gun fights, he was put in the dirt with 14 bullets he claimed were lodged in his body.[62] His command of profanity was second to none, not even muleskinners could match his invectiveness.[63]

Jesse and Frank James

In 1882, Jesse James, while in St. Joseph, Missouri living under the alias Thomas Howard, was shot in the back by Bob Ford. The $10,000 dead or alive reward on Jesse James was too much for Bob Ford and his brother to resist. A jury found the two Fords guilty of murder and they were sentenced to be hanged. The governor of Missouri intervened and pardoned them. The brothers received only $500 to cover expenses.[64] In Missouri, many saw Jesse James as a folk hero. In Northfield, many say "Jesse James slipped here."[65]

Six months after Jesse James was put on ice, Frank James, fearful that his cranium was next in line to take a bullet, surrendered to the governor of the old slave state of Missouri.[66] After a trial in a Gallatin, Missouri opera house, a friendly jury let Frank off for a Winston, Missouri train robbery.[67] In Huntsville, Alabama, a jury let Frank skate on the charge of conspiracy to rob a payroll. Spectators cheered the not guilty verdict.[68] Frank James was never extradited to Minnesota to face charges for the crimes committed during the botched robbery attempt in Northfield. He went straight and had many friends. In 1915 he died at his family's farm in Clay County near Kearney, Missouri where he gave tours. His wife said, "A better husband never lived."[69]

Jack and Annie Madden

In 1886 my great-grandparents, Jack and Annie Madden, moved into a two-story cabin with mud chinking between the logs located on 70 acres of land along Silver Lake that Annie inherited from her father John Desmond. Indians used a trail in the woods behind the cabin to access the lake. In the summer, gypsies used the trail to set up camp on the banks of Silver Lake.[70] Of the 70 acres, half was marginal farmland and half was woods. A great oak "witness tree" served as a marker for the farm's boundaries.

The Madden farm was kept in Annie's name so Jack couldn't "drink it up." He liked to sleep warm, but not too dry. To keep the log cabin snug, it had several layers of wallpaper and in the fall, Jack banked the walls of the cabin with two feet of sawdust. Jack sawed and split wood for cooking and heating.

Jack and Annie's ten children took turns walking to the neighbor's farm to hand pump water into a porcelain bucket they used for drinking and a Saturday night sponge bath. The children slept in the loft on corn husk mattresses, boys on one side, girls on the other. During cool nights they covered up with quilts with cotton backing and switched to wool batten quilts when temperatures dropped. The kids, and in later years, the grandkids woke up in the morning with a dusting of snow on the quilts that came through openings in the roof from missing clapboards.

On their subsistence farm Jack and Annie tended to a large garden and kept chickens, turkeys, and a few hogs. Jack cut and stacked brome and timothy grass to feed his horses. He also raised oats, wheat, and sorghum. In the fall Jack stripped the leaves, and cut and tied the sorghum into bundles. A neighbor took the sorghum bundles to a mill where it was pressed and boiled. While hot, the molasses was poured in tin buckets. For a meal, the Madden family spread molasses on homemade bread.

A couple of times a day Jack brewed tea on the cabin's woodstove. While drinking tea he smoked his corncob pipe and snacked on crackers with a smear of lard. One evening during Lent one of his daughters told him he shouldn't be snacking. Jack jumped out of his chair and shook his finger at her saying, "Very few people went to hell for eating a cracker."

Family and friends often came to visit Jack and Annie. During get-togethers, Jack and the guests played four- or six-handed euchre. No money was involved. They played for all important bragging rights. To see the spots on the cards, Jack lit the wick on a kerosene lantern. After the game broke up, if the visitors didn't bring food, Annie served lunch—yellow cake with brown sugar frosting or homemade sweets.[71]

Green Isle

Six miles from the Weber farm on a tributary of the Minnesota River is the small village of Green Isle with shamrocks painted on its water tower. This bit of Ireland is an Americanized name for Emerald Isle. Outside Ireland no other town in the world has the name Green Isle.[72]

In 1882 a splendid ceremony in Green Isle marked the laying of the cornerstone for the new Catholic church. The cornerstone contains an iron box with church relics and a scroll with the names of the most liberal patrons of the church.[73] When the priest wasn't looking, Thomas McMahon dropped in the iron box a picture of himself.[74] It is the only church in Minnesota dedicated to Saint Brendan, a fifth-century Irish Abbot. According to legend, St. Brendan and other Irish monks discovered America in the fifth century when Ireland was known as the Land of Saints and Scholars.[75] Now it's known as the land of Guinness and Tullamore Dew.

The potato eaters of Green Isle were well known for their fist fights. Often the reason for a good fight was the rivalry between settlers from different counties in Ireland.[76] Nearly every Sunday the priest had to break up fights on the church lawn.[77] The fights were usually harmless, that all changed in the Gay Nineties when in 1897, John Sweeney got full of the fighting stuff and became unruly. The bartender told Sweeney to leave and when he refused, the barman pulled out a pistol and fired a shot to scare him. The bullet found Sweeney and a few days later he was a goner. The jury acquitted the shooter of manslaughter.[78]

Richard Sears

In 1886, Richard Sears worked as a depot agent in North Redwood Falls, located on a tributary of the upper Minnesota River. One day a jeweler refused to pay for watches he said he didn't order. Sears peddled the watches to fellow depot agents. Sales were so brisk he ordered more watches and sold them. Sears then got the idea to sell by mail. Eventually he moved to Chicago and teamed up with watch repairman Alvah Roebuck. They sent out mail order catalogs.[79] Sears & Roebuck grew to become the largest retailer in the country. It has since been surpassed.

William Rose

On a hunting trip in South Dakota, William "Spooky" Merriam hired William Rose as his guide. Insults led to punches being thrown and the two parted ways.[80] Years later, in 1888, in Redwood County, Minnesota, William Rose was charged with murder. Since Redwood Falls had only a village lockup, Rose was held in the pokey down the Minnesota River Valley in New Ulm.[81]

Rose's first two trials ended with hung juries, both in favor of acquittal.[82] At the third trial, the winds of fate turned against Rose. A jury of 12 men convicted him of murder. When passing sentence the judge said, "Rose is to be hanged by the neck until he is dead, within three months from the date of his sentence, at a time to be appointed by the governor."[83] The Minnesota Supreme Court and the U.S. Supreme Court let the trial court's conviction stand.[84] Rather than commute Rose's sentence to life in prison, Minnesota's new governor "Spooky" Merriam reportedly said, "Let that son-of-a-bitch hang."[85]

Rose made his final trip from the New Ulm jail when he boarded a train accompanied by the Redwood County sheriff and his deputy. Rose wore his grave clothes—a new store-bought black suit and a dark blue shirt given to him by the Brown County sheriff. The train stopped in Sleepy Eye where the nippers (handcuffs) were removed from Rose's right wrist and the deputy's left wrist. At a fine hotel, Rose sat at the head of the table for breakfast, the Redwood County sheriff and his deputy sat next to him. Newspapermen filled the remaining chairs. After breakfast, Rose puffed on a cigar, amused the sheriff with his storytelling, and told a newspaper reporter of his earlier run-in with "Spooky" Merriam while he was a hunting guide.[86]

While handcuffed to the deputy, Rose boarded the train in Sleepy Eye and saw a man on the platform holding a large coiled up rope staring at him. Upon arrival in Redwood Falls, Rose was put in the 12x12 sweatbox in back of the courthouse. At noon the Commercial Hotel in Redwood Falls sent him a hearty dinner. That afternoon Rose asked the sheriff for a white shirt. The sheriff complied. The sheriff and his deputy accompanied Rose to a barbershop where Rose got a complimentary shave, trim, and moustache wax. The three men went to a portrait studio where Rose had his picture taken wearing the white shirt. Next, after taking his time, Rose picked out a fine burlwood coffin and thanked the undertaker for his courteous assistance regarding "this ugly matter." At six o'clock the sheriff brought Rose fried oysters and the two played poker until 10:30.[87]

Early the next morning, after a crying jag and eating his last meal—eggs and friend oysters—Rose met with a preacher who read from scripture and prayed with him. The sheriff read Rose his death warrant, and then the sheriff and deputies accompanied Rose, wearing the black suit and dark blue shirt, on his death march to the gallows.[88] Rose was fitted with the rope necktie, and as the black hood was pulled over his face, he said, "Goodbye all." The trapdoor dropped, the rope broke, and Rose fell unconscious to the ground. Many took the rope snapping as a sign from God of Rose's innocence. Deputy sheriffs and the coroner carried Rose back to the top of the scaffold. With a second rope, Rose was hanged again until he was good 'n' dead. There was heavy bleeding from his nostrils.[89] A newspaper called the scene a "hog killing."[90]

Rose's funeral took place at his parents' house a few miles south of Tracy. After the funeral, the burlwood box was loaded on a buggy. Over one hundred teams followed the buggy to the Tracy Cemetery. On a cold, dreary October day in 1891, the man it took the State of Minnesota three trials and two ropes to kill ended with a graveside service and a male quartet singing "Amazing Grace." As the mourners were leaving, the key witness at Rose's three trials told those at the gravesite, "Gentlemen, this is awful." Rose's friend John replied, "It certainly is. Are you sure you got the right man?" The key witness said, "I don't know, John, but I hope so."[91]

During the entire ordeal Rose maintained his innocence. The jailer in New Ulm who watched over Rose for three years believed he was innocent.[92] The judge who presided over all three trials was not entirely convinced Rose should swing.[93] A couple of years later the heavy drinker who prosecuted Rose was sentenced to 39 months in Stillwater State Prison for committing perjury in another trial.[94]

Michael Collins and Jimmy O'Neil

Irishman Michael Collins from Faxon Township in the Lower Minnesota River Valley served in Minnesota's Second Regiment. He fought in bloody Civil War battles across the south and participated in Sherman's March to the Sea. After marching in the Grand Review, the old salt fish returned to the rich soil on his farm where he was greeted by his wife and kids.[95]

In 1889, Collins' neighbor boy, Jimmy O'Neil, 28, and Collins' stepdaughter, Marcie, 16, fell in love. Marcie went into early labor and delivered a stillborn boy. The two wanted to marry, but Marcie's mother and stepfather, Michael Collins, wouldn't have it. They didn't like O'Neil's kind. The relationship between the neighboring families went downhill.[96] The feud led to a dispute over the property line on lowland between their farms. In November 1890, the dispute went to court in Henderson where Judge Francis Cadwell ruled Collins owned the land.[97]

Despite Judge Cadwell's ruling, in September 1891 the O'Neils dug a well on the lowland to supply water to a steam engine that ran the threshing machine. Jimmy O'Neil became enraged when he saw the Collins' backfilling the well. He got his gun and shot Michael Collins dead.[98]

Old man Collins' wife wound her husband's brown rosary beads he carried from his native County Kerry, Ireland through his stiff fingers. The rosary beads were a parting gift from his mother when he, his twin brother, and his sister left on their voyage to the promise of America. The evening before they left they were given an American Wake. For the family in Ireland, leaving was the same as dying.

The Kerryman's wake was held at his house. The Rosary was recited, men and women smoked tobacco in small clay pipes, and there were several whiskey toasts. The men made sure they didn't get too much blood in their alcohol stream. In accordance with Irish tradition, someone needed to remain at Michael's side throughout the day and evening.

The next day, after the wake, Collins' body was placed in a hand-hewn coffin made by his son and twin brother. The lid was nailed on the wooden box and slid into a horse-drawn wagon for the trip to St. Thomas Church in Jessenland.[99] After the Requiem High Mass it took three different shifts of six pallbearers to carry Collins' coffin up the steep slope behind the church to his final resting place. After the coffin was sprinkled with holy water it was lowered in the grave and dirt was shoveled in the hole.[100]

For shooting Collins, a jury of 12 men at the Henderson Courthouse found Jimmy O'Neil guilty of murder in the first degree.[101] Judge Francis Cadwell spared O'Neil from "stretching hemp" and gave him hard labor at the Stillwater State pen for the term of his natural life. O'Neil thanked the judge for showing him mercy.[102]

Jimmy O'Neil, accompanied by the sheriff, was on his way to the train depot two miles east of Henderson when a buggy pulled up. The sheriff stopped and, from the other buggy, out jumped Jimmy's younger brother. He approached Jimmy and said Marcie was with him and she wanted to say goodbye. With tear-filled eyes, Jimmy declined to meet her. Before long Jimmy was on a train to the prison in Stillwater.[103]

While still a "fresh fish" at Stillwater, O'Neil began building Minnesota Chief threshing machines.[104] After a few years he got tuberculosis of the bones and joints, and was confined to a hospital cell. O'Neil became friends with inmate Cole Younger, the head nurse at the prison's hospital. O'Neil reminded Younger of his brother Bob who died in the Stillwater dungeon from tuberculosis.[105]

O'Neil's right arm and leg were amputated. Judge Cadwell visited O'Neil in prison and was moved to petition the governor for a full pardon, which the governor granted. In July 1895, O'Neil, age 35, died in his mother's arms. O'Neil is buried in an unmarked grave outside the Catholic cemetery in Assumption, Minnesota. The murder O'Neil committed prevented him from having a traditional Catholic funeral Mass and from being buried in a consecrated cemetery.[106]

Timothy Traxler

Harriet Traxler, a native of Faxon Township, is the great-niece of the murdered man, Michael Collins. The information on him and Jimmy O'Neil comes from her book, *A Murder In Faxon* and from my conversations with her. In January of 1916, Harriet's grandfather, Timothy Collins, was on his way home from a public house in Belle Plaine when the engineer of a steam locomotive pulled the cord. The whistle spooked the team pulling Timothy's sled. The horses ran up a steep hill in the Minnesota River Valley, and the box—the back of the sled that holds cargo—tipped on Timothy's chest. He died with his boots on. In 1965 a new road in the cemetery behind St. Thomas Church in Jessenland was laid over Timothy's grave.[107]

Henry Cingmars and Dorman Musgrove

In 1896 two foot travelers near Glencoe, some 30 miles northwest of the Minnesota River Valley, shot the McLeod County Sheriff dead. A day later a posse of 400 men aided by a keen-eyed woman captured Henry Cingmars and Dorman Musgrove in a swamp in Sibley County. A pat down of the two desperados turned up ammunition and a set of skeleton keys. The two lock cleaners were held in the county lockup in Glencoe. Knots of people gathered at the jail to make short work of the fiends. The mayor ordered all taverns closed. At ten o'clock a message was sent to the governor requesting help. The militia arrived at midnight, just in time to prevent two lynchings. They took the prisoners to a St. Paul jailhouse, and after the hysteria calmed down, they were transported back to the clink in Glencoe.[108]

Once there, one fiend was tried and convicted of murder in the second degree. Unable to secure a jury, the other fiend was to be tried in another county. Not satisfied with justice, a sober mob of 100 men ascended upon the Glencoe jail to give the tramps their just desserts. The mob overpowered the turnkey, and using a sledge hammer ripped open the cell doors. The prisoners were gagged and dragged away. Cingmars was hanged on one side of a railroad bridge and Musgrove on the other side of the railroad bridge.[109] The coroner was notified and the bodies were cut down from the "hangman's bridge" and taken to the morgue.[110] An untrue rumor circulated that invitations decorated with a string forming a hangman's noose were sent out to attend the lynching party.[111]

Chapter Four
Spanish American War and WWI

John Curtin

Due to religious persecution, the MacCurtin family left Scotland and settled in County Cork, Ireland where they dropped the "Mac" from their name. Sick of living under British oppression, a couple of the Curtin family members immigrated to Memphis, Tennessee around 1855. From there they moved to a farm in Jessenland two miles from the Weber farm, where John Curtin was born in 1874.[1] Farm work delayed John from graduating Henderson High until he was 22.[2] In 1897, John mustered into the Army at Fort Snelling. He received his training at Fort Harrison near Helena, Montana.[3]

In February 1898, explosions in Havana Harbor, Cuba caused the USS Maine to sink resulting in the loss of her crew. Blame was cast upon the Spanish government, and those seeking war cried, "Remember the Maine."[4] Yellow journalism (an old phrase for fake news) contributed to the U.S. declaring war on Spain. As many a man said, "The first casualty of war is the truth." Ending our country's policy of staying out of foreign entanglements, the U.S. went to war in Cuba and in the Philippines to support those colonies' revolt against Spain.

In the summer of 1898, the Army sent Curtin to Cuba where he saw plenty of action. In his diary entry of July 2, 1898 he wrote, "Reached the firing line at about 3:00 P.M. and was in time to receive heavy fire from the enemy....We had a very hard fight last night and beat the enemy off."[5]

As Curtin's unit bugged out of Cuba, he suffered a relapse of malaria and was left to fend for himself.[6] The Army was slow to notify his family of his death. A storekeeper in Arlington on a tributary of the lower Minnesota River, noticed Curtin's name on a newspaper casualty list and notified his mother by letter.[7] After receiving the storekeeper's letter, his mother wrote letters to the Army asking if her son was still living.[8] The war department sent a letter to his mother confirming he died August 15, 1898 in Santiago, Cuba.[9] With help from the Catholic Order of Foresters his remains arrived in Jessenland the following spring.

At Curtin's funeral the parish priest at St. Thomas celebrated the Requiem High Mass. Wearing his bison robe coat, Father Jensen, Honorary Chaplin of the Sibley County Grand Army of the Republic Post, at the graveside service said in part, "The old patriarchs of the people of Israel, the people of God's choice, before it entered the land of Gessen, the land of God's promise and blessing, requested it as a last favor, and a duty to their children, that they should be buried in the land where they had been born."[10]

The "splendid little war" ended with a cease fire agreement in August 1898. In December 1898 the U.S. and Spain signed a treaty. The U.S. paid $20 million to Spain for the Philippines, and Spain ceded Puerto Rico and Guam to the U.S.[11] The treaty gave our country overseas colonies. Spain pulled out of Cuba.[12] The victors celebrated by hoisting Cuba Libres. Aided with American oversight, Cuba became an independent country.[13]

Henry and Katherine Weber

In 1893, Grover Cleveland was president and that year my great-grandparents, Henry Weber and Katherine Hunt, exchanged vows at St. Thomas Church. Their two sons, Edward, born in 1894, and Aloysius, "Alo," my grandpa, born in 1895, both came into the world in their two-story farmhouse. St. Aloysius from Italy is the patron saint of youth.

After delivering Alo, Katherine came down with childbed fever. On her deathbed she gave Alo her $20 Lady Liberty gold coin. Two weeks after giving birth, Katherine, at age 29, died. Henry liked to sing, but after the death of his wife he only sang in the church choir.[14] Henry had stained glass installed in a window at St. Thomas Church in memory of his wife. He never remarried. Alo and his brother were raised by their father and grandmother, Margaret, who nursed Alo. When Alo was a young boy he pulled through smallpox.[15]

Hinckley Fire

Before 30,000 lumbermen went to work, millions of acres of white pines in northern Minnesota covered the Great North Woods. The Lost Forty in the Chippewa National Forest contains a stand of virgin old grow white pines. Due to a surveying error, these majestic pines were spared Paul Bunyan's axe.[16]

During the Golden Age of Lumbering the Great North Woods was logged to build our magnificent country. The loggers only cut the trunks of the white pines. The slash was left on the ground, creating a tinderbox. On September 1, 1894, during a severe drought, several small fires combined, causing an uncontrollable force of nature called a firestorm. A firestorm has as much energy as an atomic bomb and travels as fast as a tornado. The Hinckley firestorm reached 1,600 degrees Fahrenheit, created hurricane force winds, hurled flames four and a half miles into the sky, and bubbles of glowing gas ignited over the city of Hinckley.[17] Seeing the smoke and glow of the Hinckley firestorm, Anton and his son, Henry, worried it might reach the farm.[18]

The "insatiable greed of the red demon" blackened over 480 square miles in four hours and engulfed six towns. The ground burned, leaving a layer of black ash everywhere. The firestorm took some 400 lives, not including backwoodsmen, hundreds of Indians, and thousands of animals. Boston Corbett, the Union soldier who supposedly killed John Wilkes Booth, is listed as a casualty of the firestorm, although his body couldn't be identified. Tourists came to see the dead bodies and to grab souvenirs. To help victims of the firestorm, the Sultan of Turkey sent 300 Turkish pounds. James Hill donated $5,000 and 5,000 acres of land. Montgomery Ward sent 500 pairs of shoes, and a storekeeper in Duluth said to a relief worker, "Our store is at your disposal. Go and get what you want."[19] The superintendent of the Duluth District of the Minnesota Anti-Saloon League found a silver lining in the fire—it got rid of the area's saloons and stills.[20]

Jessenland Celebrates Independence Day

In 1895, Jessenlanders celebrated Independence Day on the banks of the Minnesota River near St. Thomas Church. Those in attendance rode a merry-go-round, played baseball, and participated in sack, potato, and buggy races. Some chased a greased pig or tried to climb a greased pole. Everyone enjoyed an all-American dinner.[21] From 1898 until the early 1960s, Jessenland held several 4th of July celebrations in the Weber's cow pasture on the shores of Silver Lake.[22]

Anton Weber Dies

In 1899, Anton deeded the Weber farm over to his oldest son, Henry. Three years later, at age 79, Anton's pioneer life came to an end. During his regimented life he was a locksmith, prisoner, soldier, farmer, and public servant. After Anton's soul left for the Big Woods in the Sky, the men in the Weber house started eating with the women and children.[23]

St. Paul Trip

A couple of years after Anton's death, Henry, Alo, and their cousin, Ralph Kreger, hitched the buckboard to a team of horses. At Blakeley they took the ferry across the Minnesota River and then ferried across the Mississippi River. It was an all-day trip to St. Paul where they stayed with relatives. The next day, to protect Grandma Margaret from harsh weather, Henry purchased a carriage with a dashboard to shield the teamster from dirt and manure kicked up by the horses. On the third day, after the horses were rested, they hitched the buckboard to the carriage for the trip back to the farm. The team snorted to get through the sand at Shakopee.[24]

Hanley Falls

The plat of Hanley Falls on a tributary of the upper Minnesota River, is laid out like Washington, D.C.[25] Hanley Falls is home to the "Y" petition in which shippers asked the Railroad and Warehouse Commission for switching tracks configured like a "Y" so railcars could transfer from one railroad company's track to another's, resulting in shorter freight runs. Both railroads fought the petition. In 1901, Henry Weber was pleased to read newspaper write-ups of the U.S. Supreme Court allowing Hanley Falls to get its "Y" switching tracks. It was the first town in the United States to have a railroad transfer facility.[26]

Hamilton Judson

Beginning in the early 1900s mail carriers delivered and picked up letters and packages at the end of the Weber farm's driveway. The carriers also sold stamps and money orders. Prior to rural free delivery (RFD), most country folks had to journey to the town post office. Fearing a decline in business, shopkeepers and private mail carriers fought the change.

For 29 years, Postmaster Hamilton Judson of Farmington, Minnesota, some 40 miles east of the Minnesota River Valley, made a name for himself working during the harvest seven days a week, 15 hours a day.[27] Congress agreed to let Judson try RFD. The experiment was a huge success that led to RFD and the construction of a model postal road from Duluth to St. Paul.[28] Judson's obituary states, he "was the greatest of all our citizens."

By an act of Congress, the post office in Farmington is named in his honor.[29]

Henry Weber

After the assassination of President William McKinley in 1905, Teddy Roosevelt became our nation's youngest president. He believed in a Square Deal for everyone.[30] Also in 1905, Henry Weber purchased a steam engine on steel wheels and a saw mill. In the winter he felled trees near the shores of Silver Lake. He used a team of horses to skid the logs on the frozen lake to the mill. He sawed lumber for many of the frame houses and buildings in Jessenland that replaced log buildings. During the winter Henry sawed ice from Silver Lake and stored it in an ice house he built. For insulation he covered the blocks with saw dust from the mill. During the summer Henry put blocks of ice in his home's icebox to keep food cold.[31]

A few years after he purchased the saw mill, Henry bought a threshing machine and a corn shredder. He used the same steam engine, known as a "donkey," to power the new machines. The donkey was pulled from place to place by a team of horses. Henry filled the steam engine with water from Silver Lake, and stoked the firebox under the boiler with slabs from the saw mill.[32]

Threshing was the biggest annual event in Jessenland, and Henry's crew threshed the neighbors' grain. To feed the men, women prepared three meals a day "fit for a king" and a little lunch in the morning and afternoon. After the crew left, the women washed the antimacassars. To avoid fights and hard feelings from words spoken when "full," Henry didn't have a "make merry after the harvest" party.[33]

When a mysterious fire caused the farm's barn to go up in smoke, Henry and his sons sawed lumber and built a new barn. Permits for dances were nailed to a beam in the barn. The dances were fundraisers for St. Thomas Church. Women scrubbed and waxed the hayloft floor, and at one dance, a calf with two heads was on display. Mike Carroll often served the dancers hamburgers he fried at the shop next door.[34]

The ground floor of the new barn had three horse pens, one for each team, 14 stanchions, and a feed room. When the cow in the stanchion next to the door started swishing people with her tail, Henry sold her and left the stanchion empty. Sitting on a one-legged stool, Henry and his sons, Edward and Alo, milked by hand the herd of 13 Holsteins.[35] Breeders from the Netherlands developed Holsteins to be the best milk producers in the world. The most famous Holstein was Mooly Wooly, the last cow at the White House. She gave President Taft and his family fresh milk.[36]

During the summer Henry donned his top hat and rode his buggy to Arlington. Over a pail of beer, he talked politics in High German with other Dutchmen at Zimmerman's Saloon where the motto was: "Do as you would be done by." Zimmerman's advertised "choice wines and liquors, and such other necessaries as will best satisfy the inner man."[37]

In the early 1900s, Henry and his family enjoyed beverages from John Hepp & Co. The business used artesian well water from Henderson to bottle temperance drinks—"cream beer," pop, cider, ginger ale, seltzer, and mineral water.[38] It was said cream beer "has 'em all skinned to a frazzle."[39] John Hepp offered a $500 reward to anyone proving his "cream beer is inferior to any like beverage manufactured in the state."[40] When John Hepp was buried in Brown Cemetery in Henderson, it was said his cream beer recipe went with him.[41]

Henry, known for his wise money-management, served as Clerk of the Jessenland Township Board and as Treasurer of Silver Lake School.[42] In 1914, Henry installed a Vote-Berger telephone in the two-story farmhouse. When the telephone was patented, Western Union called it a toy.[43] That summer Henry won a Ford Model T Horseless Carriage at the Sibley County Fair in Arlington. The Tin Lizzie was gravity-fed from the gas tank to the inline four-cylinder engine, causing the driver to back it up steep hills. When it rained, the dirt roads turned to mud and the "T" often got stuck.[44]

Alo Weber

During the winter Henry hitched his buckskin driving horse to the cutter, so his mother could visit her sister. Everyone's cutter had distinct bells, the Weber's cutter could be identified before it was seen. While at his aunt's farm, the driving horse was fed oats for the trip home. At home, the horse would break out of the fence and trot to his aunt's farm for more of those tasty oats. As a young boy, Alo walked six miles to his aunt's farm and rode the buckskin bareback to the Weber farm.[45]

When Grandpa Alo was a young boy, his Grandma Margaret asked him to shoot a mess of blackbirds. Armed with one load in the 12-gauge double barrel shotgun, he snuck up on a tree flush with blackbirds, startled them, and fired a wing shot dropping 17. He plucked the feathers and carved out the breasts. For supper the family had blackbird pie.[46]

At home Alo and Edward spoke German and English. During their formative years they liked to box, play baseball, mumblety-peg, cards, ante over, and pitch horseshoes. They made whistles out of small green tree branches, and ropes out of used twine. When Alo and Edward got older they went to Saturday night polka dances. They could tell how far someone traveled to the dance by how much they smelled of horse.[47]

Silver Lake Schoolhouse

Henry sent Alo to Catholic school in St. Paul where they spoke English only. He stayed with relatives. Lonely for farm life, Alo completed grades three through eight at the one-room country schoolhouse, District 10, known as the Silver Lake School. Alo walked a half mile to school carrying his lunch in a woven stick basket.[48]

The teacher at Silver Lake School was qualified to teach after completing three years of high school and a year of training at a normal school.[49] The schoolmarm's contract dictated she had to start a fire in the wood furnace, shovel snow, clean the outhouses, and launder the linen hand towels.[50] Back then, county school rules of conduct prevented schoolmarms from getting married during her contract, from keeping company with men, and from loitering in ice-cream parlors. Schoolmarms couldn't smoke cigarettes, dress in bright colors or dye their hair, and they had to wear at least two petticoats.[51]

One day at country school Alo committed a minor misdeed. The schoolmarm took him outside and beat him with a stick. When Alo got home, his brother, Edward, (he was smarter than the teachers) told on him and his dad, Henry, took him to the summer kitchen and gave him another walloping with a stick. After country school, Alo completed a year of "farm school" in Henderson where during the week he stayed with relatives.[52]

Joseph Brown Monument

In 1909 while Teddy Roosevelt was president, the Minnesota legislature appropriated $1,000 toward a monument for Joseph Brown. Additional funds were raised locally.[53] In September 1910 my great-grandfather Henry and his son Edward attended the dedication of the 32-foot-high monument to Joseph Brown in the Brown Cemetery in Henderson. Alo stayed on the farm to skin a cow that died the night before. The hide was sold to a tanner.[54] At the dedication, a politician said of Brown's steam-powered wagon, "All traction engines and automobiles...are built on the same line of thought and invention; and they are in a way a far greater monument to him than this granite shaft."[55] Sinclair Lewis in the appendix to his novel *The God Seeker* wrote of Brown, "Perhaps as much as anyone he was the inventor of the automobile."

Sibley County Seat War

Five times my great-grandfather Henry voted to keep Henderson the Sibley county seat. After each election there were

77

cries of election fraud.[56] On the fifth vote in 1915, the taxpayers decided to move the county seat to the central location of Gaylord and the great county seat "war" came to an end.[57] It didn't help Henderson that it's Masonic Lodge was openly anti-Irish.[58]

On December 1, 1915 a motor truck, six autos and 30 teams pulling wagons left Henderson carrying the county's records, files, books, furniture and employees to Gaylord. An anonymous contributor to the newspaper called the sad procession "a monster funeral."[59] In 1917 the county's employees moved into a beautiful new courthouse in Gaylord.[60]

Ziehers

The Webers' neighbor, Christian Zieher, got a bounty land warrant containing a replica signature of President Abraham Lincoln. In 1885, Christian and his wife Elizabeth gave their son Jake a "Bread and Butter Deed" for their farm. To keep the farm, Jake had to furnish his parents a house and staples, including pork, potatoes, flour, coffee, sugar, tobacco, tea, cornmeal, apples, butter, ticking, sheeting, calico, shoes and clothes—for life. He also had to pay their doctor and medicine bills. Jake fulfilled the conditions of the deed and kept the farm.[61]

Jake's grandson, Vietnam vet Mike Zieher, and his wife Trisha now live on the farm. The Ziehers and Webers have been friends and neighbors over 150 years. Generations of Ziehers and Webers joke that they gave the Doheny brothers a helping hand off the Black Oak steamboat when she docked in Jessenland.

Sibyl Carter

In the late 1800s, Episcopal Deaconess Sibyl Carter noticed Indian women were skilled at sewing and beadwork. She went to Japan to learn the art of lace making, and upon her return she organized lace making at Indian missions. The Dakota women in Redwood County in the Upper Minnesota River Valley made some of the finest lace in the world. Their lace won a gold medal at the World's Exposition in Paris, and hoity-toity women from the east coast sought out their intricate creations.[62] Bishop Whipple presented lace made by Indian women to Queen Victoria.[63] With the coming of the "machine age," handmade lace disappeared faster than a taxpayer dollar in Washington, D. C.[64]

Henry Benjamin Whipple Dies

Episcopal Bishop Henry Benjamin Whipple was comfortable among Indians, blacks, tycoons, presidents, Queen Victoria and her royal court, and the cake-eaters at Oxford and Cambridge.[65] After the death of his first wife, Bishop Whipple, at age 74, got the old hens cackling when he married 35-year-old Evangeline Marrs Simpson in St. Bartholomew's Church in New York City.[66] When Whipple died in 1901, his wife received condolences from the four corners of the earth.[67]

Bishop Whipple is buried under the altar at the Cathedral of Our Merciful Saviour in Faribault, Minnesota, which was built under his watch.[68] A Cathedral tower was built with funds that arrived after Bishop Whipple's death. Masons embedded a bottle of strong drink in the tower's brick.[69] The tower was dedicated On All Saints' Day, November 1, 1902.[70] It bears this tribute written by Dean Slattery: "This tower is the thanksgiving of many people for Henry Benjamin Whipple, first Bishop of Minnesota and is the symbol before men of the supreme value of a righteous man."[71] After the Sioux Uprising, Whipple was detested for standing up for fairness and rights for Indians; now he's revered as a man ahead of his time.

Theodore Wallert

In 1889, Minnesota passed the "Midnight Assassination Law." It required hangings take place an hour before sun-up within the walls of a jail or within an enclosure taller than the gallows. The only persons allowed to attend hangings were the sheriff and his assistants, a minister, a doctor, three persons invited by the condemned person, and up to six persons invited by the sheriff. The gag law prevented newspaper reporters from attending executions, and newspapers could only print that the condemned person was duly executed. Violators were subject to a misdemeanor.[72]

Those born on February 29, 1896 had to wait eight years for their first birthday as there was no leap year in 1900. Also in 1900, Theodore Wallert, who lived near Arlington, went haywire with a butcher knife, stabbing to death his estranged wife and four of her five children. He said he was sorry the fifth child escaped.[73] A day after the killings, the Sibley County Sheriff apprehended Wallert near his sister's house.[74]

Wallert told the court, "My wife and stepchildren refused to work and made a slave of me and abused me by calling me an ox, bull, fool and all sorts of names. They told me I had no rights whatsoever."[75] His words didn't sway the jury. At the sentencing there were chants of "Hang him, hang him." A tearful Judge Francis Cadwell sentenced Wallert to be hanged to which the crowd vigorously applauded.[76]

In the wee hours of March 29, 1901 the hangman, using a new $5 rope, placed the noose around Wallert's neck.[77] After a black hood was placed over his head a priest recited the Lord's prayer, and before he finished, the sheriff sprung the trap door and "dropped Wallert into eternity."[78] The newly elected attorney for Sibley County, George MacKenzie, kept a close eye on the events surrounding the killing of Wallert.[79]

My great-grandfather, Henry Weber, attended the hanging of Wallert in Henderson. Henry saw Wallert's neck stretch causing the hood to pull up over his head. Blood gurgled out of Wallert's mouth and nose, his eyes bulged out and 11 minutes went by before he was dispatched. Most in the crowd were "in the tank" and some lost their supper, which caused a stampede. It was the only time Henry came home drunk and it took him several months to get over seeing a man hanged.[80]

Andrew Tapper

In 1902 the same gallows used to shorten Wallert's life were erected down the Lower Minnesota River Valley in Chaska for hanging Andrew Tapper. While working as a bartender in Carver, jealousy got the best of him and he slit the throat of a young waitress with his pocket knife. In pronouncing the hanged-by-the-neck-until-dead sentence, Judge Francis Cadwell, who opposed capital punishment, said, "It is an unpleasant duty I have to perform, and I would gladly be excused, but as a duty I must perform it...." The judge found no exceptional conditions to commute the sentence to life in prison.[81] Before the state of Minnesota got a whack at him, he tried to hang himself three times.[82] In February 1902, while ministers sang a hymn, the sheriff asked his deputies to remove their hats and he sprang the trap. Tapper felt the rope and 14 minutes later the self-confessed murderer was pronounced dead by the coroner.[83]

Ole Olson

My great-grandfather Henry had a brother, Tony Weber, who married Mary Knipple, a teacher at the Silver Lake schoolhouse. Tony took over a dairy farm in Aitken County, Minnesota his wife inherited from her father. Tony and Mary followed the saga of Aitken County Farmer Ole Olson.

Lonely on his farm, Olson sent money for his daughter, Josephine, age 18, and his 16-year-old son in Sweden to come live with him. They moved in with their father who wanted to make Josephine his wife. It wasn't long before Josephine fell in love with a neighboring farmer. The day before Josephine was to be married, her father ran a knife through her heart.[84]

Olson received a date with the scaffold. After quibbling about whether or not Olson departed from his right mind when he stabbed his daughter, in March 1903 the sentence was carried out in the middle of the night. The rope slipped, cutting Olson's throat, almost decapitating him and tearing the skin off his face.

His jugular vein was severed and sprayed blood on the sheriff and ministers.[85]

William Williams

In 1905, Cornish immigrant, William Williams, was sentenced to hang for shooting dead his underage gay lover and the kid's mother.[86] Potential jurors who indicated they were against the death penalty weren't seated.[87] When the Ramsey County hangman tripped the trapdoor, he was surprised when Williams' feet touched the floor. The sheriff didn't take into account the condemned man's neck and the rope stretching. For the next 14 minutes three deputies held the rope up to slowly strangle Williams to death. Spectators cut up the rope for souvenirs.[88] An autopsy showed Williams had criminal brains akin to the brains of a wild animal.[89] The botched hanging started a movement in Minnesota to abolish the death penalty. Williams was the last person to be exterminated by the state of Minnesota.[90]

George MacKenzie

In 1911, State Representative George MacKenzie from Gaylord, located on a tributary of the lower Minnesota River, made an eloquent anti-death penalty speech on the floor of the House in support of his bill to abolish capital punishment in Minnesota. In his speech he said, "Let us bar this thing of Vengeance and the Furies from the confines of our great State; Let not this harlot of judicial murder smear the pages of our history with her bloody fingers, or trail her crimson robes through our Halls of Justice, and let never again the Great Seal of the Great State of Minnesota be affixed upon a warrant to take a human life..."

After his speech, the bill passed both houses and the governor signed it into law.[91] Since 1911, bills to restore the death penalty in Minnesota have been dead on arrival.

Elias Clayton, Elmer Jackson and Isaac McGhie

Minnesota ended hangings by the state, but in 1920 that didn't stop a mob of thousands in Duluth, Minnesota from pulling three young African-American circus workers out of jail cells and lynching them.[92] They were among several roustabouts accused of raping a white woman. A few days after Elias Clayton, Elmer Jackson, and Isaac McGhie were hanged, stores in Duluth sold postcards with a picture of the lynchings.[93] Most Minnesota newspapers condemned the lynchings, but the Mankato Daily Free Press in the Minnesota River Valley gave editorial support to the mob.[94]

For the mob lynching, 19 men were indicted on a variety of charges from rioting to murder. Two men were convicted and went to prison. They were both paroled after serving twenty-six months. A third man was convicted of rioting and sent to the reformatory at St. Cloud.[95]

One black man, riddled by a bumbling defense team, went to prison for raping the white woman.[96] In an unprecedented move, the man sent to prison for the rape was released after serving four years. At the time, rape carried a minimum twelve-year sentence, and for being black he normally would have served close to thirty years. All records concerning the matter were destroyed.[97] Someone in a position of authority must have figured out the white woman wasn't raped.

It's likely more blacks would have gone to prison had it not been for the good work of a brilliant black defense attorney, Charlie Scrutchin, from Bemidji, Minnesota, the first city on the Mississippi. Scrutchin married a white woman. In Bemidji people said, "The colored lawyer is one smart man."[98]

The ugly lynchings in Duluth led to Minnesota's anti-lynching statute. The politicians in Washington, D.C. never passed a national anti-lynching law.[99] A book written on the Duluth lynchings was originally titled "They Was Just Niggers."[100] My dad told me, "Mobs are very dangerous and nothing good comes from them. A mob crucified Jesus."

Dan Patch

The city of Savage in the Lower Minnesota River Valley, is named after businessman Marion Savage. In 1902, Savage forked over the hefty sum of $60,000 for pace horse Dan Patch, a mahogany bay stallion with a white star on his forehead. A pace horse moves the two legs on the same side of his body forward together while pulling a sulky. Some enthusiasts consider Dan to be the greatest race horse of all time and our country's first sports superstar.[101]

In 1906 at the Minnesota State Fair, harness horse Dan Patch paced the mile in 1.55, a record that stood for more than three decades.[102] Despite having a deformed hind leg, during his career Dan only lost two heats. He was stabled at the International 1:55 Stock Food Farm in Savage, and as a member of the Wesley United Methodist Church in Minneapolis, he didn't race on Sunday. Dan loved crowds, raising his head toward spectators as though communicating with them. As a celebrity, Dan traveled in his own private railcar, two songs bear his name, and *The Great Dan Patch* movie debuted in 1949.

In 1916, Marion Savage lay in a Minneapolis hospital recovering from minor surgery when he received word Dan had died. The next day Marion died, his death attributed to the shocking news of the loss of his beloved Dan Patch. Being Dan Patch was a household name, when news of his death spread, the entire nation went into mourning. Dan is buried on the banks of the Minnesota River in a secret location passed on to a select few.[103]

John Ireland Dies

In June 1907, Henry Weber put on his well-cut suit and at the Blakeley depot boarded a streamline train to St. Paul to attend Archbishop John Ireland's ceremony for the laying of the cornerstone for the new cathedral in St. Paul. It's written in the book of donations in the narthex of the cathedral that Henry donated $30 to the building fund in the name of his late wife Katherine.[104]

When Archbishop John Ireland died in 1918 his funeral at the St. Paul Cathedral was one of the largest in Minnesota. Eight archbishops, 30 bishops, 12 monsignors, 700 priests and thousands of the faithful attended the Pontifical Mass of Requiem. For a half century the "Consecrated Blizzard of the Northwest" was one of the most dominant religious figures in America.[105]

John McGovern

In 1909, William Taft was president and Henry Weber and his sons, Edward and Alo, read newspaper accounts of the University of Minnesota Gophers football team Big Nine Conference win led by the Gophers first All-American quarterback John "Duffy" McGovern from Arlington, Minnesota.[106] During the 1908, '09 and '10 seasons, except for one game, he played every minute of every game. He won many games with his drop kick.[107] In January 1910, Duffy's coach, Dr. Henry Williams, performed an emergency appendectomy on his star quarterback.[108]

In the 1930s, John McGovern practiced law in Washington, D.C. where he was one of the founders and later president of the Washington Touchdown Club.[109] In 1937 he moved to Le Sueur in the Lower Minnesota River Valley, where he negotiated contracts with Mexico and the Bahamas to send workers to pick vegetables for Green Giant.[110] He died of a heart attack in 1963 while watching a football game. Three years later he was elected into the college football Hall of Fame.[111]

Hugh McGovern

John McGovern's father, Hugh McGovern, Arlington's town Marshall for 58 years, was called the "dean of Minnesota policemen."[112] His salary was $45 per month in 1911, in 1935 his salary was $50 per month.[113] He was caught off guard in the wee hours of an October morning in 1924 when a band of yeggs drove into town, forced their way into the telephone exchange and cut the switchboard cables. The bandits locked Hugh and two other men in a railroad refrigeration car. The outlaws broke into the First State Bank and blew the door off the vault with a blast of nitroglycerine.[114] Across the street, Tom Burke, who lived upstairs over his cafe, fired at the outlaws until his revolver was empty. When the bandits shot out the cafe's front window, he thought it was best to lay low.[115] The safecrackers left without gaining access to the $15,000 stored in the safe inside the vault. The cracksmen may have run out of nitroglycerine or they may have been afraid to enter the vault after a charge of nitro used to explode the safe failed to detonate. Hugh McGovern was upset with himself for letting the crooks get the jump on him.[116]

Clams and Turtles

Starting in the 1890s, clams were dug from the mudflats of the upper Minnesota River. The clams were boiled, the meat removed and sold for pig feed. The shells were shipped by rail to button factories. Occasionally a valuable pearl was found, but like politicians, most were worthless. Turtles were put in barrels and shipped to various locations.[117]

Mudcura

In 1909 the sanitarium Mudcura opened across the river from Shakopee in the Lower Minnesota River Valley. People suffering from rheumatism, nerve diseases, alcoholism and other diseases stayed in rooms for $15-$25 per week. In hope of a cure or to relieve pain, patients were wrapped in heated sulphur mud from the Minnesota River, hosed down and given a sulfur water bath and a massage. Given the treatment, disease, including alcohol, was rubbed out of a patient's body. Some drank the sulfur water and some took electrical treatments. In the early 1950s, the fad petered out.[118]

Guy DeLeo

From 1854 to 1929 trains carrying children from various East Coast orphanages—mostly from New York City—dispensed orphans throughout the West. The plan was to get the street Arabs out of crowded cities and into nurturing family homes in the West. When an orphan train arrived the children were sorted. Couples examined the orphans and were asked to choose a child. Some adopted a boy to gain a farmhand.[119]

In 1916, Guy DeLeo, born in New York City's Foundling Hospital, arrived on an orphan train in St. Paul. He was adopted by a couple from New Ulm. His long, dark curly hair caused people to think he was a girl. It didn't take long before his adopted mother cut his locks and dressed him in boy's clothes. In 1932, DeLeo graduated from MacPhail College of Music in Minneapolis. Shortly after graduation DeLeo formed and directed a 16-piece orchestra. It became a popular show and dance band throughout the upper Midwest. Going from New York to New Ulm did him a world of good as he believed he was the "luckiest man on earth."[120]

New Ulm During WWI

In June 1914 the heir to the Austria-Hungary throne and his wife were assassinated in Sarajevo, Bosnia. Austria-Hungary blamed the assassination on Serbia and declared war. The central powers of Austria-Hungary, Germany, and the Ottoman Empire (modern-day Turkey) went to war against the allied countries of Belgium, France, Great Britain, Russia, and Serbia. After German submarines sank unarmed U.S. passenger ships, in April 1917 our country joined the allies.[121]

When the U.S. was about to enter World War I, influential citizens from New Ulm in Brown County gave speeches on the constitutionality of the draft, questioned the U.S. entering the war and backed getting combat exemptions for New Ulm soldiers.[122] In neighboring Sleepy Eye, named for a Dakota Chief with a drooping eyelid, a banner strung across Main Street read "Berlin—ten miles east."[123]

The speeches of influential citizens caught the attention of the overzealous Minnesota Public Safety Commission that had broad enforcement powers from the Feds to shut down opposition to the war.[124] In August 1917 the governor of Minnesota suspended New Ulm's mayor, city attorney and the Brown County auditor.[125] The Public Safety Commission forced the resignation of the President at Dr. Martin Luther College in New Ulm.[126] Throughout the country the Feds required all aliens over 14 to register and threatened to take their property. After registering they had to receive permission to move.[127] On August 7, 1917 the Chicago Tribune printed: "The anti-draft meetings in New Ulm, Minn., remind us that fifty-four years ago the Indians massacred the population of that town. That is, fifty-four years too soon."[128]

Before and during WWI, agents hired by the state of Minnesota inundated New Ulm looking for any hint of disloyalty. The agents shut down dancing and cabaret performances in saloons, and questioned people who didn't purchase war bonds.[129] Some feared the entire town would be interned.[130] The agents made it a stiff row to hoe, but New Ulm was a loyal red, white, and blue city. Its citizens only wanted free speech; the federal and state politicians made sure they didn't get it. In 1920, the mayor, who had been suspended earlier by the governor of Minnesota, was elected mayor by a two-to-one margin. His first act was to hire back the suspended city attorney.[131]

Rathskeller

In the basement of the Minnesota State Capitol in St. Paul there is a *rathskeller*, a German restaurant in the basement of a town hall, complete with German artwork and mottoes. In 1917, by order of the governor, the *rathskeller* artwork and mottoes were painted over.[132] During WWI, "liberty cabbage" was the politically correct name for sauerkraut.[133]

Blakeley

During WWI the manager of a moving picture show came to Blakeley in the Lower Minnesota River Valley to show a pro-German movie. Those in attendance at the Village Hall took thousands of feet of his film and set it on fire. Many in attendance cheered, "Down with the Kaiser" and "Up with the flag" The manager escaped on the first train out of town.[134]

Edward and Alo Weber

During the Great War, original name for WWI, Grandpa Alo received a draft notice. His father applied for and received an exemption for his son. Alo wished he could have served, but he was needed to work on the farm. Already in the Army, his brother Edward made tent poles while stationed in the forest of the Pacific Northwest. The Army's Spruce Division logged high quality wood to build planes, ships, and other armaments for war.[135]

Dawson–"Ladies in White"

Ladies in Dawson and the surrounding area in the Upper Minnesota River Valley organized during WWI. Under the watchful eye of the American Red Cross, they rolled bandages, made helmet warmers, pads, knitted wool socks, and other items to send to our troops in Europe. The ladies were required to wear a white uniform and they had to bring their own silver knife, ruler, pencil, notebook and thimble.

To buy supplies the "Ladies in White" in and around Dawson held fundraisers. In September 1917 the farmers in Lac qui Parle County pitched in by donating a portion of their crops, four hogs, and five calves. When a hometown serviceman on furlough at a Red Cross rally spoke highly of the Ladies in White, those in the crowd contributed $4,338 to their cause. After the fighting in Flanders Fields ended the Ladies in White collected clothing to send to the people of Belgium.[136]

John Klancke

Woodrow Wilson was president during the war "over there." To set an example for energy conservation, he kept a flock of sheep to graze on the White House lawn, including a ram named Old Ike that liked to chew tobacco.[137] Also during WWI, John Klancke from Hamburg on the outer ridge of the Lower Minnesota River Valley, converted his Harley Davidson motorcycle into what is believed to be the world's first snowmobile.[138]

Ray Zieher

During WWI, Grandpa Alo's friend of 85 years, Ray Zieher, served as a doughboy in the trenches of France. As an ace machine gunner he took several Huns. After a battle he went missing for a few days. His buddies were relieved when he reappeared; he had stayed in the trenches waiting out German snipers. He survived taking a dose of mustard gas.[139]

Charlie Stroebel

Grandpa's brother-in-law, Charlie Stroebel, landed in free France during WWI. Having no food, Charlie and other bean boilers got up early and went to nearby villages where they got oil, flour, and eggs. While flipping pancakes on a sheet of metal over burning wood, Charlie looked up and saw a line two miles long for breakfast. That evening rations arrived.[140]

John Meints

In 1918 a group of men from Luverne, Minnesota forcibly removed German-American farmer, John Meints, from his house for being disloyal to the U.S. They drove to South Dakota where masked men gave him a whipping, threatened to shoot him, and tarred and feathered him. Meints sued his abductors for $100,000 in federal court in Mankato.[141] The judge instructed the jury that the evidence was overwhelming that Meints was disloyal.[142] The jury found for the abductors. On appeal Meints won a new trial and the case eventually settled out of court for $6,000.[143]

Leo Albrecht

In December 1903 the doctor in Belle Plaine in the Lower Minnesota River Valley told Leo Albrecht's father, "The boy is in God's hands now." Later that day, Leo's mother gave her 13-year-old son a couple of teaspoons of water her cousin brought from the grotto in Lourdes, France. Within two days the miracle water cured Leo of double pneumonia.[144] During his childhood Leo dynamited fish in the Minnesota River.[145]

During WWI, Leo Albrecht was stationed at Camp Dodge in Iowa where, due to the influenza pandemic, he saw corpses with identification tags on big toes stacked up like cordwood.[146] The fort was under quarantine.[147] The Spanish flu of 1918 was the worst public disaster since the bubonic plague.[148] More than 600,000 Americans died from the viral disease. Worldwide, the pandemic claimed 21 million lives.[149]

While Leo was at Camp Dodge, all soldiers were marched to the drill field before several gallows. The band played while four blacks were led in. The blacks were caught talking about a white girl they raped a few days earlier. One man died of fright before he reached the gallows. One of the men in his last words admitted he did wrong and asked the Lord for forgiveness. To set an example, the commander made the soldiers watch as the executioner tripped the trapdoor.[150]

After WWI, Leo ran a dog and pony show in the Albrecht Circus, where he also tumbled and walked on a slack wire. In a week Leo could teach a dog to climb a 40-foot ladder and jump into a tub of water.[151] For a time, fearless Dick Clemmons and his fighting lions went town to town with the Albrecht Circus. Every four days Clemmons bought an old nag and cut her up to feed the lions. He saved a couple of steaks for himself.[152]

At age 83, Leo was still walking the slack wire and balancing an 85-pound wagon wheel on his chin. In 1989, at age 98, Leo's soul left for the big mushroom tent in the sky. Leo was a small-town circus legend. His motto borrowed from Oscar Hammerstein II was: "Love in your heart isn't put there to stay... Love isn't love till you give it away."[153]

Jay Gould

Jay Gould from Glencoe, Minnesota operated Jay Gould's Million Dollar Gems. Later called Jay Gould's Million Dollar Circus. Jay opened all performances with a prayer and a patriotic song.[154] Jay gave Lawrence Welk from German-speaking Strassberg, North Dakota, his first job as an accordion player.[155] In Gould's "Chautauqua," blacks played banjos, actors presented a Tom show, Hawaiians danced and played ukuleles, Indians danced, and three-time presidential candidate, William Jennings Bryant, gave lectures.[156] Started in Chautauqua Lake, New York, the show combined culture and entertainment and spread throughout the U.S. President Teddy Roosevelt referred to Chautauqua as "The most American thing in America."

Jay took the gamble of his life when he booked the *Birth of a Nation*, a silent motion picture, complete with a 25-piece orchestra in his hometown of Glencoe.[157] A portion of the film sings the praises of the Ku Klux Klan.[158] The naysayers said Glencoe was too small to support such an expensive show. Gould arranged a special train to bring in spectators. For three days they were "hanging from the rafters" to watch the story of the Civil War and Reconstruction.[159]

In 1938, Jay Gould had the John Wilkes Booth on Tour show that displayed the mummy of President Abraham Lincoln's assassin at circuses throughout the country. In 1903, a man living under an alias, on his deathbed told his friend he was John Wilkes Booth. The debate on whether he was actually John Wilkes Booth continues to this day. Jay's daughter-in-law, Vi Gould, who lives in Glencoe, has Jay Gould's receipt for John

Wilkes Booth's corpse. The body was stolen while in Arlington Heights, Illinois and has not been recovered. Vi strongly believes the body is that of John Wilkes Booth. The body has a fractured ankle and a scar on its back from an infected boil. Both of which Booth had.[160]

Leo Jr. and Gloria Albrecht

Leo Albrecht's son, Leo Jr., and Jay Gould's granddaughter, Gloria, fell in love. At age 17, Gloria flew to Hawaii where Leo, Jr. was stationed in the Navy and the two took their vows. After Leo Jr. was discharged from the Navy, he and Gloria joined the Albrecht Circus. Gloria performed on the swing ladder. In addition to being master of ceremonies, Leo Jr. performed magic, and ran a dog and pony show. He should have been a politician. After having three kids on the road and performing circuses every day in two to four towns a week, they settled down in Belle Plaine, Minnesota so their eldest son could start school. They had three more "curtain climbers" and they still live in Belle Plaine.[161] Their house is a circus museum.

Michael Dowling

In 1880 14-year-old Michael Dowling sat on a soapbox in the back of a lumber wagon in southwestern Minnesota. While crossing a plowed field in a fierce snowstorm, Dowling got bounced out of the wagon. During the whiteout Dowling burrowed into a straw pile. The next morning, after the blizzard blew itself out, Dowling stood up and discovered his arms and legs were frozen. His legs below the knee, left arm below the elbow and most of the fingers on his right hand were amputated. The surgery lasted so long the chloroform wore off before it was over.[162]

Dissatisfied with life, the feisty young Irishman went before the Yellow Medicine County Board in Granite Falls in the Upper Minnesota River Valley and told them, "Give me artificial limbs and one year at Carleton College and I'll never cost the county another cent." By one vote the board acquiesced.[163] His artificial limbs allowed him to skate and dance.[164] At Carleton College in Northfield, Minnesota, Dowling got a five-year college education in one year.[165]

After graduating, Dowling taught school, started a newspaper and a bank, owned several businesses, served as a state legislator and toured the world for the cause of the handicapped. He married a wonderful woman and fathered three daughters who never thought he was handicapped in any way.[166] Dowling said, "Handicap? Why, a handicap is just a chance for a good honest fight. There is only one really insurmountable handicap, so far as I can determine. That is the loss of the inner power we call mind. Nothing else is unconquerable."

After the Spanish American War, President McKinley sent Dowling to the Philippines on a special education commission.[167] Years later Dowling told disabled WWI soldiers, "From the neck down a man is worth about $1.50 a day; from his neck up, he may be worth $100,000 a year." And, "The fun and glory of danger and achievement are known only to those who have something to struggle against and who come out smiling." After his death in 1921, Minnesotans raised $100,000 to build the Michael Dowling School for Crippled Children.[168]

Margaret Weber Dies

In 1920, at age 78, my great-great-grandmother Margaret's kind-hearted soul left for the everlasting kingdom. The Weber yard and driveway were lined with buggies of those attending Margaret's wake in the farmhouse. At the wake, her son Henry led mourners in saying the rosary.[169] The next day at St. Thomas Church in Jessenland, the Henderson choir sang the Requiem Mass and she joined her husband Anton in the cemetery. In her obituary, her grandson Edward wrote: "Of her it may be said that she always walked faithful in the path of duty, whether strewn with thorns or flowers; now she has reached that land of beauty where no storm of sorrow lowers. Requiescat in peace!"

Chapter Five
Prohibition and the Roaring Twenties

Temperance

Prohibition, one of the most remarkable crusades in modern history dating from 1840 to 1920, was led by Protestants. "Backsliders," those who drank, were shunned by their church. Protestants voted overwhelmingly against "wet" politicians.[1] A popular ballad among women's temperance groups was "Lips That Touch Liquor Shall Never Touch Mine," written by Englishwoman Harriet Glazebrook. In Henderson, Minnesota, the Good Templars voted lager beer a nuisance.[2]

During the "dry crusade" my great-grandfather Jack Madden hitched his bobtail mare to his buggy for a trip to the Farmer's Home Saloon in Green Isle owned by John Ryan. If he had a few coins, he'd plunk them in the slot machine in the backroom of the man's bar. During the winter he took the short-cut across Silver Lake to Green Isle. On a warm spring day he took the dirt road to Green Isle. On one occasion after imbibing, he started home and passed out in the buggy. Instead of taking the dirt road home the old nag pulled the buggy across Silver Lake. Neighbors watched as the crowbait sloshed through six inches of slush on thin ice. When the mare stepped on shore everyone let out a sigh of relief, except Jack; he burped.[3]

In Patricia Condon Johnston's book, *Minnesota's Irish*, there is a picture of Jack Madden and his drinking buddies. The caption reads: "Temperance was a thing of the past for this group when this photograph was taken in John Ryan's saloon in Green Isle about 1919."[4] A mural of my great-grandfather Jack Madden with his drinking buddies is painted on a wall in the Club New Yorker in Green Isle, Minnesota.[5]

Pussyfoot Johnson

An outspoken leader of the teetotalism movement, William "Pussyfoot" Johnson, was a quick draw with his revolver and good with his fists. He was a fearless gumshoe and took pleasure in arresting men who had any association with illicit alcohol, enjoying an opportunity to smash booze bottles and gambling machines.

Since most treaties prohibited the sale of liquor in Indian country, "Pussyfoot" was given the task of ridding the Indian Territories of alcohol. In the history of bureaucratic titles, his was one of the longest: Special Officer of the Government, Indian Bureau, for the Suppression of the Liquor Traffic in Indian Territory. Johnson acquired the nickname "Pussyfoot" for his cat-like stealth in disarming and arresting a pool hall keeper in the Oklahoma Territory who had put out the word he'd shoot Johnson on sight.[6]

In 1909, "Big Bill" Taft was President, and that year "Pussyfoot" and his agents showed up in northern Minnesota. "Pussyfoot" gave the grog dealers in Mahnomen County adequate time to close up their drinkeries and move their inventory out of Indian Territory. Most complied; some thought he was bluffing.[7]

During a saloon raid in Mahnomen County, Minnesota, "Pussyfoot" and his agents were smashing up a joint, when he heard "we are the mayor and city council, we are going to stop this." "Pussyfoot" replied, "I am busy." Next, the city marshal and a posse approached. "Pussyfoot," setting the standard of arrogance for federal officers, stuck his revolver in the marshal's face and said, "I represent the United States Government and you and your men had better get out of here until we finish our work." With furrowed eyebrows, the marshal and posse left for the street. After "Pussyfoot" and his men tore up the inside of the bar, the bedlam continued when "Pussyfoot" went out to the street and asked the marshal, "Do you want to arrest me?" As nervous as a politician in church, the marshal went ahead and arrested him. "Pussyfoot" called for his agents to be arrested until the marshal wouldn't arrest any more of them.[8]

"Pussyfoot" and his agents were arraigned before a justice of the peace. "Pussyfoot" did all the talking and refused to enter a plea, so the justice pleaded not guilty for the bunch of them. When "Pussyfoot" refused to post bond the justice said, "We have no jail to keep you in." "Pussyfoot" replied, "We will wait here until you build a jail."[9]

"Pussyfoot's" action was meant to settle the question: as a federal agent, did he have the authority to do what he was doing? After a trial, the court ruled "Pussyfoot" not only had the right, but the duty to do what he was doing. In 1914 the U.S. Supreme Court took up the question and sided with "Pussyfoot." A newspaper journalist in Minnesota wrote: "'Pussyfoot' Johnson has put more saloons out of business in a given time than any man on earth."[10]

Eighteenth Amendment

After a long battle, in 1920 the Goody Two-Shoes got their way. The beer taps ran dry as the Eighteenth Amendment to the U.S. Constitution took effect and the lawless decade got started. Humorist Don Marquis said, "Prohibition makes you want to cry into your beer and denies you the beer to cry into." The Ku Klux Klan vigorously supported Prohibition and they also conducted liquor raids.[11]

Prohibition closed for good the brewery in Glencoe, Minnesota founded in 1877. The brewery was known for its popular Uncle Sam Beer.[12] To survive, the Schell Brewery in New Ulm turned to making root beer, "Near Beer," and a tonic called U-No. They distributed Hershey bars until they discovered the owners of Hershey's were ardent prohibitionists.[13]

My great-grandfather Jack Madden drank as much as a good Catholic could, but he didn't drink during Prohibition. He said, "Moonshine will kill you." During this time of disallowance, a neighbor told Jack he was sick for two weeks after drinking bathtub gin from a moonshiner in Green Isle Township. Jack told him he was one of the lucky ones.[14]

Andrew Volstead

The city of Granite Falls in the Upper Minnesota River Valley is home to rocks formed 3.8 billion years ago, making them some of the oldest rocks in the world.[15] It was also home to Congressman Andrew Volstead. During the time of abstinence, he made himself the most cursed man in the country by sponsoring the Volstead Act, which provided funding and enforcement of Prohibition.[16] At least it left a loophole for medicinal alcohol. Volstead chewed a pound of tobacco a day and served homemade wine to his family.[17]

Laura Volstead Loman and J. Edgar Hoover

Andrew Volstead's daughter, Laura Volstead Loman, and J. Edgar Hoover became friends while attending George Washington University in Washington D.C.[18] The hard-boiled Hoover, FBI Director from 1935 to 1972, had his agents spy on his personal enemies including President Franklin Roosevelt's wife, Eleanor.[19] Laura and Hoover corresponded by letters for 30 years. The letters Laura received from Hoover are kept at the city offices in Granite Falls and are available to read. In Hoover's brief typewritten letters, he often mentions their friendship. He expressed alarm at recent Supreme Court decisions and an interest in the Minnesota State bird, the Common Loon (a close relative to most politicians). He thanked Laura for congratulating him on the James Earl Ray case and for sending him silver brandy cups. In a letter, he brings up the stir caused by an investigation in a labor racketeering case. In another he mentions the Warren Commission report.[20]

Medicinal Alcohol

Before and during prohibition, medicinal alcohol was prescribed for most ailments. Cocaine-laced Vin Mariani wine was the "salvation for overworked men, delicate women and sickly children." Pope Leo drank it from a flask that never ran dry. Advertised as a medical remedy, Pabst Malt Extract claimed it "causes sweet sleep, restores faded looks, lightens weary minds and builds up the body," giving you "vim and bounce."[21] Even temperance advocate John North, founder of Northfield, was drinking alcohol. He drank doctor prescribed stimulants to spare his family.[22]

Moonshine

During the no-no era there were rollicking parties in the Weber farm's cow pasture next to Silver Lake. The barn burners lasted all night, the band played, and the moonshine flowed. Grandpa Alo wasn't among the merrymakers. The next morning he'd give passed out revelers a lift home.[23]

During Prohibition at the Lake Marion Ballroom near Hutchinson, Minnesota the devil hid in the rafters. While the Lindy Hop was in full swing, the devil slid down the pole in the center of the dance floor. The sinners dashed out in a panic. The next morning pieces of clothing could be seen caught on the barbed wire fences near the ballroom. The devil was a minister with a red light in the tail of his costume.[24]

In 1921 a spate of revenuers who operated independently of local authorities were in the Lower Minnesota River Valley looking for blind pigs—businesses with fake storefronts that provided cover for the sale of illicit alcohol in the backroom. In Carver, in the Lower Minnesota River Valley, their raid on the backroom bath and steam parlor owned by my great-uncle, Herman Lenzen, turned up empty. In the front of the building Herman had a barbershop. In those days, single men working on farms and in the woods came to town to shake the dirt off their boots, take a bath, and get a shave and a haircut before wetting their throats with hooch. Oftentimes after a drinking spree, men showed up at Herman's business for a steam bath to sweat alcohol out their pores.[25]

During the sweep, revenuers arrested around 20 people for selling and makin' moon. All the seized liquor, except for a small quantity for evidence, was destroyed. In the Lower Minnesota River Valley city of Jordan, named after the Jordan River in Palestine, high-priced liquid gold ran in the gutter like rainwater.[26] Grandpa Alo heard stories of men getting down on their hands and knees to lap up as much as they could.[27]

The University of Minnesota improved Minnesota 13 seed corn for the short, cool growing seasons on the northern edge of the corn belt.[28] The cookers in Stearns County, Minnesota used it for the mash in their finest quality aged whiskey called "Minnesota 13." Henchmen from the Twin Cities and Chicago distributed the moon.[29] Stearns County was overwhelmingly German and overwhelmingly against Prohibition.[30] Some thought temperance types were fanatics.[31] After WWI, low farm prices caused many farmers to turn to moonshine—distilling at night while the moon shone—to make a living.[32] Most clergy in Stearns County didn't think making moonshine was a sin and looked at it as a way for people to make a living. One priest in Stearns County posted bail for parishioners arrested for making moonshine.[33] During Prohibition the beer monks at St. John's Abbey in Sterns County thought the Volstead Act was hogwash and kept right on brewing their favorite beverage.[34]

Suffrage

In 1900 in a Jordan Independent newspaper article, an unidentified suffragist said women can get anything from men if they adequately flatter them.[35] Also in 1900 in 37 states a married woman had no right to her children. In 16 states a wife had no rights to her earnings. In eight states a wife had no right to her own property after marriage. In seven states there was no law obligating a man to support his wife and children.[36] In 1901 a man gave notice in the Jordan Independent newspaper not to trust his wife or give her or any member of her family goods on his account. She'd left his bed and board and he wasn't responsible for her or her family's debts.[37] As they say on the farm, "she flew the coop."

In the Lower Minnesota River Valley, Grandpa Alo heard "soapbox militants" speak in favor of women voting. Also in the Valley to promote suffrage, female pilots performed aerial shows.[38] Believing women would cast their ballots for "dry" candidates, distillers and brewers were against women's suffrage.[39] The first president of the National American Woman Suffrage Association, Elizabeth Cady Stanton, blamed the suppression of the weaker sex on church law.[40] There were almost as many anti-suffrage groups as pro-suffrage groups.[41] They called suffrage a "dangerous experiment" and some believed women were intended to be homemakers and child-bearers.[42]

Ku Klux Klan

In the early 1920s my great-grandfather, Jack Madden, got agitated when the Ku Klux Klan set crosses on fire in front of the Jessenland Township Hall. The cross-burners didn't like the Catholics of Jessenland.[43] White-hooded Klansmen burned crosses because they believed Catholics adored a worthless and dead cross.[44] In the 1920s the Invisible Empire considered Catholics one of the country's worst problems. At Klan rallies in Minnesota, speakers told the audience the Pope was determined to take control of the U.S.[45] At the height of the night riders' influence in Minnesota, they had 51 chapters in the state—ten in Minneapolis alone.[46] There were women's Ku Klux Klan chapters, Klan weddings, and some local newspapers told how to make a Klan cross that burns late into the night.[47] Minnesota highway patrolmen wore black jackets with white "KKK" letters on the back.[48] The largest Klan parade in Minnesota occurred in July 1925 in Northfield.[49] Until the 1930s, homecoming activities at Carleton College in Northfield included stringing up blacks in effigy.[50] The Klan tried, but couldn't get a foothold in New Ulm.[51]

John O'Connor

In the early 1900s, St. Paul Police Chief, John "The Big Fellow" O'Connor, and his brother Richard, "The Cardinal"—he was more powerful than Archbishop Ireland—came up with the "O'Connor System."[52] The system allowed criminals from across the country to lay low in St. Paul. They were allowed to cool off as long as they followed the "layover agreement," that is, checked in with the fixer, "Dapper" Dan Hogan, handed over "green tributes" to the police, and didn't commit any serious crimes in the mob's capital city of St. Paul.[53] "The Big Fellow" allowed bootlegging, gambling, and prostitution. To further aid visiting hoods, the police had a tipoff system that made it difficult for other jurisdictions to capture criminals in St. Paul.[54] Anyone who didn't follow the agreement had a short life expectancy.[55] John Dillinger, George "Machine Gun Kelly" Barnes, Lester "Baby Face Nelson" Gillis, Alvin "Creepy" Karpis, and Ma Barker and her boys were among those who took advantage of the safe harbor in Minnesota's capital city.[56]

There were so many dirty birds in St. Paul, an infrastructure supported the gangster industry. It included defense attorneys, repairmen to patch bullet holes in vehicles, dealers that sold untraceable Chicago typewriters (machine guns), and experts who could identify banks containing stacks of cash, timing for robberies, and jail breaks. There was a mob "doctor" who specialized in abortions, treating sexually transmitted diseases, and gunshot wounds.[57] Mob speakeasies included fine liquor, gambling, jazz, and nude dancing girls.[58] The same pleasures enjoyed by most politicians.

Dan Hogan

From his Green Lantern Saloon in St. Paul, Irish mobster Dan Hogan ruled the criminal underground in St. Paul for a decade. On a December morning in 1928, "Dapper" Dan stepped on the starter pedal of his Paige coupe and a bomb under the floorboards detonated. The explosion blew off Hogan's right leg causing his death.[59]

Hogan had one of the grandest funerals ever seen in St. Paul. St. Mary's Church was filled with flowers, gangsters, businessmen, and police detectives. The priest at the funeral said, "Somehow, one would rather be in Mr. Hogan's place than [in] that of his murderers."[60] The car bombing was never solved.[61]

Nina Clifford

During the days of the "O'Connor System," Nina Clifford (an alias for a Jewish name) ran a house of sin, where some became of age.[62] As long as Clifford didn't cause problems, "The Big Fellow" gave her immunity to run her elegant two-story brick brothel located close to the police station.[63] In 1900, census records show her thriving house of ill repute had nine prostitutes (Clifford warned them not to sunburn their backs), a cook, a Norwegian housekeeper, three chambermaids, and a male porter. A Scotsman provided music.[64] All types of drinks were available to patrons.[65] Cabbies who brought "laundry loads" (johns) to the sportin' house were paid more than the working girls.[66]

An old widow had an attorney in St. Paul draw up her will. She left $25 to her wayward daughter who worked for Clifford. After the widow died, the executor gave $25 from the widow's estate to the attorney to deliver to the daughter. The attorney made five trips to see the dame, each time he gave her $5. On the fifth trip, when the attorney was leaving her room, the widow's daughter asked, "Will I be seeing you again?" The attorney replied, "No, you just received the last installment on the inheritance from your mother."

Soon after Nina Clifford's death in July 1929, a group of men called politicians to inform them Clifford had died and they were named in her will as a pallbearer. As the story goes, the day before her funeral, trains to Chicago were full of politicians from Minnesota.[67]

After Clifford's cathouse was razed, a tunnel was discovered between it and the nearby Minnesota Club. A portrait of Nina Clifford hangs at the Club's bar. A brick from Clifford's house of ill repute attached to a plaque at the Club reads: "This brick from Nina Clifford's house was presented to the Gentlemen of the Minnesota Club for their great interest in historic buildings."[68]

The "O'Connor System" started to erode when Congress gave the Feds more power to control organized crime. J. Edgar Hoover's FBI agents could arrest criminals without involving the corrupt St. Paul police.[69] The system of protecting criminals began to fade away with the kidnapping of brewer William Hamm, Jr. in 1933 and of brewer Edward Bremer in 1934. Fearing they would be the next victims, St. Paul's elite called in the Feds.[70]

Edward Weber

During the gangster days of prohibition Grandpa Alo's brother Edward had a printing business in Chicago. While Edward was stopped at a red light a gangster jumped in his car and stuck a pistol in his ribs and said drive where I tell you. The mobster had Edward pick up another gangster. They had Edward drive to the country where they tied him to a tree. The gangsters had a discussion on whether or not to shoot Edward. The gangsters left with Edward's car. The next morning a farmer untied Edward and gave him a ride home. The car was never recovered.[71]

F. Scott Fitzgerald

The gaiety of the Roaring Twenties was captured in the writings of St. Paul lush F. Scott Fitzgerald. He was named after his ancestor, Francis Scott Key, who wrote our national anthem.[72] As the golden boy of the Jazz Age, F. Scott Fitzgerald was the first Irish Catholic to become a major American novelist.[73] His most famous novel is *The Great Gatsby*. Fitzgerald died in 1940 believing he was a failure.[74] The old sports at his alma mater, Princeton, refused to buy his papers from his widow for $3,750. They saw him as a hack writer from the Midwest.[75] Now he's considered one of the greatest novelists of all time.[76]

Being a lukewarm Catholic, F. Scott wasn't allowed to be buried in the Fitzgerald family plot as he failed to receive communion for a year and his writings were undesirable. He was buried in a Protestant boneyard. Thirty-five years later he was given a Catholic burial in the family plot at St. Mary's Cemetery in Rockville, Maryland.[77] His epitaph, chosen by his daughter Scottie, is the last sentence of the Great Gatsby: "So we beat on, boats against the current, borne back ceaselessly into the past." Empty booze bottles litter his grave.[78]

Charles Lindbergh, Jr.

Charles Lindbergh, Jr. was born in Detroit, Michigan and raised on a farm on the banks of the Mississippi River near Little Falls, Minnesota. After graduating high school, he continued farming and acquired a milk machine dealership. In April 1923 he purchased a WWI army surplus plane known as a Jenny.

On June 6, 1923 Lindbergh was on his way to see his father on the campaign trail when he flew into a thunderstorm, causing three cylinders to cut out. He made an emergency landing in a swamp near Savage, Minnesota. The Jenny flipped over leaving Lindbergh upside down hanging by his seat belt. For a few days Lindbergh stayed with the railroad depot agent in Savage until a replacement prop arrived.[79]

At age 11, my maternal grandmother, Lillie Gildea, watched Lucky Lindy fly his plane in the skies over Glencoe, Minnesota.[80] He was shuttling his father, Charles A. Lindbergh, Sr., from town to town stumping for the U.S. Senate. On June 9, 1923 after taking off from Buffalo Lake, Minnesota with his father on board, Lindbergh landed near Glencoe between two farms. On the attempted takeoff for a flight to Litchfield, Minnesota the Jenny "cracked up"—"crash" wasn't in Lindbergh's vocabulary—resulting in a broken propeller, landing gear, and wing. Neither Lindbergh was injured. The elder Lindbergh alleged the Jenny had been sabotaged, possibly by a political rival.[81]

The damaged Jenny was taken to nearby Oak Leaf Park in Glencoe. With the help of a welding shop and a hardware store, the Jenny was repaired in three weeks. When the broken prop was removed from the plane, Lewis Miley cut the good half off with a hand saw and kept it. During the repair of the Jenny, Lindbergh and Lewis Miley became friends. They attached tin cans to a string and laid the string across a road. When a car came by it would catch the string and drag the cans down the road. When Lindbergh stayed at the Miley farm he gobbled up all the strawberry jam. Lewis Miley and Lindbergh remained life-long friends. In 1973 while Lindbergh was in Little Falls, Lewis Miley had Lindbergh autograph the half prop he sawed off years earlier.[82]

Lindbergh also became friends with Herbert, Florian, and Francis Hain. While in Glencoe, he often landed in the Hain's cow pasture. He usually slept under his Jenny to prevent cows from eating the covering on the wings. Herbert Hain gave Lindbergh gasoline in return for plane rides. Herbert said, "We all liked Lindbergh very much, he was a nice fellow." Once, while giving rides, the propeller clipped tree branches, causing a hard landing in the Hain's hayfield. Droves of people trampled the hay to see the Jenny. After repairs were made, Lindbergh gave rides to pay Patrick Hain for the ruined hay.[83]

Lindbergh left a broken prop tip at the Hain farm. In 1925 when the Hain family moved to California they left it in a shed. The new owner of the farm lent the broken prop tip to the meat market in Glencoe where it was displayed in the front window with a sign that read: "Prop from Lindbergh's plane." The prop tip was damaged by a fire at the meat market and is now owned by Brett DeMott from Agua Dulce, California. He is the grandson of Herbert Hain and a historian on Charles Lindbergh, Jr.'s life prior to 1927.[84]

Lindbergh took in $70 from 14 passengers on July 4th and 5th, 1923 flying in and out of Arlington, Minnesota. Lindbergh's diary on July 4, 1923 states: "Ran away from storms. Landed NE of Green Isle, then returned to Arlington." In the summer of 1923, Lindbergh's barnstorming in Minnesota included Biscay, Hamburg, Belle Plaine, Savage, and Shakopee.[85]

On the morning of an unannounced Sunday air show in Mankato, it was brought to Lindbergh's attention that he needed an affidavit regarding the condition of his plane. Thanks to an on-the-ball notary public an affidavit was made out, signed, sealed, and delivered, and the show went on. Verbally the notary called the plane a crate. While staying at a hotel in nearby Madison Lake, Lindbergh closed the door to his room with a greasy hand, leaving his handprint on the door. The owner of the hotel left the handprint intact. After Lindbergh's historic flight guests asked to see it. The handprint vanished when the hotel went up in flames.[86]

On May 20, 1927 Charles Lindbergh, with virtually no sleep the night before, took the Spirit of St. Louis down a muddy dirt runway at Roosevelt Field on Long Island, New York. Thirty-three and a half hours later after circling the Eiffel Tower he landed near Paris, France. He was the first person to fly solo and nonstop across the Atlantic. His flight epitomized the can-do American spirit. On his famous flight he took his address book containing the names and addresses of three Glencoe residents—Heston Benson, George Miley, and Francis Hain.[87]

After his historic flight, the world greeted the man known as "Lone Eagle" with one of the biggest hero's welcomes of all time. While barnstorming in the Lower Minnesota River Valley, the ultimate flyboy dropped a large greeting card weighed down with BBs to show his appreciation for the hospitality the mayor of Savage and townspeople showed him while he stayed there.[88]

During the 1930s Lindbergh often visited Nazi Germany. He hailed the German Air Force and applauded Hitler's leadership. In October 1938 Lindbergh accepted Hitler's Service Cross of the Order of the German Eagle. After a speech in September 1941 in which Lindbergh criticized the Brits, Jews, and the Roosevelt Administration, the Lone Eagle went from hero extraordinaire to public enemy.[89] After Japan's attack on Pearl Harbor in Hawaii, he wised up. He got back in the public's good graces by flying civilian combat missions in the Pacific theatre. In 1954, President Eisenhower made Lindbergh a general.[90]

Cancer ended Lindbergh's flight in 1974. He's buried barefoot in a rough-hewn eucalyptus casket lined with a Hudson's Bay blanket in the Palapala Ho'omau Church Cemetery in Kipahulu, Maui, Hawaii. His epitaph from Psalms 139:9 reads: "If I take the wings of the morning, and dwell in the uttermost parts of the sea." Buried between Lindbergh and his friend Sam Pryor are Pryor's six gibbons.[91]

Alo and Anne Weber

In 1922, Klan member Warren Harding was President, and in that year, my grandparents Alo Weber and Anne Madden wed at St. Thomas Church.[92] They fasted starting at midnight so they could receive Holy Communion at their wedding Mass. Anne wore a navy blue dress; in those days the bride and groom didn't purchase or rent special clothes to wear only on their wedding day. The reception meal was prepared by neighbors.[93]

Also in 1922, Anne and other members of the Rosary Society presented *Aaron Slick from Punkin Crick*, a play about a widow tricked into selling her farm to a scammer who is outwitted by a farmer who in the end marries the widow. The proceeds from the play purchased an ornate baptismal font for St. Thomas Church. A few years later, Alo and Anne purchased the church's twelfth station, "Jesus Expires on the Cross."[94]

Alo pitched for the Green Isle baseball team. The games were played in a cow pasture. He had a lively fastball and a roundhouse curve he threw at a batter's head. When the pitch worked, the batter bailed out and the ball curved down over the plate for a called strike. After getting married, Alo hung up his mitt. On a Sunday afternoon Alo and his bride were watching the team from New Germany, Minnesota (during WWII the town changed its name to "Motordale") rough up Green Isle's pitcher.[95] At the urging of the fans and his former teammates, Alo came out of retirement for a day and in his Sunday shoes pitched in relief. Green Isle still lost the game.[96]

In 1927, Alo and Anne watched Anne's youngest sister Helen play forward for Arlington High's undefeated girls' basketball team. Back then, girls' teams had six players; three forwards and three guards. Only the forwards were allowed to shoot the ball.[97]

Alo didn't drink, smoke, swear, or use profanity. He read the newspaper every day. He went to Mass every Sunday and holy day, and every night he got down on his knees and prayed to the Lord. He didn't work on Sunday. He had big muscular hands from milking cows by hand. He'd put an apple in the palms of his hands, twist, and the apple would split in half. Alo's favorite meal was fried chicken, sweet corn, and cake, and he put a dollop of butter on just about everything on his plate.

Henry Weber Dies

In 1927, Alo's dad, Henry, got dropsy (congestive heart failure) and told Alo to get ready to take over the farm. Alo liked to log and run the sawmill, but he shut it down because he didn't like dealing with the hirelings.[98] In 1928 Calvin Coolidge was President, the same year that at age 66, the man who lived the

Machine Age, my great-grandfather, crossed over to run the big steam engine in the sky. There've been more clouds ever since. Henry's obituary, written by his son Edward states: "The deceased was an exemplary husband and father, a good neighbor and a man of many friends. He served the people of his community for many years as a town and school officer, always performing his duties in a flawless manner." When I was growing up, a few old timers told me Henry Weber was the finest man in all of Jessenland.

Henderson's Diamond Jubilee

During Prohibition, in August 1927, 18,000 people poured into Henderson to celebrate its founding 75 years earlier by Joseph Brown.[99] A millstone from a pioneer mill west of Henderson was made into a monument and dedicated to John Other Day.[100] It reads: "In memory of John Other Day Noble Sioux Chieftain who piloted 62 whites to safety in the outbreak of 1862. I commend him to the care of a just God and liberal government. Maj. T.J. Galbraith."[101] During the festivities, badges with a picture of Other Day sold for 15 cents. Soft drinks sold for a nickel a bottle; at other celebrations they sold for a dime.[102]

During the jubilee, Dakota in costume, some whose fathers and grandfathers had gone on the warpath, performed tribal dances and rites.[103] Dakota Chief Wetasimini conducted a ceremony to adopt Dr. J. Felix Traxler into the lower agency tribe of the Sioux. He was christened "Watabiska" meaning White Eagle. The Dakota also presented the doctor with a war club. On Saturday night, Heinie's German band played old time dance music.[104] A good time was had by all.

Chapter Six
The Great Depression

Black Monday

On Black Monday, October 29, 1929, the financial bubble burst and the stock market crashed. When the Great Depression hit, barbers in Arlington charged 25 cents for a haircut. Business was so slow, barbers gradually lowered their price to 15 cents. Then a barber lowered his price to 10 cents and served patrons a complimentary glass of beer.[1] To create more business, my great uncle Herman Lenzen in Carver installed a hair growing machine in his barber shop. A helmet like device was lowered over the patron's head and Herman flipped the switch. Much to the consternation of his wife, Herman gave customers the option to roll the dice. If Herman won, the customer paid double. If the customer won, the haircut was free.[2]

Alo and Anne Weber

The 1930s were the leanest years on the Weber farm.[3] My grandparents, Alo and Anne Weber, contended with low prices caused by the Great Depression and poor crop yields caused by the Dust Bowl. No doubt the next dust bowl will be blamed on global warming. A few local farmers went broke. Farmers too old to find work and nowhere to go went to the county poor farm. At the poor farm able-bodied residents had to work for three hots and a cot.[4]

Grandpa Alo scratched out a living during the Great Depression by being frugal. He lived and farmed at a time when stretching a dollar was a virtue. He ran out of deposit slips in his checkbook before he ran out of checks.[5]

In the early 1930s drought caused the two marshes on the Weber farm to dry up. Alo cut the reeds from the two marshes, stacked them in the barn, and used them for bedding. The neighbor's horses got so thin a strong wind blew them over.[6]

During the Dirty Thirties, Silver Lake dried up except for a soft spot in the middle. Grandpa Alo dug a well in the soft area; when he hit water he quit digging. The well was used to water the garden, livestock, and the fruit trees planted by Anton.[7]

In 1932, Grandpa Alo seeded the farm's fields. The fields got a shower of rain, sprouted, and grew a few inches. That was it for rain; the crops dried up and died. It was Grandpa's worst year farming.[8] Crop insurance wasn't available and he didn't get taxpayer money for the disaster.

A few miles south of Green Isle, a 40-acre swamp dried out and the bog caught on fire. When Grandpa Alo looked at the burning soil he saw large holes in the ground. The bog smoldered a few years until the heavy snowfall of the 1935-36 winter put out the peat fire. The winter of 1935-36 was so cold that six inches of ice formed on the inner walls of the barn. In stark contrast, the summer of 1936 was the hottest of Grandpa Alo's life.[9]

Each spring during the Great Depression a salesman from Mankato showed up at the farm with White Rock roosters. Grandpa purchased one for every ten to 15 hens. Every day Grandpa Alo and Grandma Anne gathered the eggs from the laying bins in the chicken coop. They brought the eggs in the house, wiped them with a dry cloth and stored them in a warm place. Once a week they put the eggs in wooden cases. Grandpa lifted them onto the bed of his 1928 Chevy truck and delivered them to the hatchery in St. Peter. By the end of spring the roosters were no longer needed and were usually sold to H.M. Noack & Sons Produce Plant in Arlington to be butchered.[10] White Rocks were developed in the mid-19th century in New England. The hens are good layers, and the broilers have large tasty breasts that make them a favorite for Sunday dinner on the farm.

Green Giant

During the Depression, rather than stand in line at a soup kitchen, a few of Grandma Anne's nieces and nephews from St. Paul stayed at the Weber farm. They didn't go hungry as the farm produced meat, eggs, milk, wheat for flour, and seasonal fruits and vegetables. Sundays on the farm were spent going to church and making homemade ice cream. Another favorite activity was going to Saturday night dances at the pavilion in Arlington.[11]

When vegetables grown in lowland were ready to harvest, the nieces and nephews worked the pea run and corn pack at a canning factory in Le Sueur run by Minnesota Valley Canning Company, which in 1950 changed its name to Green Giant Company.[12] The only year the company lost money was 1932.[13] The company went on to develop the Jolly Green Giant as one of the most famous trademarks in advertising.[14] Ho, ho, ho. When prosperity returned, the nieces and nephews often talked about the good times they had on the farm during the Great Depression. After the Depression they often visited the farm. One of the nephews married a gal from Green Isle.[15]

Charlie Strobel and Charles Klein

During the Depression, Grandpa's brother-in-law and friend, Charlie Strobel, kept money in the First National Bank in Chaska. As manager of the farmer's co-op creamery in East Union in the Lower Minnesota River Valley, Charlie and the banker, Mr. Charles Klein, were well acquainted. In 1933 the banks went on holiday (politically correct term for closed) up to 11 days. If the bank reopened, it could not pay out gold or gold certificates, nor could it permit withdrawals of currency for hoarding. Hoarders were subject to a $10,000 fine or ten years in prison.[16] Charlie was anxious to get his money out of the bank. If the First National Bank was insolvent and closed its doors, Charlie would have lost his deposits. Mr. Klein told Charlie, "Tomorrow afternoon, if the blinds are wide open come in and withdraw your money." The next afternoon seeing the blinds were wide open, Charlie went in and withdrew his money.[17] Fortunately, the First National Bank in Chaska survived the Great Depression. The First National Bank is now Klein Bank with its main office in Chaska.

Mr. Klein kept a flock of sheep. On a snowy fall day while Alo visited Charlie at his house in East Union, one of Charlie's truck drivers stopped and told them a dog killed a bunch of Mr. Klein's sheep. Klein and the sheriff were going house to house checking dogs' mouths for wool. When Charlie checked his German Shepherd's mouth it was full of wool. Alo dug a hole and Charlie shot his dog. They shoveled the red snow behind a building. There wasn't a smidgen of evidence left when they heard a knock on the door. The sheriff asked Charlie if he had a dog. Charlie said his dog just died. The sheriff thanked Charlie and moved on. Mr. Klein had a good chuckle when the story got back to him.[18] Charles Klein was a farmer, bookkeeper, teacher, manufacturer, banker, and state legislator.[19] He was a man with progressive ideas, good morals, sound principles, and apparently a good sense of humor.

After being examined during the bank holiday, the Citizens State Bank of Green Isle (where Grandpa Alo banked) was found to be sound and permitted to reopen. During the ensuing years the bank's deposits grew rapidly. During the 1960s the Citizens State Bank of Green Isle had the highest book value per share of any bank in the United States.[20]

Allie Weber

In 1931, Herbert Hoover, a drinker who defended Prohibition, was President.[21] Also in 1931, Alo's wife, Anne, prayed novenas asking the Lord for her to conceive a child. After the ninth novena, her prayers were answered.[22] Later that year

Anne gave birth to her only child and one of the most wanted children ever.[23] Aloysius "Allie," my dad, marked the fourth generation of Webers in the New World. He was delivered by country doctor, J. Felix Traxler from Henderson, in the two-story farmhouse in the same bedroom Grandpa Alo came into the world. Lighting in the room came from bulbs powered by a 32-volt Delco Light Plant hardwired in the house. A one-cylinder air-cooled gas engine powered the generator to charge the 16 batteries in the house's basement.[24]

Anne's hobby was photography, her main subject was her son Allie. She'd put a roll of film and a check in the mailbox. A couple of weeks later the rural mail carrier delivered the pictures and negatives. In the fall of 1934, Alo dropped a Sears & Roebuck order form and a check in the mail for a new bed for Allie. Two weeks later he got a postcard notifying him the bed arrived at the warehouse in the train depot in Arlington. The bed arrived in a "less than carload lot." At the depot, the agent released the new bed to him.[25]

Dad attended grade school in the one-room Silver Lake schoolhouse. For lunch he often brought a can of peas or corn he warmed in a pan of water on top of the school's stove. The school had two "environmentally friendly" outhouses—they didn't use electricity or water. On a miserable snowy November morning Dad and another student walked to a neighbor's well and hand pumped water into a three-gallon polished metal pail. As the teacher poured the water into a dispenser, a ground-up frog fell out of the pail and hit the floor. Some of the students still drank the froggy water.[26]

In county school Dad got a basic, so-called "prairie chicken" education. The teacher taught reading, arithmetic, history, geography, grammar, spelling, citizenship, and hygiene. Music, art, and sports weren't offered at the Silver Lake schoolhouse. Discipline was not a problem. In the school's book of presidents, when students saw Herbert Hoover's picture most gave him a slap in the face as they blamed him for the Great

Depression. Dad, to this day, remembers when a girl at the school told him, "I hate Santa Claus. All I asked for was a dolly and I still got nothing." Twice a year the county nurse showed up at the school. She checked the students for scoliosis and rickets. She had an eye chart to see which students might need glasses. The nurse gave the students a pep talk on the benefits of brushing their teeth. She ended by saying, "Ignore your teeth and they'll go away."[27]

Civil Conservation Corps

In 1932, Franklin Delano Roosevelt was elected president in a landslide over Herbert Hoover. The voters connected with FDR; he gave them hope. Eleanor Roosevelt's lesbian lover, Lorena Hickob, moved into the White House where she lived on and off during FDR's presidency.[28] Polio confined FDR to a wheelchair, but it didn't prevent him from having an affair with Eleanor's secretary.[29] He told the nation, "...the only thing we have to fear is fear itself." FDR ushered in New Deal legislation creating programs and agencies to help people get back to work and to restore confidence in the financial system. Many of the programs provided assistance to farmers.

Out of the New Deal came FDR's pet project, the Civil Conservation Corps (CCC). The program reflected FDR's interest in conservation and managing natural resources.[30] "Roosevelt's Tree Army" was designed to put jobless young men to work on conservation projects.[31] They built roads, flood control projects, parks, and buildings in remote areas, and they planted trees, trees, and more trees.

The bill creating the CCC provided: "in employing citizens for the purpose of this Act, no discrimination shall be made on account of race, color or creed." Beginning in 1933 CCC camps were set up in the Minnesota River Valley under the supervision of the Army. Following the Army's strict segregation policies, black CCC enrollees in Minnesota's camps had separate living quarters away from whites.[32]

As the CCC went on, fewer blacks in Minnesota were accepted. In 1938 an order from the Feds required blacks in Minnesota camps to report to all-black camps in Missouri or be expelled from the program. No more blacks would be accepted to camps in Minnesota. Despite protests from black leaders who had the support of some Minnesota politicians, the Feds and the Army kept most black men in Minnesota out of the CCC and the few that got accepted were shipped south where Jim Crow laws were in effect.[33]

Rural Electrification Administration

In 1934, Alo, Anne, and Allie rode the train to Chicago to attend the World's Fair. They saw the latest in technology, including cigarette-smoking robots. Also in 1934, Alo purchased the first tractor on the farm, a Huber with a crank start gas engine and steel wheels, manufactured in Marion, Ohio. A year later in 1935 President Franklin D. Roosevelt established the Rural Electrification Administration (REA). In 1941, poles were set and wire strung to bring electricity to the Weber farm. A few of the neighbors didn't get electricity, deeming it too expensive.[34] Alo purchased a new General Electric refrigerator. It was the only fridge he ever purchased. He called it the icebox.

Alo installed an electric Hindman milk machine in the barn that milked the cows using a pulsating vacuum. Music from a barn radio added to the rhythm. Once the cows got used to being milked by machine they preferred it over being milked by hand.[35]

Before Christmas came from big-box stores, the Weber Christmas tree glowed with candles. Eventually, colored electric bulbs replaced the candles. Electricity replaced small gasoline engines to pump water and to run washing machines. Electric motors supplied power to run machines on the farm previously powered by hand, such as fanning mills and grinders. In the early 1950s the farmers in Jessenland started plugging in televisions and visited less often.[36]

Prohibition Repealed

In 1933 beer was back—Congress passed the Twenty-First Amendment to the Constitution repealing Prohibition. Our government couldn't enforce Prohibition without more support from citizens. Forbidden liquor turned out to be the sweetest fruit. Prohibition caused an explosion in organized crime. It was a good example of how things go wrong when government interferes with freedom of choice. "Pussyfoot" Johnson, the Prohibition Party, the Women's Christian Temperance Union led by six-foot-tall Carrie Nation who used a hatchet to tear up saloons, and the Anti-Saloon League failed to heed Ben Franklin's statement: Beer is proof God loves us and wants us to be happy.

Shortly after the failure of Prohibition, a neighbor stopped by the farm and asked Grandpa Alo if he wanted to go to Green Isle for a pail of cold beer. Grandpa told the neighbor, "To tell you the truth, I wouldn't give a dime for a washtub full of that stuff." The neighbor went to Green Isle by himself.[37]

Before the noble experiment of Prohibition, most saloons didn't allow women and many had a gutter under the bar. During Prohibition, cigarette puffing, booze-chasing flappers joined men in the beastly habit of drinking at speakeasies, which also provided a nook for cheaters. Before Prohibition, Irish lasses cooked like their mothers; after Prohibition many drank like their fathers and considered a baked potato and four pints of ale a five-course meal.

Browns Valley Man

In 1933, William Jensen, a businessman and amateur archaeologist, discovered a skeleton in a gravel pit in Browns Valley, a town founded by Joseph Brown in the Upper Minnesota River Valley. Radiocarbon dating put the Browns Valley Man's age somewhere around 9,000 years, making him one of the oldest ever found in the New World. The skeleton indicated he was a Paleo-Indian man about five feet, five inches tall. Experts believe he was a relative of the northern Asians who crossed the Bering Sea land bridge over 12,000 years ago during the last Ice Age.[38]

A couple miles west of Browns Valley is the north/south Continental Divide. On the north side of the divide, water flows into the headwaters of the Red River on its way to Hudson Bay. Water on the south side flows into the headwaters of the Minnesota River and eventually into the Gulf of Mexico.[39]

Jack and Anne Madden

Often during the Great Depression, my dad and his parents went to the Madden's log cabin for Sunday dinner. Upon arrival, Anne's sister, my great-aunt Mag, used a six-foot metal rod with a half-circle bend on the end to hook a couple of roosters by the neck, and then she whacked their heads off with an axe. While carrying on a conversation, Mag would pluck, gut, butcher, soak in salt water, and fry the roosters in a cast iron skillet on the woodstove. They ate the chickens along with bread rubbed in the frying pan's grease. The next evening, Mag rolled the chickens' livers, gizzards and hearts in flour and fried them for supper.[40]

On holidays and special occasions, Jack and Anne's children and grandchildren brought hams, chocolates, and at Christmastime everyone's favorite—homemade fruitcakes for gatherings at the log cabin. At a Fourth of July get together, Jack's dog, King, bit down on a lit firecracker. It went off and blew off the side of his mouth. The dog looked grotesque and Mag asked Alo to take care of King. Early the next morning Alo came to the rescue. He walked over to the Madden farm with his .22 rifle and plugged King. Grandpa dug a hole and when the hole was deep enough to bury King, he quit digging. When no one saw King, they speculated he wandered off in the woods and died. Alo didn't say a word.[41]

During the Great Depression on a freezing cold December night, everyone gathered at the log cabin to celebrate Jack's birthday. At night when it came time to leave, Jack's son-in-law,

Herman Lenzen, had a late model Chevy that wouldn't start. When the partiers jeered at Herman, he put gasoline in a coffee can, lit it on fire, and set it under the Chevy's crankcase. Herman, three-fourths stiff, let the crankcase get so hot the oil in it crackled. The Chevy started and Herman loaded up his wife, Helen, and the kids, and sped home to Carver in the Lower Minnesota River Valley.[42]

Martin Bacon

From 1913 to 1938 at the Dawson school in the Upper Minnesota River Valley, the students had a special friend in janitor Martin Bacon. He knew the name of every pupil and when he made his rounds cleaning he visited with students. When he passed in 1938 his body lay in state in the school corridor for several hours. After a service at the schoolhouse, children lined the streets for his funeral procession. His ability to relate to kids and teach by example made him an institution in Dawson.[43]

Armistice Day Blizzard

Armistice Day, November 11, 1940 started out mild and flowers still had their color. The forecast called for colder weather with a few flurries.[44] Without warning, a blizzard hit hard and fast, dumping heavy snow. Temperatures plummeted and the wind howled 50 to 80 miles-per-hour creating high drifts.[45] While there was still visibility, Grandpa Alo strung twine from the house to the barn and chicken coup. While the blizzard was in full force, he ran the twine through his hand so he didn't get bewildered on the way to and from chores.[46]

During the Armistice Day blizzard, Dad, at age 8, was stranded for five days at his cousin's house in East Union.[47] The early blizzard claimed the lives of 49 Minnesotans and over 150 across the country.[48] Many were hunters who were enjoying the holiday until the sudden change in the weather left them unprepared. Duck hunters were slow to leave as the storm caused ducks to fly low and because of the high winds some ducks were flying backwards. It made for good shooting.[49]

After the blizzard, some people had to crawl out of a window to shovel snow away from the doors to their homes.[50] In the Lake Pepin area a pilot dropped whiskey and food to stranded hunters. Turkey farmers in Minnesota, Iowa, Nebraska, and Wisconsin lost half their birds.[51] One of Minnesota's deadliest blizzards, the Minnesota Climatology Office ranks the Armistice Day blizzard as the state's second biggest weather event of the 20th century behind the Dust Bowl.[52]

Chapter Seven
WWII and Baby Boomers

Pearl Harbor

On December 7, 1941, a day that will live in infamy, Japan launched a sneak attack on Pearl Harbor in Hawaii, killing or injuring some 3,500 Americans and destroying U.S. ships and planes. On that day, 736 men in the U.S. were arrested for being Japanese.[1] Resistance to the U.S. entering WWII abruptly ended. The nation united to fight evil. Faster than a politician ducking a tough question, the U.S. declared war on Japan, Germany, and Italy. Lyndon Baines Johnson from Texas was the first U.S. Congressman to report for active duty.[2]

Internment during WWII

Soon after the surprise attack on Pearl Harbor, President Franklin Roosevelt told his attorney general, "I don't care so much about the Italians. They are a lot of opera singers, but the Germans are different: they may be dangerous."[3] Shortly after the attack on Pearl Harbor, Congressman John Rankin from Mississippi publicly said, "I'm for catching every Japanese in America, Alaska and Hawaii now and putting them in concentration camps...Damn them! Let's get rid of them now!"[4] In its December 1941 issue, *Life* magazine ran an article entitled: "How to Tell Japs From the Chinese" that included a picture of a Japanese man's face and a picture of a Chinese man's face. Writings on the pictures pointed out differences between the two.

One difference: Japanese have an "earthy yellow complexion," Chinese have a "parchment yellow complexion." There is also a picture of a man with a note pinned to his overcoat that says, "<u>Chinese Reporter</u> <u>NOT</u> <u>Japanese Please</u>."[5]

In February 1942, President Franklin Roosevelt lowered the boom on Japanese-Americans by signing an executive order forcing the removal and internment of all people of Japanese descent from the west coast. Germans and Italians could also be removed and interned.[6] The order also authorized the seizure of the enemy aliens' homes and farms without due process.[7] FDR's internment order is a good example of how our freedoms are only as good as the man in charge.

Herbert Oelfke

On a crisp winter morning in 1942, instead of taking his milk cans to the creamery in Hamburg, Minnesota, Herbert Oelfke gave his son and daughter a ride to school. Herbert went to his son Harold's fifth grade classroom at Emanuel Lutheran School and pounded his fist on the teacher's table and said, "They're sticking the Japanese in California in jail, us Germans will be next. Take down the German letters above the chalkboard and speak English. I want my son to talk English." The German letters came down and everyone at the school started conversing in English.[8]

USS Sibley

To help pay for the cost of war, the Production Credit Association in Sibley County started its "Victory Pig" program. "Rooting for Victory" pigs were raised to make Spam at the Hormel plant in Austin, Minnesota for G.I. rations. The money from the sale of the hogs was used to buy bonds to help finance the war.[9] Grandpa Alo purchased a $1,000 war bond.[10] To honor the citizens of Sibley County for their outstanding purchase of war bonds, a navy attack transport ship was named the USS Sibley. She was built by the Kaiser Shipyards in Vancouver,

Washington and she was commissioned in October 1944. She transported troops, patrolled the Pacific, and participated in the invasion of Iwo Jima.[11]

How to Behave

During WWII, after being overseas for an extended period of time, the Navy gave sailors a letter on how to behave back in the states. A letter to "All Hands" tells them they'll be amazed at the large number of beautiful girls and that many of them have occupations. The letter warns sailors not to approach a girl with, "How much?" You should approach a girl with, "A beautiful day, isn't it?" or "Were you ever in Scranton?"–then ask, "How much?" The letter tells sailors when they're watching a motion picture it's not good form to whistle at every female from eight to 80 on screen.

The letter warns sailors not to go around hitting everyone of draft age in civilian clothes. First ask if he's been released from service with a medical discharge, then look at his credentials. If none – then hit him. The letter tells sailors to always salute before striking a lady.[12]

Tom and Dorothy Burke

When the U.S. entered WWII, the economy shifted to military production. The government halted the manufacture of cars and tractors. During the war, Tom and Dorothy Burke closed their café in Arlington, Minnesota. They packed up their two kids and moved to Richmond, California. At the Kaiser Shipyard, Dorothy worked in the electric shop and Tom worked as a pipe bender. One worked the day shift and one worked the night shift. After three years the Burkes returned to Arlington and reopened their café.[13] Women contributed greatly to the war effort. The iconic symbol for working women during the war was Rosie the Riveter.

Bellevue, Nebraska Trip

Grandpa Alo sent his nephew, Glen Gallatin, to welding school. Glen often worked at the Weber farm during the Depression. A couple of times during WWII, Grandma Anne and my Dad took the train from Henderson to Bellevue, Nebraska to visit Glen, who worked as a welder at the Glenn L. Martin Bomber Plant. The plant produced bombers, including the Enola Gay and Bockscar, the B-29s that each dropped an atomic bomb on Japan. After the war Glen returned to Minnesota where he was a welder for 3M.[14]

New Orleans Trip

During WWII the farm's hired man gave Grandpa Alo, Grandma Anne and my dad a ride to the train depot in East Henderson, originally called Clarksville. They boarded a train, the engineer blew the all aboard and they went clickety-clack to St. Paul. From there they rode the cushions to New Orleans where they visited Anne's brother, Leslie Madden, who was in the Army preparing to ship out to war. He ended up staying stateside. Dad remembers seeing sad mothers, wives, and girlfriends sending brave men off to war. They visited Jackson Square and strolled down Bourbon Street. Grandpa Alo enjoyed the Crescent City so much he paid to have his shoes shined.[15]

Rationing and Recycling

During the war Grandpa Alo had many friends from town, since farmers weren't subject to gas rationing. Farmers were referred to as "soldiers without uniforms." They were told to take good care of their tractors and machinery and to turn in scrap metal. The government asked farmers to plant more wheat and raise more livestock.[16] As always, farmers rose to the occasion.

During the war years, families were issued rationing books, stamps, and tokens for tires, meat, butter, sugar, and many other items. Roasted barley substituted for coffee. To save tires, drivers were encouraged to keep their speed under 35 miles per hour. An empty toothpaste tube had to be turned in before another tube could be purchased. Housewives were told to turn in fat from cooking to make explosives. In Chaska, junk rallies were held. People were paid on the spot to throw their scrap metal toward the fight. An old shovel contained enough metal to make four hand grenades. The punch line in the rally's fliers: "Let's jolt them with junk from Chaska, Minnesota."[17] During the war boys and girls collected milkweed pods to provide floss for sailors' life jackets and aviators' suits.[18]

The government restricted the use of wool because it was needed for military uniforms and blankets. People unraveled wool clothes and blankets, and used the recycled wool to make sweaters, socks, and other garments. Nylon stockings were rationed. To look like they were wearing nylons women mixed gravy browning powder in water and brushed it on their legs. For the finishing touch they used an eyebrow pencil to draw a seam down the back of each leg.[19] On the upside, to save material, bikini swim suits were introduced.

The creamery in Blakeley took advantage of the railroad tracks next to its building. They made patties of butter with the impression: Lily Sweet Cream Butter. Cases of patties were loaded onto boxcars and sold on the black market to ritzy hotels in New York City under the gilt-edged guarantee there is no substitute for good butter.[20]

During WWII while at the Silver Lake School, my dad often heard a roar in the distance. When he looked out the window he saw military planes, some towing gliders. The teacher and students looked at maps where battles were being fought. Every student and the teacher had a family member or relative serving in the armed forces. The teacher's husband was stationed in France. Being from Minnesota, on cold mornings it was his job to get up early and start the tanks. At the end of the school day the schoolmarm led the class in prayer for the safe return of those serving overseas to save the world from evil.[21]

Relief Quilts

Back when things were saved and used again, sacks replaced barrels for flour and animal feed. The sacks were turned into quilts, clothes, and pillows. To enhance sales of their product, manufacturers printed elaborate designs on sacks to appeal to sewers. During WWII my mom wore a green gathered skirt the neighbor lady in Glencoe sewed from Pillsbury's Best flour sacks. When green Pullman cars with "Hitler here we come" painted on the sides came down the tracks, Mom, wearing her green skirt, ran outside to wave at the troops. When the skirt wore out it was torn up and used for rags. During the war years, bread with butter and sugar was a treat for Mom.[22]

During WWII my Grandma Anne Weber and the neighbor ladies held quilting bees. They set up the quilting frame in the kitchen and made quilts (a Midwest art form) from feed and flour sacks and cotton. They sent the "relief quilts" to New York City where volunteers sent them to war refugees in Europe. Grandma Anne received a letter telling her they shouldn't send their fancy quilts as some volunteers in New York City were keeping the nicest ones for themselves.[23]

Lynn Kaplanian-Buller, a native of Heron Lake, Minnesota, and An Keuning-Tichelaar from the Netherlands were brought together by relief quilts. During WWII, An Keuning-Tichelaar received quilts from Mennonites in the U.S. and Canada. The two Mennonite women co-authored *Passing on the Comfort*, a book giving chilling accounts of An risking her life helping resisters during Germany's five-year occupation of the Netherlands. If the Gestapo had caught An, she would have been tortured and then shot in the head.[24]

Camp Savage

From 1942 to 1944, Camp Savage in the Lower Minnesota River Valley was home to an Army military intelligence school. The Savage site was selected because a nationwide survey found Minnesota to have the best record of racial amity.[25] I don't think the Dakota Indians were included in the survey. After proving their loyalty to the United States, second generation English-speaking Japanese-Americans called Nisei, were released from internment camps and sent to Camp Savage. They studied the Japanese language and were trained in military intelligence. Some interrogated prisoners, others were paratroopers who analyzed enemy positions and plans. Their jobs were particularly dangerous because they looked like the enemy.[26] Historians believe Yankee Samurais trained in military intelligence shortened the war with Japan by as much as two years.[27]

Port Cargill

At Port Cargill in Savage on the lower Minnesota River, Cargill Inc. was busy building auxiliary oil and gas (AOG) ships and super towboats for the U.S. military. AOG ships were used to carry fuel to other ships and to transport vehicles to battlefields. The Navy chose Cargill to build the ships and super towboats because of the company's success building ships and barges to haul grain. The Savage site was picked as it was far enough inland to avoid a Pearl Harbor type of raid and the area had hard working farm boys anxious to build ships for the war effort. Before the first AOG ship was launched, the Minnesota River was dredged from Savage to the Mississippi River.[28]

Burt Karels

Jessenland resident, Burt Karels, was a member of a bomber squadron out of England. His crew usually flew the B24 "Sleepy Time Gal." Burt, at ages 19 and 20, straight out of the cornfields of Iowa, flew 35 missions over Germany as a nose turret gunner. In case he was shot down, Burt carried a silk map with print on both sides to help guide him back to Allied territory. On one mission a bullet grazed Burt's leg and just missed his head.

After his last mission, Burt boarded a ship in England to return home. Some of his buddies tried to board a ship home, but they were turned back as the ship was overladen. The commander told the boys to fly "Sleepy Time Gal" home to the states. The plane blew an engine over Scotland and the pilot turned around. "Sleepy Time Gal" went down in bad weather. All on board missed out on a honeymoon, driving a '57 Chevy, raising kids and the joys of grandchildren. Years later an airman went to the crash site and picked up pieces of "Sleepy Time Gal" and brought them to a reunion Burt attended in Bloomington in the Lower Minnesota River Valley.[29]

Ed Scully

Jessenland native, Ed Scully, served in the Army as a medic. Ed was in Oran during the invasion of French North Africa. He and another medic were ordered to bury Allied soldiers' bloated corpses that were stacked in a church. Ed and the other medic were driven out by the stench. Ed gave two full-blooded Indians from Oklahoma a quart of whiskey to bury the dead troops.[30]

Martha Bullert

Martha Bullert was raised in Green Isle Township in Sibley County. She graduated from Arlington High in 1927. She was a member of the school's undefeated girls' basketball team, and earned a master's degree in recreation and administration from Columbia University in New York.

In 1925 the Shah of Iran opened education up to women. From 1938 to 1940 Martha lived in Iran developing an education curriculum for girls. Due to political tension she left Iran and started teaching in the Philippines. During WWII, when Japan invaded the Philippines, Martha was taken prisoner. From 1942 to 1945 she was in three different civilian internment camps. She went from 192 pounds to 103 pounds. In 1945, U.S. troops set her free.[31]

New Ulm Gets German Prisoners

After being heavily monitored by agents before and during WWI for questioning America's role in WWI, and given the action taken by the governor to suspend its mayor, who'd a thunk a camp for German prisoners would be located in New Ulm, Minnesota? In June 1944 the camp received about 140 German Air Corpsmen.[32] Other than a few uncooperative officers, the prisoners sent to New Ulm were ordinary young Germans.[33]

The Krauts were as happy as prisoners could be. In New Ulm most people spoke German and some locals gave the prisoners ice cream, beer, and cigarettes. The prisoners were paid for their work. They were able to watch movies and attended local churches. Newspapers and radios were available at the camp. The prisoners often went to work with no guards present.[34] When my Dad and his parents were at the Brown County Fair in New Ulm they saw prisoners on rides. There was a debate on whether or not the prisoners needed to purchase a license to fish.[35] For heaven's sake, only in Minnesota.

Clarence Lefto

Dad's cousin, Clarence Lefto, wasn't treated nearly as well as the German prisoners in New Ulm. In December 1944 during the Battle of the Bulge in Belgium, Sergeant Lefto and his men were taken prisoner by the Germans. Clarence's band of brothers abandoned him and his men, and he was bitter about it to the day he died.

The prisoners were taken to a camp near Schwäbisch Gmünd in Germany. Sergeant Lefto and his soldiers didn't know the type of camp they were in and lived in fear of being sent to the gas chamber. The prisoners were given bread and grass to eat and water to drink. Lice were rampant and they didn't get to shave.

A prayer chain was started by Clarence's mother and her sisters. My dad prayed with his mother and aunts for Clarence's safe return. He was set free on Good Friday, March 30, 1945. During his imprisonment he lost half his body weight. After he was liberated, the Army sent him to Hot Springs, Arkansas to recuperate. Near the end of the war and after the war the Army took over most of the hotels in Hot Springs to accommodate all the soldiers returning from overseas. In Hot Springs, Clarence received medical and dental treatment and he took therapeutic mineral baths. He went on to live a normal life in St. Paul where his widow Adella lives.[36]

Gordon Westby

Gordon Westby, from Dawson on a tributary of the Upper Minnesota River Valley, got drafted into Uncle Sam's Army. He received his training at Camp McCoy, Wisconsin, Fort Sam Houston, Texas, and in Ireland. Weighing 180 pounds on June 6, 1944, Gordon hit Omaha Beach in France. At the Battle of the Bulge he was captured by the Germans and taken prisoner.

Gordon wasn't encamped. He was marched almost every day. During the march, six to eight men a day were left for dead. Every other day the POWs were given a half a cup of lukewarm soap made by passing grassy leaves through the water. The POWs all had dysentery and were infested with lice. Prisoners who spoke or tried to obtain food took a bullet in the head. There were no Geneva POW checks or packages from the Red Cross.

On April 12, 1945, Gordon and 11 other POWs were left for dead. The human skeletons were too weak to march, their minds could only think of death. Gordon couldn't move; he had no hope. German civilians loaded Gordon and the other emaciated POWs in a farm cart and took them to an empty building. When the Americans arrived, they were flown to a hospital in England.

Gordon's condition was so grave the medics gave up on him. Gordon heard them say, "He'll never make it." Gordon's last wish to take a few sips of a milkshake provided a glimmer of hope. He started gaining weight. By June 1945 he weighed almost 90 pounds.

In July 1945, Gordon returned home to Dawson. He never fully recovered from the physical effects of being starved. He always enjoyed sucking down a milkshake. For 35 years he wasn't able to talk about his harrowing experiences as a POW. He married and had three children, and eventually retired from the Dawson Mill.[37]

Karl and Lena Diebal

Late in the war on the eastern front when the Russian army started advancing west, 14 million Germans, mostly women, children and the elderly, fled their homes.[38] The reason for fleeing: the Red Army seized all property, any German male was shot on sight, and Russian soldiers freely raped and killed German women.[39] In the "land of the dead," roadsides were lined with women's dead bodies exposed from the waist down, legs apart and the snow red from their blood.[40] The animals continued to rape long after the war was over. The Soviet government encouraged its troops to rape German women. They considered the enemy's women legitimate booty. More than two million women and children did not survive the flight to escape the communists.[41]

Karl Diebal was a medic in the German army during WWII. He was captured on the eastern front and thrown in a Soviet prison camp. While in prison, Russian soldiers forced his wife, Lena, and their two young children at gunpoint to leave their family farm in eastern Germany with nothing but the clothes they had on. Lena and the children became displaced persons. After the war, with help from the Red Cross, she found Karl in a refugee camp. On a lucky night Karl and Lena picked the right guard to bribe and they escaped to West Germany where their son, Karl, Jr., was born.

In 1952, with assistance from the Lutheran Welfare Resettlement Program, the Diebal family landed in Minnesota.

For four years Karl worked on farms to repay his sponsor and in 1956, he used his savings to purchase a farm in Jessenland. The last immigrants to Jessenland lived through the horrors of war. After Karl died, his son, Karl, Jr. took over the family dairy farm. Robots will feed and milk cows in the new barn he's putting up.[42]

Larry Tillemans and Gerry Boe

Larry Tillemans was born and raised in the town of Minneota, located between two tributaries of the upper Minnesota River. While in high school his mother insisted he take typing. He was the only boy in the class. The Army sent Sergeant Tillemans to the Nuremberg and Dachau war crime trials. After General Eisenhower toured the German death camps and saw the extent of Hitler's "Final Solution to the Jewish Question" he said, "Get all the evidence you can because down the line some SOB is going to say it never happened." Larry was a clerk and he typed affidavits of those who witnessed the atrocities of the Holocaust.

Sergeant Gerry Boe, from Minneapolis, was Captain of the Guard at the Nuremberg trials. The guards, wearing white helmets, kept watch over some of the worst criminals the world has ever seen. When Hitler's right-hand man, Hermann Goering, stood up and became arrogant, Gerry grabbed the mean sucker and sat him down. Before Goering could be hanged, he took the poison pill.

Ike was right—some SOBs say the Holocaust never happened or they doubt it happened. In some schools, lessons on the Holocaust aren't taught. After becoming upset when he heard a kooky college professor on the radio say the internment of Japanese-Americans was as bad as the Holocaust, Larry Tillemans, often with Gerry Boe, traveled throughout Minnesota giving speeches at schools, colleges, churches, synagogues, prisons, American Legions, VFWs, and service organizations. They spoke of Hitler's hatred of the Jews, and told the audiences the genocide of the Jewish people happened and the world should never forget it. Larry tells the story of two Germans, who for two years led Jews into the gas chambers every day for 14 hours a day. To do the dastardly job the workers stayed drunk on cognac. Gerry Boe died in 2015. Larry is believed to be the last living soldier at the Dachau and Nuremberg trials. Thanks to General Eisenhower and many others the Holocaust is the best-documented genocide in history.

In December 1990, Larry got nicked for his second driving while intoxicated offense. Sitting in the jailhouse in Fergus Falls, Minnesota wasn't the example Larry wanted to set for his grandchildren. Larry started praying a novena to Father Engelmar Unzeitig. He prayed so loud the jailer told him to shut up, the other inmates couldn't sleep. From that night on Larry lost his cravings for booze.

Father Engelmar Unzeitig was born in the Czech Republic. The "Angel of Dachau" died of typhoid while aiding fellow prisoners. Father Engelmar is currently going through the process of beatification. Larry is thankful Father Engelmar helped him in a time of need. Larry often reads the novena booklet of Father Engelmar. Larry currently resides in Sartell, Minnesota.[43]

Annie Weber Dies

After my great-aunt Mag Carroll lost her husband, she raised her four youngsters in the Madden's log cabin. After her kids left the roost, Mag tended to her parents Annie and Jack. Mag had to handle Jack with kid gloves as he resisted help, saying he didn't want to be a bother to anyone and insisting he could take care of himself.

After suffering for years from shingles, Annie's soul left for the everlasting kingdom. She died of pneumonia in 1945. All who knew her were endeared to her. Her wake was held in the log cabin. After her funeral, six neighbors, led by Bernie Quinn, carried her to her final resting place in the cemetery behind St. Thomas Church.[44]

Sullivan Brothers

The five Sullivan brothers from Minneapolis all returned safely home from fighting in WWII. In 1946 they all gathered around their Irish immigrant mother while she removed service stars from her window.[45] Their thoughts were with the five Sullivan brothers from Waterloo, Iowa who didn't make it home when the USS Juneau they were on went down after being hit by a Japanese torpedo.[46] During the war, the Sullivans' mother christened a Navy destroyer named in honor of her fallen sons. After the war their father took on the bottle; the bottle won.[47]

Curran Brothers

In 1946, after the death of the last of the three penny-pinching Curran brothers, Grandpa Alo's cousin, Ralph Kreger, was posted by the sheriff as a posse man at the Curran farm outside of Green Isle. It was an open secret that the Curran brothers were wealthy and had squirreled away large sums of money in their house. Nearly $20,000 in gold coins were found hidden in cans in the cellar as well as a buried stash of $1,000 in silver. Under the floor and in other places throughout the house was the tidy sum of $116,000.[48] Before the heirs sold the Curran farm the old house was torn down board by board.

After the search for the hidden money, Grandpa Alo, Dad, and the hired man, Tom Collins, went to the Citizens State Bank in Green Isle to look at a pail full of gold coins on display from the Curran house. On the way home Grandpa dropped Tom Collins off at Davitt's Saloon in Green Isle for a few malt beverages. The next morning Tom walked six miles from Green Isle to the farm. He helped milk the cows. After the milk was separated, the cream was put in cans and the skim milk was slopped to the pigs.[49] Nowadays people drink skim milk.

Walter Goede

After World War II farm prices were decent and Grandpa Alo stashed a few greenbacks. In 1949, Harry Truman was president and Grandpa Alo gave traveling salesman Walter Goede $6,000 to invest in a stock fund. A few years later Goede sold Grandpa shares of Northern States Power stock, and like the stock fund, it paid a nice dividend.

Walter Goede put many residents of New Ulm and in surrounding communities into sound investments. Walter told the story of an old widow woman in Arlington who invited him to stay for lunch. She served up chicken broth, beans, two-day old bread and pickled watermelon rinds. She poured depression coffee, new grounds sprinkled over old grounds, in cups with broken-off handles. During the conversation she told Walter she couldn't spend the interest from her investments. Walter replied, "To be honest with you it doesn't look like you're trying very damn hard."[50] If Walter was still living he'd be selling investors stock in companies that sell smoke and mirrors to the politicians in Washington, D.C.

George Stark

In September 1948 the FBI arrested George Stark at his farm near Gibbon, 30 miles west of the Lower Minnesota River Valley. Stark was charged with holding Francisco Rodriguez, born in Brownsville, Texas, in virtual slavery for some six years. He forced Rodriguez to work long hours on his farm without pay. Stark beat and used a pitchfork on Rodriguez who was forced to sleep in a locked room. Stark's house didn't have a telephone, but when a salesman called on the farm while Stark was away, Rodriguez told him to tell the sheriff of his predicament. The Sibley County Sheriff liberated Rodriguez and turned the case over to the FBI.

In February 1949, Dad's high school civics teacher took the class to the last two days of the trial against Stark at the federal courthouse in Mankato. The jury found Stark guilty of inducing Rodriguez to his farm for the purpose of involuntary servitude. Stark pulled a stretch in the federal pen. He was

139

cooped up less than 15 months before he was cut loose for medical reasons.[51]

Herman Lenzen's Country Store

In 1946, Dad's uncle, Herman Lenzen, purchased the Gotha Country Store located 15 miles west of the Minnesota River Valley near Cologne, a place where Swedish, German, and Irish farmers did their trading and spread a little gossip. Once in a while a few Hollanders from Cologne stopped in.

German kids in the area didn't speak English until they went to school. The German dialect they conversed in was no longer spoken in Germany. At age 16, most farm boys in the area dropped out of school to farm full time. When Herman became the proprietor of the store, he changed the clothing line to cater to farmers—bib overalls and work boots were big sellers. He also sold milk machine parts, seed corn, and Grimm alfalfa seed.

At the Gotha Country Store an account was kept for each farmer. The cases of eggs farmers brought to the store offset their purchases of groceries and merchandise. Every spring Herman got nervous as the farmers used their money to put crops in the fields and the balance farmers owed on their accounts grew.

Eggs were the store's moneymaker and to save time, Herman purchased an egg candling machine. Herman's son, Alan, had a successful route selling eggs to hospitals, restaurants, and grocery stores in Minneapolis and the suburbs. For a few years after WWII, food items shipped to the states such as pineapple, coconut, chocolate, bananas, and cane sugar were in short supply. Herman kept these items in large drawers under the counter. Regular customers didn't ask for them because they knew Herman would slip them in an empty egg case and add the charge to their account.

Herman and his family knew the brand of cigarettes each customer smoked. Farmers who rolled their own cigarettes asked if the store had Prince Albert in a can. Farmers were fond of saying, "You better let him out." When one of his sons got out of the service he purchased the store and Herman went back to snipping hair in Carver.[52]

Anne Weber Dies

On November 3, 1948 the Chicago Daily Tribune ran its most famous headline: "Dewey Defeats Truman." Pulling off the biggest election upset in U.S. history, "Give 'em Hell Harry" defeated Dewey. Also in 1948 the mood on the farm turned sad as Dad's mother, Anne, at age 55, left the vale of tears. She died from cancer caused by chemicals used at a radiator repair shop in St. Paul where as a young lady she worked as the bookkeeper. The Weber farmyard and hayfield were filled with cars of those attending her wake in the farmhouse. Mourners viewed Anne in the back bedroom, where she lay in an open casket. During this time of grief, Dad's cousin, Mike Carroll, milked the cows.

After Anne's death it wasn't the best of times on the farm as Grandpa and Dad missed her dearly and they had to eat their own cooking. Anne's sister, Mag Carroll, helped with household chores, including washing clothes in Grandpa Alo's electric Maytag square tub washing machine with a wringer. If trousers were run through the wringer in the wrong direction the pockets usually burst.[53]

Chapter Eight
Korean War

Ron Johnson

Ron Johnson, from Ramsey County, Minnesota, lied about his age and joined the Marines when he was 16. While stationed in San Diego on the night before his unit shipped out to Korea, he and other jar heads went to Tijuana, got liquored up and set a whorehouse on fire. The *Federales* tossed them in jail. Their commander paid the jailers for the release of his Marines. Ron spent the voyage to Korea in the ship's brig.

Ron's unit engaged in a battle near Panmunjon, Korea. Ron's hands were scarred from the heat his machine gun threw off while he gave the whole nine yards. He would have been sent home in a body bag if it hadn't been for his squad leader, Duane Dewey, from Grand Rapids, Michigan, throwing himself on a grenade just before it exploded. After President Eisenhower presented Dewey the Congressional Medal of Honor, Ike told him, "You must have a body of steel."

In his old age, Ron received an all-expense paid invitation from the South Korean government for him and his wife to attend a ceremony honoring the survivors of the battle at Panmunjon. Ron's hiatal hernia prevented him from making the trip.[1] For the last 20 years of his life, Ron survived mostly on Budweiser. Good thing beer has nutritional value.

Jessenland Township Board

Jessenland Township is governed by an elected board of five members. A sign on the grounds of the town hall reads: "Jessenland Town Hall Thriving Irish Community Plus Others."[2] In the 1950s the township board was in disarray due to drunken board members who were not taking care of business. After falling off the wagon, a board member resigned. A group of farmers asked Grandpa Alo, because of his sobriety, to take the resigning board member's seat.[3]

While Grandpa was seated on the board the township doled out welfare. It was considered a disgrace to be on welfare. All able-bodied men were expected to work. The board directed the county nurse to draw up a menu for the welfare family. The board arranged for the family to charge food items at a local store. At any given time, zero to three families in Jessenland fed at the public trough. Those receiving welfare saw their names printed in local newspapers. In about 1955, Sibley County took over the task of dishing out welfare.[4]

The township board is responsible for maintaining township roads, bridges, and cartways. The board has jurisdiction over property conditions, such as abating nuisances and controlling noxious weeds, and it has the power to levy property taxes. Until about 1955, Jessenland Township had an unarmed constable to control drunken Irishmen, to keep order at elections, and to mediate minor disputes.[5]

Thanks in part to Grandpa Alo's leadership, Jessenland Township never spent more money than it took in. Grandpa cut the township road ditches with the sickle mower attached to his Ford tractor. Unlike many self-serving politicians in Washington, D.C., Grandpa Alo was a true public servant. We need a few honorable people to run the country. Too bad all the people who say they know how are consultants for cable news.

Danny Boy

In 1951, Pope Pius XII announced Catholics could use the rhythm method of birth control. Since the priest at St. Thomas Church was too shy to explain the technique, most couples thought it was safe to have sex after a polka dance. Prior to the Pope's announcement, the only approved form of birth control for Catholics was abstinence.

In the summer of 1952, Danny Boy and his wife met with the priest at St. Thomas Church to make arrangements to have their 15th child (rhythm method) baptized. When Father asked the tater tot's name, they said Hazel. Father made a sour face and said, "Tis so many lovely Irish Catholic names: Mary, Nancy, Shannon, Bridget, Margaret, Katherine, Colleen, Brenda—why don't ye give her one of those names? Why Hazel...tis just the name of a nut."

A few months after Hazel was baptized, Danny Boy's running mate who wasn't "churched" came to Father and asked if he would say a funeral Mass for his beloved old sorrel stallion that died a few days earlier. Father said that wasn't something he did, but he should ask the Lutheran minister in Henderson. The old bachelor said, "Do you think $500 will cover the services at the Lutheran Church." Father said, "You didn't tell me the horse was Catholic."

Being a subsistence farmer, having 19 offspring and a hankering for booze, Danny Boy was poorer than a church mouse. He and his wife didn't have a bar in the gate. At the kitchen table, after he finished eating, Danny Boy took out his false teeth and handed them to his wife so she could chew on her food. At an old neighbor lady's wake, when no one was looking, Danny Boy pulled the dentures from her mouth. The choppers fit his better half pretty good.

Danny Boy's wife squirted out 12 red-headed daughters, most of whom had a roving eye. When Danny Boy took family pictures, he placed his sons-in-law on each end. That way when a daughter got divorced, Danny Boy could cut the son-in-law out of the family picture.

When spring turned to summer, the priest at St. Thomas got homesick for his mother's biscuits and flew to Shannon Field in Ireland. He left Danny Boy in charge of the church grounds. While Father was away Danny went on a two-week bender at the gin mills in Green Isle, Belle Plaine, and Le Sueur. Danny Boy knew he was full when he smelled alcohol from his pores and he shook like a dog after a swim. Danny Boy said he mostly went on two-week drunks to get away from his nagging wife. While recovering from his drinking frolic the depot agent in Blakeley rang him up. He told Danny Boy he got a wire from Father saying to pick him up in a week at Holman Field in St. Paul.

After a month of neglect the church grounds were overgrown with grass and weeds. Over the next few days Danny Boy huffed and puffed as he cut and raked the grass. He pulled weeds and trimmed bushes. After the clippings dried, Danny Boy poured gasoline on the pile and tossed a match on the heap. His eyelashes got shorter.

While one of St. Paul's finest was writing Danny Boy a ticket for jaywalking he asked the copper, "Where do you let Catholics cross the street? I only see signs for Protestant crossings." After Danny Boy picked Father up at Holman Field, they ducked into Mickey's Dining Car in St. Paul. When their sandwiches and beans arrived, Danny Boy started to say grace, Father interrupted, saying it wasn't necessary to pray as no potatoes were on their plates. On the drive home, they saw lights on at the Schmidt Brewery in Minneapolis. Father pointed to them and said, "See Danny Boy, you'll never drink all the beer." Danny Boy replied, "Yeah, Father, but I got 'em workin' nights."

The next morning Father saw the church grounds were in tip-top shape and he said to Danny Boy, "While I was away the Lord and you did a splendid job of caring for this holy ground." Danny Boy replied, "Father, you should have seen it when the Lord 'twas at it alone."

Feeling the effects of a pickled liver, Danny Boy made the rounds to see his chums one last time. Over a bucket of beer he told his German neighbor, "I'm better than you." The German said, "How's that?" Danny Boy replied, "Cuz me got no Irishmen for neighbors." The next morning it was sultry and Danny Boy, feeling a bit rough coming off a three-day runner, got in the box at St. Thomas Church. Danny Boy confessed to taking a peek at a stag film. Father shook his head, sipped his shandy, smacked his lips, and gave Danny Boy his penance of 12 Our Fathers and 12 Hail Marys. The old codger stood up, got light headed and down he went. A young girl rushed up to him and said, "Danny Boy, Danny Boy! What did Father hit you with?"

After he turned yellow, they laid Danny Boy in a hospital bed. The priest and Buzzard—no one knew he drank 'til someone saw him sober—paid Danny Boy a visit. After Danny Boy took last rites, Buzzard cut a slit with his pocket knife in the IV bag. Buzzard and Father each took a swig from a bottle of wine and Father dumped the rest of the Jesus juice in the IV bag. After ten minutes Danny Boy's eyes lit up like he was strapped in Old Sparky and the electrocutioner threw the switch. Danny Boy, who hadn't said a word in a week, mumbled, "Fellas, it's all fun and games 'til the liver gives out." After a few days passed Danny Boy's wife told the hospital's bean counter their bank account was overdrawn. That night the meat wagon hauled Danny Boy to the morgue.

At Danny Boy's wake, mourners in high glee singing Irish drinking songs took ice off his corpse and put it in their beer. A few men swore the jollity of the affair put a grin on Danny Boy's face. In the wee hours of the morning Danny Boy's widow said she preferred Irish wakes to Irish weddings. When asked why, she said, "One less drunk." It took three days to cremate Danny Boy. The Belle Plaine fire department called in extra volunteers to keep the flame down.

Madden Log Cabin Goes Up in Flames

On a September day in 1952 my great-aunt, Mag Carroll, was at the Weber farm washing clothes when a chimney fire engulfed the Madden's 90-year-old log cabin. The Henderson and Arlington Fire Departments managed to save the rock foundation. Mag was shaken by the loss of her trunk that contained her personal items, mementos and special gifts she received over the years.[6]

Mag and her father Jack moved to an apartment over a house in Arlington. While living there, Jack saw a doctor who wrote him a prescription he didn't get filled. He told his grandson, Allie, he had better things to spend his money on than pills.[7]

Silver Lake School

In 1953 the fit and dapper Harry Truman was President. He's known for "The buck stops here!" sign that was on his desk for a short time.[8] Presidents of the modern era—Bill Clinton, George W. Bush, and Barack Obama carry a sign that says, "The buck never gets here." Also in 1953 the Silver Lake School closed. Grandpa Alo, like his dad and grandpa, served as school treasurer. Silver Lake School taught Great-Grandpa Henry, Grandpa Alo, and Dad not to spend more money than they took in, whether it was from farming or in public service; can't say that for the spendthrift politicians who dictate policy from Washington, D.C.

Country schools taught students to be patriotic, hard honest workers, and to take personal responsibility. One-room country schools educated the soldiers that won two world wars and the workers who built the greatest country on God's green earth. Bigger schools gobble up a lot more taxpayer money and students lose their individual importance. The U.S. Supreme Court does its part; the more they take God out of public schools the more dangerous they become. When a student goes "postal" killing kids, the first thing organized is a prayer vigil.

Allie Weber in High School

In his high school years, Dad wadded down Seven Up bars made by the Trudeau Candy Company in St. Paul. When Dad turned 15, he pushed 35 cents across the counter at the First National Bank in Arlington and the teller issued him a paper driver's license. When he played football at Arlington High he wore an open face leather helmet. In high school Dad got a medal for his knowledge of current events. His senior year he and a friend traveled to Chaska to hear Guy DeLeo's 16-piece orchestra.

When Dad graduated from Arlington High in 1950 Harry Truman was President. He started his day off with a tumbler of bourbon.[9] Shortly after graduation, Dad purchased a used Indian motorcycle. Dad spun his Indian in circles around neighbors Ed and Mary Scully to shivaree them on their wedding day.[10]

Dionne Quintuplets

After graduating from Glencoe High in 1951, Mom worked as a bookkeeper at the Shriners Hospital for Children in Minneapolis. While the Dionne quintuplets were at the winter carnival in St. Paul they stopped by the Shriners Hospital to visit patients. Mom met them and took their picture. One of the quints said about their bulky costumes, "We feel like fish swimming upstream."[11]

The Dionne quintuplets—from one egg—were born two months premature in 1934 in a house near Corbeil, Ontario, Canada. After they were born they were put in a straw basket and placed near a wood burning stove. The house didn't have electricity or running water.[12] The Canadian government intervened and made the "miracle babies" wards of the king, removing them from their parents and using them to increase tourism and market products.[13] A U-shaped observation gallery was built so visitors could watch the quints without them

149

knowing they were being observed. Eventually the quints figured out what was going on.[14]

After a long legal battle, their parents obtained custody when the quints were nine.[15] Family life for the quints was brutal. Their siblings picked on them. Their mother (called the damn cow) was verbally abusive and she often backhanded them with a slap to the face. She demoralized them and worked their fingers to the bone, never satisfied with their efforts.[16] In 1947 she was named Mother of the Year.[17] Their father (called the old man) profited from the quints, and he and their brothers molested them. When one of the quints told a nun about the sexual abuse, the nun swept it under the rug.[18] One of the quints asked a nun if the milk they drank from black women when they were babies marked their bodies.[19]

McCloud County Fair

When Mom and Dad were dating they went to the McCloud County Fair in Hutchinson where they heard a barker using a bullhorn say, "Come in the tent and see the horror car, the killers' car, the car used in the gang war days in Chicago." The car, supposedly Al Capone's, was outfitted with metal plates and bulletproof glass. For four bits, Mom and Dad took a look at the car. Afterwards they enjoyed brats, sauerkraut, and corn on the cob. They finished off the evening checking out the latest in farm machinery and equipment.[20]

St. Louis Trip

In 1953 Grandpa Alo and Dad drove Grandpa's 1948 Kaiser with vent windows to St. Louis to visit relatives. Grandpa was a little uneasy when they left—the hired man, Tom Collins, was in the tank. Tom told Alo, "Don't worry, I know I'm drunk, but I'll sober up and get the chores and farm work done." When they got to St. Louis, Alo called neighbor Bert Berger to check up on Tom. Bert said Tom was doing fine, he just left the Weber farm and the "Calves were knee deep in straw." While in St. Louis, the relatives took Alo and Dad to their church's fish feed. Afterward they had a boxing trivia contest. To everyone's astonishment Grandpa Alo correctly answered every question.[21]

Jim Crow

In 1954, Dwight Eisenhower was President. It was also the year Grandpa sold his herd of Holsteins when Dad enlisted in the army. In December 1954, Dad sold his Indian motorcycle and shipped out to boot camp at Fort Leonard Wood, Missouri where for the first time he conversed with a black man. While there, Dad's friend from Queens told him people in New York City wouldn't travel west of the Mississippi for fear of being attacked by Indians.[22]

After boot camp, Dad was stationed at Fort Hood in the old slave state of Texas. He didn't experience any workplace violence; however, while on Army business in a one-horse town in East Texas, Dad and three other soldiers—one of whom was black—walked into a store. The waitress at the lunch counter shouted, "You three can eat inside; the baboon eats outside." They left in a huff. They purchased food at a grocery store and had a picnic. When they stopped at a filling station for gas and a bathroom break the black soldier was directed to the "colored bathroom" where a couple of rusty sheets of tin were nailed to a tree.[23]

On another trip Dad stayed in Minden, Louisiana where Jim Crow was in effect. In 1896 the U.S. Supreme Court, in *Plessy v. Ferguson*, upheld the South's "separate but equal" doctrine validating Jim Crow laws. These laws dating from about 1875 to the mid-1960s, not only segregated blacks and whites, it was a way of life. Jim Crow etiquette prevented blacks and whites from eating together or from using the same water fountain. While driving, blacks had to yield the right-of-way to whites. Blacks could never assert a white person was lying or had dishonorable intentions. It was a new experience for Dad and he didn't like it. Jim Crow wasn't only in the south. In 1940, in Pasadena,

California, blacks were only allowed to swim in the public pool on Thursdays. Then it was drained so whites could swim in clean water for the next six days.[24]

Jack Madden Dies

While at Fort Hood, Dad got word his grandfather, Jack Madden, threw his last cards. At age 94, he was taken down for good with the death rattle. Jack's favorite meal was bread rubbed in hot bacon grease. He was one of Sibley County's oldest native-born citizens and he was the last of the Irish subsistence farmers from Jessenland to bite the dust.[25] The population of Jessenland and Green Isle declined in the 1950s as many of the Irish left for the bright lights of big cities.[26] St. Paul and Chicago were favorites.

Dad hailed a hack for a lift to Love Field in Dallas where he stepped up to the Northwest Airline ticket counter for a flight to Wold-Chamberlain Field in Minneapolis to attend his grandfather's wake and funeral. Not having his checkbook, the agent threw down a counter check. Dad filled it out and a half hour later he boarded his plane—no TSA (Thousands Standing Around) and the pilot and half the passengers were smoking. Dad sat next to a young lady who volunteered him to hold one of her babies during the flight. Dad and five other grandsons carried Jack to his grave next to his wife Annie in the granite orchard behind St. Thomas Church.[27]

Royal Order of Atlantic Voyageurs

In October 1955 the Army sent Dad to Fort Dix, New Jersey. Dad boarded the USS General Harry Taylor to cross the salt to Bremerhaven, West Germany. The voyage got him a membership in the Royal Order of Atlantic Voyageurs. A North Atlantic storm caused the trip to take three days longer than usual. A crusty sailor on Dad's deck laughed at the seasick troops. A half hour later that sailor put his teeth in his pocket and started heaving. So many were sick that when the ship rolled, vomit came over Dad's combat boots. Dad felt a long way from the cornfields of southern Minnesota. After the storm, on the top deck Dad saw the Queen Mary I ahead of them.

Kaiser–Wilhelm Barracks

Dad was stationed at the motor pool unit at the Kaiser-Wilhelm Barracks in Mannheim, West Germany. He was among the second group of whites integrated with this previously all-black unit. Dad didn't experience or see any racial problems. The unit was led by a colorblind black first sergeant.

At Dad's new duty station, he hauled coal in Army tractor-trailers. The coal was used by Germans to keep warm. When Dad pulled up to a stop sign, kids scaled the trailer and chucked off clumps of coal to women who scurried off with it. When Dad got the rig rolling the kids jumped off the trailer. Dad kept his speed down so the kids didn't get hurt. While stopped at intersections Dad often waited for people on crutches and wheelchairs to clear before he accelerated.

When Dad started his guard duty shift he'd say, "Walk my post, a mile a minute, empty rifle, nothing in it." Dad's ability to read a map, always sober and his shiny boots got him the job of driving Army brass around West Germany. When Dad took the boozing company commander out on bivouac, he pulled a two-wheel trailer behind the jeep. It was full of ammo and bottles of spirits for the commander and his junior officers.

When Dad took the company commander to Schwäbisch Gmünd, Germany he looked for the prison camp his cousin Clarence Lefto was held in during WWII. A former German soldier who was held at a POW camp in Indiana told Dad in English the "bad" Germans didn't come from Schwäbisch Gmünd and the prison camp had been torn down shortly after the war. On another trip Dad went to Wittenberg, Germany and saw the Castle Church where it's believed in 1517 Martin Luther (he was a beer drinker) nailed his collection of criticisms of corruption in the Catholic church to the doors of the church. The criticisms became known as the Ninety-five Theses, and they set off the Protestant Reformation.[28]

Mannheim to Paris Trip

While stationed in Germany, Dad purchased a Horex motorcycle and took leave for a trip he still talks about. He and the black soldier who couldn't eat at the lunch counter in east Texas rode the Horex from Mannheim to Paris. They rode through the historic battlefields of World War I and II. At night they stayed at military bases. Before driving into France, Dad converted some of his military script into francs at a German bank. In France the Horex stalled because the French gas had a different formula. A Frenchmen stopped, hoisted the Horex into the bed of his truck and brought it to his garage where he adjusted the carburetor. Dad paid the Frenchman in francs.[29]

Netherlands Trip

While Dad competed with two other troops for Colonel's Orderly, the Captain in charge asked, "Who's the Secretary of Agriculture?" Dad popped off, "Ezra Benson." The Captain said, "I'll be damned." The answer sealed a three-day pass for Dad that he used to take a bus tour of the Netherlands. The bus drove over several temporary bridges built by the U.S. Army. Dad asked the guide why so many trees were dead. The guide told him during the war the Dutch people ate the bark causing the trees to die.[30] During the "Hunger Winter" of 1944, a hundred thousand Dutch starved to death.[31]

Dad saw the "Secret Annexe" on Prinsengracht Canel in Amsterdam, Holland, where for 25 months Anne Frank kept her diary of hiding from the German occupiers of Holland. In August 1944, Anne's diary abruptly ended when the Gestapo were tipped off by a Dutch snitch. A month later the Franks were on the last shipment of Jews to leave Holland. In early 1945, Anne and her sister both died of typhus at the Bergen-Belsen prison camp in Germany.[32]

Allie and Geri Weber

In the summer of 1956 in Bremerhaven, West Germany, while the band played *"Auf Wiedersehen,"* Dad left the occupation army and boarded the USS General Simon B. Bucker to the states. The voyage across the pond was calm. One evening Dad and others ate mess late and they got food poisoning. No wonder Dad won't board a cruise ship. In September 1956, Dad's hitch was up. At Fort Sheridan, Illinois, he was discharged from the Army.

In November 1956 my dad and Geri Gildea, a wonderful Irish-German lady, were married by a Monsignor at St. Helena's Catholic Church in south Minneapolis, where the beatitudes are painted on the church's ceiling beams. Their reception was held in the banquet room at a restaurant on Lake Street in Minneapolis. There was no wedding dance.

While on their honeymoon, Mom and Dad took a sightseeing flight from Key West, Florida to Havana, Cuba. The pilot flew low over the clear water so they could see dolphins and sunken ships. They stayed at a hotel in downtown Havana and couldn't help but notice young soldiers with long guns stationed at major intersections. Gun-toting soldiers and gunfire off in the distance made the newlyweds feel uncomfortable; they were glad to return to Florida.[33]

In October 1957, I came into the world in the hospital in Arlington, Minnesota. When Grandpa Alo saw me wrapped in swaddling clothes he gave me the 1888 Lady Liberty $20 gold coin his mother Katherine gave him shortly before she died.[34] I was the first of seven kids and the first in my lineage born in a hospital.

Dad sold four feeder cattle to pay the 11-day hospital bill and doctor bill for my birth. A farmer would now sell at least 60 feeder cattle to pay for the birth of his child, and mother and baby usually leave the hospital after a day or two.[35]

I was the fifth generation of Webers to live in the two-story house my great-great-grandfather Anton built on the farm. I was born towards the end of the baby boomer generation, the first generation of American children who for the most part, weren't required to work. Nowadays many adults don't know how to work because as teenagers they never learned to work, or they come from homes where adults don't work. The consumer generation bought into the concepts of buy now, pay later and paying money to lose weight.

In 1958, on a cold windy December night, my little sister Ann was ready to leave the hopper. Grandpa Alo watched me. Dad, sick with the stomach flu, loaded Mom up in the '56 Ford Victoria for the seven-mile run to the hospital in Arlington. A few miles from the hospital a front tire blew. Dad ran the '56 on the rim. When Dad pulled up to the hospital's front door the rim was glowing red. After seeing Dad's condition, the nurse put him in a hospital bed for a complementary overnight stay.[36] Two weeks later Ann left the hospital wearing cloth diapers fastened with safety pins. As she grew up she brought humor and wit to the family. As the Irish say, "She can clip a hedge with her tongue."

Growing up I realized Dad possessed all the traits of a cocky Irishman except he never took to the bottle. Like his father before him, Dad attends Mass every Sunday and holy day, and every night he gets down on his knees and prays. For 30 years Dad read the Epistles at St Thomas Church. For years he led the rosary at wakes. People still comment on the Irish tones in his voice. Dad likes to read newspapers, including the cartoon "Peanuts" created by Charles Schulz from St. Paul, Minnesota. Earning $20 million a year, Schulz became one of the wealthiest cartoonists of all time.[37] Dad specializes in drainage, fixing farm machinery, growing crops, and with Mom, attending every family, church, and social event in the local area.

In 1959, Grandpa Alo turned the Weber farm over to Dad. That spring Dad experimented with a new system of planting corn, resulting in the highest yield in Sibley County. Dad planted his corn in 20-inch rows, instead of the standard 40-inch rows. In a contest sponsored by the University of Minnesota Extension Division and Farmer Magazine, despite dry weather his crop yield was 117 bushels per acre. Dad was on to something; in less than 30 years almost all corn in the Midwest is planted in narrow rows. Dad believes he was one of the first farmers in Sibley County to have a picker shelter and a corn drying bin.[38]

John Ireland Remembered

In the St. Paul Pioneer Press on St. Patty's Day 1958, Oliver Towne recalled an earlier time when Archbishop John Ireland called on St. Brendan's Church in Green Isle. After the Archbishop gave a fiery sermon on the evils of drinking, he sought pledges to give up the sauce. The Archbishop hated alcohol more than most mortal sins. When he sought pledges for total abstinence for life not one person stirred. He then called on all in front of him to come to the communion rail to pledge abstinence for ten years. No one moved. He then spotted John McMahon, father of the St. Paul police chief. The Archbishop called on McMahon to take the pledge for only five years. McMahon hesitated and said, "Your Grace, 'tis a long time — five years." The Archbishop responded, "Won't you come to the railing and take a pledge for an indefinite time…let's say from this moment until you and I meet on the streets of Green Isle again…and I don't come here very often, you know." McMahon resolutely walked to the railing and took the pledge.

The Archbishop stayed in Green Isle for a supper given in his honor by the parish priest. After putting on the dog for the Archbishop, the buckboard was hitched up and he was driven to the depot to take the train back to St. Paul. McMahon's buggy pulled up at the other end of the depot platform and McMahon stepped down from his buggy and began walking toward the Archbishop. As McMahon approached the Archbishop, he took off his hat, bowed low and said, "Well, Your Grace, we meet again."[39]

Those who care about such things believe St. Brendan's in Green Isle is the only parish visited by Archbishop Ireland where he didn't get a pledge of abstinence. It wasn't for lack of drinkers. For the Irish in Green Isle, temperance was never in style.[40]

Chapter Nine
Vietnam War and Hippies

New House

In 1960, Dad's friend built a new two-story house on the Weber farm including a small attached house for Grandpa Alo— total cost $25,000. Dad and his carpenter friend are part of a group of high school pals who have remained lifelong friends. One of the friends arranged a blind date for Mom and Dad to meet. After high school the friends took turns hosting card parties playing "500." For the last 60 years when Mom and Dad prepared to host a card party, Dad said, "The guest who comes too late is apt to make me rather surly, but irks me less by far than the one who comes too early." After the game was over Mom served lunch. The player with the high score was awarded a small prize. The player with the low score got a booby prize, often a small bottle of ketchup.

The new house had an oil burning furnace, a round Honeywell thermostat, indoor plumbing, and a flour bin with a sifter. A wall mounted rotary dial telephone owned by the telephone company was installed in the dining room. When the phone rang everyone in the house jumped up to answer it. In the early 1960s there were up to 19 telephones on the neighborhood party line. Old ladies listening in on the neighbor's telephone conversations kept the rumor mill spinning. Those expensive long-distance calls were limited, brief and to the point. A few of the neighbors didn't have a telephone—too expensive.

Using a pinch bar, Grandpa Alo tore down the old two-story house and summer kitchen. Grandpa used some of the salvaged lumber to build a doghouse and pig crate. Grandpa herded a boar into the crate and a few men hoisted the crate into the bed of a truck. The boar was off to the next farm to "go to work." Grandpa used the crate to transport an open sow he purchased from a neighbor. The next week, after Sunday Mass, Grandpa told the neighbor the sow died. The neighbor said, "She never did that before."

In the early 1960s, Dad fastened two antennas to the roof of the new farmhouse. One pointed toward the Twin Cities and picked up five signals, the other pointed toward Mankato and picked up one signal. We had a black and white television in the living room and one in the den. To change the channel I got off the couch and turned the dial. Dad wouldn't let me watch *Hogan's Heroes*. He said the program made a mockery out of the way most prisoners of war were treated by the German army.

If Dad thought I watched too much television or a racy program, such as the *Dating Game, Newlywed Game,* or *Love American Style*, unbeknownst to me until years later, he'd go in the basement and disconnect the antenna wire. Dad told me, "The picture turned into a polar bear in a snowstorm." He said watching the boob tube causes "your eyes to be the size of oranges and your brain to be the size of a pea." He'd say, "Go outside and blow the stink off you."

My siblings and I played outside or in farm buildings year round. We built forts using bales of hay, and tree houses out of scrap lumber. On cold winter days we muffled up in snowmobile suits, and hit the snow and ice. We dug tunnels in snowdrifts. On Silver Lake we rode our bicycles on thin ice. We made mud cakes and pretended to bake them in the woodstove from the old farmhouse. We played cowboys and Indians. We played "electric chair"—I was the one blindfolded and tied in a chair. During one "electrocution" Dad caught me off guard with a jolt from the cattle prod. The only times we spent all day in the house is when we were sick or there was a blizzard.

Twins and Vikings

In 1960, after winning five NBA Championships, the Minneapolis Lakers packed their bags and left for Los Angeles. In 1961, the Washington Senators from our nation's capital, moved to Minnesota and changed their name to the Twins. The Twins' mascots are Minnie and Paul. They shake hands over the Mississippi River and are the twins original logo.[1] Also in 1961, Minnesota got an expansion football team—the Vikings. Both teams played on the grass at Metropolitan Stadium in Bloomington on the outer rim of the Lower Minnesota River Valley. Landing the Twins and Vikings was the start of the Twin Cities shedding its image as big farmer towns. In 1967, Bud Grant became the Vikings head coach. He cut Saturday practices short to go hunting. He knows Owen—"Owen four" in Super Bowls.

When the Twins arrived, Grandpa Alo was a little disappointed as the bush league St. Paul Saints—originally called the Apostles—moved to Omaha and the Minneapolis Millers called it quits.[2] For years Grandpa Alo, Dad, and relatives watched the "Big River Rivalry" teams play "streetcar" doubleheaders. On summer holidays they watched the Saints and Millers play a morning game, then they hopped on a streetcar to the other team's field to watch an afternoon game.[3] In the 1950s, the Twin Cities ended streetcar service with a little help from General Motors, Firestone Tires, Standard Oil, and Phillips Petroleum.

John F. Kennedy

In the presidential election of 1960, the "Protestant Pope," Billy Graham, organized religious leaders to defeat John F. Kennedy.[4] Despite opposition from Protestant leaders, JFK defeated Richard Nixon in one of the closest presidential elections of all time. On January 20, 1961, JFK—the first Catholic and at age 43, the youngest man elected president—gave his famous, "ask not what your country can do for you—ask what you can do for your country" inaugural speech. Dad liked the Camelot President's speech so much he memorized and often recites the following portion:

> "We dare not forget today that we are the heirs of that first revolution. Let the word go forth from this time and place, to friend and foe alike, that the torch has been passed to a new generation of Americans—born in this century, tempered by war, disciplined by a hard and bitter peace, proud of our ancient heritage—and unwilling to witness or permit the slow undoing of those human rights to which this Nation has always been committed, and to which we are committed today at home and around the world."

JFK said, "All history is gossip." Being a cocksman extraordinaire, President Kennedy created a lot of history by having numerous affairs while he was president. In response to his hanky-panky with Marilyn Monroe, Dad said, "Man with two women not to be envied but to be pitied."

On November 22, 1963, I was playing in the backyard when Mom told me President Kennedy had been assassinated in Dallas, Texas. Lyndon Baines Johnson was immediately sworn in as President. Two days later I watched on TV as strip club owner Jack Ruby shot dead Kennedy's accused assassin, communist Lee Harvey Oswald.

After the Requiem Mass, I watched on TV as President Kennedy was laid to rest under his eternal flame at Arlington National Cemetery. President Kennedy's brain was put in a container and stored in a Secret Service file cabinet. In 1966, JFK's brain turned up missing.[5] The U.S. Government is second to none when it comes to losing things, especially taxpayer money.

Silver Lake Schoolhouse Torn Down

In 1962 the U.S. Supreme Court in *Engel v. Vitale* said "no" to prayer in public schools. In the summer of 1963 Grandpa Alo, Dad, and I helped tear down the Silver Lake schoolhouse on Jimmy Quinn's land. The lumber was salvaged. Dad took a couple of the chalkboards and hung them in the house basement. My four sisters used the chalkboards to play school. Two of my sisters went on to be school teachers.

Grandpa Alo and Dad were glad to see the old schoolhouse come down as it was home to a few drifters working at Nagel Packing, a fresh vegetable packing plant. A rumor circulated that a man was murdered in the schoolhouse. Grandpa erected an electric fence around the farmyard. At night he turned the electric fence on high. Grandpa said, "If one of those roughnecks from the old schoolhouse tries to come to the farm at night we might find him under the fence."

Martin Luther King, Jr.

In 1963, Martin Luther King, Jr. delivered his "I Have a Dream" speech. A portion of the speech to live by is: "I have a dream that my four little children will one day live in a nation where they will not be judged by the color of their skin, but by the content of their character." King ended his speech with a phrase from an old Negro spiritual: "Free at Last! Free at Last! Thank God Almighty, we are free at last!"

Marie Murray

In the early 1960s our neighbors Charlie and Marie Murray built a new dairy barn on their farm. To celebrate, a polka band from New Ulm played in the barn's loft. Dancers bunny hopped 'til the cows came home. In 1963, Charlie died. Marie and the Indian children she raised took over milking the herd. Every summer Dad and I, along with other neighbors, showed up at Marie's farm with loaders and manure spreaders to clean the barnyard.

163

For dinner Marie served up a spread fit for the king and queen of Poseyville—roast beef, peas from the garden, mashed potatoes with gravy, and homemade bread. For dessert she cut homemade lemon pies in quarters. After dinner the Irishmen took a nap under the weeping willow tree. Hard-working German, Martin Zimmerman, didn't have time for a snooze. He greased and tinkered with the loaders and spreaders. Martin once told me he sold a batch of feeder pigs, he didn't make any money on them, but at least he got the work out of them.

Gravel Roads

On a nice fall day in 1963, I rode with Dad in his 1950 Packard with a flathead straight-eight thunderbolt engine, guzzling gas almost as fast as "green" companies guzzling up taxpayer money. The gravel roads in Sibley County are graded about once a month to prevent washboarding. Grading one side of the road causes a ridge of gravel in the middle of the road until the other side of the road is graded. When Dad turned onto a gravel road with a ridge in the middle, a young buck whose Studebaker we didn't recognize came barreling towards us. The Studebaker swerved to the left so it straddled the ridge of gravel. Dad said, "Hold on." He pushed the footfeed to the floor and swerved the Packard to the left so it also straddled the ridge of gravel. Dad won the game of chicken. For the last several years Sibley County hasn't been able to keep up grading its gravel roads as they are constantly tore up by politicians kicking the debt can down the road.

Dynamite

In 1964, I rode with Dad in the 1950 Ford F1 pickup truck to Eickschen's Hardware Store in Green Isle. Dad purchased a box of dynamite out of a steel-lined shed. Next stop was O'Neil's General Store for cream cheese Danish. We washed 'em down with a jug of ice cold milk from the Oak Grove Dairy in Norwood, Minnesota. On the ride home Dad told me, "When it comes to politics, I can handle my enemies, but heaven protect me from my friends."

At the farm, Dad drove the F1 to a field the government paid him not to plant we called "Idle Acres." Using a tilling spade, Dad dug a hole alongside and under a large rock. He put two sticks of dynamite under the rock, lit the fuse and yelled, "Fire in the hole!" and scurried away. The explosion caused the rock to pop up to the surface. We used the large fire crackers to bring up a few more rocks.

A couple of months later I helped blast rocks with our neighbor Bernie Quinn, except he put several sticks of dynamite under a rock. After I lit the fuse I bolted. The heavy charge blew the rocks to smithereens, showering us with flying dirt and rock fragments. During one blast, a sliver whistled my way catching me in the leg. We had every window in Jessenland rattling. When Vietnam War protesters started blowing up buildings, local hardware stores quit selling dynamite.

Gulf of Tonkin

In 1964, Lyndon Baines Johnson was President. At meetings he declared swim breaks and had everyone go to the pool where he swam nude and he expected all others to strip down and get in.[6] Also that year, North Vietnam attacked a U.S. destroyer in its territorial waters in the Gulf of Tonkin. The destroyer was unscarred.[7] After a purported second attack on two U.S. destroyers in the Gulf of Tonkin, Johnson, expressed doubts as to whether the attack occurred, he told an aide, "Hell, those dumb stupid sailors were just shooting at flying fish."[8] Johnson used the fabricated second attack to expand the war by ordering bombing raids against North Vietnam. His plan was to bring the war to a swift end.[9]

In 1965 the draft shifted into high gear. By the end of 1966 the U.S. had nearly 400,000 troops in Vietnam. Grandpa Alo told me the U.S. was using the good name of the military to fight a war the politicians didn't have the will to win. Grandpa got upset when he saw the indifference displayed by politicians when young men came home in body bags. The politicians were quick to send young men off to war and slow to care for them when they returned home.

USS Forrestal

On July 29, 1967 the USS Forrestal was positioned at Yankee Station in the Gulf of Tonkin off the coast of North Vietnam. That morning a Zuni rocket accidently launched from a Phantom jet fighter. The rocket flew across the deck of the Forrestal ripping off a sailor's arm and hitting a Skyhawk jet waiting to take off, piloted by John McCain (known for his contempt of Navy rules). The rocket ruptured the Skyhawk's fuel tank. Jet fuel ran on the ship's deck and ignited.[10] Ninety-four seconds later the fire caused an old World War II era 1,000-pound bomb from McCain's Skyhawk to cook off early and explode.[11] The fire spread, setting off many more explosions.

The disaster was made worse by the Forrestal the day before receiving old rusty and leaky WWII bombs that caused the majority of the damage. The faulty fat boy bombs should have been destroyed years ago. The Forrestal got the old bombs because President Johnson was escalating the war and there was a shortage of munitions.[12] A probe into the disaster determined that a defective slide switch failed to prevent a power surge that blasted off the Zuni rocket. The Forrestal's old man was cleared of wrongdoing, but his days of being a ship's captain were over. He was exiled to Iceland to sit behind a desk.[13]

Gone was the fun-loving grin of 21-year-old sailor, Gerald Fredrickson, out of Ortonville in the Upper Minnesota River Valley. He was among the 134 men who didn't survive the fire and explosions on the Forrestal.[14] By a whisker, John McCain got through the catastrophe. To help save the ship, he threw ordinance overboard.[15] Three months later, he was shot down over North Vietnam. McCain spent over five-and-a-half years in North Vietnam prisons—including the Hóa Lò hellhole known as the "Hanoi Hilton." North Vietnam offered him an early release because his father was an admiral, but he refused saying he didn't want to be released ahead of prisoners held longer. For that he gets respect.

Southwest Minnesota State College

The Vietnam War gave rise to a counterculture that took on the establishment. It was the start of the drug culture in America. Protest marches, long hair, anti-war songs, burning draft cards, and "free love" were commonplace. Flower children liked to say, "Make love not war."

In 1967, Southwest Minnesota State College (now Southwest State University) in Marshall on a tributary of the upper Minnesota River, admitted its first class. A year later students held a peace march that ended with a discussion on race relations and the Vietnam War. Participants included the chief of police and local Catholic clergy. The marches continued and, on May 11, 1972, 166 protesters were arrested by the Marshall police. On that day they arrested more demonstrators than any police department in the country. A group of white students who called themselves the "Rat Pack," taunted black students at sporting events. In March 1971 at a college "spring fling" celebration, black and white students went to fisticuffs. Students got arrested. Black students claims of police brutality were dismissed. After a few years, most black students left the college.[16]

Otto and Jenny Kruger

President Johnson said, "I can't stand an ugly woman around, or a fat one."[17] In 1964 he declared a War on Poverty. After he announced programs for the Great Society, he told two governors on Air Force One, "I'll have those niggers voting Democrat for the next 200 years."[18] Despite spending a granary full of taxpayer money, the War on Poverty has been a failure as the poverty rate is about the same now as it was when the programs started. General George Armstrong Custer said, "In this country, no man, particularly if moderately educated, need fail in life if determined to succeed, so many and varied are the avenues to honorable employment which open all hands before him."[19]

The War on Poverty didn't keep my Mom's sister, Jenny, and her husband, Otto Kruger who was lazier than a pet seal, from getting pushed off his family's farm between Hector and Bird Island, Minnesota. Mom and Dad allowed them to stay with us until they got on their feet. We all gathered around Otto while he played his baritone horn. After a toad hopped in the baritone and died, it quit working. From having the mumps when she was a young woman, Jenny was hard of hearing. Being married to Otto it was probably a good thing.

Uncle Otto (he ate raw hamburger patties sprinkled with salt and pepper) brought to the farm a three-foot metal rod with an electric motor and a wooden handle attached to it. After supper, Otto plugged it in, held on to the wooden handle, touched the bottom of the metal rod to soil in a shaded area, and moved the rod back and forth until he found an area where angle worms and night crawlers came to the surface. We put the worms in a tin can, placed our bamboo fishing poles on our shoulders, and walked through the cow pasture to Silver Lake. We put a worm on the hook, set the sinker and bobber and fished from shore. We had bushels of fun pulling in bullheads and sunfish. We put the fish in a five gallon bucket half full of water. When Dad hooked a sunny, he'd say, "Not even a fish would get in trouble if it kept its mouth shut."

Uncle Otto cleaned a bullhead by gutting it, nailing its head to a board, and pulling off its skin with a pair of pliers. The cats ate the skin and guts. The next night we'd have bullheads for supper. We would put any extra cleaned bullheads in half gallon milk cartons, filled the cartons with water and put them in the deep freezer. On Fridays during Lent, Mom would thaw a carton of bullheads and bake them for supper. Missing most of his teeth, Uncle Otto gummed down his fish supper. After supper we attended Stations of the Cross at St. Thomas Church. Every year Dad gave up candy for lent.

After a few months, Aunt Jenny landed a job at the Fingerhut plant in Gaylord located on a tributary of the lower Minnesota River. A few months later she got a better job at the truck capital of the world in Mound, Minnesota. She worked on the assembly line building Tonka trucks until 1982 when the company moved its manufacturing to Texas and Mexico. For years our country specialized in high paid executives and sending manufacturing jobs to other countries.

Otto went on day-long drinking binges. At the end of his drunk he'd make vulgar telephone calls. He would spend the next two days in bed recuperating. He rolled his own smoke and often blathered about how he married a hard-working Catholic woman so he didn't have to work. He'd say it was all right to give your wife a "trimming" if she had it coming. Jenny and Otto moved to Arlington and eventually, with Jenny's hard-earned dollars they purchased a small farm with a dilapidated house on ten acres of cropland, and 30 acres of swamp and woods with a small stand of maple and other deciduous trees. Jenny is remembered for being the only woman on Earth who could put up with Otto's malarkey and for her rhubarb dessert with meringue topping. In their old age, Otto and Jenny sold their farm to my sister, Janet, and her husband, Steve Geib. Otto and Jenny moved into a house in Arlington. For stealing butternuts from his tree, Otto shot the neighborhood squirrels, including a rare white one. When Otto saw a jumbo-sized woman, he'd sing the refrain from the Bobby "Polish Prince" Vinson version of the "Too Fat Polka," "I don't want her, you can have her, she's too fat for me."

Janet and Steve purchased Otto and Jenny's small farm for recreation and hunting. In the neighbor's cow pasture, a pair of bald eagles built a stick nest estimated to weigh half a ton. Almost every spring two chicks hatch in the nest. The parents watch as the larger chick eats the smaller chick. Ben Franklin pushed for the turkey to be our national symbol. In 1751 Franklin came up with "Why increase the Sons of Africa, by planting them in America, where we have so fair an opportunity, by excluding all Blacks and Tawneys (Asians) of increasing the lovely White?"[20]

St. Wenceslaus Church

In 1964, I rode with Dad in his '46 Chev farm truck, straight-six motor, four-speed to take a jag of wheat to the Robin Hood flour mill in New Prague, Minnesota. After we passed through Henderson, Dad downshifted to second gear to "walk" the load up the steep grade out of the Minnesota River Valley. When we finished the long slow climb up the grade, Dad said the ride was a "royal ass flattener." New Prague's sister city is Prague in the Bohemia region of the Czech Republic. The beautiful St. Wenceslaus Catholic Church in New Prague is styled after the Cathedral in Prague.

As wheat ran out of the '46's box, Dad chewed the fat with the young Bohemian at the mill who was sweeping wheat into the hopper grate. The young fellow told Dad he had to be back to work at five tomorrow morning. Dad gave him a line from Brown's Ferry Blues, "Early to bed, early to rise, gives your girlfriend a chance to go out with the other guys."

After Dad got his check for the wheat we went to the bakery in New Prague and got a dozen prune kolacky. On the ride home we washed the kolacky down with a jug of Clover Leaf milk bottled in Montgomery, Minnesota. Dad said the kolackies "hit his taster just right."

Big Lake Potato Run

During the 1960s, each year on a nice winter day Dad and I loaded up in the '46 Chev truck and headed north to a potato warehouse in Big Lake, Minnesota. Dad purchased a ton and a half of washed number one whites in gunny sacks and paid five to six dollars per hundredweight. On the ride home while chewing on Bavarian cream pastries Dad told me, "Never go on a snipe hunt." Dad and I delivered the potatoes to relatives, neighbors, and to Dempsey's store in Henderson. When we pulled into the farmyard in the '46 I was leaning on Dad, sleeping. Grandpa Alo helped us put the remaining sacks in the house basement. Dad made a few bucks, but most of all his taste buds enjoyed Mom's German potato salad.

St. Thomas Church Activities

In 1964, St. Thomas parish sold its cemetery sheep. The parish also sold its woodshed, stable, granary, chicken house, and sheep shed. The parish purchased a small fleet of push mowers with Briggs and Stratton motors and a walk behind Gravely self-propelled mower. The men and boys of the parish got together on certain evenings and mowed the cemetery. Once in a while the men picked up a bottle of spirits and took a swallow. Friends of the dead on a "cemetery crawl" were known to bring a bottle to graves of ole drinking buddies. They said a prayer, poured a little whiskey on the grave, pulled a finger or two, and left the jug for the next "crawlers."

After the push mowers wore out I mowed the cemetery turf with a John Deere riding lawnmower. To prevent tipping and sliding it had fluid in the tires, wheel weights, and tire chains. On steep sidehills I sat on the high side fender. Once I lost control of the mower, the skidding mower knocked a tombstone off its base. The tombstone rolled down the cemetery into the church parking lot. Wasting no time, I hauled it back up to the cemetery in a cart I hitched to the John Deere. I reset the tombstone. Good thing it wasn't damaged as the couple who paid for it were still on the green side.

While I was growing up St. Thomas Church was the center of activity in Jessenland. In addition to a full slate of Masses, there were baptisms, weddings, and funerals. Special events included polka Mass, six-handed euchre tournaments and bingo nights before Easter and Thanksgiving. Yelling "Bingo!"

was good for a canned ham or a frozen turkey. After an evening of bingo, the women served lunch–egg salad sandwiches, pickles, and homemade bars. Church activities included sledding parties, softball games, and an occasional festival with beer on ice in a cow tank. For the annual dinner held in the church basement, the women of the parish served up fried chicken, hot dish, fruit cocktail in lime Jello, pickles, and everyone's favorite— homemade pie. After the church bell ringer, Bernie Quinn, finished his dinner there was one less strawberry pie.

In 1965, I was an altar boy at St. Thomas Church for a visiting hellfire-and-brimstone Jesuit missionary priest celebrating Sunday Mass. In attendance was a consecrated virgin, a female virgin over age 35, who in a church ceremony becomes married to Jesus Christ and lives in perpetual virginity. As was the fashion of the day, my Mom and sisters each wore a colorful hat. The young people in the choir loft were horsing around, and a well-put-together high school girl in a mini-skirt tumbled head first out of the choir loft. Her fall was broken by landing on a man. As she righted herself, the missionary preacher shouted, "No one turn around; anyone who looks will go blind." A young Pat Ryan put a hand over one eye, turned around and said, "I'll take me chances with one eye."

During his sermon the missionary priest urged the faithful to dig deep. Grandpa Alo dug in his wallet; he quit digging when he gave what he could afford. The ushers took up an extra collection. On the way home I mentioned the ushers doing double duty. Dad told me, "The price of salvation is going up."

During the school year we had catechism at St. Thomas Church on Saturday mornings. During my first class, Father dropped in and told the teacher to send him any students who weren't behaving. In front of the class the teacher opened her hand and said to Father, "This should keep them in line." She taught us about St. Nicholas the Wonderworker being the inspiration for Santa Claus. She didn't mention he's also the patron saint of brewers and pawnbrokers.

Every summer for two weeks, sisters from the Twin Cities came to enlighten us. They knew how to have fun and I looked forward to their arrival. When I was 11, a nun plugged in her autoharp and we sang "Kumbaya." Since I couldn't carry a tune in a bushel basket, the nun told me not to sing so loud. My sister Ann told on me and Mom gave me an earful for singing too loud.

When Dad taught catechism to the teenagers at St. Thomas Church he gave them his advice for marital bliss: wife makes a good supper, husband is home on time to eat supper, and everything else falls in place. Mom did her part and Dad took his own advice, even if it meant shutting down the John Deere B tractor that pulled the Case combine with an air-cooled Wisconsin motor in the middle of a soybean field. Our neighbor and friend of the family, Jack Harens, Jr., sat in Dad's catechism class. After Jack got married Dad asked Jack how married life was treating him. Jack replied, "I'm still getting home on time for supper."

Visitors

While I was growing up, hunters, fishermen, trappers, boaters, swimmers, and a commercial minnow man came through the Weber farm to access Silver Lake and oftentimes they stopped to chat. Next to the driveway Dad dug a hole, put in a wood post, and nailed to it a metal box with a slot for money. On it, he painted in red: "Cars to Lake 25¢ Here Drive Slowly." Dad used the money to purchase Fourth of July fireworks that he and my uncle Bob shot off over Silver Lake to a pasture full of onlookers.

Salesmen selling encyclopedias, insurance, seed corn, investments, vacuum cleaners, and Fuller Brushes, as well as a blind man selling whisk brooms all called on the farm. Once a week, the Swan's truck and the Clover Leaf Dairy truck pulled in the farmyard. If no one was home the driver went in the back door and left his delivery in the refrigerator.

At one time or another Mom put a plate on the table for most of the visitors and vendors. One that didn't get a meal was a smelly salesman from parts unknown who was rude to Dad and slow to leave. Dad asked me to get him a pencil and scrap of paper. I gave Dad pencil and paper and he walked over to the salesman's car. The salesman asked Dad what he was doing. Dad said, "I'm writing down your license plate number. There's been a little trouble in the area; it's always nice to have a suspect." The salesman hightailed it to his car. As he sped down the driveway Dad said, "Man who change socks seldom, change friends often."

The Jehovah's Witnesses often came to visit the family. We'd sit around the kitchen table and have a cup of coffee or a glass of milk, and wad down a few cake doughnuts while chatting about religion. During one conversation, a Jehovah's Witness made a derogatory comment about the Pope. Dad pointed to a doughnut and said to him, "You seem to be looking at the hole instead of the doughnut." The Jehovah's Witnesses left and never came back.

A few times a year the farm's retired hired man, Tom Collins, rode the Greyhound from Minneapolis to Green Isle. Unless someone stopped to give him a lift, he walked six miles to the farm. He visited and pitched in with a little work. After supper Grandpa Alo gave him a few bucks and a ride to "Foam Avenue" in Green Isle. Tom said he spent most of his VA pension on whiskey, the rest he just wasted. After patronizing the drinking houses he'd sleep his drunk off in a hayloft. The next morning he'd catch the Greyhound back to the Old Soldier's Home in Minneapolis.

Joe and Lillie Gildea

After Sunday Mass, Dad often said, "It's time to help Grandma Lillie clean out her refrigerator," and we would load up in the '64 Olds station wagon with a manual choke and head for

Grandma and Grandpa's house in south Minneapolis. Once in a while Dad stopped at the cheese plant in Bongards—home to a 15-foot tall fiberglass Holstein cow—and got us a small bag of squeaky fresh cheese curds to chew on. When we kids asked, "How much longer to Grandma's house?" Dad's response was, "It's like when I cut off the puppy's tail—it won't be long anymore."

On one trip to Grandma's house just before we got to the Blakeley bridge, Dad stopped so we could look at a huge snapping turtle on the road. A man in a car pulled up, got out, grabbed the snapper by the tail, and flung him into the trunk of his car. He said he'd sell the snapper for turtle soup to a restaurant in downtown Minneapolis. On another trip to Grandma's house Dad was driving on the Blooming Ferry Bridge that had a lane for cars and railroad tracks. When a train, three feet from the Olds, whizzed past us Dad sang his version of *The Ballad of Casey Jones*:

> Casey Jones was a rounder's name
> He looked at the water and the water was low
> He looked at his watch and the watch was slow
> He turned to the fireman and said to him
> Boy you better jump
> Two locomotives are gonna bump.

Grandma got out her fine china for Sunday dinner. Wearing an apron over her Sunday dress, she served fried chicken or pot roast, mashed potatoes with gravy, rolls she baked the day before, and, when in season, fresh vegetables–usually peas, corn or green beans. Grandma served canned crab apples, which we picked from a tree on the farm planted by my great-great-grandfather, Anton Weber. For dessert Grandma served homemade pies or German sweet chocolate cake. Grandma had no need for Betty Crocker. When we were done eating Dad said, "I'm as full as a tick." A couple of times a year we went to a smorgasbord, but even in her eighties, Grandma preferred cooking dinner, including a feast on Mother's Day.

While at their house Grandpa Joe said, "Wanna play for half an hour?" Grandpa Joe took the doilies off the living room table and started throwing cards. The men and boys played dime-ante poker. We placed bets and raises with nickels, dimes, and quarters. Oftentimes other visiting relatives sat in. All players were on the square. The winner usually raked in a pot of two to three dollars. The game included a few bottles of downstream Fox Deluxe beer for Grandpa Joe and others. He liked to say, "You better have a little fun here, 'cuz you're dead a damn long time."

During times of war Grandpa Joe worked at the arsenal in New Brighton, Minnesota. During times of peace he worked construction. We liked to listen to old-timey music on 78s Grandpa Joe stacked up on his Victrola. A few times a day he took a dip of Skoal. He kept a brass spittoon on the porch floor. Besides playing poker, Grandpa Joe liked to fish, garden, shoot pool, and go garage sailing. When I went with Grandpa Joe to rummage sales he said, "Johnny, you got to get there early to get the good stuff." We were often greeted by women in housecoats. We once saw an MG (initials for Morris Garages) Midget for sale.

From living through the Great Depression, Grandpa Joe haggled everyone down on price, including the grocer. Grandpa Joe told me, "Johnny, I saved a lot of money jewing people down." One evening, after an hour of back and forth on price, a salesman just about had Grandpa Joe talked into buying a new vacuum cleaner. The salesman then told Grandpa Joe, "The vacuum cleaner will clean up this filthy house." With his short legs, Grandpa Joe kicked the vacuum cleaner out the front door. Grandma Lillie in her cotton house dress kept their house, with flower wallpaper, spotless.

A couple of times in the summer, while visiting Grandma and Grandpa we loaded up in the '64 Olds, no air conditioning and headed out to a Twins game at Metropolitan Stadium in

Bloomington. When the game got slow I'd look at barns and silos off in the distance. Other favorite activities were going to Como Park Zoo, the State Fair, the Shrine Circus (replaced by a circus called the Presidential Candidates' Debates), and Minnehaha Falls. During a dry spell in 1964, President Lyndon Johnson visited Minnehaha Falls. In order to have water flow over the falls, the city of Minneapolis opened upstream fire hydrants.[21] About once a year we went to the Chanhassen Dinner Theatre in Chanhassen, Minnesota. *Fiddler on the Roof, Oklahoma, The Music Man, Guys and Dolls,* and Sherwin Linton singing "Cotton King" are family favorites.

When it came time to leave, Grandma always sent us home with a liberal supply of coffee cakes and cookies, usually oatmeal raisin, sugar, peanut butter, and molasses. Grandma stirred batter, rolled out the dough, and stamped out Christmas cookies using metal cutters. We left with a few coffee tins full of cookies with sprinkles on the frosting. On the drive home Mom asked, "Allie, are you tired?" Dad's response was always the same, "I could drive to Omaha." By the time we reached home, we kids were fast asleep. Mom and Dad carried us to our rooms and tucked us in bed.

I stayed at Grandma and Grandpa's house in south Minneapolis from an early age. Many times Grandpa Joe and I joined the strap hangers on a bus to downtown Minneapolis. We walked from bank to bank. When it was cold we walked in Skyways. Grandpa Joe moved his money around to get a free toaster or other valuable merchandise. After a week or so, Grandpa Joe put me on a Greyhound that dropped me off at Vern's Café Bus Depot in Arlington.

Polka Bands

Grandpa Joe faithfully watched the evening news. He was interested in the economy, politics, and the price of gas. He always opposed the war in Vietnam. At wedding dances he'd usually get a snootful, which irked my Mom. The area's favorite

177

polka bands for wedding dances were the Six Fat Dutchmen (there were more than six, they weren't all fat, and they weren't all German), Fezz Fritsche and the Goosetown Band, and Whoopee John; for modern dances Clem Brau, and for old time New Ulm music Clem Brau had the Jolly Lumberjacks. The bands played old time New Ulm music. Favorite songs were: "Tanta Anna," "Beer Barrel Polka," and "There Ain't No Beer In Heaven, That's Why We Drink It Here." The family often went to wedding dances at the Pla-Mor Ballroom in Glencoe and at halls in Arlington, Plato, Hamburg, Gibbon, Waconia, and when it wasn't flooded by the Minnesota River, the ballroom in Carver. Most men brought a bottle of whiskey or brandy to the hall, and purchased set-ups and mixed their own juice. On the ride home Dad often sang his version of Glen Miller's *Little Brown Jug:* which was popular during Prohibition.

> "Old little brown jug, how I love thee.
> You're the one that makes my friends and foes.
> You're the one that makes me wear old clothes.
> Old little brown jug, how I love thee."

Bands from and around New Ulm played in towns in the Upper Midwest wherever there were Bohemians (they invented polkas), Germans, and Poles.[22] Except for the Irish, other nationalities were slow to catch on to drinking and dancing to polka music. Some bands sang in English with a heavy German accent, some sang in German, some sang in both languages, some sang in Bohemian or Polish, and some didn't sing at all. The main reason to go to the ballroom or hall was to drink and dance; there weren't many wallflowers. The bands played waltzes, polkas, schottisches, and big band numbers. At most dances farm families outnumbered city folk. In his book *Enemies of Sleep: New Ulm Musicians*, Dale Holtz claims, "In 1964, there were easily 100 musicians in and around New Ulm, each of whom was a better musician than any of the Beatles."[23]

Harold Brau

One of the best musicians was Harold Brau who raised his family in Arlington. In 1995, Harold and his brother Clem were inducted into the Minnesota Music Hall of Fame in New Ulm. During WWII, Harold played the trombone in the Army Ground Forces Military Band. He was sent to North Africa, Italy, Naples, Iran, and France. After the war Harold and his siblings, Clem, Norbert, and Hildegarde, formed a band.[24]

Verne Gagne

Grandma and Grandpa were fans of Verne Gagne's "All Star Wrestling" show. He put opponents in a slumber with his "sleeper hold." On TV we watched The Crusher, The Bruiser, Mad Dog Vachon, Killer Kowalski, Nick Bockwinkel, Baron von Raschke (signature move– "the claw"), and Buck Zumofe from Hamburg, Minnesota. The most famous brute was Navy Seal veteran Jesse Ventura from Minneapolis. While in a nursing home Gagne body slammed to the floor a 97-year-old fellow resident. The 97-year-old ended up with a broken hip and died a couple of weeks later. Gagne wasn't charged with a crime, from dementia he lost his marbles.[25]

Adnan Alkaissy

Adnan Alkaissy was born into the Sunni faith in the birthplace of humanity in Iraq. His sheikh father had two wives.[26] While growing up he learned to wrestle and became friends with Saddam Hussein. They hung out together at a coffee shop near the Tigris River.[27]

After high school, despite never playing football and not knowing the rules, Alkaissy got a football scholarship to the University of Houston. As a freshman he was a starting linebacker. He said it was basic— "just tackle the guy with the ball." He transferred his sophomore year to Oklahoma State where he walked on the wrestling team. After pinning the squad's heavyweight, he got a full-ride scholarship and became an All-American.[28] In the middle of his senior year he left Oklahoma State to become a professional wrestler.[29] He wrestled as Chief Billy White Wolf. While wrestling in Oregon he earned a master's in education.[30]

In 1969 while visiting family in Iraq, Saddam Hussein called for Alkaissy. Hussein leaned on Alkaissy to bring professional wrestling to Iraq as a duty to his country.[31] Hussein made Alkaissy Iraq's director of youth at the Ministry of Youth.[32] Alkaissy promoted wildly successful wrestling matches featuring himself. He always won and he became the most popular man in Iraq. Anyone who defeated him would have probably been shot in the ring.[33]

During his rise to power, Hussein assassinated people close to him. Alkaissy was out of Hussein's good graces by being more popular than him. Alkaissy was afraid he'd be taken out if he stayed in Iraq.[34] After seven years in Iraq, Alkaissy went to Kuwait and flew from Kuwait City to London. After spending time with his girlfriend he caught a flight to San Francisco.[35]

Back in the U.S., he signed on with Verne Gagne's American Wrestling Association as the villainous Sheikh and in Minnesota his career took off.[36] After injuring his leg he decided to become a manager—a guy who stands by the ropes, talks smack and causes problems for the ref, all to help his wrestler win.[37] Then as a manager he signed on with Vince McMahan to be the villainous General Adnan—a Saddam Hussein knockoff. He managed Sergeant Slaughter, a U.S. Army drill sergeant who was brainwashed by General Adnan and turned against the U.S.[38] During the Gulf War and during the U.S. invasion of Iraq, General Adnan and Sergeant Slaughter were heels hated by everyone—making the gig extremely popular and creating nationalism.[39]

Alkaissy married a Catholic girl. They have four children and live in the Twin Cities and in Hawaii.[40] He lived the American dream where hard work pays off. He's not a political man but he condemns Hussein's actions. He does charity events for children and he promotes peace between the Arab and Western worlds.[41]

Inclement Weather of 1965

In late February 1965 a rainstorm caused a couple of inches of ice to form on the gravel and tarred roads in Jessenland. Our neighbor spread manure on the icy roads. The warm manure stuck to the ice causing the roads to be less slippery. Politicians picked up on the procedure—spread enough B.S. and hope some sticks.

In February and March 1965 four blizzards struck the area. No potatoes were planted on St. Paddy's Day as heavy snow blew about in 60 mile-per-hour winds that shut down virtually everything for several days. After each blizzard Dad plowed snow from the farmyard and driveway using a single wing snow plow attached to the '46 Chev truck. To get more traction Dad put chains on the duals.

Late in the winter of '65 our neighbor and friend of the family, Jack Harens, Sr., came to the farm and asked Dad if he could get him a load of coal. Jack was running low on wood; the snow was too deep to cut wood and his truck froze up. I rode with Dad in the '46 Chev truck to the lumberyard in Arlington where we got a couple dumps of coal. On the ride back to Jessenland with our ear flaps down we wadded down chocolate-covered Long Johns with hot cocoa when Dad gave me a little advice: "Never run after a man; he'll turn around and whip you." We pulled into Jack's farmyard, Dad pulled the hoist lever, the box raised, and coal slid off next to the house. I helped shovel the coal through the trap door to the cellar.

In April 1965 the weather suddenly turned unseasonably warm causing the worst flooding on record in the Minnesota and upper Mississippi Rivers. Early in the flood of 1965 we were on our way to Grandma and Grandpa's house in south Minneapolis. To our surprise floodwater was over the road leading to the

Blakeley bridge. The water was clear, causing it to appear shallow. Dad rolled the dice and drove the '64 Olds down the flooded road. When he got half way to the bridge Dad got worried. The water was deeper and the current stronger than he'd estimated. If the current broke the Olds loose, there would have been six floaters in the river, not including the one in the hopper. Dad made it to the bridge, which was higher than the road. While driving across the bridge I looked down at the torrent a few inches below. After we made it across the bridge Dad said, "Never again." Some 50 years later I still have nightmares of driving on the flooded road and crossing the Blakeley bridge.

During the height of the 1965 flood a man launched his motorboat in the flood water. While driving the boat through the Blakeley bridge, he couldn't hold the boat against the current. The current banged the boat against the bridge's steel girders at the same level as live electrical wire. He too was a lucky fool.

The men who designed and built the Blakeley bridge in 1924 did a bang-up job as the bridge never budged despite almost yearly ice jams, log jams or floods. I can't say the same for the I-35W bridge over the Mississippi River in Minneapolis that in 2007 collapsed from a design flaw and lack of maintenance, killing 13 people. After the bridge collapsed, an acquaintance of the family, using a broom, pulled three people from the mighty Mississippi.

In 1961, Sibley County graded-up and blacktopped County Road 6 through Jessenland in the Lower Minnesota River Valley. Dad attended the opening ceremony for the rebuilt road. He heard a county official say, "This road will never flood." In April 1965 the road was under water. The county official said crow tastes like chicken. The flood waterlogged cities and towns in the Minnesota River Valley. Families were forced to evacuate their homes and property damage was extensive. In Henderson, the Red Cross set up a disaster center in a law office. During the spring, Mom and Dad loaded up us kids in the Olds to look at the floodwater. After the water subsided Dad drove across the Blakeley bridge to the Blakeley Store and got us a "treatment." We could have any treat we wanted as long as it was an orange sherbet push-up.

In the spring of 1965 a hurly burly French farmer from Jessenland who lived on a tributary of the Minnesota River showed up at the farm. He told Grandpa Alo the township road by his farm was in need of fill and riprap as it was partially washed out from flooding. Grandpa told him it was too early in the spring to repair the road. The Frenchman got out of sorts, and as he was leaving, he squeezed his rubber coin purse and gave my sister Ann and me each four bits for having such a stingy Grandpa. Grandpa felt bad the hopping mad frog involved his grandchildren in the fray.

The long winter and heavy snowfall of 1964-65 caused a winter fish kill. The shores of Silver Lake were lined with dead fish. It took several years for the fish to return. Currently Silver Lake has some of the best walleye ice fishing in southern Minnesota. The good fishing will last until a fish kill wipes out the walleyes.

In 1965 the deep frost combined with the late wet spring caused the gravel roads in Jessenland to be so soupy they were nearly impassable. School busses couldn't drive on gravel roads. Dad put tire chains on the F1 Ford pickup truck to bring my sister Ann and me to the school bus two miles away on a paved road. The tires on the F1 sank five inches in the gravel and spun continuously.

After the gravel roads dried out, the county road supervisor was inspecting the farm-to-market gravel road past the Weber farm. Dad asked him, "Why not blacktop the road?" The supervisor replied, "The traffic count isn't high enough." Dad told the supervisor to double the traffic count as the road isn't fit to drive on half the time. Dad's comment made it to the county board and years later the county tarred Jessenland Road.

183

The spring and early summer of 1965 were full of thunderstorms, hailstorms, tornados and a storm where chunks of ice fell from the sky. During one nighttime thunderstorm when we heard glass break and the attic door bouncing around on the upstairs floor, we beelined for the basement. On the way I saw the attic door on the floor and the girls' playhouse halfway through the picture window in the living room. When the wind blew the playhouse through the window the pressure in the house changed, causing the attic door to shoot up and come down through the opening. Dad and I put on our duds and in a driving rain, Dad hooked a log chain to the playhouse and with the "B" John Deere, I pulled it from the window. Strong wind made it difficult to nail plywood over the picture window. That spring and summer the family spent many hours in the basement listening to tornado watches and warnings on the transistor radio. A tornado touched down in the farmyard and tore apart an empty tin grain bin. Dad and Grandpa straightened out the pieces of tin and put the bin back together.

The late wet spring of '65 caused the fields to be too muddy to plant on time. The spring wheat, corn, and soybeans were planted late. Dad finished planting soybeans on the fifth of July. The harvest revealed what Dad suspected—the crops didn't bushel worth a tinker's damn. The only thing lower was grain prices, making 1965 Dad's worst year farming.

In July 1965 a bill collector knocked on our neighbor's front door. Our neighbor told him, "I told you a month ago I'll pay the bill at harvest. I have a loaded .38 Special in my dresser and if I see you on this farm again I'll shoot you." The bill collector didn't come back and at harvest the bill was paid.

On a balmy summer day in 1965, Dad and I were at the PV elevator next to the railroad tracks two miles east of Henderson. Dad had just received a small check for the corn he dumped off his '46 Chev truck. He opened the top of the pop machine at the elevator and slid out two bottles of Hires Root Beer. Dad offered to buy one for our neighbor who was also there. The neighbor said, "Times are so tough Allie I'd rather have the nickel." Dad gave him a nickel.

Mike and Jim Kehoe

On the way home from the PV elevator Dad pulled into Graham's pit in Jessenland next to the Minnesota River. The pit was busy loading aggregate as the flooding and the inclement weather caused heavy erosion and road damage. As we were waiting in line for a dump of gravel for the driveway to the farm, we noticed County Commissioner Mike Kehoe talking with the manager of the pit. We watched the two men walk behind a pile of sand. As the two men took nips from the owner's mickey, four men hoisted a large flat rock into the trunk of Mike's car.

For the next couple of months we chuckled when we saw Mike's car go by the farm. Eventually Mike heard a howling from the rear of his car. When Mike took his car to a garage in Green Isle he wondered why so many people were showing up. He knew why when the mechanic popped the trunk. Upon seeing the rock Mike said, "Boys, it's time for a pint." The merriment continued at the Corner Bar.

After Mike retired, his grandson and my best friend, Jim Kehoe, age 14, was killed in 1970 when the pickup truck Jim was driving hit the ditch, and he was ejected and run over. The day he died the luck o' the Jessenland Irish ran out. At age 12, I was scared and stricken with grief. At his graveside service in the cemetery behind St. Thomas Church, his sister Jean lay on his casket and cried uncontrollably. For the rest of his life Mike Kehoe had a tear in his eye. He died of a broken heart.

National Farmers' Organization

Every year Dad farmed he depended on the government's farm programs started by President Franklin Delano Roosevelt. Some years the farm programs from the politicians in Washington, D.C. didn't make much sense, but the programs usually funneled Dad enough taxpayer money to make ends meet. The Agricultural Stabilization and Conservation (ASC) office in Gaylord was helpful with explaining the programs and assisting with forms. One year the acronym for the farm program was "PIC." Under the program Dad planted only a small portion of the farm's cropland. Not having much field work Dad told everyone he was on a summerlong "PIC"nic. When Dad dies he's going to be buried face up so he can still get a handout.

During the 1960s, Dad often stated the golden rule of farming, "Never farm bigger than your wife's paycheck." Mom stayed home raising seven kids, so Dad couldn't spend more money than he took in. If he took on too much debt or made a couple of blunders the family farm would be lost. Our county commissioner took a trip to Washington, D.C. to meet with members of Congress to discuss the farm crisis. While paying his check at a D.C. restaurant the waitress glanced over to the table where he left a tip and said, "Are you sure you can afford it?" He walked over to the table, put the tip in his pocket and said, "No, not really."

In the 1960s low farm prices caused Dad and many other farmers in Sibley County to join the National Farmers' Organization (NFO). Some farmers thought NFO stood for politicians: Nuts, Freaks, and Oddballs. In 1964 the NFO attempted to prevent non-NFO member farmers in Sibley County from taking cattle to market in order to force slaughterhouses to raise prices paid to farmers. Concerns for law and order led the Sibley County attorney to consider requesting assistance from the National Guard. In March 1967, to protest low milk prices, members of the NFO dumped 35,000 pounds of milk on our neighbor's icy hayfield. That evening I watched myself on the WCCO evening news sliding around on two inches of milk.

Dad and other farmers from Jessenland attended an NFO rally at the livestock yard in South St. Paul. During the rally, tensions escalated between Jessenland farmers and farmers with contracts with slaughterhouses. After a heated exchange, a donnybrook broke out. Two cake-belly policemen tried to keep the peace. Our neighbor, Mike Skelley, let fly a haymaker that landed on a cop's forehead and laid him out as straight as a fireplace poker. The other cop started swinging his billy. Sensing trouble, Dad walked away and watched the action from a distance. Dad was relieved no one was arrested or seriously injured.

On the evening news, a reporter asked a Norwegian farmer with lapped teeth about the brawl at the livestock yard. His only comment was, "Ach, those Irishmen from Jessenland aren't so tough. Between me, my son, and my hired man we almost licked one of them." The NFO tried but couldn't control production. The NFO received strong opposition from the Department of Agriculture.

Shop

On a bone chilling spring day in 1964, Dad's 1941 Minneapolis Moline model "U" tractor—sales jingle: "Minneapolis Moline has more power, does more work per hour"—sat in front of the farm's shop as he tried to figure out if the battery was shot or if it wasn't getting a charge. The work bench in the shop was built by my great-great-grandfather Anton. If I had known that when I was a kid, I wouldn't have drilled so many holes in it. Dad took the battery out and I rode with him in his '56 Ford Victoria with three on the tree to the Ford implement dealer in Arlington. The battery tested negative. The dealer said the battery tester was the best machine he ever purchased—it never found a good battery. The tester was like the "machine" in Chicago—it never found an honest politician. On the way home with glazed donuts out of the bag, a little kid on a bicycle with training wheels came down a hill and darted into the street. Dad skidded the '56's tires, veered left and missed the kid by a hair's breadth. When the '56 came to a stop, Dad got out and the kid took a spanking.

Dad, in front of the shop, used his "buzz box" welder to repair his and the neighbors' implements. On a crisp fall morning when a repair on the "Rube Goldberg" Minneapolis Moline one row corn picker wasn't going so well, Dad told me, "I cut it off twice and it's still too short." If a part was broken, to save money Dad welded it rather than buy a new one. Dad said, "The easiest money you can make is the money you save." Too bad Dad's words never made it to the politicians in Washington, D.C. Dad believed in a good dose of fudge factor. While welding he'd often say, "If a little is good, a lot is better."

Under a late fall beaver moon while plowing under corn stalks, I stayed cozy in the heat houser on the 70 horsepower 1650 Oliver, the first diesel tractor on the farm. The new four-bottom Oliver moldboard plow went cattywampus and broke loose from the 1650s three point hitch. When Dad arrived he lost a little religion. It's a good thing the Oliver dealer from Norwood was nowhere in sight. The next morning using the manure loader on the "B" John Deere I bucked the plow onto the stoneboat. Grandpa Alo used the Ford tractor to pull the stoneboat to the front door of the shop. I thought the plow was beyond repair, but by using a liberal amount of angle iron over three hours of welding Dad had me back plowing by noon. For the next 12 years the plow turned over thousands of acres of wheat stubble and corn and soybean stalks.

In 1966, Lyndon B. Johnson was President (he wore a girdle, ate off other people's plates and belched loudly), and on a windy spring day that year I helped Dad put a weld on neighbor Bernie Quinn's disk.[42] Our rawboned neighbor tapped on his box of Skoal and his dog spun in circles; Bernie took a dip and put a plug in his dog's mouth. The dog was addicted to nicotine almost as much as the politicians in Washington, D.C. are addicted to wasting taxpayers' money. Yeah, ya betcha! A few years later Bernie's dog died of "lead poisoning to the brain." Being a bachelor, Bernie was afraid if he died at home his dog would eat him before anyone knew he bought the farm.

Farm Creatures

In 1966, Dad and Grandpa started noticing signs of rats on the farm. Grandpa Alo used a pinch bar to pry up pieces of plywood from the floor of the old abandoned brooder house and rats scurried all about. The farm's dog, Perkie, went berserk hunting down the rats, killing several. Meanwhile, Grandpa, Dad, and I stepped on nests of pinkies. After Dad put rat poison in the subfloor, Grandpa and I nailed the plywood back down. After time passed for the rats to eat the poison, Dad put a bald tire in the brooder house, poured diesel fuel on it, and flicked a lit match. The old brooder house went up in flames and the rats were cleaned out.

One spring morning in 1967 while down in the basement, Dad put on his work pants; he didn't care for the garter snake slithering down his leg. Fearing snakes would infest the house, Dad decided to rid the farmyard of snakes. He placed a few hoes around the yard that we used to hack up snakes. When I mowed the lawn, I'd run over snakes. The first summer we killed 80 snakes. The second summer, Dad found a snake's den in the backyard close to the house. He poured drain oil in the hole leading to the snake den. When Dad saw oily snakes, he mixed left over weed spray with water and poured it down the hole. The farmyard has had fewer snakes ever since.

In the late 1960s at springtime, tiger salamanders crawled out of the mud around Silver Lake and the swamp on the farm and migrated across the farmyard. Every couple of days, I used a small shovel to scoop salamanders out of the house's window wells. My sister, Ann, told her fourth-grade teacher the salamanders were a foot long. The teacher told Ann they weren't nearly that long. The next morning, Dad and Ann put a 14-inch-long salamander in a glass juice jar. Ann sat the jar on the teacher's desk.

In the fall of 1969, a flock of sparrows took up residence in the chicken coop. Grandpa Alo and I couldn't shoo the sparrows out. Grandpa Alo, my cousin, Dan Carroll, and I each pounded a nail into the end of a stick and ground the nail to a sharp point. We used our spears to corner sparrows and stab them. After a couple of hours of wicked fun, the chicken coop was free of sparrows and the cats moved in. When bats built up in the machine shed we started a couple of tractors and closed the doors.

Mike Carroll

When I was a kid I helped my dad's cousin, Mike Carroll, set and check traps along Silver Lake and throughout the marshes and woods of the Madden and Weber farms. He trapped mink, muskrat, weasels (in the winter their fur turns white and Dad called them ermine), raccoon, and fox. When he trapped skunk, I could smell his pickup truck a quarter mile away. He used his pistol to shoot animals while their foot was squeezed in a trap. Mike strung animals from a tree branch and skinned them. When snowmobiles became popular Mike used his Polaris to run over furry animals. He stretched and sorted the pelts. He purchased pelts from other trappers and sold them for a profit to a furrier in Mankato or at fur auctions.

I helped Mike catch frogs along the shores of Silver Lake. When we caught a frog we dropped it in a gunny sack. Mike cleaned the frogs by tightly gripping the frog's head with one hand and with the aid of a coat hanger, he pulled the frog's legs with his other hand. The result was a frog with no hind legs and frog legs ready for the frying pan.

One summer evening after I helped Mike dig ginseng, we were fishing for channel cats in the Minnesota River on the Blakeley loop when two hippies showed up to pick buds from their marijuana patch. They asked what we were doing and Mike said, "We have licenses and we're fishing." When the men told us to leave, Mike said, "We're not going anywhere." One of them piped off, "How would you like to get thrown in the river, old man?" Mike grabbed the fillet knife from his tackle box and asked, "Who wants to be the first to get in the river with me?" The hippies freaked out and scrammed.

Mike died in 1991. He was the last of the fur trappers in Jessenland. With more and more land under cultivation, and with most of the potholes and marshes drained for crops, there aren't many furry animals to trap. After being in vogue for hundreds of years, furs are no longer chic in America. The hides of cattle remain popular. Even vegans like leather jackets, boots, belts, purses, and leather car seat covers.

Hemp Patch

During the 1960s, I hitched up the Radio Flyer wagon to the riding lawnmower. My sisters sat in the wagon as I pulled them around the cow pasture between the farmyard and Silver Lake. We often stopped to pick gooseberries or a posy of wild flowers. A favorite place to ride was on cow trails through ten-foot tall hemp plants.

When Grandpa Alo read the hippies in San Francisco and the overdose-prone crowd in Hollywood were smoking dope, he hooked the sickle mower up to the Ford tractor and cut the hippy hay. After the hemp dried, we used pitchforks to stack it in a pile. We doused it with diesel fuel and set it on fire.

Anderson Machine Shop

In 1966, President Charles de Gaulle pulled France out of NATO and ordered all U.S. troops off French soil. President Johnson had his Secretary of State ask President de Gaulle if his order included the 60,000 U.S. troops buried in France.[43] Also in 1966, farm prices were lower than a snake's belly. For pocket money Dad went to work at Anderson Machine Shop in Chaska. He got time off for seeding and the harvest. The shop foreman told Dad he was the only man he hired whose lunchbox was bigger than his toolbox. The foreman told Dad as WWII drew to a close, a wheelbarrow full of sterling silver wouldn't buy two chickens. After the war he left Austria and ended up in Minnesota.

Workers at the machine shop told Dad a story about the "Dog House," a bar in Carver. The owner of the bar, who was distraught over his wife, went to their house and thought his wife was in bed with a man. He shot both of them. When he discovered he shot his daughter instead of a man, he shot himself. The new owners of the bar ran a drink special: "Three shots for a dollar."

The Anderson Machine Shop made machines for the bedding industry and it did machine work for the Gedney Pickle Factory a few miles down the road. At my request, Dad planted cucumbers for Gedney. My sisters and I weeded and picked the cucumbers. Dad took them to the Gedney Plant and brought home a small check. After a summer of slaving over cukes, I decided to stick with selling sweet corn.

Sweet Corn

A few evenings in August, Grandpa Alo and I filled the back of the '64 Olds station wagon with sweet corn. The next morning I'd ride with Dad to Chaska. Dad parked the Olds in the town square and he hitched a ride to the machine shop. I pounded a post in the ground with a wood sign nailed to it. In red I painted on the sign, "Sweet corn 35¢ a doz, 3 doz for $1." My first sale was usually to the town cop. I'd sell out by noon, making $15-$20.

Grandpa Alo took me to Belle Plaine and Henderson where I sold sweet corn door to door. Sales were always brisk. I chose those towns as neither had a sweet corn packing plant. I didn't go to Green Isle because Grandpa's cousin Ralph Kreger sold sweet corn to every house in town.

Now in our "nation of regulation," I'd probably be prohibited from selling sweet corn. In 2008 the "Claremont Cookie Monster," Mayor Ellen Taylor, called the police to shut down six young girls from selling Girl Scout cookies on a street corner in Claremont, California. By the time an officer arrived the girls left.[44] If the girls had been begging for money—no problem. Kids learn valuable lessons selling sweet corn, mistletoe, and Girl Scout cookies. Their first lesson shouldn't be getting shut down by their government.

192

Late summer and autumn were special months on the farm. We'd eat melon and a mess of sweet corn almost every supper. Grandpa Alo and I easily put down a dozen ears of Golden Jubilee sweet corn dripping with butter. Favorite desserts Mom made were pie from a sugar pumpkin, and angel food cake with Land O' Lakes cream whipped in a Red Wing beater jar and then topped with fresh strawberries from Ray Zieher's patch. At the supper table Mom told us kids, "Don't play with your vegetables—eat them." Now people say, "It's okay to play with your vegetables—just don't reelect them."

John Joyce

In the summer of love, 1967, LBJ was President. He was frequently drunk and he had a harem of women for sex, including young secretaries.[45] Also that year on a summer evening hotter than a Pennsylvania blast furnace, I ate a hearty supper of head cheese, mashed potatoes with gravy, stewed beets, and homemade bread at the Joyce farmhouse in Jessenland. It's where Father John Joyce, priest at St. Patrick's Catholic Church in Shieldsville, Minnesota, lived with his sisters. Father John liked to say, "In this neck of the woods the Germans taught us how to farm, the French taught us how to cook, and the Irish taught us how to live." Father John also liked to say his ancestors moved from Louisiana to Minnesota to get away from the ruthless treatment of slaves.

While Bernie Quinn made a boardinghouse reach for his fourth helping, Father John said, "Bernie, you're more than welcome to eat all you want, but it's not healthy to eat so heavy." Bernie grabbed his paunch with both hands and said, "Well Father, it's about all you take with you." For dessert Bernie and I each put down six baked apples covered in glazed sugar.

To wash the dishes the Joyce sisters pumped water by hand from the cistern into a porcelain coated cast iron sink. One of the sisters, Mary, taught at the Silver Lake country school.

During WWII she enlisted in the Women's Army Corps (WAC). After boot camp she worked in a prisoner of war hospital.

Hubert H. Humphrey

In November 1968, Hubert Horatio Humphrey, Jr., in one of the closest presidential elections of all time, lost to Richard Nixon. HHH was a champion of civil rights and one of the most honorable politicians in American history. While in school I listened to the "Happy Warrior" give a speech in front of the canning plant in Arlington. Humphrey made his home in beautiful Waverly, Minnesota. The Hubert Humphrey Museum in Waverly burned down in 1997 and it hasn't been rebuilt.

Mike Sanken

Every summer during the 1960s, Grandpa Alo and I had the saws on the farm sharpened at Mike's Saw Filing on Woodchuck Knoll in Blakeley. The owner, Mike Sanken, wore large rubber boots. He got jungle rot in his feet from fighting in WWII in the South Pacific. While in the jungle Mike carried a knife in case a python tried to crush him.

After leaving Mike's shop we usually stopped at the Hillside Tavern in Blakeley owned by Mark "Buzzard" Berger to have a greasy hamburger. After one trip, when we got back to Grandpa's house I got out the boxing gloves and we exchanged blows. Grandpa connected with a right and I got a bloody nose. Next we played gin rummy and washed down Old Dutch potato chips with room temperature Grape Crush pop. While playing cards Grandpa told me about Senator Ted Kennedy from Massachusetts hosting a party on Chappaquiddick Island near Martha's Vineyard. He left the party with campaign worker Mary Jo Kopechne riding shotgun in his car. Kennedy drove the car off a bridge into a tidal channel. Kennedy swam to safety and fled the scene. Kopechne died in the car. Being well-heeled the Lion of the Senate pled guilty to leaving the scene of an accident and got a slap on the wrist.

Vetter Stone

In the winter of 1967-68 Dad purchased a brand new Motoski snowmobile with a one cylinder, two stroke motor and a cutter to pull behind it. After the spring thaw, Dad and I threw a load of scrap metal on the '46 Chev truck and hauled it to a junk dealer near Kasota in the Lower Minnesota River Valley. For the scrap, the junk dealer paid in cash from a wad in his pocket the size of a flophouse pillow. The next stop was the Vetter Stone Quarry between Mankato and Kasota. Dad used some of the cash from the sale to buy limestone to build a planter in front of the house. On the way home, we passed by the Silica Sand Mine near Ottawa in the Minnesota River Valley. Next we stopped in St. Peter where Dad bought us ice cream cones dipped in chocolate. We licked the black tops down and Dad gave me a few words of wisdom. "Don't be telling others your problems; half the people don't care and the other half think you deserve your problems."

"Kasota" is Dakota for "cleared off" to describe the prairie plateau of limestone between Kasota and Mankato. The limestone from the Vetter Stone Quarry has dolomite, which makes it hard, and when polished it has a glossy shine. Vetter Stone has been a family business since 1954. Its limestone is in buildings and structures around the world, including the Smithsonian National Museum of the American Indian in Washington, D.C., the Japanese National Museum in Osaka, Japan, the U.S. Embassies in Moscow and Abu Dhabi, and the Minnesota Twins ballpark, "Target Field" in Minneapolis. Vetter supplies replacement limestone for Lincoln's tomb in Springfield, Illinois.[46] While on his whistle stop campaign, President Harry Truman slept overnight in a Pullman car at a railroad siding in Kasota.[47]

Henderson Levee

The winter of 1968-69 was long with heavy snowfall. By then, Dad had purchased a rear mount snow blower for the 1650 Oliver tractor. Early in the spring of '69 the Army Corp of Engineers predicted flooding similar to the flood of 1965. At the

195

11th hour, the Henderson City Council decided to hire a blademan to build a levee to hold back the floodwater. The cat skinners worked around the clock, the levee held, and Henderson was spared from another devastating flood.

Built in 1969, it was called a temporary levee by the federal government and wasn't designated permanent until 21 years later. The permanent levee had roughly the same alignment as the temporary levee with a few minor improvements. The cost of the name change from temporary to permanent was estimated at $2,400,000 of taxpayer money.[48]

Spike Nevin

Every day Grandpa Alo picked the white eggs laid by White Rocks. In later years he picked the brown eggs laid by Rhode Island Reds. They were originally bred in Adamsville, Rhode Island. One of the founding cocks was a black-breasted Malay from England. He's stuffed and on display at the Smithsonian in Washington, D.C. If a hen got clucky (setting on her eggs) Grandpa Alo locked her in the cage in the chicken coop for a few days and the problem was over.

On many a rainy afternoon Grandpa and I washed the eggs and put them in cases that held thirty dozen. We'd hoist the cardboard cases of eggs into the trunk of Grandpa's '63 Ford Galaxy. Grandpa drove to Spike's Mercantile in Green Isle. Upon arrival Grandpa and I handed the cases off to owner, Spike Nevin. While Spike candled the eggs in the back room, Grandpa gathered his groceries and set them on the counter. He usually bought summer sausage, Spam, Cheerios, coffee, raisin bread, Dannheim butter and ice cream from New Ulm, Old Dutch potato chips, and Fig Newton cookies–and whatever clothes he needed, such as Lee overalls, and Munsingwear long johns. The thirty years I knew Grandpa he bought two pairs of Sunday shoes. He purchased a new pair of nine-inch-high Redwing work boots about every eight months.

About the time Grandpa finished shopping, Spike had the eggs candled. Using a mechanical adding machine, Spike totaled up Grandpa's grocery bill and they squared their accounts. Spike threw in the grocery box a handful of Nut Goodie Bars made by the Pearson Candy Company in St. Paul. On the way home Grandpa drove thirty-five miles an hour in the middle of the road. We ate the Nut Goodies and turned the AM radio to KNUJ out of New Ulm and listened to polka music. On one ride, an ad came on the radio claiming steel burial vaults will last for eternity. Grandpa told me, "Steel burial vaults will rust out before eternity is half over."

One day the priest from Green Isle was in Spike's purchasing a box of cereal, a tin of coffee and a pack of Red Man chew. The priest told Spike he was saving money by "cuttin' out the middle man." He was buying his meat, milk and potatoes directly from a local farmer. A couple of months later the priest met Spike on the street and asked how his relationship was with the Lord; he hadn't seen him at Sunday mass. Spike said he was praying every evening, confessing his sins every week, giving groceries to the needy and at Christmas he gave his customers a Red Wing beater jar. Spike ended by saying, "To save money I'm cuttin' out the middle man."

Shillelagh

On an Indian summer day Grandpa Alo and I were shopping at Spike's Mercantile when, lo and be glory, in hobbled Shillelagh. He was limping from beer toe (gout.) He'd step over seven nude women for a pint of stout. A few years earlier he spent four days in the "spin dry." While delirious Shillelagh got the shakes and he was seeing snakes. He checked himself out and declared rehab was for quitters. He said, "Boys, it's time for a pint."

Shillelagh told Spike he needed to buy a brassiere for his ne'-do-well neighbor lady. Spike went over to an old cardboard box full of bras and asked if grapefruits were the size. Shillelagh

197

said, "smaller," Spike asked if oranges were the size, he said, "Smaller." Spike asked if eggs were the size and he said, "it tis." Spike pulled out a brassiere and Shillelagh said, "Smaller." Spike said, "You said the size of eggs." Shillelagh said, "Fried eggs." Spike found the right size bra marked $4.00. Shillelagh asked if he could see something cheaper. Spike rummaged through the box and found a brassiere marked $2.50. Shillelagh asked if he could see something cheaper. Spike handed him a mirror.

Shillelagh was "ginned up" when he stacked wet hay in a barn. When he saw the hay smoldering he called the Henderson fire department. The volunteer fireman asked, "How do we get to the farm?" Shillelagh replied, "Don't ye still have the lil red fire truck?" The Henderson bucket brigade arrived in time to save the foundation. An old Laplander asked Shillelagh how it was to be he was down on his luck. The comment stuck in Shillelagh's craw. He snapped, "If you're lucky enough to be Irish, you're lucky enough." Shillelagh wrote a letter to his relatives back in Ireland telling them about the blaze. He ended the letter by writing, "I was going to send $5.00 but I already sealed the envelope."

One day Shillelagh got the idea to make out a will. While smoking a cigar Shillelagh strolled in an attorney's office in Gaylord. The attorney was reading the newspaper. Shillelagh asked him, "Whatcha readin'?" The attorney said, "The obituaries." Shillelagh said, "What fer?" The attorney said, "So I can see who finally quit smoking." When the two finished up, Shillelagh asked, "What's me will going to cost me?" The attorney told Shillelagh "I screwed the last client to save you money. I'll only charge you $800."

After seeing the attorney, Shalelee played a round of barnyard pool at the course near Winthrop. The next day Shillelagh was telling me about his round of golf. He said he only hit two balls hard and that was when he stepped on a rake.

Coon Feed

198

In 1969, while Dad was cashing a check at the Green Isle Citizens State Bank, the girl took a dollar for his Lion's raffle ticket. Dad told her, "Be sure to fill out the stub." A couple of weeks later a man drove a rusted-out big fender Chevy full of groceries to the farmyard. Dad won the raffle—the groceries and the car.

In 1969, Neil Armstrong was the first man to walk on the moon, and that fall Grandpa Alo and I drove the jalopy Dad won to a coon feed in Cologne, Minnesota. The feeds were popular fundraisers for VFWs, American Legions, fire departments, sports teams, and hunting clubs. Late in the feed they were running out of coon. One of the workers grabbed a big tomcat, skinned it, gutted it, butchered it, and threw him on the grill. After everyone finished chowing down, a state representative told us the raccoon he ate had small bones and tasted like chicken.

A few months later, Dad met up with Shillelagh and told him he could have the big fender Chevy. Shillelagh said he didn't want it. When Dad asked why not, he said, "Anything I ever got for free cost me so much I couldn't afford it."

Chapter Ten
Vietnam War and the Seventies

The Minnesota 8

In 1970, anti-draft activists broke into the St. Paul Post Office and other federal buildings, and destroyed thousands of selective service records. FBI agents were called in to track down the culprits. That summer, Brad Beneke from Glencoe, and seven other young men broke into government offices in Winona, Alexandria, and Little Falls, Minnesota to destroy draft documents. They got caught. One pleaded guilty and received probation. During their trials on attempted burglary, they contended they were opposed to the war in Vietnam and forcing men into battle. All seven were convicted and sentenced to five years in the big house. No one served more than 20 months. Decades later their story was made into a play called *Peace Crimes: The Minnesota 8 vs. the War*.[1]

Monuments to the Irish

Ed McCormick lived every day like it was St. Patrick's Day. He got his nickname "Swance" from skinny dipping in the Minnesota River. He was the last of the old-time Irishmen in Jessenland. One day while I was at his farm, "Swance" looked forlorn. "What's wrong?" I asked. He turned his bull neck toward me and said he bought a bottle of bug juice in Belle Plaine, and on

201

the way home he took a few snorts, but when he laid the jug down, the cap fell off and the whiskey ran on the floorboards.

On a splendid November day in 1970 the Weber family attended big doings at St. Thomas Church for the dedication of a monument to recognize the Pioneer Settlers of Jessenland donated by St. Paul sand and gravel magnate Joseph Shiely. His grandfather, Michael Shiely, is buried in the cemetery. Joseph Shiely jokingly told his grandchildren that he and railroad tycoon James J. Hill "built the Great Northern Railway."[2] The bishop of the St. Paul Diocese blessed the monument. The dedication marked the 100th anniversary of the present church. The bishop of the New Ulm diocese celebrated Mass for those buried in the cemetery. The theme of Father Jerry Berger's homily was: "If these old walls could talk."

After Mass, Dad and I walked in the parsonage, and with several men and women of the cloth present, an old spinster asked Dad how "Swance" got his name. It was the only time I saw Dad's jaw move but no words came out. Father Berger gave Dad a wink and changed the subject.

In 1972 a monument honoring Jessenland's first settlers, Thomas, Walter, and Dennis Doheny, was constructed next to St. Thomas Church. The monument was donated by Thomas Doheny's great-grandson, Earl Doheny, and his family. The ornate wrought iron cross originally on the steeple of the present church is incorporated in the monument.

Confirmation Mass

Since the opening of St. Thomas Church, the parishioners have been known for their tradition of standing around after Mass and visiting. The adults talked about crops, commodity prices, weather, and politics. Farm business included such things as: "Do you have a little seed corn left over?" "Can I borrow your grain auger?" or "Can I bring the cultivator over tomorrow to weld a crack?" Not much money changed hands and no need for a handshake. We kids often had snowball fights in the winter and ostrich fights in the summer. While standing around after Mass an old Irishman told me he needed to get a paper notarized. He asked me if I knew a "notorious republican." Sounds like something former Vice President Dan Quayle would say.

Every few years the bishop of the New Ulm Diocese (created in 1958 by Pope Pius XII) presided over the confirmation Mass at St. Thomas Church. It was customary for the bishop to ask the confirmation candidates questions. At a confirmation Mass during the early 1970s, the bishop asked his first question, "What sacrament are you receiving today?" A boy wearing a cornfield green polyester suit raised his hand and said, "Matrimony." The chuckles got pretty loud and the bishop didn't ask any more questions.

Jack Harens, Sr.

When our neighbor and friend of the family, Jack Harens Sr., died in 1975, seven of us gathered on a pleasant summer evening to dig his grave in the cemetery behind St. Thomas Church. Joe Zeiher, thinner than an Irish cookbook and too old to dig, brought a bottle opener and a case of returnable bottles filled with oh-so-good Buckhorn beer from the upstream Schell Brewery in New Ulm. The last digger was 79-year-old Grandpa Alo. When the grave was deep enough he quit digging. The men handed Grandpa the old plywood template. It cleared the grave by an inch all the way around. A couple of men grabbed Alo under the arms and hoisted him out of the grave. A few days later Jack was lowered into the grave. Jack's widow, Eleanor, was a nice lady originally from North Dakota. A few years after Jack's death, Grandpa Alo said to me, "I'd ask Eleanor to marry me if I wasn't so damn old."

Nagel Packing

In 1970 Hanoi Jane told an audience at the University of Michigan, "If you understood what communism was, you would hope, you would pray on your knees, that we would someday become communist."[3] Explains why East Germany built a wall to keep its citizens from escaping to West Germany. Also in 1970 on the last day of sixth grade, instead of walking to my great-aunt, Mag Carroll's apartment for yellow cake with brown frosting, a classmate and I walked to the Nagel Packing plant in Arlington, and applied for jobs. Ten minutes later I punched the time clock. As I sat on a stool, radishes passed by on a conveyor belt and I threw out the deformed or damaged ones. My first job off the farm paid a dollar an hour.

After my first day on the job I caught a ride home with our neighbor, Bert Berger, the head mechanic at the plant. The Bergers and Webers have been neighbors and friends over 150 years. During the dirty thirties, to find work Bert moved his family to Stockton, California where he became the head mechanic for Del Monte. In 1943 he moved his family back to his farm in Jessenland. Bert invented the "shank on" corn picker that keeps sweet corn fresher longer. I asked Bert how it was working at Nagel Packing. He told me, "the hours are long, the work is hard, and the pay is poor." When I got home I told Mom and Dad I got a job.

I only worked on the radish belt a couple of weeks before I transferred to where farm boys wanted to be—in the fields. Back then there were no porta-potties in the field. I worked on a radish combine in the peat tying and slinging gunny sacks full of radishes. On a hot summer afternoon, a fellow worker put a firecracker in a Coke bottle. Flying glass hit me in the teeth and in the right arm. I pulled the glass out; it was bleeding pretty good you know. I wrapped a rag around my arm to stop the flow. We picked radishes late into the night. After we shut the combines down, I rode home on my minibike with a Tecumseh motor, it conked out two miles as the crow flies from the Weber farm. I wheeled the minibike in the ditch and started walking cross country, and with no help from a new moon, I walked into the neighbors' black cow and electric fence. I made it to Silver Lake and walked along the shore until I reached home about one in the morning. After I woke up, Dad and I got in the '50 Ford F1 and retrieved the minibike. Dad repaired it and I rode it to the radish patch for another day of adventure.

Beer in the Ballot Box

In 1972, Richard Nixon, who used winnings from playing poker to finance his first campaign, was President, and the law in Minnesota prohibited the sale of alcohol on Election Day. On Election Day 1972 a township board member brought a church key and a case of Hamm's beer to the Jessenland Town Hall. For a little talking humor, another board member showed up with a bottle of Jameson. When the priest from St. Thomas Church pulled into the parking lot, a board member shouted out, "Hide the beer!" A board member hid his bottle in the ballot box. When Father inserted his ballot in the slit in the box it wouldn't drop. He shook the ballot box, tipping the bottle of beer. Father's ballot dropped and he left.

Grandpa Alo drove home and picked me up along with a spool of bale twine and clothespins. We strung a line of twine from a tree to the back of the town hall and clipped the beer-soaked ballots to the line. When the poll closed the ballots were dry. Grandpa, the only sober board member, and I delivered the ballots to the county seat in Gaylord.

Maurice Stans

In the election of 1972, "Tricky Dick" soundly defeated George McGovern for his second term as President. Twenty-one months later Richard Nixon became the first president to resign for his part in covering-up (obstructing justice) a break-in in June 1972 of the Democratic Headquarters at the Watergate Hotel in Washington, D.C. Of the five burglars, four were Cuban.[4] On an August day in 1974 Nixon got liquored up and eventually he went fetal. Laying on the floor of the Lincoln sitting room in the White House, while crying like a baby he asked a close aide,

"What have I done?"[5] Two days later he announced he was stepping down from the highest office in the land.

Nixon's Secretary of Commerce, Maurice Stans, also served as chairman of Nixon's 1972 Reelection Finance Committee. Maurice Stans, of Belgium heritage, was born and raised in Shakopee in the Lower Minnesota River Valley. He found himself in the wrong place at the wrong time in history. Stans had no involvement with Watergate, but during the investigation he was charged in federal court with ten felony counts of conspiracy and perjury in connection with a campaign donor's contribution. The jury acquitted Stans on all ten counts.[6] A day later overzealous Watergate special prosecutor, Leon Jaworski, went after Stans for trifling campaign finance violations. Tired of fighting, declining finances and concerned for his wife's health, Stans reluctantly pleaded guilty to five petty misdemeanors. The judge found no willful violations by Stans and he fined him $5,000. The witch-hunt against Stans was finally over.[7] The General Accounting Office found apparent violations in the campaigns of the five other presidential candidates in 1972; however, no one from those campaigns were ever charged with crimes.[8]

Belle Plaine Sales Barn

Late in the winter of 1971-72, I rode with Dad in the '46 Chev truck to the sales barn in Belle Plaine (home of a two-story outhouse.) Dad sold a load of straw bales at the weekly sales barn auction. Dad said the sales barn had "auctions with action and sales with satisfaction." Most of all he liked the certified check he received from selling the straw. After Dad got his check we stopped at the best bakery in the area for our favorite—a dozen jelly-filled doughnuts. As we got back in the truck, we noticed a lady's car stalled on Main Street and an old guy behind her laying on the horn. The lady got out of her car and walked back to the man and said, "Do you want to try to start that car while I press down on the horn?"

On the ride back to the farm as we were sliding the doughnuts down with Bubble-Up pop, we saw a young dude with long hair wearing love beads walking in the ditch near Blakeley. Dad pulled the '46 over and asked the hippie if he needed a lift. He replied, "No I'm an environmentalist and I don't believe in vehicles or roads." Dad asked him how he was going to cross the Minnesota River. He said he was going to walk across the Blakeley bridge. Dad and I laughed the rest of the way home about the flaky environmentalist who talked the talk, walked the ditch, but wasn't green enough to swim across the river. Years later I surmised the young man was Al Gore.

Russell Bryan

In 1972, Itasca County in northern Minnesota mailed Russell Bryan, a Native American, a $147.95 property tax bill for his mobile home. Bryan refused to pay the bill, claiming he lived on a res, which meant state tax laws didn't apply to him. In 1976, I read about *Bryan v. Itasca County*; the U.S. Supreme Court unanimously sided with Bryan. The case paved the way for Indian casinos in the Minnesota River Valley and throughout the United States.[9] Since casino Indians found white man's weakness, they're buying back some of the land they were gypped out of with slot machine profits.

Northern States Power

In the early 1970s Northern States Power (NSP) needed to build a coal-burning power plant to meet increasing electrical demand in the Twin Cities. A site for the plant that included the Weber farm was proposed in Jessenland. A group called Save America's Vital Energy (SAVE) opposed the site, believing farmland shouldn't be used for a power plant. The opposition caused a rift in Jessenland between those in favor of the site and those opposed. In case the Weber farm was condemned for the power plant, at Mom's urging Dad used the option money Northern States Power paid him and took out a loan to purchase

240 acres of mostly grade A farmland—fields with black soil that are fairly level and have good drainage—two miles west of Arlington near Kissner's mink farm. In those days mink were fed dead horses, livestock and fish.

Buying the land was the best business decision of Mom and Dad's life. The price of land has steadily increased and the rent from the cropland gives them a comfortable retirement. NSP built its new power plant near Monticello, Minnesota, and Mom and Dad kept the family farm. Those opposed to a power plant in Jessenland claimed victory.

Duck Hunters

On a cold windy evening in the fall of 1972, two duck hunters from the Twin Cities were crossing Silver Lake when their boat capsized. The cork decoys under the boat kept it afloat and the hunters hung on until they made it to shore. Seeing the all-night yard light, the hunters walked a mile to the Weber farm and knocked on Grandpa Alo's door. He was the only one home. By the time Grandpa reached the door, the hunters had collapsed on his doorstep. To get their core temperature up, Grandpa put them in a hot shower, dry clothes, and warmed their innards with coffee. He gave them a ride to their pickup truck at the public access to Silver Lake. The next day they retrieved their boat and decoys. They gave Grandpa a ham and a box of chocolates.

In 1973 the devil did a jig when the U.S. Supreme Court's decision in *Roe v. Wade* legalized abortion in our country. Justice Harry Blackmun, former counsel to the Mayo Clinic, wrote the majority opinion. That fall, the day before duck hunting season, Grandpa Alo and I walked to Silver Lake. With the 12-gauge shotgun in his hands Grandpa snuck up to the shore and took a pot shot. I took off my shoes, socks and pants and waded in the water and pulled out five redhead ducks. I didn't bother with the coot.

In front of the shop Grandpa and I plucked the redheads—made difficult by all the pin feathers—and gutted and butchered them. Just as we were finishing up, Dad came home and said the neighbor told him the game warden was looking for the person shooting on Silver Lake. I gathered up the feathers and guts, and Grandpa started digging a hole. When the hole was deep enough to bury the evidence, Grandpa quit digging. We hid the butchered ducks in Grandpa's refrigerator. When Dad told the story he said Grandpa and I were lucky the game warden didn't get the pinch on us.

Farm Animals

When I was growing up most farms in Jessenland were so small they didn't need a tomcat. Farms had cats to keep the mice and rat populations down. The Weber farm usually had three to eight pussies and several kittens. Most were barn cats, though a few elevated their status to porch kitties. Snowball was a cross-eyed albino puss. She'd walk to Silver Lake and snag small bullheads to feed her kittens. When I got the stomach flu Dad told me to go outside and give the cats a warm meal. When there got to be too many cats on the farm, my brother Brian tossed a few in a gunny sack and drowned them in the cow tank.

In Jessenland, German shepherds were the farmer's dog of choice. A good dog on the farm keeps livestock in line and protects the farmyard from intruders such as snakes, skunks, and the county weed inspector. The first dog on the farm I remember was a German shepherd named Sport. In 1965 on an autumn day, my Dad held my sister Nancy as she ate a hotdog. Sport jumped up to snatch the hotdog and nipped her just below the eye. For that stunt Grandpa Alo put Sport down with a ball of lead behind his ear. Grandpa grabbed a shovel, and when the hole was deep enough to bury Sport, he quit digging. After Sport, we got Perkie, a border collie who hated rats and loved to round-up livestock. The next dog was a rat terrier that Nancy named Smokey. After Smokey got a hind foot caught in Mike Carroll's muskrat trap on a 20-below-zero day, he became a three-legged dog. Two inches of his leg fell off and he developed a callous on the bottom of the stub. Smokey growled every time he saw Mike Carroll's pick-up truck go by the farm.

On the farm, Dad kept a flock of 90 White Suffolk sheep. Once in a while the recessive black gene popped up and a ewe dropped a black lamb. White Suffolks were developed in Australia and produce high-quality white wool. The meat from the lambs and ewes is yummy.

In the spring the shearer made his annual appearance at the farm. Grandpa Alo held each sheep down while the shearer clipped the wool off in a single piece. Dad and I skirted and rolled the fleeces, and tied them with paper twine so the wool didn't get contaminated. We stacked the fleeces in the box of the '46 Chev truck. I rode with Dad to Henderson. One year when we pulled into town we saw a band of gypsies dressed in white on Main Street. At the Henderson Egg and Poultry Company we helped the owner put each fleece in a plastic bag. From the store, the fleeces were shipped to the Wool Owner's Association in Minneapolis where the wool was sorted. Dad was always disappointed with the check he got for the fleeces. After paying the shearer's bill and with deductions for tags–dirt and stickers imbedded in the wool, there wasn't much to show for the effort.

After leaving the Henderson Egg and Poultry Company, Dad and I went to Bender's drugstore. At the counter we each chewed on a Pearson's Salted Nut Roll softened up with fountain pop. The year the gypsies were in town the pharmacist and the soda jerk were in a tizzy, as earlier in the day the gypsies came into the store and gave themselves the sticky finger discount. On the ride home Dad told me, "There's no fool like an old fool."

The Wool Growers Association sold the wool to mills, some to the St. Peter Woolen Mill established in 1867 in St. Peter. It's one of the longest-running family-owned enterprises in Minnesota. The mill still uses a carding machine from the 1930s to make sheets of wool batting.[10] Carding combs through raw wool transforming it into batting, a fluffy sheet of wool that is used for quilts and spinning wool into yarn.[11]

Large amounts of wool were sold to the Faribault Woolen Mill in Faribault, Minnesota. In 1915 the mill started making blankets for the cadets at West Point and during WWI they made olive drab blankets for the Army.[12] During WWII volunteers at the mill helped make blankets and sleeping bags for the troops.[13] After the war, G.I.'s German girlfriends used the blankets to make shirts and skirts.[14] In 1949, "Fabco" introduced the Pak-a-Robe. President Eisenhower called it an "ingenious gift."[15]

Early one summer a roving pack of wild dogs killed some lambs. On a windy afternoon Dad spotted the pack in the hayfield between the house and Jessenland Road. Dad went in the basement and got his .303 Lee-Enfield rifle. He opened the window in the house's den, said, "Lock and load," laid the barrel on the sill, and using Kentucky windage, squeezed the trigger and dropped the big dog in the pack. It was the only time I saw Dad shoot an animal. I dragged the German shepherd by the tail to the edge of the wheat field where I buried him in a shallow hole.

In 1971, Dad sold his flock of sheep because he was losing a few ewes each summer to liver flukes. As their first host, the parasites used snails around Silver Lake and the swamp. The ewes were the liver flukes second host. Dad sold the flock to a man who pastured the sheep at closed cemeteries.

Our square-dancing German Lutheran neighbors and friends, Hillard and Elaine Dehning, and their four children lived two miles from the Weber farm. Hillard made "old country" smoked sausages and was well known for his beautiful herd of fawn and white Guernseys that produced the highest butterfat content of any dairy herd in the countryside. Guernsey's were originally bred on the British Channel Island of Guernsey. The cows are curious and gentle. The bulls are aggressive. In the mid-1980s, Hillard had no choice but to slaughter his herd of Golden

Guernseys when they got Johne's disease, a fatal infection in the small intestine.[16]

Cousin Donny Strobel milked a herd of Holsteins on his farm in Jessenland. His kids named each cow; they called the mean cow "LBJ." When the cows were in their stanchions Donny's kids—he had 12 of them—crawled from cow to cow. During the summer at the evening milking I saw a brown snake slither to the barn door. Donny grabbed a teat of the cow in the stanchion closest to the door and squirted milk at the snake and it opened its mouth for a drink. After a couple of squirts, the snake slithered away. On a nice summer evening the Strobel kids and I were sliding down a tin lean-to roof, landing eight feet below in the barn yard. When Dad picked me up I was dirty and my forehead was skinned up. I told Dad, "By God, that's a wild place, but I sure had fun." Dad said, "The dog says the place is 'ruff.'"

In the 1960s and '70s artificial insemination of dairy cattle gained in popularity. To increase the fertility rate, dairy farmers try to inseminate cows while in heat. A gomer bull is a horny bull that has had a vasectomy. The gomer bull detects when a heifer or cow is in heat and mounts her. The farmer then knows to artificially inseminate the cow with sperm from a well-bred bull. The desired results are cows that produce more milk. If a cow doesn't have a calf each year she doesn't give milk. "Pasture pets" are ground into hamburger.

In the spring of 1971, Grandpa Alo and I came to the rescue of three cows in the swamp. The cows broke through a layer of crusted topsoil and sank to their bellies in the muck below. Grandpa and I laid down planks to walk on and grabbed a rope that saw better days pulling bales on a hay fork into the barn's loft. Being careful not to end up in the muck, we tied the rope around each cow's belly just behind her front legs. We tied the other end of the rope to the hitch on the "B" John Deere and one by one the "B" pulled each cow heavy with calf out of the muck. The cows were so tired from trying to get out of the ooze they could barely walk.

One spring day in 1972, a heifer couldn't drop her calf. Grandpa and I pulled and pulled on the calf's feet, but we couldn't get any movement. Grandpa didn't want to call the vet. To save money, he got a small chain and I backed the '46 Ford tractor up to the heifer. Grandpa wrapped the chain around the calf's feet and I hooked the other end to the Ford's draw bar. I put the Ford in gear, let off the clutch and out popped the calf. Grandpa cleaned out the calf's nose and he began to breath. The bull calf's feet were sore, but he could walk.

In 1972 a cow came up lame after she cut her foot on a piece of hardware. The wound festered and Dad was going to call the vet. To save money, Grandpa said he'd make a poultice to draw out the infection. I spent all morning with Grandpa making the poultice in a gunny sack, putting the gunny sack on the cow's foot, and attaching the gunny sack with bale twine to the cow's leg. Within a minute the cow kicked off the gunny sack. Dad said, "The ecstasy of a cheap price is soon overcome by the anguish of an inferior job," and he called the vet. The cow took a shot of penicillin in the rump and a couple of days later she was walking normally.

On a hot summer afternoon in 1973, Grandpa Alo and I smeared ointment on sunburned Chester White weaner pigs. Chester Whites were developed in the early 1800s in Chester County, Pennsylvania by breeding large white sows from the northeast to a white boar from Bedfordshire, England. After we finished with the weaners, we went in Grandpa's house where we played checkers and slid mincemeat pie down with soft Land-O-Lakes vanilla ice cream. We talked about the early days on the farm. I asked Grandpa how his grandpa, Anton, and his dad, Henry, both full German, liked being around all the Irishmen in Jessenland. Grandpa, a McKraut (Irish and German) said, "They really didn't like Irishmen, but they tolerated them." When the Irish arrived in droves in the late 19th and early 20th century,

Yankees considered them only slightly better than blacks. New York City was the worst, where Irish just off the boat lived in squalor.

On a sweltering hot summer afternoon, I drove the '46 Chev truck to a neighbor's farm to borrow his Hereford bull. I backed the '46 up to the side door of the barn. We hooked the loading chute to the back of the livestock rack. The bull had a ring through his nose with one end of a rope tied to the ring and the other end tied around a post. When the bull saw me, the neighbor, and his German shepherd, he pulled the rope so hard he pulled the ring through his nose. Blood splattered about as the bull started banging his hornless head into a corner of the barn causing boards to fly. The neighbor got his Irish up—both he and the bull were foaming at the mouth. The neighbor screamed at the bull that he was going to turn him into a steer. Fortunately, he couldn't find his pocket knife. Just then a neighboring farmer walked in the barn. He opened the back door and after a few minutes the bull ran to the cows, ending the commotion. We didn't get the bull loaded that day. His nose never healed.

To keep the gene pool fresh, the farmers in Jessenland borrowed their bulls and boars to each other. In the 1970s, Dad had a big docile Hereford bull named Nightworker who went from farm to farm. Dad didn't see him for three years. For a while Dad didn't know where he was working. The borrowing farmer drove his truck in the pasture, dropped the loading chute, and if there were no heifers or cows in heat, Nightworker ran in the livestock box. Like gomer bull Bill Clinton, he was anxious to meet fresh breeding stock.

To ensure calves were born in the spring the bull was penned up in the barn until the time was right. On a summer day in 1974, Grandpa Alo, Dad, and I opened the side door on the barn and out came the bull, madder than ego-inflated California Senator Barbara Boxer telling an Army colonel at a congressional hearing to address her as "Senator." Heckuva statement for old bossy to make to a man willing to die for her freedom. The bull aggressively took after 78-year-old Grandpa. He sidestepped the bull a few times and got behind a lumber pile. After a few minutes the bull lost interest in goring Grandpa and ran to the heifers. That evening, after Grandpa Alo and I finished pasting S&H Green Stamps in a book, we sat on the couch in Grandpa's house throwing a rubber ball against the front door while watching the evening news with Walter Cronkite. When a politician talked in favor of redistributing wealth, Grandpa said the problem was it would have to be done every five years. After supper Grandpa Alo and I went to Henderson where we watched a game of donkey basketball.

Almost every spring we got chicks from the Henderson Egg and Poultry Store and raised broilers. After the store closed, we ordered chicks from the Murray McMurray Hatchery in Webster City, Iowa. The postman delivered chirping chicks in cardboard flats. To keep the clutch warm, we put them under a brooder set up in the old ice house built by my great-grandpa Henry Weber. In the fall the family butchered the broilers. We also butchered the laying hens Grandpa culled from the flock. Dad was nowhere to be found. I'd place a chicken's neck between two nails protruding from a block of wood and, with the whack of a hatchet, the head came off. The chicken would run around with his head cut off, much like politicians looking for campaign money.

Dehorns

In 1974 former model President Gerald Ford pardoned former President Nixon for crimes he committed during the Watergate scandal, and on a winter day, we castrated and dehorned the young stock.[17] It was my job to pull up the tail while Grandpa made steers. After each cut, to prevent infection, Grandpa Alo slid the knife into a potato, a procedure he learned at farm school in Henderson. The cats ate the mountain oysters. When the weather turned unseasonably warm, maggots invaded the wounds caused by cutting off the horns. The maggots in the steers' brains caused them to go crazy.

Before they were fed out, Dad decided to ship the most dangerous steers to the stockyard in South St. Paul. By using an electric cattle prod, we got four of the softheaded steers loaded in the livestock rack on the '46 Chev truck. One steer got his front legs over the top board of the rack. I stuck a pitch fork in his nose, but that didn't stop him from tearing apart the back of the livestock rack. Luckily, I got out of the way and fortunately the steer didn't break any bones. The other three critters jumped out of the busted livestock rack. After Dad's experience with these steers, he used the term "dehorns" to describe perverts, misfits, and politicians, such as town clown Al Franken, former U.S. Senator from Minnesota. He got egg on his face when it came to light he groped several women. The pervert of the Senate resigned his seat.

Larry Pangburn

My uncle, Bob Gildea, married Marlene Pangburn. Her father, Larry Pangburn, was a retired brick layer with a gift for laying brick and stone. He hand cut stones used in many of the churches, synagogues, and schools in the Twin Cities and surrounding area. He built his brick retirement house on the shores of Sauk Lake in central Minnesota.

A couple of times each summer Mom and Dad loaded up us kids and we headed out to Larry's house. It was a good two-hour run. On the way we passed St. John's College, home of the Johnnies NCAA Division III football team. For 60 years the Johnnies were coached by John Gagliardi. His record of 489-131-11 gives him the most coaching victories in all of college football. Gagliardi insisted on being called John. He didn't use playbooks, and at practice, whistles and tackling weren't allowed. If the Minnesota state bird—mosquitoes—were thirsty, or if the weather turned nasty, he cut the 90 minute practice short. Since 1993 the Gagliardi Trophy is given each year to an outstanding

Division III football player. In 2006 he was inducted into the College Football Hall of Fame. In 2012, at age 86, Gagliardi went out the gate with dignity into a well-deserved retirement.[18]

When we arrived at Larry's house he welcomed us with open arms, and the main event was fishing from Larry's boat. He loved to catch, clean, and eat fish. He liked to gab about the big one that got away. Once he reeled in nine fish on one hook; he'd snagged someone's string of fish that broke loose. On one fishing expedition white caps splashed water in the boat. We were the only boat on the lake and it was the only time everyone, except Larry, wore a life jacket. Trolling with Red Eye lures, we caught a fine string of large Northern Pike, including an albino caught by Grandpa Joe. When we weren't out in the boat we'd hook crappies and perch from Larry's dock. Uncle Bob placed chum off the dock by punching small holes in cans of dog food.

Larry liked to clean and eat fish almost as much as he liked to reel them in. Us kids gathered around the cleaning table as Larry filleted the fish, explaining every cut and the anatomy of each fish. To add to the spectacle, he was swilling beer and smoking cigarettes. After the fish supper the men and boys went to get bait and a couple of 7UPs in Sauk Centre, the original main street. One evening we all dined at a supper club on the outskirts of Sauk Centre. For serving Grandma a spoiled steak, the owner took half off the price of Grandma's meal. He said he'd chop up the rest of the rotten steaks and put them in chili. The next summer we noticed the supper club was closed.

Sinclair Lewis

In 1973, at age 77, Larry got lung cancer. As we left his hospital room Larry said to Dad, "It's been nice knowing you Weber." Larry is under the sod in the Greenwood cemetery in Sauk Centre close to Sinclair Lewis's headstone, which reads: Author of "Main Street." Sinclair Lewis was the most famous American writer of his time. The brick used in Sinclair Lewis' boyhood home is from the Pangburn brickyard started by Larry's grandfather.[19]

Published in 1920, *Main Street* was named the most sensational novel of the 20th century.[20] Lewis won a Pulitzer Prize in 1926 for his novel, *Arrowsmith*. Angry that *Main Street* had been snubbed earlier by the judges, he declined the Pulitzer.[21] In 1927, Lewis' *Elmer Gantry* was published. It's a novel about a wayward man who becomes a minister and continues his adulterous ways. Preachers across the nation were outraged by the work and it was banned in Boston and elsewhere. Banning and criticizing the novel was good advertising–it had the largest first printing in the history of American literature.[22] In 1930, Lewis was the first American to win the Nobel Prize for Literature.[23] He and his wife sailed to Stockholm and a sober Lewis received his Nobel Prize from the King of Sweden.[24] The head of Princeton University said the award to Sinclair Lewis "was an insult to America."[25]

Charlie Strobel the Butter Maker

In 1975, Grandpa Alo and I were visiting with Grandpa's brother-in-law, Charlie Strobel, while his wife, Irene, attended a baby shower. The two hard-working, clean-living men had married sisters and were friends over 60 years. Irene told Grandpa the doctor put Charlie on a low-fat diet. He couldn't have butter, only oleomargarine. For our supper she put a Velveeta cheese Spam hot dish in Grandpa's refrigerator. Oleomargarine didn't set well with Charlie as he made a living running creameries and selling his award-winning butter. At suppertime Grandpa opened his old GE refrigerator to take out the hot dish when Charlie said, "Hell, Alo, fry us up some eggs in butter." Charlie, Grandpa, and I ate eggs and summer sausage fried in butter along with butter on our toast. When Irene picked up Charlie, the smell of grease permeated the air and she gave Grandpa a little hell for making Charlie a high-fat supper. The two old-timers looked at each other and grinned. Charlie's death certificate states his occupation as butter maker.

Clancy

On a fall day I was driving the "B" John Deere in road gear pulling a flarebox of soybeans to the elevator in Blakeley. I saw Clancy curled up in the corn stalks next to his Farmall "H" tractor with the plow in the ground. When I brought the "B" to a stop Clancy woke up. He told me he hadn't been getting much sleep. The old "ball and chain" stays up til one in the mornin' and he can't break her of the habit. I asked why she stays up so late. He said, "She's waitin' for me to get home."

Early one morning Clancy's wife was doubled over with pain in her abdomen. Clancy rang up the doctor and told him his wife was having an appendicitis. The doctor told Clancy he'd taken out his wife's appendix several years ago. The doctor asked him, "Have you ever heard of a second appendix?" Clancy responded, "Have you ever heard of a second wife?"

A year after Clancy's second wife ran off with the gismo player from New Auburn, I bumped into Clancy shining coon in Zeiher's woods. Seeing his nose was bandaged, I asked what happened. He said, "I got seenus." I said, "Sinus?" He said, "No, seenus. I took a young buxom woman out for a wine supper at the Coachlight Inn Supper Club a ways outta Henderson. Afterwards we went to the tractor pull at the Scott County Fair. She forgot to tell me she had a boyfriend and he seenus!" After Clancy's nose healed he told me he picked out a bride from the Monkey Wards catalog. A couple of weeks later, after I helped him clean-out his farrowing barn, I asked Clancy when his new wife was going to show up, he said, "She'll be here any day, her clothes were in yesterday's mail."

After a few months Clancy gave up on the catalog bride. He married Greta–a pigeon-toed Swede with an otherwise nice chassis. Clancy was Greta's third husband. The first one died from eating poison mushrooms, the second from a blow to the head–he wouldn't eat the mushrooms. Using Greta's life insurance money, the newlyweds spent their honeymoon in San Francisco. While on Fisherman's Wharf, a panhandler hit Clancy up for beer money. Clancy told him, "How can I be sure you won't waste the money on food?"

After being married to Greta for a couple of years, I asked Clancy how married life was treating him. He said, "Darn good, every Friday me ole lady brings me home a paycheck for her work as a diesel fitter." I said, "She doesn't look like she works in a repair shop." He said, "She works at a fancy boutique in Le Sueur. When a woman walks in me wife holds up a couple of dresses and yells out, "Diesel fitter."

After they were married several years, I was visiting Greta and Clancy. After supping radish soup, we took turns playing checkers. After a while Greta got fussed-up and left the room crying. I asked Clancy what was wrong. He said, "A few days ago she had that cataract surgery to clear-up her vision. She took a look in the mirror and saw her face has more wrinkles than a Beverly Hills nudist party."

Years later Clancy's second wife, who ran off with the gismo player, saw him at a wake. She rushed up to Clancy and put her arms around him to give him a hug. Clancy backed off. After she left, while Clancy and I were bending our elbows, I asked him why he stepped back from the hug. He said, "I felt her hand goin' for me wallet."

Ray and Liz Zeiher

Grandpa Alo's friend, Ray Zeiher, and his second wife, Liz, had a "moonshine farm" a few miles outside of Green Isle. They planted a large garden with a beautiful patch of strawberries, and canned their fruits and vegetables. They knew the location of every butternut tree and stand of raspberries and blueberries in the countryside. They caught catfish and carp in the Minnesota River. Ray smoked the carp in an outhouse. Ray made pop, ketchup, and mustard, and he boiled maple sap to make syrup. He also rolled his own cigarettes. They raised rabbits, ducks, geese, and chickens, and kept a Holstein cow for milk, butter, and cream. Ray hunted deer and squirrel. One autumn Ray went squirrel-hunting in Washington, D.C. It's too bad he was such a good shot; we're now left with a bunch of nuts.

On a drizzly summer day, Grandpa Alo started digging with a spade. When he saw worms he quit digging. After I put the worms and night crawlers in a bean can, Ray rolled in the farmyard in his turquoise 1955 Mercury. Grandpa and I secured our bamboo poles in holders attached to the roof of the Merc. Ray drove Liz, Grandpa, and me to Halstead's Bay on Lake Minnetonka where we fished from shore. We waited out a downpour in the Merc by eating our deer sausage on home-baked bread with freshly churned butter and washing it down with sauerkraut juice. Ray adjusted my sinker and bobber, and the fishing picked up. We all caught our limit, and then some, of walleyes and crappies. During the entire fishing expedition, Ray chawed on a quid of tobacco and the juice drooled from the side of his mouth.

On a February day colder than a well driller's ass, Ray got cabin fever and told Grandpa and me he wanted to try a restaurant. After we finished eating liver and onions at a café in Belle Plaine, the waitress left the check with Ray. He told Grandpa, "I just can't pay it." Grandpa paid the check and left a tip.

After I used an axe to chop a hole in the ice on Silver Lake to water the cows, Grandpa Alo, my sister Ann, and I went to Ray and Liz's house to borrow Ray's mechanical adding machine and to play Buck Euchre for a dime a game. All players paid the winner a nickel for each time they were "bucked" during the game. While playing, we washed down butternuts with Ray's homemade ginger ale. As Ann reached for more butternuts, Liz slapped her hand. Grandpa was peeved; the butternuts were from a tree in our woods. Someone like Liz should be guarding taxpayers' money in Washington, D.C.

For supper Liz fried up squirrel and scrambled duck eggs in an iron skillet on the woodstove. For dessert she served up gooseberry pie with homemade ice cream. It was a delicious and wholesome supper, fresh with no preservatives. It may be the reason it took 94 years for Ray to cross over. Nowadays people eat food so laced with preservatives that when they die their corpse doesn't decay as fast as when people ate fresh food off the farm. Some "organic" farmers spray at night, leading to crates of vegetables like those amazing coffee pots that pour both regular and decaf.

When I was on the farm, except for winter, chickens in Jessenland spent their days scratching in the farmyard and their nights roosting in the chicken coop. Grandpa Alo fed the hens crushed oyster shells and during the winter he gave them sand for their gizzard. The hens lowest on the pecking order often had missing tail feathers and bled from behind. Today, chickens are raised by the hundreds of thousands in steel barns. They're fed steroids and antibiotics to grow faster and bigger, and live in crowded cages. It makes for drumsticks twice the normal size.

Except for winter, in the 1960s and 70s the dairy and beef cattle in Jessenland spent their days in the pasture. Dairy cattle came into the barn mornings and evenings to be milked and were fed ground feed. In the winter, cattle were fed alfalfa and ground feed, and on nice days they wandered about the barnyard. Nowadays most cattle are confined and never walk in a pasture. Cows are given hormones to produce more milk, and to steers to grow faster. On the Weber farm we ate plenty of wholesome meat—free of hormones and other additives. As Erma Bombeck said, "I didn't fight my way to the top of the food chain to be a vegetarian."

In the 1960s and early '70s most farmers in Jessenland took their pickup trucks with a small load of corn and alfalfa to the feed mill in Green Isle. The corn and alfalfa were milled to make ground feed for livestock. While the farmer's grain was being milled, he would visit a bar or two so he wouldn't be declared a "fire hazard." When the farmer had his fill of fire retardant, he'd return to the feed mill and stack gunny sacks full of ground feed in his pickup truck. I soon learned to give pickup trucks returning to Jessenland the middle of the road. Even though the pickup truck wasn't the only thing running with a full load, the farmer always gave the customary "pointer finger" wave from his hand on the steering wheel.

Milton Engelman

In 1957, Milton Engelman, a farmer who lived a few miles north of Green Isle, invented the portable feed mill for use on the farm. Mounted on tires, it could be pulled around the farmyard by a tractor. The tractor's power take-off shaft provided the power to run the portable feed mill. In 1958, Engelman, along with local investors, built a plant in Green Isle to manufacture the portable feed mills. In 1961, Engelman's Green Isle Manufacturing Company merged with Farmhand, Inc. Engleman stayed on as plant manager until his sudden death in 1964. During the 1960s and '70s the portable feed mills sold well throughout the U.S. and Canada. The plant was a major source of employment in the local area. The portable feed mills and the vanishing small farm ended trips to feed mills in town. The feed mill in Jordan, Minnesota was converted into the Jordon Feed Mill Restaurant. It still has the sweet smell of ground feed. In the early 1980s, Farmhand closed its plant in Green Isle.

Port Cargill

In the early 1970s farming picked up and Dad quit Anderson Machine Shop. He started hiring a grain hauler to truck his grain to Cargill and other grain terminal elevators at Port Cargill some 40 miles down the Minnesota River Valley in Savage. Even after paying to have his grain trucked, he came out better than if he had hauled his grain to a local elevator. At Port

Cargill grain is augured into cargo barges. After several barges are loaded, they're hooked together and pushed by towboat down the Minnesota and Mississippi Rivers. The barge line boat tows go through approximately 26 locks on the Upper Mississippi River on their way to New Orleans where the grain is loaded onto ships bound for foreign ports. On the return trip up river, the barges dead head or they're loaded with fertilizer or other bulk items.

Trucking grain to terminals at Port Cargill was the beginning of the end of small local elevators. The elevators Dad hauled grain to in Arlington, Gaylord, Blakeley, Cologne, and East Henderson are no longer elevators. The elevator in Blakeley now mixes bird seed. The land where the elevator once stood as the tallest building in Arlington is now a patch of weeds. By the 1990s, Arlington changed from a rural farming community to a retirement and bedroom community. Even though Arlington is surrounded by corn and soybean fields, it doesn't have an implement dealer or a farmer store. Arlington now has Arli-Dazzle—the largest lighted Christmas parade in Minnesota.

Most farmers in Sibley County now own at least one semi, and ship at least some of their grain to Port Cargill in Savage. My brother Pete runs the family farm and 11 other farms that 50 years ago provided each family a living. He owns three semis and hauls grain year-round except in the spring when weight restrictions are posted on certain roads. To prevent damage to roads when the frost is coming out the state limits the weight of trucks. Like other farmers in the area, in addition to hauling grain to Port Cargill he has two local markets, the chicken barns in Gaylord, and local ethanol plants. He also hauls grain to regional elevators in Brownton, New Ulm, and Buffalo Lake, where the grain is loaded onto unit trains bound for west coast ports.

Cargill

Cargill is a privately-owned company with its headquarters in Wayzata, Minnesota. Cargill's main business is food production and is by far the largest in the country. Cargill touches almost everyone's daily life. It sells eggs in liquid form to McDonald's, slaughters more cattle than anyone in the U.S., and if you eat candy, pretzels, soup from a can, ice cream, yogurt, anything salted, sweetened, preserved, fortified, emulsified, texturized, chew gum or drink beer, chances are it includes an ingredient from Cargill.

Cargill is worldwide; it operates nearly 1,000 river barges and charters 350 ocean-going vessels that call on some 6,000 ports, making it one of the world's biggest bulk shippers of commodities. Its ships will pick up a load of soybeans at its deep-water Amazon port in Santarém, Brazil and unload it in Shanghai, then take a load of coal from Australia to Japan before cleaning out and returning to Brazil for more soybeans. Cargill takes grain and just about any other commodity from places of supply to places of need.[26]

Bernie Quinn

Starting in the late 1970s, I noticed the small family farmers in Jessenland were retiring and selling or renting their farms to a few young men who were running more and more land. Modern farm machinery allows a single farmer, with help during planting and harvest, to run a couple thousand acres. As they say, modern farmers don't covet thy neighbor's wife, they covet thy neighbor's farm. When our neighbor Bernie Quinn sold his farm, he told a salesman he was moving to Henderson. The salesman told him, "When you move to town you can catch up on all the gossip." Bernie responded, "It's better for your mind and soul if you don't hear gossip."

Pat Quinn

Our neighbor and friend of the family, Pat Quinn, had a hearty appetite for chocolates. After his wife removed all boxes of chocolates from their house, Pat went to town and bought more chocolates and hid them in the garage. Pat told me, "It's a good thing I don't have the same appetite for whiskey as I have for chocolates."

When Pat saw the doctor in Arlington, the doctor gave him hell for eating too many chocolates and wrote him a prescription. Pat went to the drugstore and while he was waiting for the pill mixer to fill a bottle, he bought a box of Fanny Farmer chocolates. As he was putting chocolates down the hatch, the doctor walked in and in front of everyone he lit into Pat. Years later when Pat told me the story, he would end by saying, "I've already outlived that son-of-a-bitch by ten years."

Pat told me another story on himself. On a Friday afternoon he went to a city-owned bar in Arlington called the "Muni" or "Snake Pit." After Prohibition, Arlington formed a municipal liquor store to control the liquor business and to use the profits for other city services.[27] Pat bought a couple of rounds of "liquid candy" and others had the bartender set up drinks for Pat—back then beer was 20 cents a glass. When Pat was ready to leave, the realtor and the auctioneer who recently sold his farm and machinery strolled in. They each had the bartender set up a drink for Pat. Not used to drinking, Pat needed help getting up the "Snake Pit" stairs. When he got to the top of the stairs he sat down, wiped his face with a red hanky, and assured everyone if he could find his car he could drive home. When Pat was a mile from his farm he saw his neighbor's pickup truck and wondered why the neighbor was driving in the ditch.

When Pat got to his farmyard he pumped a bucket of water to splash on his face. His wife came out of the house, shook a finger at him and said, "Most men wash their face before they go to town." Pat responded, "Don't start on me woman—twice in all these years."

Edmond Fitzgerald

In November 1975, I read about the SS Edmund Fitzgerald steaming out of Superior, Wisconsin and heading for Detroit with 26,000 tons of taconite pellets. Taconite ore provides the steel to build and defend our magnificent country. He was tailed by the SS Arthur M. Anderson that departed Two Harbors, Minnesota laded with taconite pellets for Gary, Indiana. The Fitz and the Anderson ran into a monster storm, the kind that only occurs on Lake Superior once or twice in a decade.[28] Captain Ernest McSorley radioed the Anderson's skipper to say the Fitzgerald was listing, its rail was gone, there was damage to vents, the radars were out, the pumps couldn't keep up, and the mighty ship was sinking. The seasoned old man's gritty run for Whitefish Bay came up short.[29]

As Gordon Lightfoot's song "The Wreck of the Edmund Fitzgerald" goes, the old cook told the crew, "Fellas, it's been good t'know ya." The Titanic of the Great Lakes broke in two and sank in the "ice-water mansion" of Lake Superior. All 29 souls perished; their bodies were never found.[30] Every November tenth, at the Split Rock Lighthouse on the north shore of Lake Superior, there is a memorial for those who went down in the wreck of the Edmund Fitzgerald.[31]

Super Bowl Blizzard

In January 1975 the storm known as the Super Bowl Blizzard hit the Upper Midwest. Just as visibility neared whiteout conditions, I busted through a few drifts with the help of studded snow tires on the '68 Nova to make it to the farmyard. The blizzard caused some of the lowest barometer pressures on record. Mom had the kitchen cabinets and deep freezer full of goodies. We had an ample supply of heating oil as Dad recently installed a second tank in the basement. We played cards and board games. In the evenings Mom popped white popcorn that we munched down with pop.

When the electricity went out, Dad and I carried in the standby generator; it was mostly needed to run the furnace. For ventilation we set it up in the outside entrance to the basement. The generator ran until electricity was restored. If the generator quit, we would have fired up the wood furnace Dad purchased during the Cuban missile crisis.

The blizzard lasted four days and it took us five days to dig out. Thanks to Mom and Dad's good planning, we got through the blizzard without a problem. The blizzard claimed the lives of 58 people in the Midwest, and in the Southeast, tornados took 12 lives.[32]

Alan Page

During the blizzard, Dad and I watched the Steel Curtain of the Pittsburgh Steelers beat the Purple People Eaters of the Vikings on our black and white antenna TV in the den. Super Bowl IX was played at Tulane Stadium in the Big Easy. The Purple People Eaters were led by defensive tackle Alan Page. In 1971 he was the first of only two defensive players to be league MVP. When my sister, Ann, worked at an orthopedic surgeon's office in the Twin Cities, Alan Page came in for an appointment. Ann handed him a client information sheet for him to fill out. He wrote "Alan Page" on top of the sheet and handed it back to her.[33]

After retiring from football, in 1992 Alan Page was the first African-American elected to the Minnesota State Supreme Court. In 1998 he was reelected earning the distinction of the biggest vote-getter in Minnesota history. He was also reelected in 2004 and 2010.[34]

Paige and his wife have a collection of slavery, Ku Klux Klan, Jim Crow, and African-American memorabilia. They have an Abraham Lincoln linen funeral banner that greeted the slain president's funeral train. One side of the banner reads: "Our Country Shall Be One Country!" and the other side: "Uncle Abe We Will Not Forget You!" Their collection also includes a slave branding iron, a slave collar, a 1964 poster that says, "Notice! Stop Help Save the Youth of American Don't Buy Negro Records" and a White House brick made by slaves.[35]

Leo Thorsness

In 1967, Leo Thorsness, a farm boy from Walnut Grove, Minnesota that drains into the upper Minnesota River, was flying his F-105 on a mission over North Vietnam when his Wild Weasel was hit by an air-to-air missile from a MiG. Ejecting at 690 miles-per-hour caused serious damage to his knees. As he parachuted to the ground, the enemy shot at him. The Air Force officer was captured and taken prisoner.[36] Thorsness' back was broken and his knees got worse from being tortured.[37]

Tortured by Cubans working for the Viet Cong, some servicemen's minds stopped working, they no longer felt pain and died. Others were tortured so hard and so long they withered away and died.[38] Thanks to his iron constitution, Thorsness, barely able to hobble around, endured almost six years of torture in North Vietnam prisons, some of them in the "Hanoi Hilton." Prisoners were fed rice with pebbles to crack and cause abscesses to their teeth. While in prison, Thorsness received the Congressional Medal of Honor for his heroics in a dogfight that occurred less than two weeks before he was shot down.[39]

Hanoi Jane was on top of the prisoners' list of people they would never talk to.[40] In the summer of 1972 Hanoi Jane slapped all GIs and their families in the face when she traveled to North Vietnam to willingly have her picture taken on a North Vietnamese anti-aircraft gun used to shoot down American planes. In the picture she is surrounded by men whose goal was to kill American servicemen.[41] Patriotic men enjoy peeing on Hanoi Jane's face on stickers in bathroom urinals.

Early in 1973 the guards opened the cells and the POWs gathered outside. The prison camp commander told the POWs, "The war is over."[42] In March 1973, Thorsness, who had a high temperature, along with fellow POWs boarded a C-141. He was given a cold beer and left hell for Clark Air Force Base in the Philippines.[43] Since his release from prison Thorsness wrote: "I've never had a really bad day."[44] Thorsness came home to an ungrateful nation.

The war wasn't really over. The Paris Peace Accords provided for the release of the POWs and a cease fire that was violated at will. With no more support from the U.S., in the spring of 1975, South Vietnam surrendered to North Vietnam. After almost 20 years, the war in Vietnam finally ended in April 1975.[45] No thanks to the politicians the Vietnam War was a huge disgrace for the U.S. Over 58,000 young Americans were killed. Those that came home were disgraced out of their uniforms, spit on and called baby killers. They were ridiculed by fellow citizens. The war itself and the treatment the vets received when they came home led to homelessness, drug addiction, and a high rate of suicide.

Baseball

Starting in the early 1970s, I often rode my minibike to the outskirts of Arlington for baseball practice, games, and to hang out with friends. I'd hide the minibike in tall weeds and walk to town on the railroad tracks. One time I was walking on the trestle over High Island Creek when a train came barreling down the tracks. I sat on the end of a railroad tie with my feet dangling over the end as the train whistled by behind me.

After a baseball game in Arlington, rather than walk home, I put a dime in a payphone in a booth and called Grandpa Alo to see if he could pick me up. We drove to the Supervalu store and he had me run in to get a treat. I returned with Bazooka bubble gum. Grandpa got a funny look on his face and said, "Go back in and get us something good." I returned with a six-package of Hostess snowballs and two cans of room temperature orange Fanta pop. On the ride home we washed the snowballs down and Grandpa told me, "There's not a chimney big enough to take the smoke of two women."

On nice summer evenings, Grandpa Alo, the Weber kids, and the neighbors had fun throwing shoes, and playing ante over and kitten ball. Grandpa Alo told stories about Ty Cobb, Babe Ruth, Charles Bender, and Jackie Robinson. In 1947, while playing for the Brooklyn Dodgers, Robinson became the first African-American in the modern era to cross the "color line" in the big leagues.[46] His number, 42, is the only major league number permanently retired.

In 1953, Charles Bender was the first Minnesotan elected to the baseball Hall of Fame in Cooperstown, New York. He was an Ojibwe Indian born on the White Earth Reservation in northern Minnesota. The "Chief" is credited for inventing the slider; it helped him win 212 games in the big leagues. When he pitched, he put up with Indian chants. He pitched for the Philadelphia Athletics and the Chicago White Socks.[47] After the players strike in 1972, Grandpa Alo lost interest in major league baseball. He said the game was too much about money.

In 1974, President Nixon, in order to conserve oil, signed a bill lowering the speed limit nationwide to 55 miles per hour. After the change, I was on my way to a baseball game when a highway bull pulled me over and wrote me a ticket for going the old speed limit of 65. Dad was none too happy he had to go to court with me in Gaylord. His disposition improved when he found a "Jackson" on the courtroom floor.

Like Grandpa Alo, I was the baseball team's pitcher. In my senior year in high school, I rode with a friend to Gaylord for a playoff game. We sat in his car and drained a 12-pack of Oly as a pelting rain soaked the ballfield. The sky cleared and the ground crew from Gaylord poured gasoline on the infield and set it on fire. An hour later the umpire yelled, "Play ball!" I pitched the Arlington-Green Isle Indians to a 2-0 victory over arch rival Gaylord. After the game Dad said to me, "That's the loosest I've ever seen you play."

A few games later I pitched our team into the high school state tournament with a complete game shutout over rival Glencoe. Player for player Glencoe was a better team, but that night the "Indians" from Arlington-Green Isle were better, thanks to my fast ball tailing in on right-handed batters, sound defense, and a couple of timely hits. Our ragtag team had three players from the small village of Green Isle and two farm boys from obscure Jessenland. In the state tourney we lost the first game to Sleepy Eye in a thriller.

After high school football and baseball games, my siblings and I threw a few parties in the cow pasture next to Silver Lake. We gathered around a bonfire and drank keg beer. We listened to the rock and roll music of Bob Dylan from Hibbing, Minnesota and of other rockers from our car speakers.

Arlington and Green Isle are both baseball towns. To recognize its baseball tradition the water tower in Arlington is painted like a baseball, complete with seams and stitches. The Arlington A's town team has five Minnesota State Amateur Championships under its belt. The Irish from Green Isle have one state championship.

I played town team baseball for the Green Isle Irish led by the big stick of Joe Kreger. Our player-manager harped on us not to drink the night before a Sunday afternoon game. At a game in Plato our player-manager showed up with a bell ringer. A few times between innings we tee-heed when he upchucked behind the dugout. After the sixth inning he took himself out of the game. We had a comfortable lead, thanks to his three home runs.

After I pitched a game against Winstead, I drove the tail happy Nova to New Brighton to see my girlfriend. On the way home, my eyelids got heavy and I pulled into a filling station to nap in the Nova. Seeing flashing cherries in the rearview mirror, I woke up from sleep driving and pulled in the rubbard (shoulder). Not having any road beers, I walked a straight line and the county mountie let me go. I drove a couple of miles before I realized I was driving the wrong direction. I veered onto the gravel shoulder, made a high-speed drifting turn and was wide awake for the drive home.

Arlington-Green Isle School

When I was in school in Arlington the teachers had a lounge where they smoked. In junior high as I stood in line waiting for the gym teacher to unlock the door to the locker room, I snapped my buddy with a rubber band. The gym teacher's right fist connected with my jaw, bouncing my head off the wall. My school didn't give timeouts. On the last days of each school year my buddies and I had fun shooting each other with squirt guns. We tried to surprise each other with shots to the face.

In high school during lunch some of my classmates walked to Stu's or Burke's beer joint for a hamburger and a cigarette. In the back room old-timers played *Schafkopf* cards where there was at least one kibitzer. Since the drinking age at the time in Minnesota was 18, some high school seniors legally poured down a couple of 3.2 Grainbelts before returning to class. Tom Burke ran his ten-cent joint for 71 years.[48]

Club New Yorker

The Club New Yorker in Green Isle featured the Irish Dutchman band and it was well known for hosting snowmobile parties. While I was in high school, one night a week the New Yorker laid a sheet of plywood on a pool table for strippers to dance on. It was a popular hang-out for local politicians.

In 1980, Green Isle had its largest voter turnout in its history—the ballot box overwhelmingly said, "No-no to the go-go." After the vote, one of the Club New Yorker's owners said, "I don't know what all the fuss is about. The girls usually aren't even that good looking."[49] After the vote, the Club New Yorker sold T-shirts that read, "Green Isle—the city with no pity on the titty."[50] The New Yorker won an injunction to keep dollar bills in the girls' G-strings. In the 1990s interest in erotic dancing waned and the Club New Yorker threw away its scuffed-up piece of plywood.[51]

Thomas Bros. Hardware

In 1975, Dad purchased a new International, model 1066, from Thomas Bros. Hardware in Arlington, the first tractor on the farm with duals and a cab. Thomas Bros. is the oldest continuous family-owned hardware store in Minnesota.[52]

On a nice spring day, Dad, being a road farmer, was on the road driving the 1066, pulling a wide disk to the fields west of Arlington when he came to a portion of the road with guide posts on the right shoulder causing him to cross over the centerline. The semi truck behind Dad couldn't pass. When the guide posts ended, Dad moved over and the semi passed. The driver went a half mile down the road and parked the semi crossways blocking the road. He jumped out of the cab. Dad throttled down the 1066 and came to a stop. Dad stepped off and pulled a two-foot steel rod from the toolbox. With the rod clutched in his right hand he headed toward the trucker. The trucker took a hard look, climbed back in his rig and started shifting.

Yellow Mustache

In his mid-'80s, Grandpa Alo slowed to working seven to eight hours a day in the fields during planting and at the harvest. During seeding, Dad sprayed the field with herbicide and Grandpa followed close behind with the 1066 disking the weed killer into the soil. The herbicide made his lips and teeth yellow. On a day so humid it felt like a *schwitz*, I took a break from planting bin-run soybeans–soybeans from a grain bin rather than from a seed company, and relieved Grandpa for a couple of hours. The spray turned my mustache yellow. When I got off the 1066, I told Grandpa the rough field had me bouncing all around. Grandpa said, "You never spent all day walking behind a one bottom plow pulled by a team of plugs." At dusk we shut the tractors down and left the field in a late model Chevy Suburban with the air conditioner blowing. On the way home Grandpa said, "It's cooling off nice this evening."

Beach Boys

In 1976 Jimmy Carter defeated Gerald Ford for what would turn out to be a one-term presidency. Carter said,

"Whatever starts in California unfortunately has an inclination to spread." That same year at my high school graduation party, Dad gave me a suitcase with wheels. That summer my cool cat friend, Scott "Bert" Herman, and I loaded up a couple of "spring chickens" wearing hip huggers in my '68 Nova with a bench seat. We motored to Metropolitan Stadium in Bloomington, Minnesota. The concert started off with Frisbees flung into the crowd from the top of the stadium. We listened to Boz Scaggs, Tower of Power, Todd Rundgren, Utopia, and the "California Sound" of the Beach Boys. The deck where we sat bounced a few inches to the beat of the music. On the way home, we listened to Journey on the eight-track tape player I jury-rigged to the bottom of the dashboard.

Watershed Board

In January 1977, peanut farmer Jimmy "Gritz" Carter was sworn in as President with Minnesota's Walter "Fritz" Mondale as Vice President. On his second day in office Carter pardoned Vietnam War draft dodgers. The pardon wiped clean the criminal slate of those who defied their country's call to duty.[53] To look like the common man when the cameras were rolling, President Carter carried his own luggage. When the press wasn't around, he had secret service agents carry it.[54]

Also in 1977, Dad was on the Sibley County Watershed Board when a drainage dispute went to trial in the courthouse in Gaylord. An old farmer took the witness stand. An attorney asked him the width of a drainage ditch. The farmer replied, "That ditch is so narrow I can pee across it." The Judge scowled and rapped his gavel on the bench saying, "You're out of order." The old hayseed replied, "I know I'm out of order and I can still pee across that ditch." The judge called a recess.[55]

A couple of years after the court hearing in Gaylord, during a dry spring, a fire started a few miles west of Arlington in the dead meadow grass in the High Island Creek and in the flood plain next to the creek. Burning the dead grass off in the

235

spring makes it a lot easier to cut the new growth of meadow grass. The fire burned on Dad's land and on the land of two neighboring farmers. The game warden, a man from the Department of Natural Resources, a few hunters and the two neighboring farmers were all watching the blaze when Dad pulled up. He had been planting peas in a field a mile down the road. The brother of one of the farmers, Augie Mueller, who rode in on his old Ford tractor, was also there. The game warden, the man from the DNR and the hunters were upset that the fire was destroying wildlife habitat. They were asking who set the fire. No one knew. They said they'd be at the next watershed board meeting demanding to know who set the fire.

At the next watershed meeting, the neighboring farmers whose dead grass burned off weren't in attendance, but their attorney from New Ulm was in the crowd. The chairman called the meeting to order. When the High Island Creek came up on the agenda, the crowd demanded to know who set the fire. Dad, who was on the board, said he wasn't at the scene of the fire when it started, but a neighbor had seen a couple of cars stopped at the bridge over the creek, so he got on his Ford tractor and drove to the bridge to see what was going on. As everyone knows, on those old Fords the exhaust pipe comes off the manifold and runs down below the back axle. The hot exhaust pipe probably rubbed on the dry grass starting the fire. A few in the crowd mumbled and the chairman called the next item on the agenda. After the meeting, the attorney from New Ulm raced up to Dad and said, "Weber, that was pure Irish blarney, Irish blarney, and I tell you Weber, they believed every word of it."[56]

American Agriculture Movement

The American Agriculture Movement (AAM) was formed by farmers in 1977 to increase commodity prices and to save family farms. Dad followed their activities closely. Politicians in Washington, D.C. considered farmers an annoyance. A congressman from California, the largest agricultural state in the land, told farmers in his office he had no time for them. Apparently the congressman forgot where his food came from.

In March 1978, 30,000 farmers marched down Pennsylvania Avenue in Washington, D.C. As the protesters approached the Capitol, some goats from Missouri broke loose and climbed on the steps and statues of the Capitol. After the farmers left the Capitol, they decided to visit the Department of Agriculture. Hearing farmers were on their way, Department of Agriculture officials locked the doors and the Secretary of Agriculture escaped through a window. The farmers were left to stand in a cold drizzle.

In February 1979 thousands of farmers driving their tractors, including bonanza farmer, Valentine Miller, who farmed the field across Jessenland Road from the Weber farm, converged on Washington, D.C. The event known as Tractorcade angered the bureaucrats. Nineteen farmers were arrested and put in a pen on the Washington Mall.

While the farmers were in Washington, D.C. a storm dumped 20 inches of snow, which paralyzed the city. To keep our capital city running, farmers gave doctors, nurses, firemen, and government officials rides in their tractors. Farmers gave blood. Their wives—some of the best women in the country—cooked and cleaned in hospitals as employees were busy digging out.[57]

Willmar 8

During the late 1970s, women workers at the Citizens National Bank in Willmar, some 35 miles northeast of the Upper Minnesota River Valley, made a whole lot less money than the men employees. The women held mostly clerical jobs, worked overtime without additional pay, and didn't get promoted. The women got their panties in a bunch when they weren't allowed to apply for an officer position and were told to train the newbie hired for the job. When the women complained, the bank president told them, "We're not all equal, you know."[58] Sounds like the treatment women get in Arab countries.

Steamed up, the women wrote out a gender discrimination charge with the Equal Employment Opportunity Commission and an unfair labor complaint with the National Labor Relations Board. Both claims went nowhere fast. The women created Minnesota's first bank union. In December 1977 the women went on the first bank strike in the U.S. On their first day walking the picket line, the wind chill was 70 degrees below zero.[59] Some neighbors ridiculed the strikers. They got lip service from other labor unions and no support from laws that were supposed to help them.[60] The bank put financial pressure on a gas station that let the strikers use its bathrooms.[61]

After almost two years on the picket line without results, the strike was declared a failure. Initially only one of the strikers got hired back, and she was demoted and teased by co-workers.[62] But their efforts were not in vain. The media spread their story throughout the country and two films were made about their plight. Their ordeal significantly advanced the movement for equal pay.[63] Banks and other employers took notice. They gradually increased pay for women and began to promote them. There's still a lot of progress to be made as actresses get paid significantly less than their male counterparts. You would think the powerful and privileged Hollywood actresses would do something about the discrepancy.

Biloxi

During the afternoon of September 19, 1977, before men put fruit in their beer, I threw back a few intoxicating agents with the big boys at Schmidt's Bar in Green Isle. The next day this innocent farm boy from Minnesota shipped out to boot camp at Lackland Air Force Base in Texas. My bobbing up and down while I marched upset the drill sergeant to the point where he ordered the platoon to march in half step a couple of miles. When I told Dad the story, he told me when he was in boot camp the drill sergeant gave him a rock to carry to rid him of his farm boy bounce.

After boot camp Uncle Sam put me on a Greyhound to Keesler Air Force Base in Biloxi, Mississippi. At the time, Biloxi was flowing with drugs and fancy girls. My friend from Wilmington, North Carolina and I went to a seedy dramshop cantilevered over the Gulf of Mexico. While sliding down oysters and swilling a few frosties we noticed a picture on the wall of John, Bobby, and Teddy Kennedy with the caption: "All countries have three stooges, ours have the same last name."

During the holidays Dad loaded up the family and towed the '68 Nova behind his Suburban to Biloxi. I waited for them beneath a Sambo's Restaurant sign. While in New Orleans we toured Jackson Square, and on a Mississippi River tour we heard about the Battle of New Orleans on the Chalmette Battlefield. When my youngest brother, Pete, returned to school, the teacher asked him what he did over Christmas vacation. He told the class he walked down Bourbon Street. The teacher told him not to make up stories.

Minot

A few weeks after the family left Dixie, I received orders to go to the John Moses Hospital in Minot, North Dakota, part of Minot Air Force Base. I slurped down a bowl of grits, and after adjusting the gap on the points and throwing a can of oil in the Nova, I drove up to the farm. I wore my dress blues to Sunday Mass at St. Thomas Church. After communion, Joe Zeiher, a WWI veteran as mild as a pet lamb, stopped and shook my hand while thanking me for my service to our country. After WWI, Joe stayed in the Army to bury dead American soldiers in France.

After installing a new block heater in the Nova's engine, on a January day in 1978, so cold even the politicians in St. Paul had their hands in their own pockets, I drove up to Minot and reported to a buck sergeant for duty. The hospital compound was on 20 acres in the middle of town. It treated military, veterans, and Indians. Air Force formalities were almost non-existent. We had a coed barracks. Our parties were well attended as the

239

drinking age on the hospital compound was 18 and the drinking age in North Dakota was 21. The hospital cantina sold Billy Beer and other necessities. Billy Beer was the brainchild of President Jimmy Carter's brother, Billy. He came up with one of the most profound statements of all time: "Beer is not a good cocktail party drink, especially in a home where you don't know where the bathroom is."

I worked in the hospital's business office where about half the people smoked at their desk. Using carbon paper, I typed reports in duplicate or triplicate on an IBM Selectric II typewriter. Good thing I took typing in high school. I went to Medical Supply to use a machine that punched holes in Hollerith cards. In the office a civil service employee kept track of the hospital's food inventory on 3x5 cards, one card for each food item. During my peacetime stint, the Air Force started "Operation Golden Flow" to test for drugs.

1891 photograph of St. Thomas Catholic
Church, Jessenland Township

Madden log cabin banked with sawdust
to keep the floors warm

241

Weber Farm in 1950's

Weber Farm in 1976. Recognized by Governor, Wendell R. Anderson for continuous agricultural operation since 1858 and making contributions to the community, state, nation, and the world.

Alo Weber watching his grandmother Margaret Weber operate a spinning wheel

Allie and Alo Weber fishing in Highland Creek, Jessenland

Brian Weber taking a load of straw to Canterbury Downs racetrack in Shakopee

Allie Weber feeding orphaned piglets

Geri Weber, pregnant with the author, and her mother Lillie Gildea, 1957

Grandpa Joe Gildea in front of his gardening shed

Oldtimers talking after mass – Bert Berger, Alo Weber, & Swance McCormick

Alo and Anne Weber 1940

Weber kids
Janet, Mary, Brian, and Ann holding Pete
1946 Chevy loaded with sweet corn

Ann and John Weber in front of
sign for access to Silver Lake

Jack Madden with drinking buddies at Farmer's Home Saloon in
Green Isle, Jack is third from the left

245

Jesse and Allie Weber discussing WWII
German Helmets

John Weber, Jesse Weber,
Allie Weber, and Matt Weber

Allie, John, and Geri Weber, with
Larry Tillmans (seated right)
believed to be the last known
participant in the Nuremberg Trials

Melissa Weber
and dad John Weber

Chapter Eleven
Gulf War

"Miracle on Ice"

My Air Force buddy from Alpena, South Dakota asked me to watch his hunting dog while he took his family on vacation. Every day I fed the hound. When my pal returned home he chewed me out for letting his dog get fat. The next summer he asked me to watch his bird dog. I forgot all about the pooch until the evening before he returned home from vacation. I rushed to the hound's kennel and thank God he was breathing. He drank three gallons of water and gulped dog food for 20 minutes. When my friend returned home he said it was good to see his dog's ribs and thanked me for taking the time to exercise his dog. I told him, "It was the easiest job I ever had."

In 1980, Jimmy Carter who was hazed for refusing an upperclassman's command to sing General Sherman's battle hymn "Marching Through Georgia," was President.[1] Also in February 1980, after adjusting the rabbit ears on the TV in the barracks, my Air Force buddies and I gathered to go watch the U.S. hockey team defeat the heavily favored Soviet Union in a nail-biter in the semi-finals of the Winter Olympics in Lake Placid, New York. The victory by our country's young amateurs over the "Big Red Machine" made us wing nuts proud of our

247

miracle country. In the Mediterranean Sea the USS Nimitz flashed the score of the game to a nearby Soviet spy ship.[2]

The underdogs were coached by Herb Brooks from St. Paul. Twelve of his 20 amateur collegiate players were from Minnesota.[3] Star player, Rob McClanahan, from St. Paul, was featured on a Paraguayan postage stamp.[4] The "Miracle on Ice" is considered by most Americans to be the best sports moment of all time. Before the final game against Finland, Coach Brooks told his players, "If you lose this game, you'll take it to your fucking grave."[5] The U.S. skaters put the biscuit in the net more times than the Finns to win Olympic gold.

Hermann the German

In 1980, I watched pig farmer Ron Lieske from Henderson, Minnesota show off his 840-pound white boar to Johnny Carson on the "Tonight Show." That fall, four of my Air Force buddies and I loaded up in an old Ford station wagon for a road trip to the Weber farm. One of them was a woodsman from northern Minnesota. They have a sharp eye you know, they're some of the best hunters and fishermen in the country. Several times on the trip he pointed out wildlife no one else noticed. The next morning we went to New Ulm. While in the most German town in America, we climbed to the top of the Hermann Monument, a statue commemorating Hermann the Cherusci, also known as Hermann the German. In 2000 the U.S. Congress designated it as our national symbol of German heritage. It's the third largest copper statue in the U.S. behind Liberty Enlightening the World (the Statue of Liberty) and Portlandia in Portland, Oregon. In 9 AD, Hermann led a motley army over Roman legions saving Germany from Roman conquest.[6] Later we toured the picturesque Schell Brewery and dined on German fare at the Ratskeller in Turner Hall.

Glockenspiel

In downtown New Ulm my buddies and I watched the revolving figurines on the Glockenspiel. The figurines include a farmer with his wife and son, two polka dancers in traditional German garb, a brewer raising a beer, a worker loading a barrel of beer, a bricklayer, a polka band, and for political correctness, a Dakota Native American. New Ulm relishes its strong German heritage through groups, organizations, festivals, and the greatest German tradition of all—drinking beer.

5th Avenue Club

On Friday evening we went to the Metropolitan Sports Center in Bloomington to watch a fight and a hockey game broke out. The North Stars lit the lamp more times than the Chicago Black Hawks. On Saturday evening we went to the 5th Avenue Club in the "MiniApple" for a few suds and listened to the Minneapolis sound of Prince. While there I shook Jesse "The Body" Ventura's hand. His motto: "Win if you can, lose if you must, but always cheat."[7] After one of my buddies left an airport tip (a small tip because you'll never see the waitress again) we went to the lounge at the Marriot Inn for a few lubricants and chatted with Vikings' and Buccaneers' coaches and players. The barmaids wouldn't talk to us flyboys. Taped to the back bar was a sign: "Notice players—sexual harassment will not be reported at this bar but it will be graded." The next day we watched the Vikings and Bucs toss the pigskin on the gridiron at Met Stadium. Most in the stadium were drinking from flasks. The Vikes even won the game.

Hibernians

In 1980 members of the Ancient Order of Hibernians, a few in full regalia, converged on St. Thomas Church in Jessenland to revive their centuries old organization. The shamrock degree was given to local men to reestablish the Le Sueur County division. The Hibes were founded in Ireland in the 16th century

249

for the preservation of the church and to protect priests from the English. When the Irish immigrated to the U.S. the Hibernians protected the clergy from bigotry. The Hibes are now genealogists. They work to preserve Irish history (storytelling) and Irish culture (drinking). When the Hibernians asked me to be a member, I borrowed a line from Groucho Marx and said, "I don't care to belong to any club that will have me as a member."

San Lucas Tolimán, Guatemala

During the summer of 1980 the Air Force gave me time off without leave to go with a group of youths, including my sister Mary, to a mission in San Lucas Tolimán, Guatemala. The New Ulm diocese runs the mission along with a church and school; it assists with food, shelter, and health care. In San Lucas Tolimán most people live in corn stalk huts, sleep on the ground, and eat ground corn and beans. The economy is centered around coffee. On a day trip the mission's bus pulled into the city of Antigua. When the bus stopped it was surrounded by soldiers with guns drawn. After a missionary priest had a brief discussion with the leader the soldiers moved on.

Oil of Chrism

In the New Ulm Diocese holy oils to anoint the sick and those being baptized and confirmed are blessed by the bishop at the annual Chrism Mass. The oil of chrism is distributed to the parishes in the Diocese. Usually the special Mass is held at the Cathedral Church in New Ulm. In April 1982, for the first time, the Chrism Mass was held at St. Joseph's Church in Montevideo, in the Upper Minnesota River Valley. The town is named after Montevideo, Uruguay.[8]

Metrodome

In 1982, President Ronald Reagan's economic policies known as Reaganomics brought the economy out of a ten-year funk and into a long period of prosperity. You had to put on sunglasses to look at the "shining city on the hill." Also in 1982 the Minnesota Twins and Vikings said good riddance to Metropolitan Stadium in Bloomington and started playing on carpet in the Metrodome in Minneapolis. It's the only sports facility to host a Super Bowl, a major league baseball All-Star game, the World Series, and the NCAA Final Four.

In 2012, on the way to a game with my sons Matt and Jesse, we stopped at Matt's Tavern in south Minneapolis. In 2014, President Obama stopped there for a burger.[9] We each put down a Jucy Lucy, a hamburger with melted cheese in the middle. After the Twins won the game, we ran the bases at the Metrodome—a stadium that's hosted some of the greatest games and moments in sports. In 2014, the Metrodome was demolished to build U.S. Bank Stadium. It's built in the shape of a Viking ship.

Mall of America

The Mall of America is built on the site of the old Metropolitan Stadium in Bloomington on the north bank of the Lower Minnesota River Valley. Home plate is embedded in the floor of the indoor amusement park. The Mall of America is the largest shopping center in the country. It has more visitors per year than Disney World, the Grand Canyon, and Graceland combined.[10] It's a great place to go when the winds of winter are howling.

Henderson Sells Potholes

In 1983, Ronald Reagan occupied the White House. He enjoyed watching "Little House on the Prairie."[11] President Reagan didn't want anyone to know he wrote personal checks to people who wrote him hard-luck letters. He said he was once poor.[12] In the same year, Henderson, Minnesota, home of Sauerkraut Days, received national publicity for selling potholes in its streets. For ten dollars, a cavity was filled in and the buyer received a Certificate of Ownership stating where his patched-up pothole was located. The chuckholes were sold throughout the U.S. and one was sold in Germany.[13]

Prince

In 1984, Ronald Reagan, who said, "I've noticed that everyone who is for abortion has already been born," carried 49 states to win his second term as President. He beat Walter Mondale in a landslide, losing only to Mondale's home state of Minnesota. Mondale's running mate was Geraldine Ferraro, the first woman to run for vice president. When the "Gipper" was asked what he wanted for Christmas, he jokingly said, "Minnesota would have been nice." Also in 1984, for his movie *Purple Rain*, Prince filmed a scene two miles east of Henderson. In the scene, actress Apollonia Kotero jumped into the chilly backwater of the Minnesota River.

The multi-talented Prince was born and raised in Minneapolis and he made his home at his Paisley Park estate on a tributary of the Minnesota River in Chanhassen. He was a singer-songwriter, musician, actor, and film director. He had some of the biggest selling records of all time, received numerous awards, and at Super Bowl XLI he put on one of the best half-time performances of all time. He was a vegan and donated to good causes. In 2001 he became a Jehovah's Witness. The nasty lyrics in his song "Darling Nikki" led to Parental Advisory stickers on CDs.[14] Despite being a superstar, he was always a Minnesotan. In 2016, at age 57, Prince departed this life from an overdose of an opioid painkiller. President Obama said of Prince, "Nobody's spirit was stronger, bolder, or more creative."

Garrison Keillor

In 1987, silver-tongued Irishman, President Reagan, during a speech at the Berlin Wall, told the leader of the Soviet Union, "Mr. Gorbachev, tear down this wall!" According to Secret Service agents, Reagan didn't show any symptoms of Alzheimer's during his two terms as president.[15] Also in 1987, I read *Lake Wobegon Days* by Garrison Keillor. His spot on observations of life in the Gopher State made him a great storyteller and humorist. He hosted *A Prairie Home Companion,* a long-running Saturday evening live radio program. Performers on the program included the Powdermilk Biscuit Band and the singing Rhubarb Sisters. In 2017, Minnesota Public Radio canned Keillor for sexual harassment on the job.

Minnesota Twins

To commemorate the 125th anniversary of the Sioux Uprising, Minnesota's governor declared 1987 to be a Year of Reconciliation.[16] It was about time. Also in 1987 the Minnesota Twins squared off against the St. Louis Cardinals in the World Series. On the morning of game seven of the World Series, the Twins' first baseman, Kent Hrbek, born and raised in Bloomington, Minnesota, and a buddy drove to a slough near Litchfield, Minnesota and hunted bluebill ducks.[17] By golly, it doesn't get more Minnesotan than that. A few years earlier a player was cleaning fish in the trainer's room. That caused the manager to ban fish in the clubhouse.[18]

Trailing two to one in game seven of the World Series, during the fifth inning break the public address announcer at the Metrodome went to the restroom. A Twins' player held the door shut and another player put shaving cream in the announcer's earpiece and soaked his towel in shaving cream. When the announcer returned to the booth he got shaving cream in his ear. He grabbed the towel to wipe off his ear and got shaving cream all over his suit. The Twins won the game four to two to win the World Series.[19]

In 1991 the fall classic featured the Twins and the Atlanta Braves. In game seven of the World Series, St. Paul native, Jack Morris, tossed nine innings of shut-out ball. The Twins were also held scoreless. After the ninth inning, Manager Tom Kelly told Morris his night was over. Morris refused to leave the game and walked back to the mound. Kelly told the pitching coach, "What the heck, it's just a game."[20] Morris had a three-up three-down tenth inning. The Twins scored in the bottom of the tenth to win the World Series. Hanoi Jane was in the stands at the Metrodome, cheering on the Braves by swinging her arm up and down doing the tomahawk chop. Morris was game to the backbone turning in one of the gutsiest pitching performances of all time.

Game seven of the series had my favorite play of all time. In the eighth inning Atlanta's Lonnie Smith was on first base and with the hit and run on, the batter ripped a double into the left center gap. The fleet-footed Smith normally would have scored, but he held up at third base because shortstop Greg Cagne and rookie second baseman Chuck Knoblauch faked the start of a double play pretending to force Smith out at second base. Smith took the decoy and paused. The hesitation caused Smith to lose several strides and prevented him from scoring—most likely costing Atlanta the World Series.

Allie Weber in the Washington Post

On September 7, 1987, Dad made the front page of the Washington Post. The article discussed Vatican II, the priest shortage, and new roles for lay persons in the Catholic Church. The article called Dad a "corn farmer." A picture on page ten shows Dad walking down the Weber farm driveway with Sister JoAnne Backes. Dad is quoted as saying "Why shouldn't she be ordained?"

Alo Weber Dies

At age 88, Grandpa Alo missed a step at St. Thomas Church and did a somersault down the concrete steps, putting a gash in his forehead. On the ride back to the farm Grandpa said his legs were "playing out." My sister, Mary, suggested a cane for his tottering; he wouldn't have it. The misstep didn't keep him from his 40-year tradition of eating Sunday broasted chicken dinner with his cousins, Ralph and Mildred Kreger, at the Hillcrest Café located between Hamburg (home to a classic tinman water tower) and Norwood Young America. Suffering from hardening of the arteries, Grandpa Alo went to the undertaker's holding tank, and over the next couple of years the Good Samaritan nursing home in Arlington relieved Grandpa of his life savings.

In 1988 the pride of New Ulm, Minnesota catcher Terry Steinbach, was named most valuable player of the All-Star game and on a Sunday afternoon that summer, Dad and I went to Arlington to see Grandpa in the nursing home. After visiting Grandpa, we called on a few blue hairs, including Dad's friend's mother, Kate. When we walked in her room, Kate asked Dad, "Where's your wife?" Dad said she was working in the kitchen at the nursing home in Waconia. Kate said, "It's too bad people work on Sunday, it should be a day of rest." Dad told Kate, "Someone's got to feed you old beezers."

In August 1988 former WWII navy fighter pilot President George H. W. Bush said, "Read my lips: no new taxes." As President he raised taxes, leading to his title as a one-term president. In October 1988, one month shy of 93, Grandpa Alo's soul left for the waist-high grass of the green pastures of the great beyond. He worked the farm's fields for 80 years. In his lifetime he went from traveling a few miles per hour on a buckboard pulled by a team of horses to going over 500 miles per hour in a jet plane to visit his brother Edward in St. Louis. On a splendid autumn day with leaves in full color, Grandpa Alo took his last ride through his beloved Jessenland past the Weber farm and Silver Lake and down the church hill into the Minnesota River Valley. At his funeral my sister, Janet, read: "A Tribute to Our Grandfather." The tribute concluded with these words:

"Spring was always a special time with Grandpa, he liked being in the fields the best. Every year for almost ten years we thought would be Grandpa's last year in the fields, but Spring brought new life to Grandpa and in the fields he was.

Many fun times were shared with Grandpa— playing cards and baseball, gathering butternuts, walking along the shore of Silver Lake. He shared his patience and kind ways with us that made him a great and loveable Grandpa.

As could be seen in Grandpa's smile and peaceful ways he shared his contentment. Content to be Grandpa Weber, the farmer, from Jessenland.

Faith, prayer and generosity were a natural part of Grandpa's life. He valued this dear church and community. He told us the Lord had been good to him."

There wasn't a dry eye in church. Grandpa Alo was laid to eternal rest next to his wife, Anne, in the cemetery behind St. Thomas Church.

Jessenland Project

In 1990 the Jessenland Project culminated with the Irish Genealogical Society from St. Paul publishing three books. One covers the civil records of Jessenland and Faxon Townships, another covers the marriage records of St. Thomas Church, and the third has gravestone transcriptions and burial records. A year later, thanks to Sister JoAnne Backes, St. Thomas Church, parsonage, and cemetery were entered on the National Registry of Historic Places. The church represents what is believed to be the earliest Irish agrarian community in Minnesota.[21]

Peter Anderly

In 1990, Iraq was angry at Kuwait for overproducing oil. Iraq invaded Kuwait and claimed its land. The United Nations authorized a coalition force led by the U.S. to put down the invasion. In seven months the Gulf War, code name Operation Desert Storm, drove the Iraqis from Kuwait. Jessenland leatherneck Peter Anderly's unit was on the march to liberate Kuwait City. Peter's biggest fear was that Saddam Hussein would unleash chemical weapons. On the second day of the march, smoke from burning oil fields was so thick Peter couldn't see his hand in front of his face.[22]

St. Paul Saints

In January 1993, draft dodger and tireless gomer bull, Bill Clinton was sworn in as commander in chief and the St. Paul Saints baseball team was resurrected. The Saints play in the American Association of Independent Professional Baseball—not affiliated with the big leagues. The Saints have a tradition of a feeder pig bringing baseballs to the umpire in return for a snack. One season the pig's name was Kim Lardashian. In 1996 Saints players included Darryl Strawberry, Jack Morris and Dave Stevens. Prior to playing a season with the Saints, Dave Stevens attended Augsburg College in Minneapolis where he lettered in football and baseball. Stevens was born without legs. He runs with his hands.[23]

Minneapolis Police

In 1993, two Minneapolis police officers rolled up on a couple of Indians sleeping off a drunk. The subject officers cancelled the call for an ambulance, and cuffed and dragged the Indians into the trunk of their squad car. The officer behind the wheel drove erratically to the hospital, causing injuries to the Indians trapped in the trunk. To pay for the police brutality, "Mill City" paid each Indian $100,000.[24] For the love of Pete. Fortunately, cell phone video cameras are reining in police brutality and unwarranted shootings. Some officers would have fewer problems if they treated people with respect.

Brian Weber

In 1993 at St. Thomas Church in Jessenland, my brother Brian took the leap and married Bonnie Oakes from Aberdeen, South Dakota. Bonnie was surprised that Brian usually had the TV on the weather channel. Brian knew the weather everywhere

257

in the world where corn and soybeans grow. Plans to till the soil, spray, plant, harvest, and cut hay are all based on the weather forecast. Marketing is probably the most challenging and stressful part of modern farming. A good marketing strategy is to listen to the experts on the farm channel and do the exact opposite of what they advise. Government programs and crop insurance are important, too. By the 1990s the small family farm became a thing of the past.

Brian liked to raise, butcher, and eat rabbits and pheasants. He also hunted white tail deer, pheasants, geese, and puddle ducks on the swamps and fields surrounding Silver Lake. A couple of times Brian and his hunting buddies went to the Lac qui Parle refuge near Watson in the Upper Minnesota River Valley. During the fall migration, Canadian geese rest and feed at Lac qui Parle. In the fall as many as 150,000 honkers flock to the refuge area—makes for good shooting.

In 1994, President Bill Clinton, he had a romp in the White House with former Vice President Walter Mondale's daughter Eleanor "the wild child," said the era of big government is over.[25] Eight years later President Barack Obama proved him wrong. Also in 1994 on a 20-below-zero evening, my brothers Brian and Pete loaded up two steers in a trailer and hauled them to Ruck's Meat Processing in Belle Plaine for butchering the next morning. After two hours of battling to unload the big steer that weighed 1,800 pounds, he got exhausted and down he went. There was no getting him up. Brian and Pete were afraid the steamed-up steer would get pneumonia and die. They hauled him to my brother-in-law Steve's heated shop in Arlington where the butcher loaded his rifle. The butcher shot the steer in the trailer. They fastened a chain to each hind leg and with a Bobcat, dragged the steer out of the trailer and strung him up from the loader on the Bobcat. While cutting meat the butcher ran a finger into the band saw, even with blood squirting into the meat, he continued to saw. He wouldn't take the time to get stitches or wrap the wound. By 4:00 in the morning the steer was butchered. Cold storage wasn't a problem.

Corn is King

In our country of plenty, corn is the largest crop by volume and value. A bushel of corn produces almost three gallons of clean burning ethanol, it doesn't pollute the water, it improves engine performance, and it's a renewable resource. The byproduct, called distiller's grain, provides high-protein livestock feed. Fructose in corn syrup is the same sugar found in fruit. It's used to sweeten cereal, snacks, and soda. There are over 3,500 uses for corn, including mash for bourbon.[26]

Olivia, Minnesota, is located some 15 miles north of the Lower Minnesota River Valley and located on the original Yellowstone Trail that ran from Plymouth Rock to the Puget Sound. The Minnesota Senate designated it the Corn Capital of the World. Olivia is home to a 50-foot monument in the shape of an ear of corn. It also has the world's largest seed corn broker and nine experimental seed centers.[27] They do their part to feed the world as corn yields have roughly doubled in the last 25 years. While in high school, I wore my bell-bottoms and a green bead necklace to Corn Capital Days in Olivia.

Pheasants Forever

In 1996, President Clinton's economic policies known as Clintonomics had the economy purring like a new John Deere combine at full throttle taking out 200-bushel-to-the-acre corn. Also in 1996, at a Pheasants Forever banquet at the ballroom in Gibbon, Minnesota, Mom and Dad received a plaque recognizing their outstanding support for the preservation of wildlife habitat in Sibley County. Dad put 40 acres of marginal cropland in a Reinvest in Minnesota (RIM) program for wildlife habitat. He had to plant a portion of the 40 acres in Nebraska switchgrass to provide cover for ground nesting birds. After he sold his herd of Herefords, instead of clearing two pastures for crops, he put the pastures in conservation easements for deer, pheasants, wild turkeys, wood ducks, doves, and other wildlife. The local chapter of Pheasants Forever raises money for preserving wildlife habitat and to provide winter feeding by raffling off shotguns and rifles.

Jesse Ventura

In the election for governor of Minnesota in 1998, Dad voted for Jesse Ventura, who'd asked retired Twins slugger Kent Hrbeck to run as his Lieutenant Governor.[28] Mom voted for Skip Humphrey, son of Hubert Humphrey. After pulling off an upset for the ages, Governor Ventura got his own action figure doll. On the David Letterman show, when referring to the crooked streets in St. Paul, Ventura said "Whoever designed the streets must have been drunk...I think it was those Irish guys. You know what they like to do."[29]

Monster Wedge

In April 1998, a gang of Webers loaded up to see the damage in St. Peter, Minnesota caused by a monster wedge–a tornado that spins horizontally. It was a mile and a quarter wide. It tore up St. Peter and pretty much everything else in its 18-mile path of destruction. Debris from St. Peter was found 80 miles away in Hudson, Wisconsin. One lady went back to where her house once stood and found two bottles of wine. The bottles were intact with the corks in place, but the wine was missing. The Gustavus Adolphus College campus in St. Peter was heavily damaged, including 2,000 downed trees.[30] After touring the devastation, we downed a burger and a pint at Patrick's on 3rd in St. Peter.

Pete Weber

In 1991 on a Friday afternoon my brother Pete applied for a truck driving job at Gresser Construction in Eagan in the Lower Minnesota River Valley. He didn't get the job. The man who got the job showed up Monday morning with alcohol on his breath.

The owner sent him home and shouted out, "Call the farm boy who was here last Friday." The office girl reminded the owner the farm boy was too young to drive a commercial truck. The owner said, "Call him anyway." An hour later Pete pulled into the Gresser parking lot. In no time Pete was the company's number one driver, delivering equipment and materials to construction sites around the Twin Cities. Being fluent in blarney, Pete quickly learned to handle people. Like Dad, he could easily wash down custard-filled bismarcks while shifting gears. Pete eventually moved into management. While my brother Brian would never admit it, Pete got him a job as a union bricklayer at Gresser.

On a dog day in August with a load of K-rails on the truck, Pete took an exit ramp too fast and one of the K-rails tipped off the flatbed and tumbled into the grass. Pete pulled the truck off to the side. The first vehicle to come along was a crane truck. The driver stopped and without talking to Pete, used the crane to set the K-rail back on the flatbed. Pete walked toward the crane truck to give the driver the $100 bill he kept in the glove box for emergencies. Before Pete could deliver the Franklin the driver tore out yelling, "I'm getting the hell out of here before the cops show up." There's nothing better than the luck o' the Irish and there's nothing worse when it runs out.

In 2001, Pete dropped anchor and married Shannon McKasy at St. John the Baptist Church in Excelsior, Minnesota. Pete and his Irish bride had a first-rate reception and dance at a hall on the shores of Lake Minnetonka. They built a new house on Silver Lake next to the Weber farm.

Chapter Twelve
Big Debt

Chris Kyle

In 2015 my son Jesse and I saw *American Sniper*. The blockbuster movie tells the story of war hero and crack shot, Chris Kyle from Texas. During the Iraq war, Kyle picked off more bad guys than any sniper in American military history. After serving four tours in Iraq, Kyle was discharged from the Navy SEALS. He and a friend, Chad Littlefield, attempted to help Marine veteran Eddie Ray Routh. They went to a shooting range where Routh, who suffered from post-traumatic stress disorder and was high on weed, wasted Kyle and Littlefield. Kyle's funeral was at Texas Stadium. He left a widow and two youngsters.

Two days after *American Sniper* was released, documentary filmmaker Michael Moore in two tweets stated, "My uncle killed by sniper in WW2. We were taught snipers were cowards. Will shoot u in the back. Snipers aren't heroes. And invaders r worse."[1]

Former Minnesota Governor and former Navy SEAL, Jesse Ventura, said he won't see the movie. Chris Kyle, in his book *American Sniper*, alleged in 2006 he punched out a man in a San Diego bar for saying the SEALS "deserve to lose a few" in Iraq. He later identified the man as Ventura. In federal court in Minnesota, Ventura sued Kyle's estate claiming the story was a fabrication. The jury awarded Ventura $1.8 million. A federal appeals court drug a few reasons out of the woods to toss the jury's judgment against Kyle's estate.[2] The case eventually settled.

Dove Season

The Minnesota legislature during the 2003-04 session took up a bill to permit a dove hunting season for the first time in almost 60 years. Dad, unlike Grandpa Alo, didn't shoot or butcher animals. Dad wrote his local state representative a letter stating his opposition to a dove season. Dad wrote, there's no sport in shooting doves, there's not enough meat on doves to make hunting them worthwhile—a dove dresses out at less than two ounces of meat—and the dove is the symbol of world peace.

Dad's letter got less attention than most politicians give the constitution. He received a wish-washy letter from a staffer touting the economic benefits (more taxpayer money) from having a dove season.[3] Politicians should be more concerned about middle-class jobs leaving our country faster than the mayor of New York shuts down the city for a three-inch snow fall. The politicians passed the bill and Minnesota is collecting the almighty fee to bag the symbol of world peace. Not even Sven and Oly from the North Wood in Minnesota shoot them cute lil love birds, ya' know.

St. Thomas Church Becomes an Oratory

In 2006 the Bishop of the New Ulm Diocese in a *fait accompli* made St. Thomas Parish in Jessenland the first Oratory in the New Ulm Diocese. Under Canon Law an Oratory is for small parishes whose membership is declining but has financial means of support. The drawback is not having a regular Sunday Mass.

St. Thomas no longer being a parish marked the end of an era. The small family farms the parish served over 150 years no longer exist. St. Thomas was the mother parish of the Minnesota River Valley, the oldest church in the New Ulm diocese and one of the oldest in the state. It was the nucleus of Minnesota's first Irish farming settlement. When its former parishioners attend Sunday Mass in a different church they feel like a duck in a hen house. I was saddened by the change, but it was necessary as Jessenland doesn't have enough parishioners to justify a parish, and those left have one foot in the grave.

Brian Weber Dies

In 2006, Mom and Dad moved to Arlington, Minnesota and they turned the Weber farm over to my brothers, Brian and Pete. Brian was the fifth generation of Webers to live on the farm. On a bitter cold December day in 2008 my brothers, Brian and Pete, were dumping a load of sweet corn silage from a local canning factory off their tandem axle truck to feed a small herd of Angus steers and heifers. As the hoist was raising the box, Brian held the tailgate open. The silage on the passenger side of the box froze to the box and the silage on the driver's side slid off the box. The weight of the frozen silage on the passenger side of the raised box caused the truck to tip over and it landed on Brian. Instantly his soul left for the endless cornfields of the Great Beyond.

Brian is buried in the cemetery behind St. Thomas Church along with a few farm tools and a die cast model John Deere tractor. In his memory the family purchased a stained glass window in St. Mary's Catholic Church in Arlington. So far there have been over 60 memorial Masses at St. Brendan's in Green Isle, St. Mary's in Arlington, and at St. Thomas in Jessenland for the repose of Brian's soul to heaven. Brian's two children, Toney and Ashlie, represent the sixth generation of farmers on the land settled by their great-great-great-grandfather, Anton Weber.

Barack Obama

In 2008, 144 years after President Lincoln issued the Emancipation Proclamation, Barack Obama became the first African-American elected president. My mom was a proud member of his Honorary Kitchen Cabinet. His father was from the Luo tribe in Kenya.[4] From Obama's mother's side he's Scots-Irish. He called his maternal grandmother a "typical white person."[5] On the "Tonight Show," referring to his 129 bowling score, he said, "It's like—it was like Special Olympics or something.[6]

Under President Obama the higher ups in the IRS, FBI and Department of Justice used their positions to advance their political agenda. Not a good thing for our constitutional democracy. After spreading B.S. about Obamacare (if you like your health plan you can keep it), he found out he couldn't put it back in the bull. In a prepared speech, nuttier than a Stuckey's pecan log roll, U.S. Congresswoman Nancy Pelosi from California, said, "But we have to pass the bill (Obamacare) so that you can find out what is in it away from the fog of the controversy."

Lindsey Vonn

Born in St. Paul and raised in the Lower Minnesota River Valley in Burnsville, Lindsey Vonn is the greatest Alpine skier in U.S. history and one of the greatest in the world. In 2010 she became the first American woman to win Olympic gold in the downhill. She has 81 world cup victories and she's still competing. She's really competitive and pretty too, dern tootin'!

Matt Weber

In 2010 my kids, Matt, Melissa, and Jesse, and I were at a kiosk at McCarran Airport in Las Vegas to print our boarding passes for a flight to Minnesota. The screen said to see an agent. At the counter the ticket agent told Matt he was on the No Fly List. Gee willikers! Without much hassle he was able to obtain a boarding pass. I asked the agent if Matt was now off the No Fly List. The agent said he will be on the No Fly List the rest of his life and he will always need to check in with an agent to obtain a boarding pass. Since then Matt's obtained several boarding passes without seeing a ticket agent. That summer the Weber bunch spent the better part of a day at Canterbury Park in Shakopee betting on the ponies. There weren't many trips to the window. The younger generation of Webers learned the meaning of Phil Baker's words of wisdom, "Horse sense is what keeps horses from betting on people."

Meteorite

In 2011 the Navy's SEAL Team 6 raided terrorist mastermind Osama bin Laden's compound in Pakistan. He's best described with words used to clean the calf pan with a pitchfork. Navy SEAL Rob O'Neill, a native of Butte, Montana, blew bin Laden to hell. Pumping lead in bin Laden put an end to the rumor he was hiding out in the Northwoods of Minnesota under the alias "Ole's bin Loggin."

Also around 2011, Nelva Lillenthal, from my high school class, and her husband Bruce, were picking rocks in their field a few miles east of Arlington when Bruce picked up a 33-pound meteorite. It weighs about three times the weight of an earth rock with the same dimensions. Tests at the University of Minnesota show it's a rare iron meteorite originating from an asteroid.[7]

Jerry Berger

One Sunday, Father Jerry Berger started off his homily by relating a story about seeing his cousin who was attending a prep school for the seminary. Father Berger said he was peddling his bicycle in Green Isle when his front tire got wedged in a groove at the railroad track crossing, which caused him to fall and hit his head. While he laid unconscious on the railroad tracks, the Virgin Mary came to him and told him to follow his cousin into the priesthood. He regained consciousness just in time to crawl away from an oncoming freight train. At that moment he decided to be a priest. Father Berger hesitated and said, "If you believe that you'll believe anything."[8]

Knights of Columbus

In 2012 the unthinkable happened. A thief made off with the preserved heart of St. Laurence O'Toole from the Christ Church Cathedral in Dublin, Ireland where it had been on display since the 13th century.[9] Also in 2012, with his new bovine heart valve, Dad celebrated 60 years as a member of the Knights of Columbus (President Kennedy was also a member). The KCs are named in honor of Christopher Columbus. They were founded in 1882 in New Haven, Connecticut to help Catholic immigrants. Now they help those in need and defend Catholicism.[10]

Blakeley

The best thing to happen in Blakeley in my lifetime occurred in 2012 with the establishment of u4ic Brewing in the old creamery building. It's the only place on earth that brews pints of Old Corn Crib and my favorite Luskey's Irish Stout. Their motto is: "to boldly brew what no man has brewed before." The hops for their pints of liquid happiness are grown in the Minnesota River Valley. They make their handcrafted beer using grain from the Rahr Malting Company down the Valley in Shakopee.[11]

A few years before the brewery opened, my sons, Matt and Jesse, and I went zip-lining on the newly constructed Kerfoot Canopy in Jessenland, a few miles from Blakeley. We went lickety-split through and above the trees on the bluffs and glens of the Minnesota River Valley. We saw majestic oaks, a doe and her fawn, and a pair of bald eagles.

Butchering

In 2012 a computer programmer's error created Precinct 3B in Minneapolis. The precinct was entirely in the eastern half of beautiful Lake Calhoun.[12] Surprisingly, the politicians failed to get the fish registered to vote. Also, that spring on the Weber farm, an Angus cow pushed out mixed twins. As is generally the case, a few minutes after giving birth, the cow sniffed both calves, accepting the bull calf and rejecting the usually sterile heifer calf. Twice a day my sister-in-law, Bonnie Weber, bottle-fed the sterile female, called a freemartin. When the twins hit about 1,200 pounds my brother Pete finished them with a mixture of ground corn and crushed soybeans. After packing on a couple hundred pounds, Pete called a livestock hauler to truck the twins along with other steers and heifers to Central Livestock in Zumbrota, Minnesota where the critters were auctioned off. From there the bovines were shipped to slaughterhouses. The meat ends up on the plates of some of the finest Midwest and Eastern steakhouses.[13]

Also in 2012 my brother Pete asked a retired neighbor if he had any land for rent. The neighbor told him the only thing he had left to rent out was the tomcat. That fall, Pete and his son Ryan, shot a 12-point whitetail deer three times. The buck ran a half mile before he bled out. Pete took the buck to Pekarna Meats in Jordan, Minnesota, a family-owned business since 1893. The butcher carved out the tenderloin chops and ground up the remaining venison, and mixed it with pork to make deer sausage.[14]

During the summer of 2013 a group of family members gathered at my auld sod, the Weber farm, to butcher ducks and chickens. The night before, a weasel—also called a "Comey"—got in the coop and thinned the flock by sucking the blood out of six chickens. My niece, Ashlie, took over my old job of whacking off the heads with a hatchet, dunking the headless chickens in boiling water and plucking the feathers. After butchering the fowl, my nephew, Toney, gave Jesse and me a ride around Silver Lake in his small motor boat. It reminded me of rowing the neighbor's leaky wooden dinghy on Silver Lake with Grandpa Alo and my friend, Jim Kehoe. After boating, my brother-in-law, Steve Geib, and I quenched our thirst with a couple of Kato Lagers from the Mankato Brewery.

William Marvy Company

In 2013, Jorge Mario Bergoglio from Argentina became Pope Francis. His Holiness said the Church's ban on birth control doesn't mean "breed like rabbits."[15] In September of that year I visited with Robert Marvy, owner of the storied William Marvy Company in St. Paul's Macalester-Groveland neighborhood. The Marvy family operates the last barber pole factory in North, South, and Central America. Their poles are all over the world, including Navy ships. President Clinton had one installed in the White House barbershop. Marvy's been making the iconic poles since 1950. Pole number 75,000 is in the Smithsonian.[16]

A Marvy pole hangs on Dickie Downs' barber shop in Henderson. When Dickie cuts my hair, I sit in a classic old barber chair with a neck rest and an attached round stool that swivels around the chair for Dickie to sit on when he's tired of standing. When he's done snipping, he shaves my neck with a straight razor sharpened on a leather strop. When Dickie retires, his vestige of the last male domain will be a thing of the past.

Climate Change

In 2013-14 the sixth generation of Webers in the Minnesota River Valley experienced the harshest winter of their young lives. For six months the mercury in Arlington didn't reach 60 degrees Fahrenheit.[17] Where's some of that global warming when you need it? The harsh winter provided the youngsters with plenty of climate change (new phrase for a change in weather pattern) for sledding. Al Gore's 2007 prediction that all Arctic ice would be melted by 2014 didn't pan out.[18]

When the long winter finally ended, the trophy-for-everyone sixth generation of Webers held a few bashes in the cow pasture next to Silver Lake. They gathered around bonfires and drank beer while listening on their iPods to hip-hop music, and gangsta rap from the Niggaz Wit Attitudes (NWA) label. The young bloods are carrying on the timeless tradition of getting under their parents' skin. One of the partiers, my niece Ashlie, got married in August 2018 in the cow pasture.

Pioneer Power

In 2014 my son Matt ran with the bulls in Pamplona, Spain. In August of that year, I went to the annual Pioneer Power Show six miles east of Le Sueur, Minnesota. On display are buildings similar to the ones mentioned in this book, including a log cabin like my great-grandparents, Jack and Annie Madden's, a creamery outfitted with original equipment similar to the ones managed by my great-uncle, Charlie Strobel—his picture hangs on the wall—and a one-room schoolhouse like the one Grandpa Alo and my Dad attended. At certain times the machines of yesteryear are fired up, including a threshing machine and corn shredder. An old saw mill like the one my great-grandfather Henry ran is still ripping logs into boards. There is quilt making, a large display of working steam and gas engines, machinery, vintage automobiles, and acres of every farm boy's favorite—old tractors. On the way home, I stopped off at the Henderson RoadHaus—voted best happy hour by the Betty Ford Center—for a couple of snappers. A sign on the front window read: "For your safety legal conceal guns permitted here." After the barmaid beered me with a Grain Belt Nordeast, I asked the tatted-up biker on the stool next to me, "What ya' packing?" She said, "Dirty Harry" (.44 Magnum). I asked why she was carrying, she said, "Dat's 'cuz I can't fit a police officer in my purse."

National Debt

Showman P.T. Barnum said, "There is scarcely anything that drags a person down like debt." The same can be said for a country. Just ask the citizens of Greece, Argentina, and Cypress. The politicians, starting with President George W. Bush, accelerated by President Barack Obama (in keeping with his values, he increased the nation's debt more than all other presidents combined), and continuing with President Donald

Trump, got the taxpayers owing over $21,000,000,000,000. Oof-da! That's irresponsible and unpatriotic. Every day politicians dig the debt hole deeper. What would Grandpa say? President Obama said, "Raising the debt ceiling, which has been done over a hundred times, does not increase our debt."

Over the last fifteen years taxpayers paid approximately $5,250,000 on hair care for the U.S. Senate. Taxpayers shell out some $3,600,000 per year so former presidents George W. Bush and the "Gomer Bull" can live high on the hog. U.S. taxpayers forked over $1,400,000,000 per year on President Obama and his family. Taxpayers in the United Kingdom spend about $58,000,000 per year on the entire royal family. In 2012 the dehorns in Washington, D.C. saw fit to spent $27,000,000 to teach Moroccans how to design and make pottery.[19] How about Congress between 1997 and 2007 paying out some $17,000,000 from a secret fund of taxpayer money to settle cases of their inappropriate behavior, including "hush" money to women they sexually harassed.[20] Politicians adhere to the old axiom: sin concealed, sin forgiven.

Unlike Grandpa Alo, the politicians in Washington, D.C. don't know when to quit digging. The cheese gets more binding as the swamp creatures in Washington, D.C. ignore the debt problem and keep overspending and digging the hole deeper. The politicians are creating a colossal bubble. When the house of cards falls, the financial collapse will be faster than top FBI agents covering up their wrongdoing.

Dahir Ahmed Adan

Dykes on Bikes, Queer Nation, other gay and lesbian groups, and those who care about equality celebrated in 2015 when the U.S. Supreme Court, in *Obergefell v. Hodges*, legalized gay marriage in our country. Also in 2015 the radical Islamic terrorist group al-Shabaab from Somalia threatened to blow up shopping malls. Of particular concern is the Mall of America. From Lutheran Aide's relocation program, Minneapolis has a large population of Somalis. Some of them haven't assimilated into life in Minnesota and a few lean toward al-Shabaab.

In September 2016, wearing his private security guard uniform, Dahir Ahmed Adan went in the Crossroads Mall in St. Cloud, Minnesota. He pulled out a small knife, made reference to Allah and sliced ten people before a fast acting off-duty police officer smoked him. It appears Adan was a lone-wolf Islamic terrorist.

Irish Festival

In August 2016, Mom, at age 83, helped put on another Irish Festival at St. Thomas Church. The day before the festival, I walked to the Minnesota River and stood on an outcropping of rock that may have been the site of Doheny's landing, where some 160 years earlier the first settlers arrived in Jessenland. After the Irish Festival Mass, Father Berger and I told a few Irish stories and talked about the history of Jessenland and St. Thomas Church. With a few others, I went on a cemetery crawl to see the grave markers of those mentioned in this book. We walked on the road that is over a few graves. We took with us a bottle of Irish lemonade.

The festivals are complete with push pole tents, a band playing Irish music, cloggers, and a bog jumper on the bagpipes. I enjoyed a chicken dinner and canned beer chilled on ice in a cow tank. Descendants of the original settlers were plentiful. People waited in line to hear Dad's stories of days gone by. Some just liked hearing the Irish tones in his voice.

Hazeltine

In the fall of 2016, the Ryder Cup was held at the Hazeltine National Golf Club in Chaska (home of the best pillow ever—Mike Lindell's My Pillow) in the Lower Minnesota River Valley. For the first time since 2008, the U.S. team took home the cup. Golf legend Arnold Palmer died a week before the matches. At Hazeltine, the U.S. and European teams paid tribute to "The

King." The U.S. team dedicated its victory to Palmer. Legend has it, after a round of golf, Palmer would survey the golf course with binoculars for any last-minute autograph seekers before heading to the clubhouse. Arnie quenched his thirst with an Arnold Palmer—three parts unsweetened iced tea and one-part lemonade.

Donald Trump

In 1988, Dad and I were having lunch at a coffee shop in Manhattan. By the cash register a sign on a bucket read: "Help keep Donald Trump from going bankrupt." I dropped in a few bucks for the Donald. In the election of November 2016, Republican presidential candidate and billionaire real estate developer, Donald Trump, lost the popular vote to Democrat Hillary Clinton. Except for Illinois—a state the politicians put in dire financial straits, and Minnesota, the voters in the heart and soul of our country threw old sourpuss Hillary Clinton in the furrow and Trump plowed her under in the electoral college to become our 45th commander in chief. U.S. Supreme Court Justice Ruth Bader Ginsberg said if Trump won it would be time to move to New Zealand. Hopefully, she gives her legal opinions more thought.

Dad and I knew Trump was a shoo-in for president as a couple of weeks before the election boxelder bugs congregated at St. Thomas Church in Jessenland. When that happens a Republican is elected president. If they don't congregate before the election, a Democrat wins. Boxelder bugs, or lack of them at the church is a better predictor of who'll be elected president than the so-called media experts and pollsters.

Allie and Geri Weber's 60th Wedding Anniversary

In November 2016 the Weber family celebrated Mom and Dad's 60th wedding anniversary at the Old Log Theatre in Excelsior, Minnesota. After chowing down, we took our seats in the theatre and enjoyed the *Million Dollar Quartet*—a musical based on a December night in 1956 when Johnny Cash, Sam Perkins, Jerry Lee Lewis, and Elvis Presley and his girlfriend, all unexpectedly showed up at Sun Records in Nashville, Tennessee. The four musicians jammed the night away.

New Ulm Diocese Goes Bankrupt

In 2017 the New Ulm Diocese in Minnesota filed for bankruptcy. The diocese "took a bath" from having received over 100 claims for sexual abuse committed on children by clergy. The Minnesota legislature extended the time for molestation victims to bring their claims.[21]

For years, instead of notifying law enforcement, those high up in the church's hierarchy, operating in a shroud of secrecy and not wanting to tarnish its image, covered up the heinous crimes. Bishops often moved pedophile priests from parish to parish without notifying the police. In 2011 and 2012 Pope Benedict defrocked 384 priests for child sex abuse.[22]

Summer Fish Kill

In early July 2017 there was a rare summer fish kill in Silver Lake and in other shallow lakes in southern Minnesota. Theories as to the cause include the weather suddenly turning warm, parasites, a virus, and the old whipping boy—man-made climate change. The lake was lined with decaying fish, mostly carp. The odor was almost as bad as the stench coming from the U.S. Senate. American white pelicans, commonly called Great Lakes pelicans, covered the lake to feast on the dead fish. Wildlife around the lake also got in on the all-you-can-eat fish.

Lindsay Whalen Greve

In the fall of 2017, Minnesota basketball fans celebrated when point guard Lindsay Whalen Greve, born and raised in Hutchinson, led the Minnesota Lynx's basketball team to the Women's National Basketball Association title for the fourth time. All-star Whalen Greve also has two Olympic gold medals.

Henderson Roll In

Every Tuesday evening during the summer, Henderson has a "roll in." People in classic vehicles and motorcycles enjoy the beautiful ride through the Minnesota River Valley to Henderson. On arrival they have a cold brew and a hamburger while hanging out on the sidewalks of Main Street. Henderson has one of the most historical Main Streets in Minnesota.

Grim Reaper

Wherever I go and whatever I do, my memories of growing up in the Minnesota River Valley are with me. May the star the wise men followed shine upon you with God's grace. When the grim reaper calls may your soul pass through purgatory and take its place in heaven a half-hour before the devil knows you're dead.

Boys, it's time for a pint!

Endnotes

Chapter 1

1. Julius A. Coller, II, *The Shakopee Story*, p. 9.
2. William E. Lass, *The Treaty of Traverse des Sioux*, pp. 4-6.
3. Evan Jones, *The Minnesota*, p. 11 and E. Sandford Seymour, *Sketches of Minnesota: The New England of the West: With Incidents of Travel in that Territory During the Summer of 1849*, p. 38.
4. Seymour, p. 41.
5. Thos. Hughes, Esq., *Introduction* in Revs. Thos. E. Hughes and David Edwards, and Messrs. Hugh G. Roberts and Thomas Hughes, Editors, *History of the Welsh in Minnesota: Foreston and Lime Springs, Ia. Gathered by the Old Settlers*, p. 8.
6. Wayne E. Webb and J.I. Swedberg, *Redwood: The Story of a County*, p. 9.
7. Curtis A. Dahlin, *Words vs. Actions*, in Mary Hawker Bakeman and Antona M. Richardson, editors, *Trail of Tears: Minnesota's Dakota Indian Exile Begins*, p. 35.
8. Webb and Swedberg, p. 10.
9. Jones, pp. 14-15.
10. Ibid., p. 15.
11. Hughes, Esq., p. 8.
12. Jones, p. 15.
13. Benjamin Ives Scott & Robert Neslund, *The First Cathedral: An Episcopal Community for Mission*, p. 1.
14. Hughes, Esq., pp. 7-8.
15. Jones, p. 59.
16. Irving H. Bartlett, *John C. Calhoun: A Biography*, p. 218.
17. John Stauffer, *Giants: The Parallel Lives of Frederick Douglass and Abraham Lincoln*, p. 79.
18. Jones, pp. 56-59.

Endnotes

19. Gwenyth Swain, *Dred and Harriet Scott: A Family's Struggle for Freedom*, p. 30.

20. Ibid., p. 26.

21. J. Fletcher Williams, *A History of the City of St. Paul to 1875*, p. 46.

22. Mary Lethert Wingerd, *Claiming the City: Politics, Faith, and the Power of Place in St. Paul*, and St. Paul biographer, in Wingerd, p. 20.

23. Williams, pp. 85-86 and Edmund Brissett, in Williams, p. 85.

24 Wingerd, p. 20.

25. Williams, p. 147.

26. Seymour, p. 19.

27. Chaska Bicentennial Committee, *Chaska: A Minnesota River City*, Vol. 1, pp. 18-19.

28. Rhoda R. Gilman, *Henry Hastings Sibley: Divided Heart*, p. 38.

29. Ibid., pp. 75-76.

30. Ibid., p. 136.

31. Ibid., p. 165.

32. K Pederson, *Makers of Minnesota*, in Sibley County Sesquicentennial Publication Committee, *Bits & Pieces: Celebrating 150 Years of Sibley County History*, p. 116.

33. Gilman, (*Henry Hastings Sibley*) p. 87.

34. K Pederson, in Sibley County Sesquicentennial Publication Committee, p. 116.

35. Rita Zurst, interview and discussion.

36. Kathleen Krull, *Lives of the Presidents: Fame, Shame (and What the Neighbors Thought)*, p. 31.

37. R.I. Holcombe, in Henderson History Book Committee, *Henderson Then and Now 1852-1994: In the Minnesota River Valley*, 3rd Ed., p. 7.

38. Gilman, (*Henry Hastings Sibley*), pp. 104-108.

39. Krull, p. 32.

40. Gilman, (*Henry Hastings Sibley*), p. 109.

Endnotes

41. Webb and Swedberg, p. 30.
42. K Pederson, in Sibley County Sesquicentennial Publications Committee, p. 116.
43. Author's visit to the Pipestone National Monument near Pipestone, Minnesota.
44. Jones, p. 114.
45. Lass, (*The Treaty of Traverse des Sioux*), p. 40.
46. Ibid., p. 22.
47. Author's visits to the Traverse des Sioux Treaty Center near St. Peter, Minnesota.
48. Lass, (*The Treaty of Traverse des Sioux*), p. 32.
49. Ibid., p. 35.
50. Original Notes of James M. Goodhue written for The St. Paul Pioneer, in Thomas Hughes assisted by Brigadier General W.C. Brown, *Old Traverse des Sioux: A History of Early Exporation, Trading Posts, Mission Station, Treaties and Pioneer Village*, Edited by Edward A. Johnson, p. 43.
51. Ibid., p. 37.
52. Lass, (*The Treaty of Traverse des Sioux*), pp. 35-36.
53. Goodhue, in Hughes assisted by Brown, Edited by Johnson, p. 45
54. Lass, (*The Treaty of Traverse des Sioux*), p. 44.
55. Ibid., pp. 46-47.
56. Ibid., p. 47.
57. Gilman, (*Henry Hastings Sibley*), p. 127.
58. Lass, (*The Treaty of Traverse des Sioux*), pp. 57-58.
59. Henderson History Book Committee, p. 7 and William Watts Folwell, *A History of Minnesota, Vol. 1*, p. 283, Fn. 37.
60. Lass, (*The Treaty of Traverse des Sioux*), pp. 54-55.
61. Article 5 in *The Treaty of Traverse des Sioux* and Article 6 in *The Mendota Treaty*.
62. Author's visits to the Lower Sioux Agency near Morton, Minnesota.
63. Henderson History Book Committee, p. 169.
64. Pioneer, November 21, 1850, in Williams, p. 274.

Endnotes

65. Williams, pp. 323-324.
66. George Doheny, interview and discussion.
67. John Gerald Berger, *A History of St. Brendan's Parish, The Village of Green Isle and Minnesota's First Irish Settlement*, p. 2.
68. George Doheny, interview and discussion.
69. Bishop Cretin, in Berger, pp. 10-11.
70. Berger., p. 13.
71. Ibid., p. 6.
72. Ibid., p. 35.
73. Alo Weber, stories he told.
74. Henderson History Book Committee, p. 1.
75. Gilman, (*Henry Hastings Sibley*), p. 159
76. Henderson History Book Committee, p. 4.
77. Gilman, (*Henry Hastings Sibley*), p. 59.
78. Henderson History Book Committee, p. 7.
79. Henderson History Book Committee, p. 1 and Don Osell, in Henderson History Book Committee, p. 12.
80. Henderson History Book Committee, p. 42.
81. Sibley County Sesquicentennial Publications Committee, p. 3.
82. Seigneuret, in Henderson History Book Committee, p. 44.
83. Henderson History Book Committee, p. 415.
84. Gibbon Gazette, Jan. 2, 1941, in Sibley County Sesquicentennial Publications Committee, p. 17.
85. Dann Woellert, *Cincinnati Turner Societies: The Cradle of an American Movement*, p. 15.
86. Daniel J. Hoisington, *A German Town: A History of New Ulm, Minnesota*, pp. 2-3.
87. Fredrick Beinhorn, in Hoisington, (*A German Town*), p. 3.
88. Hoisington, (*A German Town*), p. 4.
89. Peter Mack, in Hoisington, (*A German Town*), p. 5 and Webb and Swedberg, p. 30.
90. Elizabeth Scobie, *A History of Sleepy Eye, Minnesota*, p. 17.
91. Jones, pp. 155-156.

92.   Hoisington, (*A German Town*), pp. 6-7.

93.   Jones, p. 159.

94.   Woellert, p. 14.

95.   Hoisington, (*A German Town*), p. 10.

96.   Woellert, p. 9.

97.   Hoisington, (*A German Town*), pp. 11-12.

98.   Dr. Thomas O. Kajer, *They Ate From One Bowl: The New Prague Area Its First Forty-Four Years*, p. 95.

99.   Author's visits to the Brown County Historical Society & Museum in New Ulm, Minnesota.

100. Kajer, pp. 8-9.

101. Ibid., p. 21.

102. Ibid., p. 100.

103. Ibid., p. 75.

104. Ibid., p. 20.

105. Ibid., p. 103.

106. Ibid., p. 106.

107. Joseph R. Brown's letter in the Henderson Democrat, March 12, 1857, in Henderson History Book Committee, p. 146.

108. Gilman, (*Henry Hastings Sibley*), p. 149.

109. Jones, pp. 173-175.

110. Williams, p. 372.

111. St. Peter State Hospital Museum Committee, *The St. Peter State Hospital Museum: Minnesota's First and Oldest State Hospital Serving the Mentally Ill and Mentally Ill and Dangerous 1866-present*, p. 2.

112. John Stoever report in the Democrat, *Francis Bassen Hung in Effigy*, in Henderson History Book Committee, pp. 146-147.

113. Henderson History Book Committee, p. 147.

114. Gilman, (*Henry Hastings Sibley*), p. 153.

115. Ibid., pp. 156-157.

116. Winona Times, May 15, 1858, in Gilman, (*Henry Hastings Sibley*), p. 156.

Endnotes

117. Alo Weber, story he told.

118. Ibid.

119. Kajer, p. 12.

120. Alo Weber, stories he told.

121. Berger, p. 4.

122. Kajer, p. 24.

123. Ibid., p. 34.

124. Ibid., p. 33.

125. Henderson Democrat, 1860, in Henderson History Book Committee, p. 254.

126. Alo Weber, stories he told.

127. Allie Weber, stories he tells.

128. Sibley County Independent advertisement, 1908, in Henderson History Book Committee, p. 7.

129. Allie Weber, stories he tells.

130. Don Osell, *On the Road With Joseph R. Brown In Search of Joe Brown's Life & Work in Early Minnesota Transportation*, p. 35.

131. Alo Weber, story he told.

132. William E. Lass, *Joseph R. Brown And His Times*, p. 23.

133. Osell, p. 35.

134. Mary Rose Volberding, *Emily's Story*, in Henderson History Book Committee, pp. 546-547 and Rita Zurst, interview and discussion.

135. Author's visit to the Grimm Farm Historic Site near Victoria, Minnesota.

136. Jones, pp. 225-226.

137. Dale R. Albrecht and Leo Albrecht, Jr., *Tales of a Small Town Circus Legend*, p. 43.

138. Author's visit to the Grimm Farm Historic site near Victoria, Minnesota.

139. Deacon Donham, Article in magazine called *Donham's Doings*, in Hon. William G. Gresham, Editor-in-Chief, *History of Nicollect and Le Sueur Counties Minnesota: Their People, Industries and Institutions*, Vol 1, pp. 542-544 .

140.   Walter N. Trenerry, *Murder in Minnesota: A Collection of True Cases*, pp. 34-39.

141.   John D. Bessler, *Legacy Violence: Lynch Mobs and Executions in Minnesota*, p. 88.

142.   Trenerry, p. 41.

143.   Ibid., p. 219.

Chapter 2

1.   Mary L. Hagerty, *Meet Shieldsville: The Story of St. Patrick's Parish Shieldsville, Minnesota*, p. 9.

2.   Stauffer, pp. 122-123.

3.   William Henry Condon, *Life of Major-General James Shields: Hero of Three Wars and Senator From Three States*, p. 49.

4.   Ronald C. White, Jr., *A. Lincoln: A Biography*, pp. 115-116.

5.   Patricia Condon Johnston, *Minnesota's Irish*, p. 26.

6.   Hagerty, p. 10.

7.   Johnston, p. 26.

8.   Alan Axelrod, Ph.D., *The Complete Idiot's Guide to American History*, Fifth Ed., p. 130.

9.   Joseph Farr, in St. Paul Pioneer Press article, May 5, 1895.

10.   Stauffer, pp. 148-149.

11.   Swain, pp. 43-44.

12.   Ibid., pp. 3-4, 49-50, 55.

13.   Ibid., pp. 69-73.

14.   Susan Hvistendahl, Originally published in the Entertainment Guide presented here in partnership with the Northfield Historical Society, *Historic Happenings*, Vol 1, NHS History Series No. 1, p. 79.

15.   Emily Willey Skinner, *Reminiscences of Early Days*, in *Pioneer Women: Voices of Northfield's Frontier 1856-1876*, compiled and edited by Jeff M. Sauve, p. 24.

16.   John North and his daughter Emma, in Hvistendahl, pp. 37-38.

17.   Stauffer, p. 105.

18.   Harold Holzer, *The World Book Encyclopedia*, v. 12, p. 321.

Endnotes

19. Hvistendahl, p. 39.

20. Ibid., p. 40.

21. Merlin Stonehouse, *John Wesley North and the Reform Frontier*, p. 169.

22. Hvistendahl, p. 41.

23. Enthralled Writers, *Singing Hutchinsons* featured frequently, in McLeod County Historical Society, *McLeod County History Book 1978: McLeod County Minnesota*, pp. 652-653.

24. Jones, pp. 149-150.

25. Author's visit to the McLeod County Heritage Center in Hutchinson, Minnesota.

26. Henry David Thoreau, in Henderson History Book Committee, p. 33.

27. Littlecrow, in Jones, pp. 185-186.

28. Jones, p. 186.

29. Andrew Myrick, in Jones p. 186 and Jones p. 186.

30. Kenneth Carley, *The Dakota War of 1862: Minnesota's Other Civil War*, pp. 7-9.

31. Ibid., p. 14.

32. Alo Weber, story he told.

33. William Cairncross, *His Biography: December 19, 1829 Dundee Scotland, April 23, 1921, St. Paul, Minnesota*, p. 131.

34. Henderson History Book Committee, p. 27.

35. Carley, (*The Dakota War of 1862*), pp. 30-31.

36. Henderson History Book Committee, p. 27.

37. Carley, (*The Dakota War of 1862*), pp. 60.

38. Blesser, p. 38.

39. Helen Clapesattle, *The Doctors Mayo*, p. 34.

40. Woellert, p. 35.

41. Henderson History Book Committee, p. 159.

42. David M. Grabitske, *Mary McDonald, Would-Be Warrior of Faxon Township, 1862*, in Sibley County Sesquicentennial Publications Committee, pp. 33-34.

43. Carley, (*The Dakota War of 1862*), p. 41.

44.   Cairncross, p. 140.

45.   Pamphlet on Historic Sites of Renville County and Surrounding Areas, p. 3.

46.   William Kahlow, in Win Working, Independent, 1925, in Henderson History Book Committee, pp. 29-30.

47.   Carley, (*The Dakota War of 1862*), p. 44.

48.   Ibid., pp. 64-65.

49.   Curtis A. Dahlin, *Words vs. Actions*, in Mary Hawker Bakeman and Antona M. Richardson, Editors, *Trail of Tears: Minnesota's Dakota Indian Exile Begins*, p. 37.

50.   Cairncross, p. 140.

51.   Gilman, (*Henry Hastings Sibley*), p. 184.

52.   Gregory F. Michno, *Dakota Dawn: The Decisive First Week of the Sioux Uprising, August 17-24, 1862*, pp. 1-2.

53.   Cairncross, pp. 127, 138.

54.   Duane Schultz, *The Earth I Came*, in Henderson History Book Committee, p. 30.

55.   Sam Brown, in Henderson History Book Committee, p. 30.

56.   Rhoda R. Gilman, *The Story of Minnesota's Past*, p. 120.

57.   Carley, (*The Dakota War of 1862*), pp. 69-70.

58.   Ibid., p. 70.

59.   Gilman, (*Henry Hastings Sibley*), p. 188.

60.   Vernard E. Lundin, *At the Bend in the River: an Illustrated History of Mankato and North Mankato*, p. 20.

61.   Carley, (*The Dakota War of 1862*), p. 71.

62.   Scott and Neslund, p. 17.

63.   Bessler, p. 25 and Gilman, (*The Story of Minnesota's Past*), p. 123.

64.   Bessler, p. 45.

65.   Ibid., pp. 25-26.

66.   Ibid., p. 46.

67.   Abrahm Lincoln, in Kate Roberts, *Minnesota 150: The People, Places, and Things that Shape Our State*, p. 186.

68.   Bessler, pp. 37, 52 and Carley, (*The Dakota War of 1862*), pp. 72-73.

Endnotes

69. Bessler, p. 64.

70. Scott W. Berg, *38 Nooses: Lincoln, Little Crow, and the Beginning of the Frontier's End*, p. 233.

71. Eric Dregni, *Weird Minnesota: Your Travel Guide to Minnesota's Local Legends and Best Kept Secrets*, p. 21.

72. Bessler, p. 61.

73. Gilman, *(Henry Hastings Sibley)*, p. 189.

74. Henderson History Book Committee, pp. 42, 279.

75. H.J. Seigneuret, M.D., History of Sibley County, State of Minnesota, *From the Remotest Time Up to the 4th Day of July, 1876*, in The Sibley County Independent, Henderson, Minnesota, July 5, 1876, Vol. 4, No. 13., back page.

76. Bessler, p. 62.

77. Elizabeth Johanneck, *Hidden History of the Minnesota River Valley*, pp. 99-100.

78. Entered according to Act of Congress, by J.E. Whitney, in the year 1862, in the Clerk's Office of the U.S. District Court for Minnesota, in Dregni, p. 10.

79. Clapesattle, p. 36.

80. Johanneck, p. 100.

81. Clapesattle, p. 42.

82. Elizabeth Dorsey Hatle, *The Ku Klux Klan in Minnesota*, p. 44.

83. W. Eugene Mayberry, M.D., Foreward, in Clapesattle, pp. v-vi.

84. Carley, *(The Dakota War of 1862)*, pp. 83-86.

85. Bessler, p. 65.

86. Dregni, p. 20 and Carley, *(The Dakota War of 1862)*, p. 75.

87. Adrian J. Ebell, in Harper's News Monthly Magazine, in Curtis A. Dahlin, *Words vs. Actions*, in Mary Hawker Bakeman and Antona M. Richardson, Editors, *Trail of Tears: Minnesota's Dakota Indian Exile Begins*, pp. 38-39.

88. Carley, *(The Dakota War of 1862)*, p. 76.

89. Notes by Nancy McClure Huggins, in Hughes, p. 130.

90. Henderson History Book Committee, p. 27.

Endnotes

91.   Author's visits to the Brown County Historical Society & Museum in New Ulm, Minnesota.

92.   Lass, (*The Treaty of Traverse de Sioux*), p. viii.

93.   Daniel John Hoisington, *Chanhassen: A Centennial History*, pp. 50-51.

94.   William Lochren, Company E, in Kenneth Carley, *Minnesota in the Civil War: An Illustrated History*, p. 14.

95.   Author's visit to Statue of Josias R. King in St. Paul, Minnesota.

96.   Henderson History Book Committee, p. 170.

97.   Richard Moe, *The Last Full Measure: The Life and Death of the First Minnesota Volunteers*, p. 261.

98.   Brian Leehan, *Pale Horse at Plum Run: The First Minnesota at Gettysburg*, p. xiv.

99.   Moe, pp. 264-272.

100.   Leehan, p. 46.

101.   Author's visits to the Minnesota Historical Society in St. Paul Minnesota.

102.   Moe, p. 297.

103.   Author's visit to Gettysburg National Cemetery near Gettysburg, Pennsylvania.

104.   Calvin Coolidge, in Moe, p. 313.

105.   Program for the "Dedication of the One Hundred Thirty-Fifth Infantry Colvill Memorial" in Leehan, p. 163.

106.   Lawrence A. Frost, *The Custer Album: A Pictorial Biography of General George A. Custer*, pp. 7, 37-39.

107.   Hoisington, (*Chanhassen*), and Edwin Aldritt, in Hoisington, (*Chanhassen*), pp. 45-49.

108.   Jim O'Connor, *What was the Battle of Gettysburg?*, p. 82.

109.   Carley, (*Minnesota in the Civil War*), p. 27.

110.   The Board of Commissioners, *Minnesota in the Civil and Indian Wars 1861-1865*, p. 64.

111.   Stauffer, p. 15.

112.   Allie Weber, story he tells.

113.   Mary Scully, interview and discussion.

114. H.J. Seigneuret, M.D., History of Sibley County, State of Minnesota, *From the Remotest Time Up to the 4ᵗʰ Day of July, 1876*, in The Sibley County Independent, Henderson, Minnesota, July 5, 1876, Vol. 4, No. 13., back page.

115. Gary W. Gallagher, *An End and a New Beginning*, in Division of Publications, Harper Ferry Center National Park Service, U.S. Department of the Interior, Washington, D.C., Appomattox Court House, pp. 71-72.

116. Patrick A. Schroeder, *Thirty Myths About Lee's Surrender*, pp. 18-19, 25.

117. Winona Allanson Hagen, from undated clippings of the Gaylord Hub and Glencoe Enterprise, *Civil War Flag of 1863 Made By Betsy Rosses*, in Sibley County Sesquicentennial Publications Committee, p. 31.

118. John Stanchak, Eyewitness Books, *Eyewitness Civil War*, p. 64.

119. Ibid., p. 9.

120. Ibid., p. 67.

Chapter 3

1. Stauffer, pp. 297-298.

2. Julius A. Coller, II, *The Shakopee Story*, pp. 65-66.

3. Publisher, Belle Plaine Herald, April, 1915, *How the News of Lincoln's Assassination was Received in Belle Plaine 50 Years Ago*, in Leo J. Albrecht, *Belle Plaine 150 Years 1854-2004*, p. 398.

4. James L. Swanson, *Manhunt: The 12-Day Chase for Lincoln's Killer*, pp. 334-335.

5. Mary Scully, interview and discussion.

6. Seymour Reit, *Behind Rebel Lines: The Incredible Story of Emma Edmonds, Civil War Spy*, p. 127.

7. Ibid., pp. vii, 8.

8. Carley, (*Minnesota in the Civil War*), p. 195.

9. Bessler, pp. 8-10.

10. Ibid., pp. 10-11.

Endnotes

11. William Anderson, *Laura Ingalls Wilder: Country The People and Places in Laura Ingalls Wilder's Life and Books,* p. 29.
12. Tanya Lee Stone, *Biography Laura Ingalls Wilder: A Photographic Story of a Life,* pp. 26-30.
13. Ibid., p. 36.
14. Ibid., p. 41.
15. Ibid., p. 61.
16. Ibid., p. 75.
17. Ibid., pp. 107-112.
18. William Anderson, *Laura Ingalls Wilder's Walnut Grove,* pp. 68-70.
19. David W. Blight, *An America Transformed,* in Division of Publications, Harpers Ferry Center, National Park Service, U.S. Department of Interior, Washington, D.C., p. 92
20. Henderson History Book Committee, p. 38.
21. New York Times, May 30, 1916 in Roberts and Roberts, pp. 74-75 and author's visit to the James J. Hill House on Summit Avenue in St. Paul, Minnesota.
22. Letter written by Joseph Shiely to Father Eugene Sebesta.
23. Berger, pp. 22-23 and Allie Weber, story he tells.
24. Le Sueur paper, October 26, 1870, in Berger, p. 23.
25. Allie Weber, stories he tells.
26. Johnston, pp. 19-20.
27. Wingerd, p. 57.
28. Kevin Duchschere, in Roberts, pp. 84-85.
29. Author's visit to the James J. Hill House in St. Paul, Minnesota.
30. Johnston, pp. 33, 40.
31. Henderson History Book Committee, p. 12.
32. George Allsonson, in Independent, 1939, in Henderson History Book Committee, p. 12.
33. Dearth, in Independent, November 20, 1885, in Henderson History Book Committee, p. 438.
34. Allie Weber, story he tells.
35. Frost, p. 154.

Endnotes

36.   Axelrod, p. 192.
37.   John J. Koblas, *Faithful Unto Death: The James-Younger Raid on the First National Bank September 7, 1876.Northfield, Minnesota*, pp. 2-5.
38.   Ibid., pp. 6, 12.
39.   Berger, p. 27.
40.   Chaska Bicentennial Committee, Vol. I, p. 163.
41.   Koblas, pp. 42-43.
42.   Ibid., p. 48.
43.   Ibid., p. 61.
44.   Koblas & John Oleson, in Koblas, pp. 67-68.
45.   R.C. Phillips, in Koblas, p. 70.
46.   Koblas, pp. 72-75.
47.   Koblas and Anselm Manning, in Koblas, pp. 77-81.
48.   Ibid., pp. 84-85.
49.   Hvistendahl, pp. 152, 155.
50.   Koblas, p. 88.
51.   Henry P. Upham, Walter Mann, John S. Prince, Committee, in George Huntington, *Robber and Hero: The Story of the Northfield Bank Raid*, pp. 105-119.
52.   Huntington, pp. 79-84.
53.   Koblas, p. 96.
54.   Dr. McIntosh, in Koblas, p. 109.
55.   Koblas, p. 119.
56.   Ibid., pp. 139-140.
57.   Oscar Sorbel, in Koblas, p. 141.
58.   Koblas, pp. 149-150.
59.   Ibid., pp. 162, 165.
60.   Ibid., p. 168.
61.   Warden Henry Wolfer, in Koblas, p. 169, and Koblas, p. 169.
62.   Harriet Traxler, *A Murder in Faxon*, p. 164.
63.   Man Who Worked for Cole Younger in the Circus, in Koblas, p. 2.
64.   Koblas, pp. 169-170.

Endnotes

65.   Jones, p. 243.
66.   Ted P. Yeatman, *Frank and Jesse James: The Story Behind the Legend*, pp. 277-279.
67.   Ibid., pp. 283-284.
68.   Ibid., pp. 287-288.
69.   Koblas, p. 171, and Annie Jesse, in Koblas, p. 171.
70.   Rita Zurst, interview and discussion.
71.   Allie Weber, stories he tells.
72.   Berger, p. 32.
73.   Sibley County Independent article, April 30, 1882, in Berger, p. 34.
74.   Margaret Mullen, in Berger, p. 35.
75.   Berger, pp. 37-38.
76.   Ibid., p. 31.
77.   Sarah Nevin, in Berger, p. 32.
78.   Berger, p. 52.
79.   Webb and Swedberg, p. 168.
80.   Elizabeth Johanneck, *Hidden History of the Minnesota River Valley*, p. 56.
81.   Patricia Lubeck, *Murder in Gales: A Rose Hanged Twice*, pp. 40-41.
82.   Ibid., p. 46.
83.   Ibid., pp. 62-63.
84.   Ibid., pp. 64-68.
85.   Johanneck, p. 57.
86.   Lubeck, pp. 85-88.
87.   Ibid., pp. 89-95.
88.   Ibid., pp. 103-104.
89.   Ibid., pp. 108-109.
90.   Twin Cities newspaper, in Johanneck, p. 59.
91.   Lubeck, pp. 112-113.
92.   Ibid., p. 84.
93.   Ibid., p. 125.
94.   Ibid., pp. 127-128.
95.   Traxler, pp. 31-36.

96.   Ibid., pp. 131-132.
97.   Ibid., p. 9.
98.   Ibid., pp. 25-27.
99.   Ibid., pp. 47-49.
100.   Ibid., pp. 51-55.
101.   Ibid., pp. 121-122.
102.   Ibid., pp. 124-125.
103.   Ibid., pp. 129-132.
104.   Ibid., p. 141.
105.   Ibid., p. 163.
106.   Ibid., pp. 169-171.
107.   Harriet Traxler, story she told.
108.   The Glencoe Register, June 27, 1896 loaned to the Enterprise by Joe Kosek and St. Paul Globe, September 7, 1896, *Hangmans Bridge*, in McLeod County Historical Society, pp. 649-650.
109.   *Hanged From a Railroad Bridge*, Alexandria Republican (Alexandria, Minnesota) September 9, 1896, p. 6. col. 4.
110.   The Glencoe Register, June 27, 1896 loaned to the Enterprise by Joe Kosek and St. Paul Globe, September 7, 1896, *Hangmans Bridge*, in McLeod County Historical Society, p. 650.
111.   McLeod County Historical Society, p. 650.

Chapter 4

1.   John Curtin, Family History, in Sibley County Historical Society, *The Boys In Blue: Diaries of John Curtin with Information on Other Sibley County Minnesota Soldiers in the Spanish-American War and the Philippine Insurrection 1898-1902*, p. 5.
2.   Sibley County Historical Society, (*The Boys In Blue*), p. 7.
3.   John A. Curtin, Diary, in Sibley County Historical Society, (*The Boys In Blue*), p. 8.

Endnotes

4. Peggy and Harold Samuels, *Remembering the Main*, book jacket, pp. 308, 310, in Sibley County Historical Society, (*The Boys In Blue*), p. 13.

5. John A. Curtin, Notebook No. 2-John A. Curtin, Co. "C" 2 Inf., in Sibley County Historical Society, (*The Boys In Blue*), p. 19.

6. John C. Mass, letter dated November 8, 1898 to Mr. James Curtin, in Sibley County Historical Society, (*The Boys in Blue*), p. 30.

7. H.D. Brown, letter dated August 17, 1898 to Mrs. Curtin, in Sibley County Historical Society, (*The Boys in Blue*), p. 27.

8. Mrs. E. Curtin's letters dated September 14 and September 29, 1898, in Sibley County Historical Society, (*The Boys in Blue*), pp. 28-29.

9. Thomas Ward, letter dated October 14, 1898 to Mrs. Ellen Curtin, in Sibley County Historical Society, (*The Boys in Blue*), p. 29.

10. Funeral of J.A. Curtin, in Sibley County Historical Society, (*The Boys in Blue*), p. 32.

11. Sibley County Historical Society, (*The Boys in Blue*), p. 4.

12. Axelrod, p. 219.

13. Ibid.

14. Allie Weber, story he tells.

15. Alo Weber, stories he told.

16. Author's visit to the Chippewa National Forest in Minnesota.

17. Author's visit to the Hinckley Fire Museum in Hinckley, Minnesota.

18. Alo Weber, story he told.

19. Author's visit to the Hinckley Fire Museum in Hinckley, Minnesota.

20. Ezra C. Clemans, in Hatle, p. 53.

21. Independent, June 7, 1895, in Henderson History Book Committee, p. 492.

Endnotes

22. Independent, June 3, 1898, in Henderson History Book Committee, p. 492 and Alo Weber, story he told.

23. Allie Weber, story he tells.

24. Alo Weber, story he told.

25. Carl and Amy Narvestad, *A History of Yellow Medicine County, Minnesota 1872-1972*, p. 453.

26. Ibid., p. 469.

27. Farmington Area Historical Society, *From Hand to Hand: The Legacy of a Post Office*, pp. 8-9.

28. Ibid., p. 11.

29. Kate Roberts, *Minnesota 150: The People, Places, and Things That Shape Our State*, p. 93 and author's visit to the post office in Farmington, Minnesota.

30. Orville V. Webster, *The Book of Presidents*, p. 77.

31. Alo Weber, stories he told.

32. Ibid.

33. Ibid.

34. Ibid.

35. Ibid.

36. Krull, p. 49.

37. Henderson Independent, Zimmerman advertisement, November 15, 1881, in Arlington Sesquicentennial Committee, p. 78.

38. Article in Independent, June 3, 1903, in Henderson History Book Committee, p. 302.

39. Article in Independent, March 26, 1926, in Henderson History Book Committee, p. 303.

40. Sibley County Independent, Advertisement, 1896, in Henderson History Book Committee, p. 302.

41. Henderson History Book Committee, p. 303.

42. Allie Weber, story he tells.

43. National Geographic, *100 Shocking Events: Disasters, Scandals, and Misadventures That Made History*, p. 10.

44. Alo Weber, stories he told.

45. Alo Weber, story he told.

Endnotes

46.   Ibid.
47.   Alo Weber, stories he told.
48.   Ibid.
49.   Sibley County Historical Society, *Remembering Country Schools of Sibley County, Minnesota*, p. 11.
50.   Allie Weber, story he tells.
51.   Gaylord Hub of Sibley County, (1915 list of rules from another state), in Sibley County Historical Society, (*Remembering Country Schools*), p. 6.
52.   Alo Weber, stories he told.
53.   Henderson History Book Committee, p. 438.
54.   Alo Weber, story he told.
55.   Congressman, in Jones, p. 133.
56.   Alo Weber, story he told.
57.   Gus Buck, Independent, September 10, 1915, in Henderson History Book Committee, p. 149.
58.   Berger, p. 62.
59.   Anonymous contributor, *A Monster Funeral*, Independent, December 3, 1915, in Henderson History Book Committee, p. 150.
60.   Henderson History Book Committees, p. 150.
61.   Mike and Trisha Zeiher, interview, discussion and review of documents.
62.   Webb and Swedberg, p. 441.
63.   Scott and Neslund, p. 71.
64.   Webb and Swedberg, p. 441.
65.   Scott and Neslund, p. 64.
66.   Ibid., p. 69.
67.   Ibid., p. 74.
68.   Author's visit to the Cathedral of Our Merciful Saviour in Faribault, Minnesota.
69.   John Wark, in Scott and Nesland, p. 165, fn. 11.
70.   Scott and Nesland, p. 76.
71.   Dean Slattery, in Scott and Nesland, p. 76.
72.   Bessler, p. 118.

Endnotes

73.   Henderson History Book Committee, p. 160.
74.   Dwight Grabitske, *Sibley County's Only Execution*, in Sibley County Sesquicentennial Publications Committee, p. 36.
75.   Ibid.
76.   Bessler, pp. 173-174.
77.   Henderson History Book Committee, p. 161.
78.   Grabitske, p. 36.
79.   Bessler, p. 140.
80.   Alo Weber, story he told.
81.   Chaska Bicentennial Committee, Vol. II, pp. 6-7.
82.   Bessler, p. 140.
83.   Chaska Bicentennial Committee, Vol. II, p. 7.
84.   *Murdered Girl Left a Letter Father Not Only a Murderer But Worse Still*, The Aitkin Age (Aitkin, Minnesota), October 28 1902, Vol. XX, No. 37.
85.   *Bungle of Hangman Decapitates Murderer*, Spokane Press (Washington) March 20, 1903, www.genealogytrails.com/minn/aitkin/news_crimehang.html.
86.   D.T. Tice, *Minnesota's Twentieth Century: Stories of Extraordinary People*, pp. 12, 14.
87.   St. Paul Dispatch, May 12, 1905, in Trenerry, p. 160.
88.   Trenerry, p. 163.
89.   Tice, p. 16.
90.   Ibid., pp. 16-17.
91.   Bessler, pp. 171-177.
92.   Roberts, p. 42.
93.   Michael Fedo, *The Lynchings in Duluth*, p. 110.
94.   Ibid., p. 118.
95.   Ibid., pp. 149-150, 172.
96.   Ibid., pp. 158-162.
97.   Ibid., p. 172.
98.   Ibid., p. 164.
99.   Roberts, p. 43.
100.   Tice, p. 45.

Endnotes

101. Jens Bohn, President, The Dan Patch Historical Society, forward, in Tim Brady, *The Great Dan Patch and the Remarkable Mr. Savage*, pp. 9-10.

102. Brady, p. 182 and Jens Bohn, p. 9.

103. Nancy Huddleston, *Images of America: Savage*, pp. 50-62.

104. Author's visit to the St. Paul Cathedral in St. Paul, Minnesota.

105. Johnston, pp. 17, 80.

106. Dwight Grabitske, *John F. McGovern University of Minnesota All American Quarterback*, in Arlington Sesquicentennial Committee, p. 154.

107. Al Papas, Jr., *Gopher Sketchbook: Drawing Sketches and Thumbnail Sketches of the Great Ones From the "U" of Minnesota's Earliest Football Days to Now*, p. 23.

108. Minneapolis Morning Tribune, *Football Coach Has Surgeon's Touch*, January 26, 1910, in Ben Welter, *Minnesota Moxie: True Tales of Courage, Muscle & Grit in the Land of Ten Thousand Lakes*, pp. 57-58.

109. Grabitske, in Arlington Sesquicentennial Committee, p. 155.

110. Author's visit to the Le Sueur Museum in Le Sueur, Minnesota.

111. Grabitske, in Arlington Sesquicentennial Committee, p. 155.

112. Dwight Grabitske, *Marshal Hugh McGovern*, in Arlington Sesquicentennial Committee, p. 46.

113. Arlington Sesquicentennial Committee, p. 47.

114. Arlington Enterprise, *Bandits Attempt to Rob First State Bank*, October 30, 1924, in Arlington Sesquicentennial Committee, pp. 91-92.

115. Marlys Buckentin, *Thomas G. (Tom) Burke*, in Arlington Sesquicentennial Committee, p. 165.

116. Arlington Enterprise, in Arlington Sesquicentennial Committee, pp. 91-93.

117. Narvestad, pp. 127-128.

Endnotes

118. Hoisington, (*Chanhassen*), pp. 96-100.
119. Renée Wendinger, *Extra! Extra! The Orphan Trains and Newsboys of New York*, pp. 11-12.
120. Ibid., p. 71.
121. The Dawson History Book Committee, *Dawson Minnesota Centennial June 15, 16, 17, 1984: History of the First 100 Years 1884-1984*, p. 115.
122. Tice, p. 19.
123. Scobie, pp. 9-10 and Hoisington, (*A German Town*), p. 133.
124. Hoisington, (*A German Town*), p. 129.
125. Ibid., p. 134.
126. Ibid., p. 136.
127. Ibid., pp. 136-137.
128. Author's visits to the Brown County Historical Society & Museum in New Ulm, Minnesota.
129. Hoisington, (*A German Town*), p. 130 and Tice, p. 23.
130. William Slade, in Hoisington, (*A German Town*), p. 138.
131. Hoisington, (*A German Town*), p. 141.
132. Author's visit to the Minnesota State Capital in St. Paul, Minnesota.
133. Axelrod, p. 224.
134. Blakeley Township Bicentennial Committee, *Blakley Township's Walk Through History*, p. 152.
135. Alo Weber, story he told.
136. The Dawson History Book Committee, p. 114.
137. Krull, p. 52.
138. Darlene Wendland Fasching, *Hamburg: History of a Central Minnesota Village*, pp. 82-83.
139. Ray Zieher, story he told.
140. Charlie Stroebel, story he told.
141. Minneapolis Tribune, *Tarred and Feathered*, November 16, 1919, in Welter, p. 80.
142. Welter, p. 81.
143. Minneapolis Tribune, in Welter, p. 80.

Endnotes

144. Albrecht and Albrecht, (*Tales of a Small Town Circus Legend*), pp. 13-14.
145. Ibid., p. 20.
146. Ibid., p. 36.
147. Iric Nathanson, *World War I Minnesota*, p. 98-99.
148. Ibid., p. 97.
149. Tice, pp. 29-30.
150. Albrecht and Albrecht, pp. 35-36.
151. Gloria and Leo Albrecht, Jr., interview and discussion.
152. Albrecht and Albrecht, p. 77.
153. Ibid., pp. 109-110.
154. Vi Gould, interview and discussion.
155. Leo Albrecht, Jr., interview and discussion.
156. McLeod County Historical Society, p. 52.
157. Ibid., p. 53.
158. Kathleen Sears, *U.S. History 101*, p. 142.
159. McLeod County Historical Society, p. 53.
160. Vi Gould, interview and discussion.
161. Gloria and Leo Albrecht, Jr., interview and discussion.
162. Narvestad, pp. 138-139.
163. Ibid., p. 140.
164. Dorothy Pritchard, in Narvestad, p. 142.
165. Saturday Evening Post, 1916, in Narvestad, p. 140.
166. Narvestad, p. 137.
167. Ibid., p. 142.
168. Ibid., p. 143.
169. Alo Weber, story he told.

Chapter 5

1. Hatle, p. 52.
2. Democrat, March 2, 1859, *Pop Factories*, in Henderson History Book Committee, p. 302.
3. Allie Weber, story he tells.
4. Johnston, p. 27.

Endnotes

5.   Author's visits to the Club New Yorker in Green Isle, Minnesota.

6.   F.A. McKenzie, *"Pussyfoot" Johnson*, pp. 73-74.

7.   McKenzie, pp. 100-101.

8.   Ibid., pp. 101-103.

9.   Ibid., p. 104.

10.   Ibid., pp. 104-107.

11.   Hatle, p. 40.

12.   Author's visit to the Glencoe Preservation Historical Society's Exhibits in the Glencoe Center building in Glencoe, Minnesota.

13.   Hoisington, (*A German Town*), p. 143.

14.   Allie Weber, story he tells.

15.   Roadside plaque erected by the Minnesota Department of Transportation, 1992, near Granite Falls, Minnesota.

16.   Elaine Davis, *Minnesota 13: Wet' Wild Prohibition Days*, p. 11.

17.   Ibid. and Dregni, p. 206.

18.   Johanneck, p. 93.

19.   Jan Jarboe Russell, *The Train to Crystal City: FDR's Secret Prisoner Exchange Program and America's Only Family Internment Camp During World War II*, p. 28.

20.   Author's visit to the city offices in Granite Falls, Minnesota.

21.   Newspaper ads, in Hvistendahl, pp.81-82, and Hvistendahl, pp. 82-83.

22.   John North, in Hvistendahl, pp. 81-82.

23.   Alo Weber, story he told.

24.   Lillie Gildea, story she told.

25.   Rita Zurst, interview and discussion.

26.   Michael Fedo, *The Pocket Guide to Minnesota Place Names: The Stories Behind 1,200 Places in the North Star State*, p. 75 and Jordan Independent Newspaper, *Prohibition Officers Active Hereabouts*, March 24, 1921, in Gail Andersen,

Endnotes

Editor, *Jordan Minnesota A Newspaper Looks at a Town*, Vol. Two, p. 360.

27. Alo Weber, story he told.
28. Davis, p. 36.
29. Ibid., pp. 1-2.
30. Ibid., pp. 2-4.
31. Ibid., p. 29.
32. Ibid., pp. 4, 34.
33. Ibid., p. 30.
34. Ibid., p. 29.
35. Jordan Independent newspaper, *How to Handle a Man*, April 26, 1900, in Andersen, Vol. Two, p. 44.
36. Jordan Independent newspaper, *Women's Rights*, December 27, 1900, in Andersen, Vol. Two, p. 77.
37. Jordan Independent newspaper, *Don't Trust Her*, January 10, 1901, in Andersen, Vol. Two, p. 83.
38. Alo Weber, story he told.
39. Davis, p. 9.
40. Barbara Stuhler, *Gentle Warriors: Clara Ueland and the Minnesota Struggle for Women Suffrage*, p. 2.
41. Sharon Hazard, *The Roosevelts Disagree: The Debate About Women's Suffrage*, www.ultimatehistoryproject.com/womens-anti-suffrage-movement.html.
42. Minnie Bronson and Kate Shippen Roosevelt, in Hazard.
43. Allie Weber, story he tells.
44. Hatle, p. 62.
45. Ibid., p. 41.
46. Ibid., back cover and p. 83.
47. Ibid., pp. 63, 57, 111.
48. Barbara Cyrus, in Hatle, p. 154.
49. Hatle, p. 134.
50. Ibid., p. 54.
51. Ibid., p. 23.

Endnotes

52.   Ann Regan, *Irish In Minnesota: The People of Minnesota*, p. 40.

53.   Paul Maccabee, *John Dillinger Slept Here: A Crooks' Tour of Crime and Corruption in St. Paul 1920-1936*, p. 2.

54.   Ibid., p. 3.

55.   Ibid., p. 6.

56.   Ibid., xi.

57.   Ibid., pp. 61-62.

58.   Ibid., p. 65.

59.   Ibid., p. 2.

60.   Ibid., p. 17.

61.   Ibid., p. 18.

62.   Ibid., p. 15.

63.   Pat Lannon Sr., in Maccabee, p. 13.

64.   Maccabee, p. 14.

65.   Gareth Hiebert, in Maccabee, p. 14.

66.   Richard Hooten, in Tice, p. 42.

67.   Fred Heaberlin, in Maccabee, p. 16.

68.   Maccabee, pp. 16-17.

69.   Ibid., pp. 180-181.

70.   Regan, p. 41.

71.   Allie Weber, story he tells.

72.   Rose Adrienne Gallo, *F. Scott Fitzgerald*, p. 1.

73.   Johnston, p. 63.

74.   Gallo, p. 15.

75.   Johnston, p. 63.

76.   Ibid., p. 67.

77.   Gallo, p. 14.

78.   Author's visit to cemetery next to St. Mary's Catholic Church in Rockville, Maryland.

79.   Brett DeMott, interview, discussion, his research documents and time line he compiled with Mike Gretz.

80.   Lillie Gildea, story she told.

81.   Brett DeMott, interview, discussion, his research documents and time line he compiled with Mike Gretz.

Endnotes

82. Ibid.

83. Ibid.

84. Ibid.

85. Ibid.

86. Elizabeth Lorentz, *Charles Lindbergh's Visit to Madison Lake and Mankato*, in Julie Hiller Schrader, *The Heritage of Blue Earth County, Minnesota*, p. 568.

87. Brett DeMott, interview, discussion, his research documents and time line he compiled with Mike Gretz.

88. Author's visit to the Scott County Historical Society and Stans Museum in Shakopee, Minnesota.

89. National Geographic, p. 13.

90. Dregni, p. 102.

91. Palapala Ho'omau Church, www.heyhawaii.com/Maui/Palapala_Hoomau_Church_K ipahulu_Hawaii.html.

92. Krull, p. 53.

93. Alo Weber, stories he told.

94. Allie Weber, stories he tells.

95. Fedo, (*The Pocket Guide to Minnesota Place Names*), p. 106.

96. Alo Weber, story he told.

97. Ibid.

98. Ibid.

99. Henderson History Book Committee, p. 493.

100. Independent, July 25, 1952, in Henderson History Book Committee, p. 616.

101. Author's visit to the John Other Day monument in Henderson, Minnesota.

102. Henderson History Book Committee, pp. 493-494.

103. Sibley County Independent, August 26, 1927, in Henderson History Book Committee, p. 493.

104. Buck, Independent, in Henderson History Book Committee, p. 494.

Chapter 6

1. Lorraine Bliss, *Depression Years Trivia*, in Arlington Sesquicentennial Committee, p. 191.
2. Rita Zurst, interview and discussion.
3. Alo Weber, statement he made.
4. Author's visit to the Redwood County Museum in Redwood Falls, Minnesota.
5. Allie Weber, story he tells.
6. Alo Weber, story he told.
7. Ibid.
8. Ibid.
9. Ibid.
10. Ibid.
11. Allie Weber, stories he tells.
12. Pamphlet, *Memoirs of a Giant: Green Company's First 75 Years 1903-1978*, p. 2 (chronology).
13. Ibid.
14. Ibid., p. 29.
15. Allie Weber, story he tells.
16. Albrecht, p. 338.
17. Allie Weber, story he tells.
18. Ibid.
19. Chaska Bicentennial Committee, Vol. 1, pp. 292-293.
20. Berger, p. 58.
21. Kenneth C. Davis, *Don't Know Much About the American Presidents*, p. 417.
22. Rita Zurst, story she tells.
23. Mag Carroll, story she told.
24. Allie Weber, stories he tells.
25. Ibid.
26. Ibid.
27. Ibid.
28. Susan Quinn, *Eleanor and Hick: The Love Affair That Shaped a First Lady*, pp. 2, 6.
29. Krull, p. 56.

30. Barbara W. Sommer, *Hard Work and a Good Deal The Civilian Conservation Corps in Minnesota*, p. 16.
31. Ibid., p. 17.
32. Ibid., pp. 22-24.
33. Ibid., pp. 24-26.
34. Allie Weber, stories he tells.
35. Allie Weber, story he tells.
36. Allie Weber, stories he tells.
37. Allie Weber, story he tells.
38. The Browns Valley Town and Country Club History Committee, *Browns Valley 125 Years: 1866-1991*, pp. 45-47.
39. Sign at the Continental Divide near Brown's Valley, Minnesota.
40. Allie Weber, story he tells.
41. Ibid.
42. Ibid.
43. The Dawson Centennial History Book Committee, p. 183.
44. Martin Keller and Sheri O'Meara, *Storms! Tales of Extreme Weather Events in Minnesota*, pp. 7-8.
45. Ibid., p. 9.
46. Alo Weber, story he told.
47. Allie Weber, story he tells.
48. Keller and O'Meara, p. 7.
49. Forest Lake Times and Babe Winkelman, in Keller and O'Meara, pp. 10-11.
50. Alo Weber, story he told.
51. Keller and O'Meara, pp. 12-13.
52. Ibid., p. 7.

Chapter 7

1. Russell, p. 159.
2. Webster, pp. 107-108.
3. Russell, p. 33.
4. Author's visit to the Japanese American National Museum in Los Angeles, California.

Endnotes

5.   Life, *How to Tell Japs From Chinese*, December 22, 1941, Vol. II, No. 25, pp. 81-82.

6.   Russell, pp. 33-34.

7.   Russell, p. xix.

8.   Harold Oelfke, story he told.

9.   Independent, September 1942, in Henderson History Book Committee, p. 181.

10.   Allie Weber, story he tells.

11.   Henderson History Book Committee, p. 181.

12.   U.S.S. Franks (DD554), c/o Fleet Post Office, San Francisco, Calif., letter to All Hands, Subject: United States - Preparation to Return To.

13.   Buckentin, in Arlington Sesquicentennial Committee, p. 166.

14.   Allie Weber, story he tells.

15.   Ibid.

16.   Alo Weber, story he told.

17.   Chaska Bicentennial Committee, Vol. II, p. 331.

18.   Lafayette Ledger, September 1, 1941, *Boys, Girls ask to Get Mildweed Floss In*, in *The History of Bernadotte Twp. 1866-2016: In Celebration of Bernadotte Lutheran Church's First 150 Years*, Bernadotte Lutheran, *Rooted in Christ, Growing in Faith*, Edited by Ruth Klossner for Bernadotte Lutheran 2016, p. 190.

19.   Lillie Gildea, story she told.

20.   Esther Beseke, interview and discussion.

21.   Allie Weber, stories he tells.

22.   Geri Weber, stories she tells.

23.   Allie Weber, story he tells.

24.   An Keuning Tichelaar and Lynn Kaplanian-Buller, *Passing on the Comfort: The War, The Quilts, and the Women Who Made a Difference*, p. 51.

25.   Huddleston, p. 73.

26.   Ibid., pp. 72-74 and Author's visit to the Japanese American National Museum in Los Angeles, California.

Endnotes

27. Russell, p. 144.
28. Huddleston, pp. 63-71.
29. Bart Karels, interview and discussion.
30. Mary Scully, interview and discussion.
31. Ramona Bade, *Martha Bullert*, in Arlington Sesquicentennial Committee, p. 179.
32. Johanneck, p. 133.
33. Local writer, in Hoisington, (*A German Town*), p. 181 and Hoisington, (*A German Town*), p. 181.
34. Author's visit to the Brown County Historical Society & Museum in New Ulm, Minnesota.
35. Allie Weber, stories he tells.
36. Julie Kaufman, interview and discussion.
37. Gordon Westby, in the Dawson Sentinel, in the Dawson History Book Committee, pp. 123-124.
38. Erika Vora, *The Will to Live: A German Family's Flight From Soviet Rule*, p. 11.
39. Ibid., pp. 24-25.
40. Ibid., p. 27.
41. Ibid., p. 12.
42. Karl Diebal, Jr., interview and discussion.
43. Larry Tillemans, interview and discussion.
44. Allie Weber, stories he tells.
45. Regan, p. 53.
46. Dan Kurzman, *Left to Die: The Tragedy of the USS Juneau*, captions under the first and seventh pictures between pp. 164-165.
47. Ibid., pp. 249-250.
48. Berger, p. 71.
49. Allie Weber, stories he tells.
50. Ibid.
51. Ibid.
52. Rita Zurst, paper on the Gotha Store.
53. Allie Weber, stories he tells.

Chapter 8

1. Ron Johnson, stories he told.
2. Author's visits to the Jessenland Town Hall in Sibley County, Minnesota.
3. Allie Weber, story he tells.
4. Ibid.
5. Ibid.
6. Ibid.
7. Ibid.
8. Krull, p. 59.
9. Krull, p. 61.
10. Mary Scully, story she told.
11. Geri Weber, story she tells.
12. Jean-Yves Soucy with Annette, Cécile and Yvonne Dionne, *Family Secrets: The Controversial & Shocking Story of the Dionne Quintuplets*, pp. 16, 196.
13. Ibid., pp. 3, 17, 22.
14. Ibid., pp. 21, 97.
15. Ibid., pp. 3-4.
16. Ibid., pp. 8, 38, 53, 68, 102-104, 117.
17. Ibid., p. 73.
18. Ibid., pp. 8, 66-67, 79-82, 104, 108, 115-116.
19. Ibid., p. 162.
20. Allie Weber, story he tells.
21. Ibid.
22. Ibid.
23. Ibid.
24. Author's visit to *Testify Americana Slavery to Today*, The Diane & Alan Page Collection, temporarily on display at the Minneapolis Central Library, Minneapolis, Minnesota.
25. Allie Weber, stories he tells.
26. Berger, p. 74.
27. Allie Weber, stories he tells.
28. Ibid.
29. Ibid.

30. Ibid.
31. Keuning-Tichelaar and Kaplanian-Buller, p. 81.
32. Ernest Schnabel, *A Portrait in Courage*, in Anne Frank, *The Diary of a Young Girl* (Afterword), pp. 278, 280.
33. Allie Weber, stories he tells.
34. Alo Weber, story he told.
35. Allie Weber, story he tells.
36. Ibid.
37. Dregni, p. 53.
38. Allie Weber, stories he tells.
39. Oliver Towne Column, St. Paul Pioneer Press, March 17, 1958, in Berger, pp. 104-105.
40. Allie Weber, story he tells.

Chapter 9

1. Rex D. Hamann, *The Millers and the Saints: Baseball Championships of the Twin Cities Rivals, 1903-1955*, p. 5.
2. Ibid., p. 7.
3. Allie Weber, story he tells.
4. Davis, (*American Presidents*), p. 484.
5. James Swanson, *The End of Days: The Assassination of John F. Kennedy*, New York Post, October 20, 2013, *RFK may have swiped JFK's missing brain*, https://nypost.com/2013/10/20/jfks-brain-went-missing-and-rfk-may-have-swiped-it.
6. Krull, p. 72.
7. Axelrod, p. 285 and *The Pentagon Papers* leaked to the New York Times, in Axelrod, p. 285.
8. Stanley Karnow, *Vietnam: A History The First Complete Account of Vietnam at War*, p. 374.
9. Axelrod, pp. 285-286 and *The Pentagon Papers* leaked to the New York Times, in Axelrod, p. 285.
10. Gregory A. Freeman, *Sailors to the End: The Deadly Fire on the USS Forrestal and the Heroes Who Fought It*, pp. 25, 103-104.

Endnotes

11. Ibid., p. 122.
12. Ibid., pp. 84-85, 272-273.
13. Ibid., pp. 267-269.
14. Ibid., p. 279.
15. Ibid., pp. 167-168.
16. John Radzilowski, *Prairie Town: A History of Marshall, Minnesota, 1872-1997*, pp. 266-270.
17. Krull, p. 72.
18. www.goodreads.com/author/quotes/ 15769.Lyndon_B_Johnson?page=2.
19. Frost, unnumbered first page.
20. Author's visit to the Japanese American National Museum in Los Angeles, California.
21. Author's visit to the Minnehaha Regional Park in Minneapolis, Minnesota.
22. Kajer, p. 148.
23. Dale Holtz, *Enemies of Sleep: New Ulm Musicians*, p. 51.
24. Author's visit to the Minnesota Music Hall of Fame in New Ulm, Minnesota.
25. Kevin Featherly, *Legendary Wrestler Verne Gagne and a Tragic Tale*, Minnpost, February 18, 2009, www.minnpost.com/politics-policy/2009/02/legendary- wrestler-verne-gagne-and-tragic-tale.
26. Adnan Alkaissy with Ross Bernstein, *The Sheikh of Baghdad: Tales of Celebrity and Terror From Pro Wrestling's General Adnan*, p. 1.
27. Ibid., pp. 9-10.
28. Ibid., pp. 16, 22-24.
29. Ibid., p. 26.
30. Ibid., p. 30.
31. Ibid., pp. 55-60.
32. Ibid., p. 79.
33. Ibid., p. 95.
34. Ibid., p. 133.
35. Ibid., pp. 137-139.

36. Ibid., pp. 143, 149.
37. Ibid., p. 175.
38. Ibid., pp. 183-184.
39. Ibid., p. 189.
40. Ibid., pp. 210-211.
41. Ibid., p. 223.
42. Krull, p. 71.
43. www.goodreads.com/author/quotes/
     15769.Lyndon_B_Johnson?page=2.
44. David Pierson, *Girl Scouts Misfortune Cookies*, Los Angeles
     Times, July 19, 2008, articles.latimes.com/2008/jul/19/
     local/me-claremont19.
45. Ronald Kessler, *In the President's Secret Service: Behind the
     Scenes with Agents in the Line of Fire and the Presidents They
     Protect*, pp. 15-18.
46. Howard Vetter, interview and discussion.
47. Fred Danner, interview and discussion.
48. Henderson History Book Committee, pp. 111-112.

Chapter 10

1. David Hawley, *'Peace Crimes' tells Minnesota 8's war story*,
    Minnpost, February 21, 2008,
    www.minnpost.com/politics-policy/2008/02/peace-crimes-
    tells-minnesota-8s-war-story.
2. Wingerd, pp. 45-46.
3. *Hanoi Jane's apology*, The Washington Times, July 7, 2000,
    www.washingtontimes.com/news/2000/jul/7/20000707-
    011718-2143r.
4. Maurice H. Stans, *One of the Presidents' Men: Twenty Years
    With Eisenhower and Nixon*, pp. 247-248.
5. National Geographic, p. 91.
6. Stans, pp. 254-255.
7. Ibid., pp. 256-260.
8. Ibid., p. 264.
9. Roberts, p. 21.

Endnotes

10.   Author's visit to the St. Peter Woolen Mill.

11.   Lisa M. Bolt Simons, *Faribault Woolen Mill: Loomed in the Land of Lakes*, p. 14.

12.   Ibid., p. 33

13.   www.faribaultmill.com/pages/our-heritage.

14.   Russell, p. 281.

15.   Simons, p. 44.

16.   Barb Mathwig, interview and discussion.

17.   Krull, p. 78.

18.   https://en.wikipedia.org/wiki/John_Gagliardi.

19.   Marlene Gildea, story she tells.

20.   Roberta J. Olson, *Sinclair Lewis: The Journey*, p. 23.

21.   Ibid., p. 24.

22.   Ibid., pp. 27-29.

23.   Roberts, p. 101.

24.   Olson, pp. 28, 33.

25.   Henry Van Dyke, in Olson, p. 33.

26.   David Whitford with Doris Burke, *Cargill: Inside the quiet giant that rules the food business*, Fortune Magazine, October 27, 2011, archive.fortune.com/2011/10/24/news/companies/cargill_food_business.fortune/index.htm.

27.   Richard "Dick" Thomas, *Richard Thomas Mayor of Arlington*, in Arlington Sesquicentennial Committee, p. 35.

28.   Chicago Tribune story about *Bulletin of the American Meteorological Society*, May 2006, in Keller and O'Meara, p. 42.

29.   Keller and O'Meara, p. 41.

30.   Ibid., pp. 35-36.

31.   Author's visit to the Split Rock Lighthouse State Park near Two Harbors, Minnesota.

32.   https://en.wikipedia.org/wiki/Great_Storm_of_1975.

33.   Ann Wiener, story she tells.

34.   https://en.wikipedia.org/wiki/Alan_Page.

Endnotes

35. Author's visit to *Testify Americana Slavery to Today*, The Diane & Alan Page Collection, temporarily on display at the Minneapolis Central Library, Minneapolis, Minnesota.
36. Leo Thorsness, *Surviving Hell: A POW's Journey*, pp. 10-13.
37. Ibid., p. 29.
38. Ibid.
39. Ibid., pp. 8-9.
40. Ibid., p. 103.
41. National Geographic, p. 59.
42. Thorsness, p. 116.
43. Ibid., pp. 117-118.
44. Ibid., Author's note.
45. Axelrod, pp. 294-295.
46. Jim O'Connor, *Jackie Robinson: and the Story of All Black Baseball*, pp. 8, 12.
47. Roberts, pp. 12-13.
48. Buckentin, in Arlington Sesquicentennial Committee, p. 164.
49. Mankato Free Press, August 19, 2012, *Go-Go Dancers Didn't Go Well in Green Isle Glimpse of the Past*.
50. Author's purchase of t-shirts.
51. Mankato Free Press, August 19, 2012.
52. Arlington Sesquicentennial Committee, p. 62.
53. History.com staff writer, 1977 *Carter pardons draft dodgers*, published 2009, http://www.history.com/this-day-in-history/carter-pardons-draft-dodgers.
54. Kessler, p. 71.
55. Allie Weber, story he tells.
56. Ibid.
57. Allie Weber, stories he tells.
58. Asa Wilson, *Decades Later, Willmar 8 Are Heroes to a New Generation*, August 6, 2006,

Endnotes

http://www.d.umn.edu/~epeters5/Cst1201/Articles/Twenty-five%20years%20later,%20Willmar%208%20are%20heroes%20to%20a%20new%20generation.htm.

59. Ibid., Roberts, p. 188.
60. Gilman, (*The Story of Minnesota's Past*), p. 209.
61. Williams.
62. Ibid.
63. Gilman, (*The Story of Minnesota's Past*), p. 209.

Chapter 11

1. Benny Wasserman, *Presidents Were Teenagers Too*, p. 151.
2. Wayne Coffey, *The Boys of Winter The Untold Story of a Coach, a Dream and the 1980 U.S. Olympic Hockey Team*, p. 247.
3. Coffey, pp. viii-ix.
4. http://icehockey.wikia.com/wiki/Rob_McClanahan.
5. Coffey, p. 254.
6. Author's visits to the Hermann Statue in New Ulm, Minnesota.
7. Roberts, p. 177.
8. Jane McKeown, *Chrism Mass Held at Montevideo*, Newsletter, Diocese of New Ulm, Vol. XI, No. 9, April 1982, p. 1 and Fedo, (*Minnesota Place Names*), p. 101
9. Rick Nelson, *Only in Minnesota*, in Star Tribune, Super Bowl LII, *The Essential Twin Cities Guide*, p. 14.
10. Patricia Schultz, *1,000 Places to See Before You Die*, p. 545.
11. Anderson, (*Laura Ingalls Wilder's Walnut Grove*), p. 70.
12. Kessler, p. 89.
13. Henderson History Book Committee, p. 75.
14. https:en.wikipedia.org/wiki/Darling_Nikki.
15. Kessler, p. 116.
16. Bessler, p. 66.
17. Kent Hrbek with Dennis Brackin, *Tales From the Minnesota Twins Dugout: A Collection of the Greatest Twin's Stories Ever Told*, pp. 101-102.

18. Ibid., p. 22.
19. Ibid., p. 105.
20. Alex Halsted, *100 Things Twins Fans Should Know & Do Before They Die*, p. 35.
21. Britta Bloomberg for Nina M. Archabal, State Historic Preservation Officer, letter dated October 22, 1991.
22. Peter Anderly, interview and discussion.
23. https://en.wikipedia.org/wiki/Dave_Stevens_(athlete) and wolfmanproductions.com/dave-stevens.
24. www.hrw.org/legacy/reports98/police/uspo86.htm.
25. Gary J. Byrne, *Crisis of Character: A White House Secret Service Officer Discloses His Firsthand Experience With Hillary, Bill, and How They Operate*, p. 112.
26. Ed Stroesser, *Amazing Corn*, Minnesota Corn Growers Association pamphlet.
27. Olivia Chamber of Commerce pamphlet, *Olivia the Corn Capital.*
28. Hrbek with Brackin, p. 185.
29. Regan, p. 1.
30. Rich Naistat from the National Weather Service, Jim Dawson with the Star Tribune, Star Tribune, Pioneer Press and *Twist of Fate*, in Keller and O'Meara, pp. 78-80.

Chapter 12

1. David Mikkelson, Fact Checker, *Michael Moore Called Chris Kyle a Coward?*, January 25, 2015, www.snopes.com/fact-check/american-sniping.
2. Dan Lamothe, *Court throws out $1.8 million judgment against 'American Sniper' Chris Kyle's estate*, Washington Post, June 13, 2016, www.washingtonpost.com/news/checkpoint/wp/2016/06/13/court-throws-out-1-8-million-judgment-against-american-sniper-chris-kyles-estate.
3. Allie Weber, story he tells.
4. Barack Obama, in Wasserman, p. 175.

Endnotes

5. Taylor March, *Obama: Grandmother "Typical White Person"*, www.huffingtonpost.com/taylor-marsh/obama-grandmother-typical_b_92601.html.

6. Scott Wilson, *Perhaps Bowling Is a Subject Best Avoided*, Washington Post, March 21, 2009, www.washingtonpost.com/wp-dyn/content/article/2009/03/20/AR2009032003420_pf.html

7. Bruce and Nelva Lillenthal, interview and discussion.

8. Father Jerry Berger, interview and discussion.

9. Shawn Pogatchnik, *Saint's preserved heart stolen from Christ Church Cathedral in Dublin*, The Star, March 4, 2012, www.thestar.com/news/world/2012/03/04/saints_preserved_heart_stolen_from_christ_church_cathedral_in_dublin.html.

10. Allie Weber, story he tells.

11. Jeff Luskey, interview and discussion.

12. S. Brandt, *Voting difficult in precinct without a snorkel*, Minneapolis Star Tribune, November 12, 2012, www.startribune.com/voting-difficult-in-this-precinct-without-a-snorkel/178166351.

13. Pete Weber, interview and discussion.

14. Pete Weber, stories he tells.

15. Steve Scherer, Editing by Tom Heneghan, *Pope says birth control ban doesn't mean breed 'like rabbits'*, Reuters, January 19, 2015, www.reuters.com/article/us-pope-airplane/pope-says-birth-control-ban-doesnt-mean-breed-like-rabbits-idUSKBN0KS1WY20150119.

16. William Marvy, interview and discussion.

17. Allie Weber, story he tells.

18. J.D. Heyes, *Al Gore's 2007 prediction that all arctic ice would be gone by 2014 now proven to be alarming fear mongering*, Natural News, September 16, 2013, www.naturalnews.com/042074_Al_Gore_global_warming_predictions.html#.

Endnotes

19. Michael Snyder, *60 Completely Outrageous Ways The U.S. Government Is Wasting Money*, The American Dream, March 25, 2013, endoftheamericandream.com/archives/60-completely-outrageous-ways-the-u-s-government-is-wasting-money.

20. MJ Lee, Sunlen Serfaty and Juana Summers, *Congress paid out $17 million in settlements. Here's why we know so little about that money*, CNN, November 16, 2017, www.cnn.com/2017/11/16/politics/settlements-congress-sexual-harassment/index.html.

21. Jean Hopfensperger, *New Ulm bankruptcy makes Minnesota No. 1 in church bankruptcies*, Star Tribune, March 4, 2017, www.startribune.com/new-ulm-diocese-files-for-bankruptcy-protection/415333274.

22. John Heilprin, *Pope Benedict defrocked 400 priests in 2 years, document says*, Star Tribune, January 18, 2014, www.startribune.com/pope-benedict-defrocked-400-priests-in-2-years-document-says/240859541.

ACKNOWLEDGEMENTS

I wish to thank the following:

My cousin Ken Strobel for the picture of St. Thomas Church.

Dennis Nelson for the picture inside the Jessenland Town Hall.

Serena Reder for her relentless research.

Terri Saenz, Spike Lynch, Janet Williams, and my sister, Janet Geib, for feedback.

Sandy Halsey for proofreading.

Teresa Hayes, my secretary for 26 years, for proofreading and for always being there to gladly help. She helped make this book happen.

Kitty Kladstrup, for editing, for believing in my book, and for helping to get it published.

ABOUT THE AUTHOR

Author, John F. Weber, and his Dad, Allie Weber, standing behind the ballot box in Jessenland Township Hall.

John F. Weber was born and raised on a farm in Jessenland Township, Sibley County, in the Lower Minnesota River Valley. He grew up at the end of the small family farm era. After high school he spent four years in the Air Force, then graduated from Minot State University in Minot, North Dakota. He went to law school at California Western School of Law in San Diego, California, and has practiced law in Barstow, California for twenty-seven years. He enjoys spending time with his three children—Matt, Melissa and Jesse. To write this book, he dragged Jesse to almost every museum, historical society and site in Minnesota. John goes back to Minnesota every couple of months. One of his favorite activities is driving around with his parents and Jesse looking at crops, drainage and farm sites. They also enjoy seeing wildlife, churches and businesses. They often talk about politics and the old days of farming. Of course, they finish the evening off with lunch.

IN MEMORY

This book is in memory of my grandfather, Alo Weber, and my brother, Brian Weber.